5.6/16

P9-DGR-034

BOOK SEVEN

THE GRAVE ROBBERS
OF GENGHIS KHAN

Children of the Lamp

BOOK SEVEN

THE GRAVE ROBBERS OF GENGHIS KHAN

P. B. KERR

ORCHARD BOOKS/NEW YORK
AN IMPRINT OF SCHOLASTIC INC.

Library of Congress Cataloging-in-Publication Data
Kerr, Philip.
The grave robbers of Genghis Khan / P.B. Kerr.
p. cm. — (Children of the lamp ; bk. 7)
Summary: While volcanoes spew golden lava around the world, djinn twins
John and Philippa, with their parents, Uncle Nimrod, and Groanin, face
evil more powerful than ever before when they try to stop the wicked djinn
trying to rob the grave of Genghis Khan.
ISBN 978-0-545-12660-1
[1. Genies — Fiction. 2. Magic — Fiction. 3. Twins — Fiction. 4. Brothers
and sisters — Fiction. 5. Volcanoes — Fiction. 6. Genghis Khan,
1162–1227 — Fiction. 7. Mongolia — Fiction.] I. Title.
PZ7.K46843Gr 2011
[Fic] — dc23
2011020803

10 9 8 7 6 5 4 3 2 1   11 12 13 14 15

Printed in the U.S.A. 23
First edition, November 2011
Book design by Elizabeth B. Parisi

In memoriam: Fiona Kerr

BOOK SEVEN

THE GRAVE ROBBERS
OF GENGHIS KHAN

CHAPTER 1

COME BACK TO SORRENTO

Nimrod, a powerful English djinn and uncle to the similarly empowered but quite dissimilar twins John and Philippa Gaunt, had absolutely no idea why he should have felt compelled to invite his young niece and nephew on his annual holiday to the southern Italian town of Sorrento and his favorite grand hotel in southern Italy, the Excelsior Vittoria. The hotel, which was built on the site of a holiday villa once owned by the Roman emperor Augustus, had never been the kind of place that seemed particularly appealing to children. It was full of old people and valuable antiques and elegant frescoes and stiff-looking waiters in white jackets. Sorrento itself offered only inlaid woodwork, spectacular views of the Bay of Naples and the volcano Vesuvius — not to mention the world's biggest super-yacht, the *Schadenfreude*, which was anchored in the bay — and a proximity to the ancient city of Pompeii, which had been destroyed and completely buried during a catastrophic volcanic eruption in

A.D. 79. But none of these amenities seemed likely to impress Nimrod's three companions.

John disliked vacationing in hotels that did not have a wide-screen television with an extensive variety of programs in English; Philippa disliked being without her laptop computer and the Internet, and the hotel's rather unreliable Wi-Fi connection soon left her feeling frustrated and bored. Nimrod's butler, Mr. Groanin, who accompanied the three djinn on their Italian journey, merely disliked any town where he could not obtain a decent cup of tea or the latest English newspaper; however, being a bit of a snob, he rather admired the Excelsior Vittoria hotel because of all the many kings and queens who had stayed there. Groanin was a big fan of the British royal family and whenever he traveled he always carried a silver-framed picture of Queen Elizabeth II in his luggage, which he would place, reverently, on his bedside table.

On their second night in Sorrento, the four sat on the hotel's panoramic terrace enjoying dinner and the twinkling lights of Naples on the other side of the bay while Nimrod talked about the last days of Pompeii and the excursion they would make there the following day as the twins listened, politely concealing their boredom.

When Nimrod had finished speaking, John frowned and said, "What's the Italian for *déjà vu*?" He shrugged. "You know: the feeling that you've seen or experienced something before."

"I suppose," said Nimrod, "it would be *già visto*. And it seems rather a good idea to have a fresh new name for déjà vu as the French one has become tiresomely familiar. I shall adopt your idea immediately." Nimrod lit an enormous cigar and blew a triangular-shaped smoke ring in the direction of the volcano. "But is it the hotel or the place that seems familiar to you, John?"

"The place," confessed John. "Especially Pompeii. I mean, I *know* I haven't ever been to Pompeii before but I sort of *feel* that I have. And I can't explain it."

"Me, too," admitted Philippa. "Ever since I saw Vesuvius I've had the strangest idea that I'd seen it already."

"Perhaps," said Groanin, "in a previous incarnation, each of you was one of them folk from Pompeii who got themselves buried in volcanic ash." He sniffed loudly. "That is, if you believe in such nonsense as reincarnation."

Of course they all spoke much more than they could know. Or could ever know. None of them was or ever would be aware that indeed they had visited Pompeii and seen Vesuvius before. While at the same time, of course, they hadn't. Their previous visit was in a previous adventure that had occurred in an alternative or parallel universe that was not within the observable universe in which they now lived. Which is to say it happened and then it didn't happen; and since this previous visit to Pompeii was far beyond their cosmological horizon, then only you, omniscient reader, might possess a more complete knowledge of why they had been there and what they had done. Suffice it to say they had no sense or memory of this previous adventure, which is exactly the kind of thing that happens when you travel through a wormhole in space-time.

But no more of that for now. In the world they currently inhabited, it never happened and when nobody took up Groanin's provocative conversational thread, he added, "Although such a catastrophe as a volcanic eruption seems hard to believe on a night as lovely as this, with the bay looking so blue and calm and the sky so clear, and Vesuvius itself — well, from here it's hard to credit that it's an actual volcano. I've seen warts that looked more dangerous than that volcano. I said, I've seen warts that looked more dangerous than that."

"Nevertheless, it is one of the most dangerous volcanoes in the world," said Nimrod. "Certainly in Europe. It probably ranks about third in the volcanic top ten. There's no telling what damage or disruption or loss of life would be occasioned if it were to erupt. Frankly, it would make Eyjafjallajökull look like an overflowing ashtray."

As might have been expected, Nimrod's pronunciation of this tongue-twisting Icelandic name was faultless.

"I-er-follow-Joe-Cole?" repeated John, as best as he was able. "What the heck's that?"

"Another volcano," said Philippa. "In Iceland. Don't you read the newspapers? It's what caused all that disruption to flights to and from Europe in the spring of 2010. Eyjafjallajökull."

"The ash cloud," said Groanin. "Of course. For several weeks no one could fly anywhere. In a plane at least. The ash affected all of the jet engines on the planes that tried to fly through it. And so they didn't. Not for weeks and weeks. People were stranded all over the world. Yes, I'd quite forgotten about that Icelandic volcano. It's amazing what you forget, isn't it?"

"It's not exactly an easy name to remember," said John, and immediately attempted to repeat the name while it was still in his mind, only it came out sounding more like, "Hey, fellow, are you joking?"

"Well, I'm happy to say, it looks quiet enough now," said Groanin. "I said, Vesuvius looks quiet enough. Not so much as a whiff of trouble brewing there."

"Yes, but looking quiet is no indication that there's nothing happening underneath," said Nimrod.

"Unless it's John you're talking about," Philippa said cruelly.

John ignored her and so, for the moment, did Nimrod.

"Vesuvius," he explained, "was quiet for eight centuries before it started erupting again, in A.D. 62. And Mount St. Helens, in Washington State, was dormant for seven hundred years before it became active in 1480. It's a bit of a mystery what causes some long-quiet volcanoes to become active again. With others, the explanation seems much more straightforward, such as an earthquake. It's remarkable that volcanoes don't cause more disruption, considering how many of them there are in this world. And the power they contain."

"How many volcanoes are there?" asked John. "In total. Does anyone know?"

"Nobody knows for sure," said Nimrod, "since there are a great many that lie unseen on the seabed. However, there are possibly six or seven hundred volcanoes that have been active on land throughout recorded time and man has learned to coexist with them. Even today there are probably fifty volcanoes erupting each year. Kilauea, in Hawaii, has been erupting since 1985. Of course, our family has good reason to remember that particular volcano."

"We do?" said John.

Philippa gave her brother a scornful look. "Duh," she said. "It was Kilauea that destroyed our mother's physical body, and obliged her to take on the shape of Mrs. Trump, our housekeeper."

"Oh," said John. "Of course. I remember now."

"It was your mother's misfortune that it was a pyroclastic flow that hit her rather than a simple blast cloud. Very likely her body would easily have survived the latter, but not the former. A pyroclastic flow can attain a temperature of eight hundred and fifty degrees centigrade or more."

"You seem to know a lot about this subject, Uncle Nimrod," observed Philippa.

"Volcanism? Oh, yes. But then again that's hardly surprising is it? Given that we djinn are made of fire? Our kind has always enjoyed a close affinity with volcanoes. Indeed, some of the world's most eminent volcanologists have been djinn."

"Being full of hot air must be a tremendous advantage, in that respect," remarked Groanin, who had enjoyed a little too much of the local Italian wine, which was perhaps the only reason he reached down and stroked one of the hotel's cats.

Nimrod smiled happily. He was in much too good a mood to feel provoked by Groanin's insult. The Bay of

Naples has a very calming effect on people, which is why they go there, of course.

"Oh, very good, Groanin. Very good indeed."

"Thank you, sir."

"I was, myself, for many years a visiting professor in the Planetary Geosciences division of the University of Hawaii," said Nimrod. "And before that I was the Corleone Professor of Volcanology at the University of Palermo in Sicily."

As Nimrod continued to list his academic qualifications in the hot field of volcanology, John tried and failed to stifle a yawn.

"Sorry," he said. "This is very interesting, I know, but I think it's bedtime for me."

"Me, too," admitted Groanin. "It's all this fresh air. It's a bit too, well, fresh, for me. Plays havoc with me pipes. Give me Manchester smoke any day of the week."

John and Groanin got up from the table, said good night, and went back into the air-conditioned hotel, which was a little too cool for John's comfort and not quite cold enough for Groanin's.

The young djinn went to his room on the fourth floor, brushed his teeth, and watched a program on Italian TV for a while, which seemed to be about a fourteen-year-old Romanian gang leader called Decebal in a town near Rome.

John, who was fourteen himself, thought fourteen was kind of young to be a gang leader and assumed he must have misunderstood. Then again the boy did look fourteen.

When the program was finished, John switched out the light. Immediately, he fell asleep and dreamed strange and improbable dreams of mountains and Tibet, aged Nazis, kind monks and fourteen-year-old gangsters and talking wolves.

Groanin did much the same. He watched TV and brushed his teeth, which were false. These he placed in a large vodka and tonic that stood beside the photograph of the queen on his bedside table. Then he read a little of *David Copperfield*, which he always found to be as good as any sleeping pill.

It was almost dawn when the butler was awoken by the tinkling of the glass chandelier hanging above his bed, as if its complex array of dangling prisms had been brushed by the hand of some invisible force or being. Groanin switched on his bedside light and looked up to see the chandelier swaying on the ceiling. The next second the whole room shuddered loudly like a Russian passenger plane in flight, and he didn't have to see the needle moving on a seismometer or be watching the BBC to know that he was experiencing an earthquake and probably quite a powerful one.

Unnerved by the movement of his hotel bedroom, Groanin replaced the dentures in his mouth and, as was his habit, earthquake or no earthquake, drank the vodka and tonic. Such are the intemperate habits of butlers the world over.

"Don't worry, Your Majesty," he said addressing the queen's picture. "I'll look after you, lass. You're safe with me." And so saying, Groanin placed her precious picture back in his suitcase before, reeling and rolling, he rambled out of his room and down the stairs where, among the other guests heading for the safety of the open air, he encountered John.

John had never experienced an earthquake before and all earlier thoughts that he would like to know what one felt like were now quite forgotten; this was much scarier than ever he had supposed.

"We have to get outside," he yelled at Groanin. "In case the building comes down on our heads."

"I know that, you young scamp," growled the butler. "I wasn't born yesterday, more's the pity."

Most of the guests walked quickly toward the safety of the poolside and the hotel's extensive gardens and orange groves. John and Groanin would probably have followed them, too, but for the fact that they caught sight of Nimrod and Philippa heading out onto the terrace at the back of the hotel where they had dined the night before. Yet it hardly seemed like the safest place given the height of the cliff below the terrace railing. This was a sheer drop of at least seventy or eighty feet and the thought that the cliff and the terrace might at any minute give way beneath their feet gave Groanin more than a pause for thought.

"Sir," he said. "Is this advisable? To be out here? Surely the garden would be safer." Nervously, he turned and pointed in the other direction. "Which is this way."

In the violet hues of the Italian dawn, Nimrod remained silent for a moment, his face pointed out to sea, his hands resting on the elegant stone balustrade, and looking more than a little like the Roman emperor Augustus whose villa had once occupied this same spot.

"Sir," persisted Groanin. "We shall perish if we remain here. At any moment this whole flipping terrace might collapse and land us in the sea. Surely caution dictates that we should follow the rest of the guests into the garden."

Nimrod waved his hand at the hotel. "It's all right," he said. "The immediate danger's past."

And it was true. The hotel had stopped shaking. Unlike Groanin's knees. What was more, the building seemed quite undamaged beyond a bit of dust that had been disturbed from some of the less accessible parts of the older public rooms and a picture of the actress Sophia Loren that had fallen off its hook.

In the harbor parking lot underneath Nimrod's gaze several car alarms were going off, and in the distance could be heard the sound of more than one approaching siren.

"I will yield neither to the song of the siren," said Nimrod, "nor to the voice of the hyena, the tears of the crocodile, or the howling of the wolf."

"Eh?" Groanin looked at the twins. "What's the man on about? There aren't any wolves about here. Nor any crocodiles, neither, I should hope."

"Legend has it that this is the place where the sirens sang to Ulysses," explained Philippa. "In Homer's *Odyssey*. Sorrento. It means the 'place of sirens.' Somewhere to avoid."

"Aye, well, I can see why," remarked Groanin. "What with earthquakes and the like. Still, we seem to have come off okay. No harm done, eh?"

"I'm afraid that's just not true, Groanin," said Nimrod.

"Eh? How's that, then?" Groanin glanced around. "Hotel looks all right. We're still here. So where's the harm? I said, where's the harm?"

John pointed across the Bay of Naples at Vesuvius. "Look, there," he said quietly. "There's the harm."

Groanin stared out to sea. For a moment he struggled to understand what the others were all talking about, and then he saw that from the four-thousand-foot-high summit of Vesuvius — so quiet and unremarkable the previous day — a long, thin plume of gray smoke was now drifting up into the violet-blue sky like a Cheyenne Indian's signal fire in some old western movie.

"Oh, Lord," he said. "Does that mean what I think it means?"

"I kind of think it does," said Philippa. "Uncle?"

"There hath he lain for ages and will lie," said Nimrod. "Battening upon huge seaworms in his sleep, / Until the latter fire shall heat the deep; / Then once by men and angels to be seen, / In roaring he shall rise and on the surface die."

"What's that, then?" inquired John.

"The kraken wakes," murmured Nimrod.

CHAPTER 2

GROANIN QUITS

Vesuvius is the most densely populated volcanic region in the world. For the three million Italians who live near the volcano, the fact that smoke had started billowing from the crater would have seemed uncomfortable enough. But Vesuvius is not the only volcano in Italy, nor indeed the largest. Mount Etna in Sicily is more than twice as big as Vesuvius and, according to the television news, began a powerful eruption minutes after the earthquake had struck southern Italy. Stromboli, another of the three active volcanoes in Italy — this one on an island off the coast of Sicily — also began its first eruption since 2003.

"Fascinating," said Nimrod as they watched the television in his handsomely appointed hotel suite. "It's highly unusual that all three volcanoes should become simultaneously active. It seems that we have arrived in Italy at a most interesting time."

"And I always thought Italy was a nice, quiet country," said John.

"Oh, but it is," insisted Nimrod. "All the same, I'd better call my friend, Professor Sturloson in Reykjavik."

"Why would you want to do that, sir?" inquired Groanin.

"Surely you remember, Professor Sturloson, Groanin?"

"Naturally, I remember him, sir. He is a rather hard man to forget."

"Then don't be a fool. He'll want to know what's happening here as soon as possible."

But when Nimrod telephoned the professor at his laboratory in Iceland he was told that Sturloson was out of the country and given a cell phone number to call. Nimrod dialed again and spoke to the professor's assistant, Axel Heimskringla, who explained that he and Professor Sturloson were by a coincidence already in Italy and up on Vesuvius, and that the professor was unable to take Nimrod's call because he was in the process of making a descent into the crater to take some rock samples.

"Please inform the professor I'm on my way to help," Nimrod told Axel Heimskringla. "And that I'll be there within a couple of hours."

"Oh, Lord," groaned Groanin and, sitting down at an antique desk, he began to write a letter.

When Nimrod had finished speaking to Axel Heimskringla, Groanin stood up stiffly and waited politely for a moment to interrupt his master, who was packing a backpack and outlining his plans.

"If we leave now," he told the twins, "we can make the seven minutes past seven Circumvesuviana train from Sorrento to Pompei Scavi. Assuming it's still running after the earthquake. From there we can take a taxi or the bus as far as the upper parking area and then walk to the summit. Assuming it's not closed because of the ash plume. If it's closed, we'll have to hike up the whole mountain so you'd better wear stout shoes, take a walking stick if you have one, and bring lots of bottled water."

"You want to go up Vesuvius?" John's tone was incredulous. "Just when it's started to get active again. Are you crazy?"

"A bit of smoke isn't going to harm you, boy," said Nimrod. "You should know that by now, being a good part smoke yourself."

"Suppose it erupts," objected Philippa, "while we're up there. What then? I'd rather not repeat the experience of my mother and end up like a flying potato chip."

"Yeah," said John. "It's not so easy to find another body. Besides, I'm kind of attached to the one I already have."

"I do have some experience of knowing when a volcano is going to erupt and when it's not," said Nimrod. "After the earthquake of A.D. 63, which seemed to have reawakened Vesuvius, it was another sixteen years before it erupted properly and destroyed Pompeii, in A.D. 79. *Sixteen years.* And Snorri Sturloson would hardly be making a descent into the crater if he thought it was about to explode. He may be mad, but he's not that mad."

Silently, John looked at Philippa, who hardly looked convinced.

"Light my lamp, don't you children want to learn anything?" demanded Nimrod. "This is a fantastic opportunity to expand your knowledge."

"It's not my knowledge expanding I care about," said John. "It's the side of the mountain."

"Nonsense," said Nimrod. "You'll be fine. Groanin, you'd better stop at the local supermarket to buy a lady's nylon stocking, or perhaps a pair of micro-mesh tights. You may need to pull one over your head to help you breathe if the ash becomes troublesome. Given your previous career as a burglar you should be used to wearing that kind of headgear."

"It's bank robbers what wears ladies' nylon stockings over their heads," Groanin said coolly. "Not burglars. And as a matter of fact, I wasn't a burglar. I were only ever a thief. Not that it makes any difference. Do say hello for me to the professor, and to Axel, sir. But I'm afraid I have no intention of wearing a lady's stocking over me head. Nor have I any intention of accompanying you and these children on this daft expedition of yours. Not now. Not ever."

He handed the letter to his master.

"What's this?" asked Nimrod.

"Me resignation," said Groanin. "I'm sorry, sir, but after our last adventure, so called, I swore I wouldn't ever do anything of a hazardous nature again. I've had enough of creepy crawlies and giant millipedes and homicidal head-hunting Indians and all manner of inconveniences that I've had to endure in your service. John's right. It's crazy to go gallivanting up a flipping volcano just when it shows signs of turning nasty. If you want to end up as toast, that's your affair, sir. But count me out."

"Honestly, there's no danger of that, Groanin," insisted Nimrod.

"I wish I had ten pounds for every time you've said something like that."

As soon as Groanin uttered these words, a small leather briefcase appeared, as if by magic, out of rippling thin air on top of the desk where Groanin had written his letter of resignation.

"Eh? What's that?" Groanin opened the briefcase and discovered that it was full of ten-pound notes.

"Sorry," said John. "That was me. It was instinctive. Subliminal wish fulfillment. Couldn't help it."

"Aye, well, this can count as severance pay," said Groanin. "I'm obliged to you, lad."

"But, Groanin." Nimrod looked and sounded bewildered. "What will you do? Where will you go?"

"Back to England," said the butler. "I'll stay with me sister, Dolly, in Heaton Park until I can find a place of me own."

"I didn't even know you had a sister, Groanin," said Philippa.

"We don't get on, she and I. Never did. But blood's blood and she'll have me to stay for a while. I shall miss you and John, right enough. But I shan't miss the foreign travel. Or the foreign grub. Or the hair-raising scrapes that we've been in. I've even started to dream that I was in a scrape. Last night I dreamt I was being chased by a flippin' grizzly bear. I woke up out of breath as if it was actually happening." He shook his head grimly. "I can't take it anymore. I said, I can't take it anymore."

"Look, old chap," said Nimrod. "You don't have to quit. You can stay here. Take it easy. Read the newspaper."

Groanin looked pained. "Thank you, sir, but no. Me mind's made up. I've been thinking about leaving your service for a while and this has just made me think that it's the right thing to do. You see, I know how these adventures start. You'll go off to the volcano, leaving me here at the hotel, but something will happen that'll be worse than if I'd come with you after all. Worse for me, that is. There'll be another earthquake or something and the whole hotel will fall down the cliff face and I'll look like a chump for not coming up Vesuvius."

"Please don't leave," said Philippa. "You're like family."

"Sorry, miss. But one of these days I'm going to end up dead or seriously injured, possibly both. Unlike you, I don't have nine lives, just the one."

"A djinn doesn't have nine lives, Groanin," objected John. "You're thinking of a cat, surely."

"Maybe I am at that," admitted the butler. "Well, if you don't mind, I'm going to go and get packed."

"Will you still be here when we return?" asked Philippa.

"It all depends on how soon I can get on a flight from Naples to Manchester, miss. But perhaps, I don't know."

Groanin wiped a tear from his eye and left Nimrod's room.

The three djinn were silent for a moment as they contemplated the departure of their faithful old friend.

"I'm gonna miss him," said John.

"Me, too," agreed Philippa.

"I shall miss him, right enough," admitted Nimrod. "But his mind seems made up, wouldn't you say?"

"Yes," agreed John.

"Totally," said Philippa.

"I mean, you heard me try to talk him out of it, didn't you?" said Nimrod.

"Yes," they agreed.

"In some ways he was a terrible butler," said Nimrod. "Insolent. Bad tempered. But in many other ways he was the best butler I've ever had." Nimrod paused for a moment and then added: "I shall especially miss his tea. No one makes a cup of tea like Groanin." He shook his head. "And his boiled eggs are perfection. I never knew anyone who could boil an egg so that it was always exactly how I like it. Soft, but not too soft. Every time. While his ironing — his ironing was without equal. There isn't a laundry in the whole of London that could press a shirt as well as Groanin." He sighed. "Still. There's no point in crying over spilled milk. We've got a train to catch."

Fifteen minutes later, the twins followed their uncle out of the hotel and along the street to the railway station where they boarded a train covered in ugly graffiti. Soon, they were rattling north, along the winding, precipitous Neapolitan coast toward Pompeii and Vesuvius.

John and Philippa were unusually quiet during the journey aboard the humid little train since they were preoccupied with Groanin's departure as well as the daunting prospect of ascending to the crater of an active volcano. This silence soon hardened, like pumice, into a mood of pessimism and depression as the reality of everyday life without the grumpy, old butler began to take hold of their young minds. Not even the arrival aboard the train of a three-piece band — guitar, double bass, and accordion — to serenade the sweating passengers with a selection of cheesy Italian hits from the 1950s such as "Volare" and "Tu Vuò Fa' L'Americano" could cheer the twins. And it wasn't long before John began to grow irritated that his enjoyment of feeling miserable should be challenged by a stupid band that nobody had asked or wanted to play and whose jaunty, happy Italian music was now quite at odds with his prevailing feelings of melancholy.

At first, he was inclined to use djinn power to turn the three unwitting musicians into stray cats, which seemed, somehow, appropriate. But better sense and Philippa's telepathic disapproval persuaded the boy djinn that this would have been something of an overreaction; so instead he merely turned the strings of the guitar and of the double bass into dry spaghetti that swiftly shattered, and the impromptu concert aboard the train immediately ended in a shower of broken pasta.

"Thank you, John," said Nimrod. "That was a real kindness to us all."

At Pompei Scavi, they left the train in the company of several hundred tourists who, despite the earthquake and the plume of smoke on Vesuvius, were still intent on sightseeing the ancient Roman city of Pompeii. But the usual bus up the mountain was canceled until further notice and while Nimrod negotiated a "danger-money" fare with a local taxi driver, the twins inspected some of the gift shops with polite disinterest.

CHILDREN OF THE LAMP

Then they were in the taxi and driving through the neglected, garbage-strewn streets of new Pompeii with its dilapidated shops and cheap high-rise apartment buildings.

"Gee, I don't know which is the bigger ruin," observed John. "Roman Pompeii or the new one."

"This is a very poor part of Italy," said Nimrod. "There's not much money here for anything in the way of public services. And of course, the houses are the cheapest in Italy."

"Why's that?" asked Philippa.

"Would you buy a house on the slopes of an active volcano?"

"Hmm," said Philippa. "Perhaps not."

In spite of this, the taxi driver, Carmine, was a happy sort and sang a song all the way up the slopes of the volcano, through a beautiful, sweet-smelling forest, to the upper parking area, where they were met by a contingent of excitable Italian police — the carabinieri — who demanded of the taxi driver and then Nimrod why they and the children had come to what was now a dangerous and restricted area.

Speaking perfect Italian, with a strong Neapolitan accent, Nimrod explained that he was an important volcanologist, a *professore*, and that he had arrived on Vesuvius to lend assistance to the famous Arlecchino; and that since he had brought his own niece and nephew with him they could all rest assured that things were not nearly as bad as they might otherwise have supposed.

After ten or fifteen minutes of lively conversation — which Nimrod had simultaneously translated for the benefit of the twins — the carabinieri allowed the three djinn to complete their journey and to ascend the remaining twenty-seven hundred feet of the volcano to the summit on foot.

The trail led up a dusty, steep, winding path that was covered with volcanic rock and pebbles.

"Why did you call Professor Sturloson, Arlecchino?" Philippa asked Nimrod. "That was the word, wasn't it?"

"Yes," admitted Nimrod. "Everyone in this part of the world calls him that. It's his local nickname. I must say the Italians can be a little cruel like that. But I don't think it bothers him. The name, that is."

"What's it mean?" asked John.

"'Harlequin,'" said Nimrod.

"Why do they call him that?"

Nimrod pulled a face. "Perhaps I should explain one or two things about the professor before you meet him and embarrass us both by staring at Snorri. That's his real, Icelandic name by the way: Snorri Sturloson. But you should call him Professor. Unless he invites you to call him something else. But never Arlecchino. That would be too impertinent."

Nimrod stopped for a moment to catch his breath, admire the view of the Bay of Naples, and to finish his explanation.

"Has either of you ever heard of Montserrat?"

"It's the surname of a famous writer," said Philippa. "And it's also the name of an island in the Caribbean. Next door to Antigua."

Nimrod was impressed. "An island in the Caribbean with a volcano. The Soufrière Hills volcano. The Soufrière

Hills eruption, which began on July eighteenth, 1995, was the first in more than two hundred years. An even larger eruption occurred two years later, which caused the deaths of nineteen people. The professor, who. was monitoring seismic activity with his wife, Björk, was hit by the pyroclastic flow and horribly burnt. One complete side of his face was burnt to a crisp. Which is why he wears the Harlequin mask. And why his wife left him, apparently: because she couldn't bear to look at him."

"Sounds a bit like the guy in *The Phantom of the Opera*," observed John.

"Yes," agreed Nimrod. "In a way. Except that the professor doesn't hide himself away. He may have been horribly disfigured but he's no recluse. His work is too important for him to stay out of the public eye."

"So, this could be dangerous, after all," said John. "This little excursion of ours. I mean, if the professor got it badly wrong once, then he could get it badly wrong again. And so indeed could you. For all we know, this whole mountain could be about to go bang. And then djinn or not, we'll be history."

Nimrod shook his head. "Really, John, there's nothing to worry about. But if you're worried, you can go back down to the car park and wait for us in the taxi."

Philippa took off her glasses and started to polish the lenses, which was always a sign that she was feeling nervous.

"Good idea," said Philippa. "Maybe it's better if you do wait for us down there. But it's all right to be scared, you know. Nothing to be ashamed of, bro." She smiled a sarcastic smile that helped to conceal her own fears. "I might be scared myself if I bothered to stop and really think about it."

"Who said I was scared?" said John. Hoisting his backpack on his shoulder he started up the path again, overtaking Nimrod and leading the way up the rocky path. "All I said was, it could be dangerous. And it is. But I don't mind a bit of danger. Never did."

"By the way," said Philippa. "Does the professor know that you're a djinn?"

"No," said Nimrod. "He thinks of me as gifted in the field of volcanology. But nothing more."

Above the cloud line, they reached the top of the cone and stared down into the depth of what looked like a huge quarry: Most of this resembled a large dust bowl, but from a glowing hole at the foot of one of the sheer walls on the opposite side of the crater was emerging an enormous plume of gray smoke, like the biggest cypress tree anyone had ever seen. John looked up its vertiginous height and thought of "Jack and the Beanstalk" and half expected to see a boy climbing down from an unseen castle several miles above his head, with a goose under his arm.

"Holy smoke," he exclaimed. "That is just amazing. Amazing."

Philippa was experiencing the same sensation as her brother. The idea of the ash plume and its little glowing origin was utterly fascinating to her and reminded Philippa of the time, soon after she and John had lost their wisdom teeth, when the trail of smoke from Mrs. Trump's cigarette had held such a strong fascination for her.

"Isn't it just the most extraordinary thing you have ever seen?" said Nimrod.

"Yes," agreed Philippa unhesitatingly. "It is."

"I think it's the rising column of smoke and ash that exerts such a strong effect on all djinn," said Nimrod. "It touches something deep and primordial within us that no mundane being could ever hope to understand. That's why I wanted to bring you two up here. So that you might understand exactly why it is that volcanoes are so special to our kind. And why it is that the destiny of our djinn tribe, the Marid, has always been inextricably linked to volcanoes.

"For it is written that when a sea of cloud arises from the bowels of the earth to turn the lungs of men to stone and the wheat in the fields to ash, then the Marid shall save the world from inflammable darkness."

CHAPTER 3

SNORRI STURLOSON

W here is it written?" asked Philippa.

She thought it was a reasonable question but Nimrod didn't answer. Her uncle had seen Professor Sturloson climbing up a long rope from the interior of Vesuvius, and was already hurrying down a desolate-looking path into the crater to greet him. Philippa and John followed him to a Matterhorn-shaped rock crest around which the professor's rappel rope had been expertly tied and where a tall, blond-haired man was carefully monitoring Sturloson's laborious ascent.

Philippa thought this tall man very handsome indeed.

"My dear Axel," said Nimrod. "How are you? Permit me to introduce my nephew and niece, John and Philippa. Children? This stout fellow is Axel Heimskringla."

The blond-haired man greeted Nimrod and the twins warmly in Icelandic but never took his blue eyes off the taut rope; and finally, a wiry-looking man, covered in dust and sweat and wearing a Harlequin's black mask, appeared at their feet, grunting loudly. He pulled himself up onto the Mars-like red dust of the crater path and sat down heavily.

John leaned a little closer, curious to see the full extent of the horrible burns that might lie behind the mask and saw an ear that was no bigger than a child's.

"Snorri, my dear fellow," said Nimrod. "I was holidaying in Sorrento with my niece and nephew and saw the ash cloud. So I thought I'd better come up here and take a closer look. Although not as close as you just did. What do you think? Is it safe?"

The professor said nothing until he had caught his breath and drank two whole quarts of water, and because of the mask it was difficult to tell if he had even registered Nimrod's presence; but finally, he nodded wearily and said, "It looks safe enough for now, I believe. I took a lava sample. From a spot as near the fissure as I dared to go. Really, it's quite imperative that I should have several more before I venture an opinion as to the volcano's long-term future, but I was overcome by heat and exhaustion. I'm not the climber I used to be."

Both the professor and Axel spoke with a strong Icelandic accent, which is a bit like a Scandinavian accent, but colder.

The professor lifted his arms and allowed Axel to untie the rope that was knotted around his middle. That was when John noticed the professor was wearing a single glove. At first, when it caught the sunlight, he thought it was a rhinestone glove, and it was another moment before he realized it was actually made of chain mail.

"Who is, dear fellow?" said Nimrod. "Who is? None of

us is getting any younger. I'm afraid my days of clambering up and down ropes like a monkey are behind me."

"I'll go," said Axel, and fed the rope around his own waist.

The professor shook his head. "You can't. You're too heavy, my boy."

"This is a good rope," insisted Axel. "Should be no problem. Besides, you said yourself, it's imperative that you get some more lava samples."

"It's not the rope I'm concerned about," said the professor. "It's the crater floor. I'm half your weight and underneath the dust, the floor felt very brittle. Like a honeycomb. You might easily fall through."

John glanced over the edge of the path and thought it looked safe enough. The volcano wasn't anything like what he had imagined. If it hadn't been for the large column of smoke that emanated from the fissure in the crater wall, he might even have said it looked a bit boring. And stung by his sister's suggestion that he lacked the nerve to climb an active volcano, he was determined to prove to his uncle — he really didn't care what Philippa thought about him — that he could do a lot more than ascend the outside of Vesuvius; he could also descend into the inside of Vesuvius.

"Why not let me try?" said John. "To gather some more lava samples, you say? Well, I can do that. And the heat is hardly likely to worry me. After all I'm —"

Nimrod covered John's mouth with his hand.

"You impetuous youth," he said. "Professor Sturloson? This is my young nephew, John. And my niece, Philippa, his sister. Like most children they think they're immortal.

Especially John. Anyone would think he had superpowers, the way he carries on. He hasn't yet learned that he is just a human being like the rest of us, and nothing more. Eh, John?"

"If you say so, Uncle," muttered John, remembering almost too late that these two humans were ignorant of the kind of beings Nimrod and his blood relatives were.

But Professor Sturloson was having none of it. He stood up, brushed off his clothes, which were those of an old-fashioned mountaineer — all gaiters, tweed, and flannel — and taking John's hand in the chain-mail glove, pumped it furiously.

"Nonsense, Nimrod," he said, and clapped John on the shoulder. "This *is* a brave lad. And you should be proud of him. Very proud. Of course, it's quite unthinkable that one could actually permit a boy to go down there to do a man's work but —"

"With all due respect, sir," said John. "Now it's you who's talking nonsense. You said yourself it's imperative you get more samples and that Dr. Kreimhingla was too heavy for the crater floor."

"Heimskringla," said Axel, trying to conceal his irritation. "My name is Heimskringla."

"Well, if he can't go, and you can't go, and Nimrod can't go, then that leaves me and my sister," argued John. "And I'm not about to let a girl go down there when I can go myself."

"Sexist," said Philippa.

"Have you ever rappelled down a rope before, boy?" asked Axel. "It's extremely dangerous. Rappelling is the highest cause of fatality among mountaineers because it looks a lot easier than it is."

"But it's a lot easier than climbing back up," added the professor.

"I can climb a rope," insisted John. "I'm a boy. It's what we boys do best. Sure, I wish I was a better climber."

And muttering his focus word, which was ABECEDARIAN, he was. For such is the power of a djinn that new skills and knowledge can be instantly learned.

"But I think I know what I'm doing."

And now, of course, he did.

John picked up a spare length of rope and began tying knots. "Here," he said. "A three-wrap Prusik." Untying the Prusik as quickly as he tied it, John began to tie another knot. "A French Prusik." And then another: "A Munter hitch."

"Impressive," said Axel.

"A rolling hitch." John was showing off now. "Can either of you do a rolling hitch?"

Axel looked abashed. "Er, no," said Axel.

"And there are easier ways to climb a rope than what I saw you doing just now, Professor," said John. "I would have assumed that knowing how to rappel, you would have brought some mechanical ascenders."

It was hard to tell if behind the mask the professor looked abashed or not; but he certainly sounded abashed. "*Nei*," said the professor.

"Then it's fortunate I brought my own rig." John dropped his backpack onto the ground and took out a Petzl Corax harness, several carabiners, a handful of ascenders, fingerless climbing gloves, an ice ax, and a helmet.

"I see you came prepared, bro," said Philippa.

"We can hardly argue with a man who brought his own harness," said the professor. "Nimrod, you didn't tell us the boy was so proficient. *Hann er alveg litla hetja.*"

"Among all his other accomplishments, it quite slipped my mind," said Nimrod.

"As long as it's the only thing that slips," observed Philippa, "then he'll be okay, I guess."

While John got into his climbing harness, she gave him a skeptical look.

"Do you really know what you're doing?" asked Philippa.

"You know I do," answered John. "You most of all."

Philippa nodded. Now that she stopped to think about it, she realized that her twin brother was right, for all twins, be they djinn or no, possess curious powers over nature and often have the true knowing of things that could not be known by means other than what might be called telepathy.

"All right," she agreed. "I guess you do know what you're doing."

Only when John was secure on the rope and standing on the edge of the crater rim ready to rappel down onto the floor of the volcano almost a hundred feet below, did he start to feel a little nervous. Because of his wish *he knew* what he was doing; but knowing and feeling are two different things. And nearly all of his confidence was inside his brain rather than in his hands and his feet. This was hardly surprising and probably just as well. For as the late Mr. Rakshasas once said, "A man who is not afraid of the sea will soon be drowned."

Axel clipped an asbestos-lined rock sample bag and telescopic scoop to John's harness while the professor advised him on what to do when he reached the bottom.

"*Illusta.* Stay as close to the crater wall as possible," he said. "The dust is treacherous and shifting underfoot, like a sand dune. What you need to do is traverse the length of the wall toward the fissure. The nearer you get, the warmer the rock will become to the touch. When it starts to feel hot, or you're as near to the ash plume as your lungs can bear, hammer a piton into the wall and then descend on the rope a little. There's a small, fresh lava flow underneath the plume. It's important you recognize the difference between rock and lava, John, because only fresh *pahoehoe* lava gives us a precise idea of what's happening underground. *Pahoehoe* lava is smooth and billowy and undulating, like it's some sort of curtain material. In fact, it's molten rock, and about twelve hundred degrees centigrade, so for Pete's sake don't touch it with your hand. Use the sample scoop. Find a toe or lobe on the edge of the main flow and pour some water on it. This should break it off the flow and allow you to pick it up with the scoop.

"Now: some do's and don'ts, *hugrakkur ungur vinur minn.* Do pay attention with all your senses. If you feel vibration in the wall of the crater, assume the worst and make your way back. The same goes if you hear an explosion. Try not to put too much weight on the ground under your feet. The ground might be thin and you could go straight through. Even if you didn't fall in, the hole you make would create enough oxygen to cause a sudden flash flame that would surely incinerate you, my boy. And watch that the rope doesn't rest somewhere too hot and start to melt. It's nylon, see? And nylon melts when it gets hot. Just like your papa's shirt when your mama gets careless with the iron."

John nodded gravely. His father had never worn a nylon shirt in his life, but that was beside the point now.

"But the thing you really have to watch out for is gas. It's the gas that's most likely to kill you, boy. And I'm not talking about the smell of sulfur and rotten eggs and all that *kjaftœði*. I'm talking about something much worse. Carbon dioxide. You can't smell CO_2. And you can't taste it. But it's denser than air and you might see it moving on the ground like a river of smoke. So keep your eyes peeled. And of course if you start to feel very sleepy, that's a sure sign that CO_2 is affecting you. If that happens, you move the other way as quickly as possible."

Professor Sturloson shrugged. "Well, there's a lot more hazards I could describe but that's probably enough to be going on with."

"Light my lamp," exclaimed Nimrod, "I swear if I hear of another life-threatening hazard, I won't let the boy go down there at all."

"It's all right," insisted John. "I'll be careful. Depend on it."

Stepping out was the worst part because this was the moment he was handing over his life to the equipment he'd created from thin air. John checked his locking carabiner and the figure-of-eight it secured and then, putting more weight on the rope, he leaned back and began walking his way over the edge and down the sheer crater wall.

CHAPTER 4

GROANIN CHECKS IN

Groanin finished packing his battered leather suitcase and took a taxi to Naples airport. Like most airports in summer this one was full of sweaty tourists with cheap luggage milling aimlessly around as if they had lost their heads on a chicken farmer's chopping block. So far so normal. But as Groanin approached the British Airways check-in desks he began to sense that not all was well. Word spread quickly through the line of strongly smelling travelers awaiting check-in that the British Airways cabin staff had called a strike. Everyone groaned loudly, Groanin loudest of all, and headed to the ticketing desks for other airlines.

Half an hour later, he succeeded in buying an easyJet ticket to Manchester and was congratulating himself on his own resourcefulness when an announcement on the Naples airport loudspeaker announced that because of the ash plume from Vesuvius, all southern Italian airspace was closed to passenger aircraft until further notice.

"When is that?" he demanded of the frazzled-looking girl manning the easyJet check-in desk. "Until when are we likely to be stranded here?"

"Until I don't know," she said. "Until someone decides it's safe. Until tomorrow at the very earliest. Until someone tells me different."

"If this is southern Italy," said Groanin, "then what constitutes northern Italy? They're flying from there, right? Where do I have to go to get on a plane home?"

"Get yourself to Rome," said the girl. "They're still flying from Rome. Is what I would do."

"How far is that, then?"

"From here, is one hundred forty miles," said the girl. She switched off her computer and then walked quickly away from the desk before Groanin or anyone else could ask her another awkward question.

Groanin bit his lip and, pulling his largish suitcase on wheels, went outside to look for transport and found the line at the taxi rank was already more than a hundred yards long with no actual taxis in sight. The line for buses into Naples was even longer and there seemed to be no train station attached to the airport.

"Flipping heck," he murmured. "This is a nightmare. A real one. Forget being chased by a grizzly bear. This is worse."

Seeing a sign for Naples city center, he followed it, hoping to hail a taxi along the way. But if the lines of tourists at the airport had been bad, the lines of traffic on the *autostrada* were even worse. All of the roads between the airport and the city center were one big traffic jam and, in spite of the

91° heat, Groanin had little alternative but to take off his jacket and walk into the city, because Sorrento was too far for him to go all the way back there.

Not that Groanin wanted to return to the Excelsior Vittoria hotel and face Nimrod like a dog with its tail between its legs. That would have been too humiliating. Worse, there was every chance that Nimrod would offer Groanin his job back and, weakened by heat and exhaustion and the sheer horror of traveling on his own dollar, he might easily accept it. Groanin knew that now was his best chance to escape Nimrod's service for good. It wasn't that he disliked Nimrod. And he loved the children, of course. But as he had explained, the hazards of working for a djinn were just too great for him to bear his employment any longer.

Four miles and two hours later, Groanin finally came in sight of a hotel that looked equal to his fastidious, xeno-phobic tastes: the First Grand Imperial Britannia Hotel. A British flag hung like a dishcloth on a flagpole outside the entrance.

Dripping with sweat, and almost faint with dehydration, Groanin trudged into the dingy lobby and approached the ancient-looking reception desk.

On the wall behind the desk was a large picture of the queen. Another good sign, or so Groanin thought.

A short, red-haired man ignored him carefully for a moment and then condescended to pay him some attention.

"Good afternoon, and welcome to the First Grand Imperial Brittania Hotel, sir," said the man behind the desk, who seemed to be British. "Can I help you?"

"Thank goodness for an English accent," said Groanin. "If it was an English accent." He collapsed against the desk and looked more closely at the man behind it. "I dunno. Was it?"

Unfortunately, Groanin was one of those people who, to the irritation of the Scots, the Irish, and the Welsh, employ the word *English* when they really mean *British*. In Groanin's case this was the result of having spent so much time with John and Philippa who, being Americans, had little or no sense of the subtle difference between what are two very different things.

Groanin frowned and peered more closely at the receptionist. The man had green eyes and skin as pale as last week's lard. "Wait a minute. You're not English. You're Scottish, aren't you?"

"I am," said the receptionist, bridling a little. "And proud of it, too."

"Then what are you doing here, sunshine?"

The man's face reddened with anger. "We're not the untraveled peasants you English think we are."

"No?" said Groanin. "Never mind. British will have to do. British is good enough under these extreme conditions. Now listen, Angus. I want a room, with a bath, and then I want some dinner. Proper food, mind. None of that foreign stuff. I say, I don't want any of that Italian muck. I want English food. Roast beef and roast potatoes and recognizable vegetables. Can you do that, innkeeper?"

The receptionist, who was from Edinburgh, and by a strange coincidence was actually called Angus, disliked the assumption that all Scotsman are called Angus almost as much as he disliked the English who were often those making that assumption. Indeed, his strong dislike of the English had, since his arrival in Italy, been many times reinforced by the fact of its being regularly assumed by the Neapolitans that he was English himself. And he had almost lost count of the number of times he had fixed a patient, snaggle-toothed smile to his fat face and corrected their mistake. In short, he was a tiresome little man with no more people skills than a guard dog. As a hotel-keeper in Scotland this would not have been a problem; but in a country as friendly as Italy, it marked him out as uniquely ill qualified for his chosen career.

"I'll have to see," said Angus unhelpfully. "Did you make a booking?"

Angus was well aware that Groanin hadn't made a booking but he still felt it was necessary to make the customer feel small and stupid and that by asking for a room he was putting the staff to enormous inconvenience.

"Should I have done?" asked Groanin.

"This is the high season," said Angus. "We're normally very busy right now."

Groanin surveyed the many keys hanging on the wall behind the desk. It looked as if the hotel was empty, which he ought to have taken as a bad sign, which it was, but he didn't.

"I'll take your word for it."

"You can have twenty-two," said Angus. "Payment in advance if you don't mind. And payment in advance even if you do."

"Very hospitable, I'm sure."

Groanin opened his money bag, took out his foreign currency wallet, and shoved some money across the desk. Angus hardly looked at the money coming his way; he was much more interested in the large amount of cash Groanin was carrying in his bag. The tens of thousands of pounds that John had put there with djinn power.

"In the morning I shall want a copy of *The Daily Telegraph*, an English breakfast, and then transport out of here," he said. "A taxi to the airport, if it's open. And the railway station if it's not."

"There's a Scottish breakfast, if that's any good to you," said Angus. "And we only get the *Daily Express*."

"I wouldn't line a hamster cage with that," said Groanin, and wearily snatching the room key from the Scotsman's hand, he went up to his room.

Angus watched him go and then picked up the telephone to report on the interesting Englishman's bag of money.

CHAPTER 5

THE DESCENT

At first, John's descent into the huge crater was slow and steady and it was only after a few minutes that, gaining in confidence, he felt equal to the task of actually kicking off and rappelling down the rock face like some black-clad special-forces soldier. Adrenaline pumping now, he whooped loudly as he bounced on and off the rock face like a racquetball.

"This is fun!" he yelled.

"He seems to know what he's doing," observed Axel.

"Let's hope so," replied Nimrod.

Reaching the bottom of the wall, John secured himself with a piton and then waved at Nimrod and the others. Down here, a strong smell of sulfur filled the combusted air, and from time to time the eerie silence of the volcano was broken by the sound of melted rock hitting the basalt beneath the plume after it cooled in the air and became pieces of hardened lava.

Underneath John's boots, the slope of red dust that covered the crater floor moved treacherously. And even through the thick rubber soles he could feel the heat of it in his socks. Pieces of rock and shale went tumbling down the length of the slope like tiny skiers caught in an avalanche and, but for the rope securing him to the wall, John might easily have followed. Instead, he started to climb along the base of the wall toward the smoke fissure. Without gravity to help him now, he made slow, laborious progress. From time to time he glanced around and caught a glimpse of a soft reddish glow and sometimes orange sparks in the space behind the smoke, as if a hidden blast furnace was being stoked by the scaly hand of some unseen demon from the infernal regions of the earth. For anyone lying on an area of grass in a quiet park, he thought, it would have seemed incredible that the ground contained such enormous violence.

"Makes you wonder exactly what lies beneath us all," he told himself.

The air was hard to breathe now. Every so often John had to stop and give way to a fit of coughing. The third time it happened he soaked his handkerchief in water and tied it around his nose and mouth. He might have remained at this position and gathered some lava samples right then and there, except that much better ones were to be had a little nearer the fissure. He started along the traverse again and, moving into the shadow cast by the eastern edge of the crater, he stopped for a moment to allow his eyes to adjust to the sudden lack of light. Glancing up he saw that his companions were now wholly obscured by smoke from the fissure.

"Man," he exclaimed. "This is hard work."

But just a few more feet to go and then he could start gathering samples of lava. And what samples they were. This lava was not like he had imagined it being at all. Was it a trick of the light that the lava looked so shiny and, almost — there was no other word for it — precious? And yet how could it be? He was in shadow now and the strong sunlight on the other side of the crater floor could have had nothing to do with this.

This lava was the color of gold.

Of course he didn't think it *was* gold. Probably the professor, being a geologist, would offer some simple explanation for this golden lava. And if he had ever paid attention in a science class, John might have devised a few explanations of his own. But as it was, he hadn't a clue what might have caused it except perhaps the idea that the golden color was what most rock looked like when it was almost twenty-two hundred degrees Fahrenheit.

He hammered another piton into the wall and let himself down until his feet were almost touching the edge of the golden lava flow. He felt like he was standing in front of an open oven door. It was, he thought, just as well the two Icelanders could no longer see him as they would surely have wondered how anyone could have withstood the high temperatures John was now experiencing.

Leaning back in his harness, John poured some water from his bottle onto the advancing toes of the lava flow, and then hammered off some pieces with his ice ax before collecting the hot, golden shards with his scoop and emptying them into the asbestos-lined sample bag. He felt like Neil

Armstrong collecting moon rocks except that he could have wished to have been weightless. Of course he didn't wish any such thing, which would only have given the game away as far as Professor Snorri Sturloson and Axel were concerned.

John smiled to himself as he worked. *How did you get a name like Snorri?* he wondered.

He drew himself back up to the piton on the wall and unclipped his rope in order to traverse back. It wasn't a particularly difficult maneuver or one that required any great physical exertion, and it struck John as odd that his pulse should start to race as if he had been sprinting. The next second, his legs weakened noticeably and he started to see stars. Suddenly, it was really hard to breathe.

Instinct told him he was suffering from carbon dioxide poisoning and that his only chance was to get away from the fissure and find some fresh air as quickly as possible. He might have uttered his focus word and wished for a fireman's breathing apparatus if his mind had been less confused by lack of oxygen, but it was all he could do to stretch one leg to his left and then bring the other alongside, and then to do this again, and again, and again.

Finally, he escaped the invisible pocket of deadly gas and was in fresh air, where he quickly managed to heave some oxygen into his lungs and started to revive. Looking up the edge of the crater, he waved at the four figures standing there and then continued back to the position where he would make his ascent.

He locked in a right- and left-hand ascender on the rope with two carabiners and attached his harness. Next, he thumbed the release button on the right-hand ascender and stretched it up above his head so that when he let the release button go, the teeth on the ascender could bite into the rope. Then he started his ascent.

All went well for about forty feet when a small explosion from the fissure behind him blew out a fragment of molten rock about the size of a cell phone. Most of it hit the crater wall but a smaller piece hit the rope above John's head.

"Holy mackerel."

John lifted the ascender to a place on the rope a few inches below the spot hit by the lava and lifted himself up to take a closer look. To his alarm he saw that the nylon rope had already started to melt under the lava's nearly twenty-two-degree Fahrenheit temperature. He poured some water onto the lava spot in the hope that this might prevent the rope from melting any further; and it did, only this hardly seemed to improve his precarious situation. The blackened rope seemed to harden and narrow as the water cooled the lava so that John was left with little choice but to quickly slide the right-hand ascender over the length of damaged rope and risk it snagging the climbing aid's mechanics. It didn't and he breathed half a sigh of relief; but before he could take his weight off the left-hand ascender and move that up the rope, it broke, which left him hanging by his right hand.

Dangling like a gibbon, John let out a gibbonlike yelp and wondered what to do. The temptation to use djinn power immediately and wish for a new rope was, of course, almost overwhelming; but he checked himself for a moment in the hope that Nimrod might see his dilemma and offer some help from the crater rim above. John then confined his focus word to making a wish that his right hand might have a stronger grip.

Seeing his nephew's vertiginous dilemma, Nimrod glanced around the crater path.

"Rope," he yelled. "We need another length of rope."

"There isn't one," admitted Axel.

"There must be," said Nimrod.

"There isn't," insisted the professor.

Philippa was beside herself with anxiety. "Do something," she yelled.

Nimrod pointed at the little concrete building farther along the crater path. "Perhaps there's one in there," he said.

"It's a gift shop," said Axel. "They sell stupid souvenir necklaces made of lava, and bottles of water, not climber's rope."

Nimrod wasn't listening. The souvenir shop was closed, of course. But he was hardly deterred by that. Nimrod kicked open the door, muttered his focus word, and collected a large coil of climber's rope that suddenly appeared against the wall of the shop.

"Found some," he said, running back to the others. He tossed it down and immediately started to tie one end around the Matterhorn-shaped rock crest.

"Well, I'm surprised," said the professor. "I was in the shop this morning and didn't see any rope."

"Me neither," admitted Axel.

"That's quite all right, my dear chap," said Nimrod, and

chucked the rest of the rope down to John. "Easy to overlook a bit of old rope, eh?"

Sixty feet below, John took hold of the new rope in his left hand and breathed a sigh of relief. Now the only problem was how he was going to get up the rope to the crater rim. Even with a newly improved strong grip in his right hand, it was going to take an awfully long time. Wrapping the new rope around his leg to secure himself, he wondered if he could attach his ascenders to the new rope and quickly realized that the only way that was ever going to happen was by using djinn power. Which — following an interval of several minutes when he made a show of fumbling around with his harness for the benefit of the two Icelanders who were watching him up on the crater rim, always supposing their eyesight was as keen as that of an eagle — is exactly what he did.

"ABECEDARIAN!"

And with the two ascenders properly attached to the new rope, John continued with his ascent.

At last he reached the crater rim where Axel, who was as strong as he was handsome, grabbed hold of his harness and hauled him over the side.

"*Ótrúlegt*," he said. "Amazing. I didn't think it was possible to attach a rappel harness to a rope when you were already on it."

"It was nothing," said John.

"*Frábœr*." Axel shook his head. "And I thought I knew a lot about rock climbing." He clapped John on the shoulder. "Hey, promise you'll show me how to do that."

"Sure," said John. "Why not?" He smiled sheepishly. "It'd be my pleasure."

"I'd like to see that myself, John," observed Philippa. "It should be fascinating."

"I still don't understand how you managed to get that close to the fissure, John," said the professor. "The heat must have been *ákafur*. Intense. If you had stayed any longer, you'd have ended up looking like me, boy. And believe me, this is not a pretty sight."

"It was kind of hot," admitted John.

"That's quite a nephew you have there, Nimrod," said Axel.

Still shaking his head, Axel went to the Matterhorn-shaped rock crest to untie the rope while Professor Sturloson emptied John's asbestos bag and examined his lava samples.

"My God, it's true," he said. "It really is gold. I couldn't believe my own eyes when I saw the lava flow down there. I thought the heat or the CO_2 was getting to me."

"The CO_2 did get to me," said John. "I almost passed out down there."

"I can't believe this knot you tied, Nimrod," confessed Axel.

"Hmm. What's that, dear boy?" Nimrod was preoccupied with his own examination of the golden lava samples.

"I never before saw a knot like this one you tied, Nimrod. And I wouldn't begin to know how to untie it."

Nimrod did not look up from the two golden lava samples that lay in the palms of his hands like two very special eggs.

"That?" he said absently. "That's a Dionysus knot. I'm afraid you're not supposed to know how to untie it. You see, as well as being the most secure knot it's humanly possible to tie, it's also a cipher. A sort of code. You had better cut it. Like your near namesake, Alexander the Great. Otherwise we'll be here all day."

Axel unfolded his lock knife and began to saw at the rope.

"Professor?" said Nimrod. "Do you have access to the research institute? Here on Vesuvius."

"I prefer to have a lab in the old observatory," said Professor Sturloson. "Not in the new research institute. I don't like the people working in the new institute to see me."

"It's quite understandable that you should feel a bit self-conscious about your mask," said Nimrod.

"No, that's not the reason," said the professor. "My mask scares the Italians. Oh, I don't mean they're afraid of me. No, it's that I don't want them to be scared of the possible consequences of the work they're doing. I don't want what happened to me to put anyone off from this important work. They're all handsome fellows. Apart from the two women who work there. And they're beauties. I just don't think any of them wants to end up with his face burnt off by a pyroclastic flow."

Nimrod nodded. "That's most admirable, Snorri," he said. "Most admirable. Well, look, we need to examine a section of this lava sample under a light-polarizing microscope. Urgently."

"You're worried about the golden color, aren't you?" said the professor. "And that ancient Mongolian legend."

"Yes. I am."

"You really don't believe that such a thing could ever happen, do you?" The professor shook his head. "Not a man of science like you, Nimrod."

"What legend is that?" asked Philippa.

Nimrod didn't answer. He was still frowning at the gold lava samples.

The professor continued to shake his head. "Surely such a thing couldn't ever be possible. Could it?"

"What legend?" repeated John.

"I don't know about any Mongolian legend," said Axel. "But I can tell you what really isn't possible. It isn't possible to cut through this rope."

"What are you talking about, Axel?" said the professor.

"This rope," said Axel. "It appears to be indestructible."

Nimrod winced as if he had been stung by a bee. In his haste to "find" a length of climbing rope to throw to John and mindful of the fate that had befallen the other rope, Nimrod had managed to create a rope that was impervious to molten rock, not to mention the sharp edge of Axel's lock knife.

"I've tried cutting it," said Axel. "And I've tried picking the fibers to pieces with the point of my knife. I've even tried burning it with my cigarette lighter." He handed the lighter to the professor. "Here, you try."

"Oh, we've no time for that now, surely," said Nimrod.

But the professor was not to be denied his opportunity to try to burn the rope himself.

"You're right," he said. "I've never seen anything like it."

"We really ought to get down to the observatory," insisted Nimrod. "To test the samples."

"I wonder what else this rope might withstand," mused the professor. "It really is remarkable. And you found this in the souvenir shop, Nimrod?"

"Er, that's right," said Nimrod.

John thought to help his uncle by offering an explanation that managed to sound even more improbable than a rope that could not be cut or burnt.

"Yeah," he said, "I'll bet it's that amazing new, indestructible, high-tech, top secret rope I've been reading about in some of the American climbing magazines. A top scientist invented it for the U.S. special forces after his son was killed climbing on the island of Antigua. It's called Nine Lines, I think, on account of the fact that it's made of nine separate cords and because it seems to have nine lives. Like a cat."

Philippa closed her eyes and wondered if she should use djinn power to make her brother shut up. Sometimes it was a little hard to believe he was her twin.

"Antigua?" said the professor.

"Yeah, it's an island in the Caribbean, near Montserrat."

"I have good reason to remember exactly where it is," said the professor. "That's where I lost my face."

"Oh, right," said John. "Sorry."

"It's just that there aren't any mountains to speak of in Antigua," said the professor. "In fact it's one of the least mountainous countries in the world."

"Well, it might not have been there exactly," said John, backtracking a little. "It could have been on another island.

Like the Bahamas. Or the Maldives. I dunno. Anyway, it wasn't a mountain he was climbing. It was a palm tree, I think. A very tall palm tree."

"Well, that explains it," said the professor. "A bit. All the same it's amazing that we should have found some top secret rope just lying around here, in a souvenir shop. Don't you think? And quite fortunate. For you."

John shrugged.

"I expect the Americans were lending it to the Italian Army," said John. "For a NATO exercise. After all, we're all on the same side these days, aren't we?"

"Yes, we are," Nimrod said firmly. "And right now, in more ways than one. We need to make a start in the lab. Before these lava samples get too hard to cut."

"You're right," agreed the professor. "There is no time to lose. Because I'm afraid our rock saw is not as sharp as it could be."

Philippa smiled at her brother. "It sounds like you and it have something in common."

CHAPTER 6

TOOTSI FROOTSI

Alone in his crummy room at the First Grand Imperial Britannia Hotel, Groanin did not enjoy his roast beef dinner. He took one look at the grisly plate on the trolley in front of him and knew without touching one congealed mouthful that the food he had ordered was quite inedible; however he was feeling a little guilty concerning the way he had spoken to Angus, the hotel receptionist, and the fuss he had made about having "proper English food" and now he was hesitant to pick up the phone and complain, which had been his first instinct.

No more did he want to injure the feelings of the poor chef. As someone who had often cooked for Nimrod, Groanin was well aware of how hurtful a customer complaint could be to those in service, and instead of just leaving the food uneaten, he decided to go the extra mile and to dispose of it in some thoughtful way. It was fortunate — for this purpose, if nothing else — that Groanin's second-floor room was immediately over the garbage at the back of the hotel and he was easily able to lean out of his grimy window and sweep the entire contents of his plate straight into an open trash can, where a family of rats ate them later.

Following a decent interval, during which time it was possible he might actually have eaten the dinner, Groanin telephoned room service and told the switchboard operator that someone could come and remove the dinner trolley; a few minutes later, Angus himself, all smiles now, turned up at his hotel room door.

"Everything all right?" the Scotsman asked Groanin.

"Er, yes, it was very nice," said Groanin.

"There's nothing like a nice roast, is there, sir?"

Groanin nodded and restrained himself from telling the Scotsman that what had appeared on his plate had indeed been nothing at all like a nice roast. What would have been the point? The man was a Scot. In Groanin's opinion, good food and the Scots were at opposite ends of life's restaurant.

"Can I get you anything else?" asked Angus.

"Er, no, that was quite sufficient," said Groanin. "I'm going to bed now. And you can forget the English breakfast. Or for that matter, the Scottish one. In the morning I shall only require transport to the station."

"I'm afraid that all the trains in southern Italy have gone on strike," explained the Scotsman as he wheeled the dinner trolley toward the door.

"Don't say they're affected by the volcano, too?"

"No, no. They want more money, that's all. And they're going on strike in order to take advantage of the fact that there are no planes flying."

"Very Machiavellian, I'm sure," said Groanin. "In which case I'd better have a taxi driver who's prepared to take me to Rome."

"Very well, sir. Good night, sir. Sleep well, sir."

"Yes, I think I shall, you know. I said, I think I shall. One way or another, it's been a most tiring, tiresome day."

The Scotsman closed the door behind him and rubbed his hands with malicious glee.

"Sleep well, you fat Sassenach," he said, and laughing at his soon-to-be-realized good fortune, Angus pushed the trolley into the elevator. "Sleep well."

It was fortunate that Groanin had not eaten his dinner because Angus had drugged it with a powerful sleeping draft. Somewhere in the wee small hours of the morning he intended to let himself into the insensible English butler's room and steal the bag of cash that John's djinn power had created for him.

Groanin ate a couple of bags of potato chips from the minibar and watched TV, which was how he learned that several other European volcanoes were also showing signs of new activity: the Montañas del Fuego on Lanzarote, Hekla in Iceland, and near the Greek mainland, Santorini. There was no doubt about it, he thought. He had to reach Rome as soon as possible to get on a flight for Manchester, otherwise he faced being stranded in Europe for the rest of the summer as the effects of the strike and the volcanoes started to bite.

This thought — about the effects of something starting to bite — prompted Groanin to remove his false teeth, and, having placed these in a large vodka and tonic, he went straight to bed.

Despite the soporific effects of *David Copperfield*, Groanin slept only lightly that night, and just before dawn he awoke to hear furtive movement in his room, which was full of light coming through the threadbare curtains from the street-lamp outside his window. Opening one eye, he saw a figure with his money bag creeping toward the door. Groanin did not hesitate. He reached for a weapon and the first weapon that came, instinctively, to hand was his silver-framed picture of Her Majesty the Queen. Hurling it hard across the room like a Frisbee, the picture struck Angus squarely on the back of the head and knocked him out, but not before it had shattered into several pieces.

Groanin switched on the bedside light, collected his false teeth, drank the vodka and tonic, leaped out of bed, and looked sadly at the scene that now met his eyes.

Angus groaned loudly and rubbed the back of his red-haired head.

"I am so sorry," Groanin said to the picture. "I'd have given anything to have avoided that, Your Majesty. That you should be used as a projectile to bring down a light-fingered Scotsman. The indignity of it. The sheer disrespect of it takes one's breath away. But in the heat of the moment, I took hold of the first thing and hurled it. I am so, so sorry."

He kicked the bag to the opposite side of the room and then picked up the pieces of the picture. He nodded at the woman in the photograph and placed her and the silver frame and the cardboard slip on the edge of his bed.

"That's all right," said Angus. "Not much harm done, I think."

Groanin bent down and flicked the Scotsman's pink ear very hard.

"Ow!" said Angus.

"No one's talking to you, Rob Roy MacGregor. Except perhaps the police when I've telephoned them."

He picked up the telephone and started to dial.

"Please, sir. Have pity on me. I've a police record and they'll throw the book at me this time. I'll be deported, for sure." Angus rolled over and adopted a begging position, consistent with someone asking for mercy.

Groanin stopped dialing. Being an ex-thief himself, he disliked the idea of turning someone in to the police; if Nimrod hadn't been such a forgiving sort, he might have gone to prison himself, too. Could he do any less than forgive this worthless man? He put down the phone and picked up the Scot. One of the butler's arms had been created with djinn power and as a result was superstrong. Mostly it came in handy for picking up Nimrod's heavy suitcases and it was rare that the butler ever used it in an intimidating way. But this was the arm he used now to slowly lift the thieving Scot up to the ceiling.

Which was very intimidating. The Scotsman squealed loudly, as his head brushed the ceiling light.

"Count yourself lucky I'm the forgiving sort," said Groanin.

"Thank you, sir."

Groanin looked at his watch. It was five o'clock and there seemed little point in going back to bed now.

"Tell you what," he said. "Get me a cab and we'll call it quits."

"Yes, sir. Yes, sir."

Groanin carried Angus to the telephone and put him down; immediately the Scotsman dialed a number and spoke in Italian. This happened several times. Finally, Angus confessed that there were no taxis to be had in the whole of Naples.

"Because of the rail strike," he explained.

"You'd better find me some transport to Rome and pronto," growled Groanin, "or you'll find there's no shortage of police cars prepared to come and ferry people to jail."

"Yes, sir," squealed Angus, and once again he picked up the telephone.

Half an hour later, Angus put down the phone with a look of relief.

"All right," he said. "I've got someone who's prepared to take you to Rome. It's not what you'd call a car, exactly, but I promise you it's all there is this morning."

"If it's not a car, what is it?"

"A van," said Angus. "The driver's name is Bruno Tattaglia. Turns out Bruno was going to Rome, anyway. To visit his mother. You won't have to pay him anything. He's doing this as a favor to me."

Groanin nodded. "A van will have to do, I suppose."

"You promise you won't call the police?"

"If this van turns up, yes, I promise. But if it doesn't, you're cell meat."

An hour later, Groanin and Angus were standing outside

the front of the hotel beside the butler's leather suitcase and waiting on his ride to Rome.

"Where is this blighter?"

"This is him coming now, sir."

A cheeky jingle heralded the arrival of a pale blue van at the front of the hotel. On the roof of the van was a large cone from which a scoop of ice cream seemed to have melted over the side while the black-and-white seats inside appeared to have been upholstered in the skin of a dairy cow. The name on the van said TOOTSIE FROOTSIE GELATI.

"It's a flipping ice-cream van," protested Groanin. "I've a good mind to turn you into the police after all, you impudent rascal."

"Honestly, sir, it's the only transport I could find." Angus shrugged. "Perhaps, if you gave me more time, I could find a suitable replacement, but today of all days —"

"It'll have to do," said Groanin. "I can't wait any longer."

The van pulled up, the jingle stopped, the window came down, and the driver leaned out.

He was a big man with short, gray hair, an ample stomach, and bulging, bullfrog eyes. He spoke with a voice that sounded like crushed charcoal. Groanin thought he was rather frightening for an ice-cream man. He couldn't imagine too many children buying ice cream from a man who looked more like a pro wrestler. And not just any wrestler but the bad wrestler, the evil, win-at-all-costs sort of wrestler.

"Is this the English?" asked Bruno.

"Yes," said Angus. "This is him."

"*Andiamo*," said Bruno. "We go. You put your bag in the back, English. Then ride shotgun, in the front. Okay?"

Groanin put his suitcase in the back as ordered and then got into the van alongside Bruno. As they moved away from the hotel, the jingle played again.

Minutes later, they were driving north on the *autostrada*, toward the Italian capital city of Rome.

It was several more minutes before Groanin noticed the shotgun behind his seat, and several more minutes after that before he had worked up the courage to mention it to Bruno himself. But not right away. He decided to come at the subject from the side, by first talking about music which, it's said, soothes the savage beast and even on occasion persuades him to buy ice cream.

"Er, that tune your van plays," he says. "Sounds familiar. What is it?"

"It's called 'Parla Più Piano.' You like it, English?"

"Very much I like, yes. Very soothing and romantic, is that music."

"Is very Italian, too."

"Yes. It is. It's the sort of music that makes you think of summer and flowers and friendly Italian people and good food and happy families. The kind of music that makes you wonder why a man should choose to keep a shotgun in an ice-cream van."

Bruno shrugged. "I can hardly ask you to ride shotgun in my van without a shotgun, English. What kind of man do you think I am?"

It was now that Groanin noticed that Bruno was wearing a bulletproof vest. It was black with a little green crocodile logo on the breast pocket.

"You mean ride shotgun like in them old Westerns?" said Groanin. "You're joking, aren't you? There aren't any Native Americans on the *autostrada*."

"Is not Native Americans we got to watch out for." Bruno laughed. "But I think maybe you can relax until we get to Rome, English. We get no trouble until then."

"What kind of trouble?"

"Ice cream in Rome is controlled by Mafia. Ice cream in Naples is controlled by Camorra. Camorra is gang like Mafia. Ice-cream people in Rome pay money to Mafia for protection. They no like Naples ice-cream people come to their city. Is bad for business. Me, I no plan to sell ice cream in Rome. But Mafia don't know that." Bruno shrugged. "So, you keep shotgun on lap just in case someone try to hijack van. Understand?"

"Listen, Bruno, all I want is a ride to Rome airport."

"Is fine. I do you favor. But you do me a favor, too, or else I leave you here at side of road. Now you decide."

Groanin thought for a moment. "Very well. Since you put it like that."

They drove for about an hour before Bruno told Groanin that they were reaching the outskirts of Rome and to pick up the shotgun.

Groanin did as he as he was told, cradling the weapon on his lap and certain that if they did encounter any trouble, there was no chance he was ever going to use it. Groanin had never shot anything except a rabbit or two. It was one of the advantages of working for a djinn that in matters of self-defense, guns were completely unnecessary.

The journey might have continued being uneventful but for two unfortunate events. The first unfortunate event was that Bruno saw a pretty girl by the side of the road waving at him and so he stopped to sell her an ice cream.

"Here, what are you doing?" said Groanin as, with the jingle playing loudly, the van drew up on the grass shoulder by the girl. "I thought you said you weren't planning to sell any ice cream in the area of Rome. The Mafia won't like it."

"I'm an ice-cream man," insisted Bruno. "I can't help it. Is what I do. Besides, she's a very pretty girl."

This was certainly true. But, as it happened, the girl didn't want an ice cream after all but a lift and, since the passenger seat of the ice-cream van was already occupied, Bruno felt obliged to refuse. So they drove off again, which was when they discovered the second unfortunate event, which was that the van kept on playing "Parla Più Piano" and would not stop.

For several miles Groanin thought this was merely annoy-ing until Bruno mentioned that the tune was considered especially irritating to the Mafia, even a little insulting.

"Can't you switch it off?" asked Groanin as they drove through a graffiti-covered suburb.

"I'd have to stop the van to do that," admitted Bruno. "And I don't like to do that in this particular area we're in now. Besides, I think they're already onto us."

"What makes you say that?"

"There's another ice-cream van following us. It's been there for the last two miles."

Groanin leaned forward and glanced in the side mirror. Bruno was correct: A green ice-cream van was about thirty yards behind them. And even as he watched, this other ice-cream van accelerated toward them.

"What will they do if they stop us?" asked Groanin.

Bruno laughed grimly. "I don't think they will buy an ice cream, English," he said. "And maybe there's raspberry sauce on the ground before this is over, yes?"

"Put your foot down," yelled Groanin. "They're gaining on us."

But the green ice-cream van was more powerful than the blue one driven by Bruno and swiftly came alongside Groanin's window.

The driver was another very fat man with a mouth as wide as a shovel and hair so thick and black and curly it looked like a woolly hat. He grinned at Groanin and then drew his finger across one of his many double chins.

"Let them have it!" yelled Bruno. "The shotgun! Let them have it!"

Groanin hardly needed telling twice. And feeling very relieved that Bruno didn't seem to want to make a fight of it after all, he leaned out of his open window and handed the shotgun, stock first, to the driver of the other van.

"What are you doing?" yelled Bruno.

"You told me to let him have it," said Groanin. "So I did."

"I meant you to shoot him." Bruno cursed loudly as the other driver pointed at the roadside.

THE GRAVE ROBBERS OF GENGHIS KHAN

"With the gun?" Groanin sounded shocked.

"Now we have to stop," said Bruno, slowing down. "Or they will shoot us." He shrugged. "Maybe they shoot us, anyway, English. I hope you know how to pray. And I hope you know how to beg. And I hope you know how to act."

"Act? What are you talking about? Act." Groanin shook his head. "I'm a butler, not some lovey-dovey thespian."

Bruno stopped the van, switched off the engine, and finally the jingle stopped.

"Well, thank goodness for that," said Groanin.

"Your one chance is to act like you are crazy," growled Bruno. "The Roman Mafia is very superstitious. They no like to kill crazy people. Not unless they're politicians. So, maybe if you act crazy, they let you go."

"I shall do no such thing," said Groanin. "I'm English. We didn't get the British Empire by acting crazy in a crisis, you know. What's required here is a bit of backbone, my Neapolitan friend. Backbone. Nerve. British stiff upper lip."

He put on his bowler hat and stepped out of the ice-cream van and prepared to face the enemy.

CHAPTER 7

ROCK ON

The old Vesuvius Observatory, an elegant, red-ocher build-ing in the neoclassical style, was located on the west flank of Mount Vesuvius, at around two thousand feet above sea level, in a verdant oasis of pine and ilex trees and yellow rock helichrysum flowers.

Professor Sturloson unlocked the rust-colored gates and opened the main doors.

"The other institute," he explained, "the modern insti-tute, is lower down the slope. But I much prefer this place. Please. Go inside."

"This looks more like a villa than a scientific institute," observed Philippa.

"True," said the professor. "But I sometimes think that everything in Italy looks better than it should. Even this vol-cano. After all, who would expect a volcano to be covered in so many beautiful flowers, and to smell so sweetly?"

"It is rather fragrant," said Nimrod. He walked straight over to the rock saw and switched it on.

"Then again," said John, "it's not much of a villa that doesn't have any windows. These ones look like they have been filled in with concrete."

"That's just one of the reasons that the building is able to resist the seismic and eruptive activity of the mountain," said the professor. "For example, during the 1872 eruption, the director of the observatory, Luigi Palmieri, although surrounded by incandescent lava, stayed to observe the electric phenomena that resulted from the large amounts of ash in the sky."

"That's a comforting thought," said John. He looked up at a picture on the wall. "Is that him?"

"No, that's Vittorio Matteucci," said the professor. "Sadly, he was killed here. As a result of his rather too close observation of Vesuvius and its related phenomena."

John pulled a face and looked at another portrait. "And him?"

"Umm," said the professor. "That would be Giuseppe Mercalli. He was killed here, too, I think."

"I'm beginning to suspect that volcanology is much more dangerous than you'd have us believe," Philippa told her uncle.

"Me, too," said John. "To have one dead director is unfortunate. But to have two dead directors — well, that looks even more unfortunate than having just the one who's dead."

Nimrod was too busy with the rock saw, cutting a section from the golden lava sample, to answer Philippa's or John's remarks.

"There's no getting away from the fact that volcanoes are

dangerous," said Axel, who was helping him. "But by trying to understand them we hope to make them more predictable and, as a result, make them less dangerous."

John look at the rock saw with curiosity. "What kind of saw is it that can cut through rock?" he asked.

"One with industrial diamonds in the blade," said his uncle.

The telephone rang and the professor answered it. As soon as he finished his call he turned on the TV, which was how everyone learned that several other countries and regions throughout the world were reporting new volcanic activity — not just Italy, but Russia, the United States, New Zealand, Iceland, and South America. The situation appeared to be worst of all in the Democratic Republic of Congo, where Nyamuragira, Africa's most active volcano, had just erupted with devastating effect. For half an hour they watched dramatic television pictures of two fiery craters throwing glowing molten rock thousands of feet into the air, and several dozen villages on the Rwandan border being evacuated.

And some of the people who had witnessed the eruption were reporting that pieces of the solidified lava *resembled nuggets of gold*.

"This is looking much more serious than I had thought," said the professor.

"Is this normal?" asked Philippa. "That all these volcanoes become active at once?"

"There's no reason why they *shouldn't* all be active at once," said the professor. "Much of the volcanic activity that occurs on the seabed usually goes unreported. But, no, it's not normal."

He looked anxiously at Nimrod, who had finished with the rock saw and was carrying his section of the golden lava to a large, white microscope that was attached to a small computer screen.

Nimrod sat down in front of the microscope, switched it on, and then placed the slide section under the lens. For several minutes he peered through the viewfinder while he fiddled with the focus knobs and the light-intensity control.

"This section of rock is now thin enough so that we can shine a light through it," explained Nimrod. "A special polarizing light that will enable us to identify its various chemical properties. And which will explain the unusual golden color."

Gradually, the picture on the screen grew sharper. And so did the professor's interest.

"There seems to be an extraordinarily high level of silica here," he said.

"More than eighty-five percent," said Nimrod. He switched the view to a powerful lens. "There we are. A normal silicon tetrahedron, as you might expect."

"What's a tetrahedron?" asked John.

"Four triangular faces," said Philippa. "Three of which meet at each point."

"Only there's something else," said Nimrod.

"I've never seen anything like it," observed the professor. "A silicon tetrahedron with four oxygen atoms at the corner of the tetrahedron and, in the center, one silicon atom and something else closely attached to it that looks like gold, which probably accounts for the lava color."

Nimrod typed some instructions into the computer. "Let's see if it is gold," he said.

They waited for a second before the computer came back with an answer.

UNKNOWN ELEMENT.

"There must be something wrong with the computer," insisted the professor. "Try again."

Nimrod retyped the instructions but the answer that came back was the same.

UNKNOWN ELEMENT.

Nimrod began typing again. "Let's try to narrow it down," he said. "It's not oxygen or silicon; and it's not aluminum, iron, calcium, sodium, magnesium, or potassium, which, together, account for all but half a percent of the elements in the earth's crust. We will get the computer to take a closer look in that half percent, and see if it doesn't resemble one of those other elements. And —"

Nimrod pressed the return key and waited for a second.

"It doesn't," said the professor.

"No," agreed Nimrod. "However, according to the computer, this mystery element does share one particular characteristic with the following list of minerals: barringerite, brezinaite, brianite, buchwaldite, carlsbergite, daubreelite, farringtonite, gentnerite, haxonite, heideite, kosmochlor, krinovite, lawrencite, lonsdaleite, majorite, merrihueite, niningerite, osbornite, panethite, ringwoodite, roedderite, schreibersite, stanfieldite, and yagiite."

"And what characteristic is that?" asked Philippa.

"These are all non-terrestrial minerals," the professor said quietly. "Found only in meteorites."

"So maybe a meteorite fell into a volcano," said John. "Wow. I can see that causing a few problems."

"Maybe," said the professor. "But unlikely. One meteor falling into Vesuvius would hardly affect all of these other volcanoes. Besides, there's no trace in this lava sample of any of these other non-terrestrial elements. Just this unknown one that's the color of gold."

Absently, the professor began to tap the edge of his black mask with a fingernail, which prompted John to wonder exactly how it remained on his head. There was no string or elastic holding it in place that he could see. Really, it was most peculiar, almost like it was actually sticking to his face.

"If only," said Axel, "we knew more about its properties."

"We don't have time to isolate it." Nimrod started to type again. "To analyze it properly. However, we can construct a computer simulation of how it might behave in the laboratory. In other words, how it would react if we were to put it in water, cool it, heat it, or bombard it with radiation. And most important of all, to see how it reacts within a lava flow."

"Good idea," said the professor.

"You mean like a pretend experiment?" said John.

"Yes, John."

Once again Nimrod started to type on the computer keyboard.

Philippa didn't know which was the more impressive: all of the scientific information Nimrod seemed to carry within his head and that he fed into the computer, or the speed with which he typed it. Even so, he was typing for almost half an hour before he announced that "the experiment" was ready. Everyone came away from watching the television news and some pictures from the island of Bali, in Indonesia, where one of the three interlocking craters on Mount Batur had suddenly started emitting ash and smoke, to watch Nimrod's computer simulation.

When the element was heated, it seemed to become more fluid, and at the same time dramatically more explosive. When added to lava the mystery element seemed to make the lava behave much more violently than might have been expected.

"I think it's reasonable to assume," said Nimrod, "that it's the mystery element that is affecting the behavior of all of these volcanoes."

"I'm obliged to agree with you, Nimrod," said the professor.

"Then perhaps you're also ready to admit the possibility that this might just have something to do with the Fu Xi legend," said Nimrod.

The professor nodded. "I'm beginning to think it does," he said.

"That's the second time you've mentioned this legend," said Philippa. "Would someone mind telling me what it is?"

"I'm not entirely sure myself," admitted the professor.

"Well, now," said Nimrod. "Where to begin? It's been a while since I told anyone this story, which, since it's almost eight hundred years old, is largely dismissed or forgotten by

most modern scholars of Mongolian and Chinese history.
Although not by me. Many years ago, after university, I wanted
to travel somewhere really remote, and Mongolia seemed
about as remote as one could get. So I learned the language
and read some books. Although to be honest, there's really
just one book that matters when it comes to Mongolia.

"*The Secret History of the Mongols* is the oldest surviving book
about the Mongols, although it is more of a history of the
rise and death of Genghis Khan in particular than of
the Mongols in general. This is hardly surprising since
he's the most important thing that's ever happened to the
Mongols. It was written sometime near his death in the early
thirteenth century. Around A.D. 1227. After he had conquered the largest contiguous empire in recorded history."

"What does *contiguous* mean?" asked John.

"It means 'connecting without a break,'" said Nimrod.
"Within a common boundary. The Mongol Empire stretched
from the Black Sea to North Korea. It was truly vast. And
what's more, it took a little over seventy years to conquer.
Compare that to the Roman Empire and the British Empire,
which took much longer to bring together and you can understand just how great a warrior Genghis Khan really was."

Philippa drew her uncle aside for a moment so that she
could speak without being overheard by the professor and
Axel; John followed.

"Wasn't he a djinn?" asked Philippa.

"Part djinn," said Nimrod. "Almost certainly."

"Well, that would help explain why he was such a great
warrior, wouldn't it?"

"Yes, but the Mongols didn't know that. You see, Genghis preferred to conquer countries the old-fashioned way. He wanted to measure himself and his own conquests against great heroes like Alexander the Great and Julius Caesar. And his military conquests would hardly have been the same in his own eyes if he'd relied on djinn power to bring them about. It's these conquests that *The Secret History* largely deals with."

Nimrod strolled nonchalantly back to the professor and Axel to continue with his story.

"However, no Mongol-language versions of this book — *The Secret History* — have come down to us today and all surviving versions derive from Chinese translations dating from the end of the fourteenth century. Only one of these — itself now lost — mentioned a secret weapon called Fu Xi that the Xi Xia Emperor Xuanzong threatened to deploy against the Mongols when Genghis Khan threatened to invade his country. The Xi Xia Empire was the largest province in ancient China."

"Isn't Fu Xi a kind of dragon?" said Philippa. "In the I Ching?"

"Very good, Philippa," said Nimrod. "Yes, that's quite right."

"So was that his weapon? A dragon?"

"Metaphorically speaking, yes," said Nimrod. "Which means it was not a real dragon. But as a figure of speech, something that was like a dragon. You see, it was said that with his dragon weapon the Emperor Xuanzong would bring ten thousand days of fire down upon the heads of not only the Mongols but the Xi Xia, too. What he called *yi wàng nián de huǒ zāi*. A kind of extreme scorched-earth policy in which one country destroys itself in order to deny it to the enemy.

"As it happened, the speed of the Mongol cavalry tribesmen was such that the Xia were completely overrun before Xuanzong could deploy his weapon; and the 'dragon' fell into the hands of the Mongols. Just like a lot of other weapons — gunpowder and siege engines and better swords. Genghis Khan was fascinated with new weapons, which partly explains his success in conquest. And he was especially interested with this 'doomsday' weapon of the Emperor Xuanzong.

"Having said that, there's little known for sure about the true nature of the weapon. Some people think it was just gunpowder, which the Mongols took from the Chinese and learned to use, but other contemporary Chinese sources mention a dragon that came out of the Yellow River and which some people have speculated may actually have been a meteorite — and more specifically some crystals from the meteorite that had the power to turn lava to gold."

"Maybe that's what turned the river yellow," offered John.

"I never thought of that," said Nimrod. "Anyway, these crystals were called Ho Tani Ya Chin Shi, 火灾医药晶体, which means 'fire medicine crystals,' and it was probably them that gave the medieval alchemists the idea of the philosopher's stone that would turn base metal into gold.

"But that was just one of the properties of the Hotaniya crystals. Incidentally, *Hotaniya* is Chinese for 'gunpowder.' Legend had it that using these Hotaniya crystals, Xuanzong could actually stir sleeping volcanoes into life, and that he had actually intended to bring about these ten thousand days of fire by bringing back to life the Emeishan volcano of southwest China."

"Never heard of it," said Axel.

"Me neither," said John.

"Perhaps not," said Nimrod. "But if you want to know why the name of Emeishan is important, then here's a fact that might interest you: There are some scientists today who believe that it was not a meteorite that destroyed the dinosaurs and all life on earth, but a catastrophic eruption of Emeishan some two hundred and sixty million years ago."

Nimrod paused for dramatic effect.

"Holy smoke," said John. "It's all beginning to make sense. And you think that someone has gotten hold of these Hotaniya crystals and may be deliberately making all of the world's volcanoes simultaneously active? Is that it?"

"As usual, you cut straight to the heart of the matter, John," said Nimrod. "But, in a nutshell, yes, I do think it's a possibility."

"Holy smoke," repeated John.

"My theory is not without its problems, however," admitted Nimrod.

"To put it mildly," added the professor.

"For someone to have gained possession of these ancient Hotaniya crystals," said Nimrod, "they would first have to have found the tomb of Genghis Khan, which has been lost ever since his death in A.D. 1227." He shook his head. "Over the centuries many people have looked for it, and failed."

"But is it such a big deal if a lot of volcanoes become more active?" said John. "After all, back at the hotel, you said yourself that there are at least fifty eruptions every year. And six or seven hundred volcanoes that are active today."

"He's right," said Philippa. "You made it sound like we have learned to coexist with volcanoes. In fact, I think you actually said that."

"Perhaps I did," admitted Nimrod. "And in a way, that is true. However, underneath what anyone including myself says about volcanoes and man coexisting on our planet, there must always be a strong note of caution. Eruptions like the one at Mount St. Helens, in Washington State, back in 1980, remind us all of the incalculable destructive power of the planet we live on. That was the deadliest and most economically devastating volcanic event in the history of the modern United States. If all of the earth's major volcanoes suddenly became active at the same time and erupted with the power of Mount St. Helens, we would face a cataclysm beyond human imagination."

"What your uncle says is no exaggeration," the professor told the twins. "That amount of volcanic ash in our atmosphere would affect everything. It would blot out the sun, and cause huge electrical storms. Transportation, communication, and energy systems all over the planet would be paralyzed. The world's weather patterns would be severely affected and affect the growth of crops. Millions of people would starve. Or die of thirst from lack of clean water. That might sound like science fiction, but it isn't."

"So," added Nimrod, "if there's one chance in a hundred that all this new volcanic activity is man-made, then I have to do something about it. We all do."

The professor was nodding but the twins knew their uncle's words were really meant for them and them alone. Neither had forgotten the gist of what he had said earlier in the morning: that in some frightening and predestined way it was down to them as djinn, and to their tribe in particular, to save the world.

CHAPTER 8

KIDNAPPED

Two men stepped out of the second ice-cream van. Neither one of them looked particularly friendly.

One, smoking a cigarette, jostled past Bruno and ducked into his van. There he inspected the ice-cream drum, which was full of vanilla flavor, switched it off, and then, as if to make sure that it was spoiled, tossed his cigarette inside.

Groanin thought this was a bit unnecessary. All the same, he smiled and tipped his bowler hat to the other, larger Italian walking toward him. The man was carrying Bruno's shotgun, which was the main reason Groanin felt an extra obligation to be courteous. In Groanin's opinion it always paid to be polite to a man carrying a gun, especially in a foreign country.

"Good morning, kind sir," he said cheerily. "Lovely day, isn't it? Perfect for selling ice cream, I should have thought. Not that we were doing that, of course. I said, not that we were doing that. We only stopped to ask for directions to the airport, which is where I am going. We certainly didn't stop to sell any actual ice cream, you understand. Indeed, the fact that my friend here is driving an ice-cream van is incidental to the fact that he is acting in the role of taxi driver, there being no taxis to be had in the whole of Naples, what with rail strikes and volcanic ash and so on. It could just as easily have been a furniture van. Or a grocery van. The important thing was that I might travel back to England as soon as possible. I have important business I need to attend to. In Manchester. I don't even like ice cream very much. It's too cold for my stomach, you see."

While Groanin was explaining himself, the man from the Mafia — whose name was Vito — looked the butler up and down with some incredulity. He saw an Englishman with pin-striped trousers, a dark jacket and matching vest, a crisp white shirt and black tie, and a bowler hat. In short, he looked very like a picture the Mafioso had once seen of Sir Winston Churchill, a former British prime minister. And it was very evident to the Mafioso that Groanin must be someone equally important. Surely only someone important would have dressed in this ridiculous and absurdly formal fashion. This impression was underlined when the Mafioso searched Groanin's bags and found one of them full of money.

"You speak any Italian?" Vito asked Groanin.

"I'm afraid not," said Groanin. "Just English."

"That's all right," said Vito. "I speak the English pretty good, eh?"

"Yes," agreed Groanin. "You speak the English very good."

Vito called the other, smaller Mafioso over and, for a moment or two, they discussed the cash, in Italian.

"How come you have so much money?" Vito asked Groanin. "What do you do for a living, Englishman?"

"I'm a butler," said Groanin.

"What is a butler?" asked Vito.

"A servant," said Groanin.

"For someone very important?"

Suddenly, Groanin thought it best not to be unemployed but to be someone who had an influential employer.

"Oh, yes," said Groanin. "Very important. And very powerful, too. You've no idea how powerful. If anything happens to me, this person will be furious."

"Is this his money, or yours?"

"It's his," said Groanin. "I'm looking after it for him."

"So this person you work for, he's rich, yes?"

Groanin laughed bitterly. "Oh, making money's never been a problem for him. If he wants some money, he makes it." He snapped his fingers. "Just like that."

"Maybe this man you work for might pay us a reward for looking after you. For protecting you, yes? For delivering you safely back to him."

"Perhaps," said Groanin. "Yes, it's possible. But I'm not in need of any protection right now, thank you. What I do need is a ride to the airport."

Vito put his hand on Groanin's shoulder.

"Everyone needs protection," insisted Vito. "Especially 'round here. This is not a safe area, Englishman. It's full of thieves and robbers who might steal your money. But don't worry. Me and my little friend Toni here, we look after you good. Eh, Toni?"

Toni grinned a gap-toothed grin and nodded.

"Rome airport is closed," said Vito. "All airspace in Italy is now closed. Because of the volcano. But we take you to a place where you can get on a truck, or a boat, yes? And then maybe you can telephone your boss and tell him you are all right, and your boss will give us a reward and everything will be fine."

"That's very kind of you," said Groanin. "If you're sure that it's no trouble."

"It's no trouble," insisted Vito. "You get in the van and I drive you somewhere safe."

Thinking that the Mafioso might just be as good as his word, Groanin stepped into the second ice-cream van and waited while Vito and Toni spoke in Italian to Bruno. Everyone bit their thumbs at each other in compliance with what Groanin assumed must be some sort of local custom, and then the two Mafiosi got into the van alongside Groanin.

They drove for several minutes before Vito asked Groanin if he had a cell phone. When Groanin said he did, Vito suggested he might like to call his boss and tell him that he was all right and being well taken care of.

Groanin hardly wanted to call Nimrod so soon after resigning, since it would look like he was already eating humble pie and begging for his old job back. Vito was very insistent, however, and since Groanin hardly wished to offend someone who was offering him protection, he quickly complied and dialed Nimrod's number.

Without success.

"That's strange," he said, looking at his cell phone. "I can't get a signal."

Toni inspected his own cell phone and said he couldn't get a signal, either; and when Vito confirmed that he, too, was unable to use his cell phone, Groanin suggested it might have something to do with all the volcanic ash in the atmosphere.

"I was watching television last night," he said, "and they said that volcanic ash particles are always saturated with electrical charge, which affects mobile phone signals."

Glancing out of the window, they all saw that a small electrical storm was already in progress in the darkening purple sky above their heads.

After a while, Vito stopped the ice-cream van and tried using a pay phone to call Nimrod but once again failed to make contact.

"All the local landlines are down," said Vito. "'Cause of the electrical storm."

This seemed to irritate Toni and, speaking Italian to Vito, he said, "If we can't even call this Nimrod guy, then how can we make a ransom demand for his fat friend here?"

"I dunno," confessed Vito.

Toni looked at Groanin and smiled reassuringly.

Only a little reassured, Groanin nodded and smiled back, understanding not a word of what was being said about him.

"Some kidnapping this is turning out to be," said Toni.

"You're right. I thought it would be easy."

"You know what I think? I've got a bad feeling about this. I think we should be happy with stealing all of the money he has in his bag and no more. We should dump this guy by the side of the road and forget about trying to extort a ransom from this Nimrod guy. Everything is against us. The volcano. The weather. The phones."

"I got a better idea, Toni," said Vito. "We should sell him."

"Sell him?" Toni looked critically at Groanin. "Why would anyone want to buy him? A bald, fat Englishman?"

"I was thinking that if this guy's boss is as rich as he says he is, then he's worth something, surely," said Vito. "I was thinking we could sell him to the Romanian Mafia. Those guys will buy anything if they think there's a possible profit in it. They're much more ruthless than we are."

"Good idea," said Toni. "Besides, kidnapping is their special thing."

"Exactly."

"Do you know anyone in the Romanian Mafia?"

"Sure. You remember that Romanian kid. What was his name? Decebal?"

"The fourteen-year-old who runs Guidonia? Sure. How could I forget? He's just about the most famous gangster in Italy since he was on that TV program. But he's ruthless, Vito. A madman. They don't call him the Wolf of Guidonia for nothing. He bites people. It's dangerous for us even to go to Guidonia and talk to that kid."

"Relax." Vito chuckled. "I'll give him and his friends a free ice cream."

Both Italians looked at Groanin sandwiched between them like a slice of salami, and smiled.

Groanin smiled back but inside he was beginning to suspect that he was in deep trouble.

CHAPTER 9

MOROCCO BOUND

So what *are* we going to do?" Philippa asked her uncle.

"We need to get to Mongolia and look for the grave of Genghis Khan as quickly as possible," said Nimrod. "Only by going there will we discover if someone has indeed found his grave and those Hotaniya crystals. And if that proves to be the case, then we may well find some clues as to who that someone might be. And what they're up to."

"That's not going to be easy," said Axel, pointing at the television. "All European airspace is now closed because of volcanic ash. And Mongolia is quite a distance from here."

"You're not kidding," said John.

"To be exact, the distance between Naples and Ulan Bator, which is the capital of Mongolia, is six thousand nine hundred and forty-four kilometers," said Nimrod. "About four thousand three hundred and fifteen miles."

"And there's a rail strike," said John.

"I think we're going to have to travel rather more quickly than any transcontinental train," said Nimrod.

"What do you suggest?" The professor uttered a dry laugh, which sounded even drier by being uttered from behind a mask. "A magic carpet?"

"You know? I was thinking the exact same thing," said Nimrod. "Especially now that it's no longer safe to travel by whirlwind. Which means we'll have to get ourselves to Morocco first. So that we can buy a carpet from the Very Special Rug Emporium of my old friend Asaf ibn Barkhiya. In the old city of Fez."

Nimrod stood up and went over to a map of the Mediterranean on the laboratory wall. "We need to charter ourselves a boat from Naples to Nador, as quickly as possible," he said. "Come to think of it, the U.S. Navy has a hydrofoil at Naples. I saw it entering port just the other day. We can probably borrow theirs. That's what, about one thousand and twenty-two miles, door to door. So we'll probably have to refuel in Cagliari on the island of Sardinia. With any luck we can be in Nador in, let's see, about seventeen hours from now."

"This is no time for jokes, Nimrod," said the professor.

"I agree." Nimrod glanced at his watch. "It's two o'clock. We can arrive in Nador by, say, eight tomorrow morning. No, wait, six o'clock. Naples is two hours ahead of Nador."

"Where's Nador?" asked John.

"It's a Rif port on the Bhar Amzzyan lagoon," said Nimrod. "And the major trading center in Morocco. Rather a nice town, as it happens. A taxi from there to Fez is about one hundred and forty miles. So that's three hours."

"Really, Nimrod," protested Professor Sturloson. "None of this is at all helpful."

"Which means we can be in Mr. Barkhiya's shop in time for lunch."

The professor walked over to Axel, shaking his head. "The man's taken leave of his senses. *Hann er brjálaður.*"

"*Ég held það líka,*" said Axel. "Must be the heat. It affects the English differently from other people, I've heard."

"Professor. Axel." Nimrod beamed at the two Icelanders. "My apologies. I know it must seem that I've taken leave of my senses, gentlemen, but rest assured, dear sirs, I haven't. There's something important I have to tell you. About myself and my young friends here. And I apologize for not having told you before; however, when I *do* tell you, you will understand why not, I think. It simply isn't the sort of thing an Englishman mentions unless he really has to."

Nimrod sighed and held out an empty hand.

"As the great Tariq Ali once said, a demonstration is better than a long speech. So, please watch carefully and, for the present moment, I would ask you to postpone all of your questions just as I shall postpone all my explanations and, for now, I merely say the following: QWERTYUIOP."

No sooner had Nimrod uttered his focus word — all djinn use a word to focus their powers — than a set of car keys appeared on his palm.

"That's a pretty good trick," said the professor. "But what is the relevance, please?"

"The relevance is quite simple, my dear Snorri," explained Nimrod. "These are the keys to a brand-new Humvee A2 of the kind used by the U.S. military. A vehicle like this will make it much easier for us to drive through the navy checkpoints in the port of Naples on our way to commandeering a hydrofoil."

Axel looked astonished.

The professor would have looked astonished, too, if he hadn't been wearing a mask.

"You can't be serious," said the professor.

"I'm very serious," said Nimrod. "The Humvee is now parked immediately outside the front door." Nimrod and the children were already heading toward the door. "Shall we go? I suggest we use it to drive to the port as quickly as possible."

"There's no Humvee out there," said Axel. "We'd have heard one arrive. Surely."

Even so, Axel and the professor still followed Nimrod outside where, as Nimrod had said, a brand-new Humvee now stood immediately in front of the door, gleaming in the sun, where no Humvee had been standing before.

John shook his head. "If I might make a suggestion, Uncle?"

Nimrod nodded. "By all means, my boy."

"The U.S. Marines would never take delivery of a Humvee without a camouflage pattern," said John. "This one's still wearing a standard factory paint job."

"Good point," said Nimrod. "Perhaps you would care to fix that yourself."

"Sure," said John. And uttering his own focus word, ABECEDARIAN, he fixed the problem in the blink of an eye.

"This is better," he said. "It's what the U.S. Marines call Woodland Digital Camouflage."

"And doubtless they think it's a modern masterpiece," said Nimrod, and climbed into the driver's seat.

"This isn't happening," said the professor.

But a few minutes later the three djinn and two mundanes were driving down the western slope of Vesuvius in the general direction of Naples.

"Remind me of why we're going to Morocco, when we really want to go to Mongolia," said the professor.

"To get ourselves a magic carpet, of course," said Philippa. "Only, correct me if I'm wrong, Uncle Nimrod, but I thought you said that magic carpets didn't exist."

"That was also my impression," the professor said weakly.

Nimrod shook his head. "I said nothing of the sort, Philippa. Previously, I said that nearly all modern djinn prefer to travel by whirlwind. Or airplane. And of course we did. But since it's no longer permitted for good eco-minded djinn to travel that way, and since it is difficult at the best of times to get to Mongolia, we must look to more old-fashioned methods of transport. Such as a flying carpet. Of the kind described — as I'm quite sure you will both remember — in night number five hundred and seventy of the *Arabian Nights*."

Professor Sturloson groaned. "This isn't happening."

"And please don't let me hear either of you twins describing it as a magic carpet," insisted Nimrod. "You know my views on the use of that word. It's a flying carpet. I know, I know — a djinn on a flying carpet is vulgar, clichéd, embarrassing. John, you would probably say it was corny, but I can now see no alternative to us owning one. A flying carpet must be procured if we are ever to get to Mongolia. Which is why, before we do anything, we must visit Mr. Barkhiya, in the Medina, which is the old part of Fez."

Forty minutes later, they reached the port of Naples, followed all the signs for U.S. naval forces in Europe, and soon they found themselves approaching a security checkpoint.

"We are just going to drive through, are we?" inquired the professor.

"Something like that," said Nimrod, and quietly muttered his focus word.

The professor glanced momentarily out of the window and when he looked at Nimrod again he was surprised to see that the Englishman was now wearing the uniform of a U.S. Navy admiral.

"How did you do that?" he gasped.

"Mind over matter," Nimrod said breezily and, drawing up at the checkpoint, he smiled at the two marines manning it and handed over his identification document. In fact, his documents were nothing more than a guide to Pompeii that Nimrod had picked up at the railway station earlier that same morning, but when the marines looked at it Nimrod made sure that they only saw what they wanted to see, and no one wants to see an admiral with the wrong document.

"I don't believe it," exclaimed Axel as the security barrier lifted and Nimrod drove the Humvee into the naval base.

"No," said Nimrod. "But the important point is that *he* believed it."

Some of the U.S. Sixth Fleet was anchored in the harbor and while Nimrod was certain he knew what a hydrofoil looked like when it was moving at speed above the water, he was less confident of identifying one when it was stationary. Once again, he muttered his focus word and this time the result was that he handed John a copy of *Jane's Fighting Ships*, an annual reference book of information on all of the world's warships.

"Here," he said. "You have keen eyesight, John. See if you can find the ship we're looking for in there."

John studied several silhouettes and photographs and then shook his head. "I dunno," he said. "They all kind of look the same."

"True."

Nimrod slowed the Humvee next to some military policemen and leaned out of the window. The policemen all saluted and listened as Nimrod, now speaking with a convincing American accent, addressed them to ask for directions to the hydrofoil.

"Is there anything he can't do?" the professor asked Philippa.

"Sure there is," said Philippa. "We're djinn, not gods or mutants or anything weird like that. And mostly it's like he says: It's mind over matter. You see, whatever is possible in logic is also permitted in physics. A thought contains the possibility of the situation of which it is the thought. So what is thinkable is possible, too."

"You make it sound like I could do it," said the professor. "Could I? Could you teach me, perhaps?"

"Well," said Philippa, "I expect you could do something. Like move a pencil across a desk. Something small. But not this kind of stuff. Only a djinn can make things appear out of thin air. Like three wishes and stuff like that."

"I see."

"But we have to learn how to do it," continued Philippa. "To develop the part of the brain where our powers are focused. The part that we djinn call the Neshamah. You just don't have a part of your brain like that. Sorry." She shrugged apologetically. "Everyone's different."

"If you want to know the way, ask a policeman," said Nimrod, when they were moving again.

"You speak pretty good American, Uncle Nimrod," observed John.

"What is English as spoken by an American?" remarked Nimrod. "Simply a rhotic consonant dropped like a plastic rattle from a baby's pram. The lazy merger of vowels, such as *a* and *o*, which like a middle C and D are played at the same time by the clumsy forefinger of some ham-fisted pianist. And a whole load of compound badland, flatland words, and incompetent nouns that properly are verbs. All in all, American is to English what the hamburger is to beef: ground-up meat in an outsized and unnecessary bun."

"Gee," said John. "And I thought you liked us."

"Oh, I do like you," said Nimrod. "Some of my best friends are American. I just wish you could all say the word *water* without sounding like you were asking a rather tentative question."

Nimrod stopped the Humvee in front of a gangplank that led off the dockside onto the USS *John Thornycroft*. The gangplank was guarded by two more military policemen.

"They're not going to like my mask," said the professor.

"And they're going to wonder why you are accompanied by two kids," said Philippa.

"Ye of little faith," said Nimrod.

"They're right, though," said John. "We're hardly a conventional bunch of visitors, are we?"

"The military mind," said Nimrod, "is especially susceptible to one thing in particular: orders. It's simply a question of making the orders appear to be from the highest authority and therefore quite incontrovertible."

Nimrod thought for a moment, imagined that he had a smart U.S. Navy briefcase handcuffed to his wrist, which was full of impressive, laminated passes for the professor, Axel, and the twins, and some top secret orders, and it was so — at least it was as soon as he had uttered his focus word.

He handed around the passes and waited for a moment while everyone got their curiosity out of the way and examined them.

"A good likeness." The professor stared at a photograph of himself in the black mask and chuckled.

"Forgive me for asking, Professor," said John as he and the others followed his uncle out of the Humvee. "But couldn't you have had a face transplant, or something? A better mask, perhaps."

Philippa threw up her eyebrows to hear this. Her brother was always keen to walk where good manners seemed to forbid that anyone should tread.

"I thought about it," said the professor. "But that kind of surgery is very time consuming, John, and really, I'm much too busy with my work to spend months and months in a hospital having someone mess around with something so inconsequential as my appearance." He tapped his head and then his heart. "It's in here where things matter. It's in here that being human counts most of all. Don't you think?"

"Er, yes," said John, who thought that not having a face would have mattered a great deal to him. Until he remembered what had happened to his mother and how she now had a completely different face to the one he'd known just a few years ago.

"Besides," added the professor, "not having a face to speak of hardly seems to matter since there are so very few people where I live, in Iceland. And hardly any mirrors. Icelanders aren't much given to looking at themselves. They're rather more introspective, like I was saying. And it's only when I visit other countries that it starts to assume greater importance. The people at customs can be rather vexing, to say the least."

"I'll bet," observed John.

"I remember one time at customs in New York, a rather belligerent immigration officer made me take off my mask and fainted after I'd done so. And she sued me for nervous shock."

The professor laughed again.

"Serves her right," said John.

"Which is why I have a microchip under the skin of my neck, so that I can satisfy even the most demanding of U.S. Immigration officials."

"You mean like a dog," said John.

"Woof, woof," said the professor. "Exactly like a dog."

John shrugged. "They treat everyone like a dog these days," he said. "No matter what you look like."

Nimrod was already presenting his credentials to the marine guard, and minutes later he and the four others were standing in front of the hydrofoil's commanding officer, Captain Rock Delaware, and watching him read the top secret orders.

"You'll note the signature on all those orders, Captain," said Nimrod who, in his uniform, looked every inch a senior admiral.

"Your credentials are impeccable, sir," said Captain Delaware.

"I'm glad you agree," said Nimrod. "And you're satisfied that you understand what you're required to do?"

"Yes, sir. I'm to take you and these VIPs to wherever you want to go."

Captain Delaware tried to restrain his curiosity, but it wasn't every day his ship was commandeered by presidential order, not to mention a senior rear admiral who was accompanied by two children and two men, one of whom was wearing a black mask. Captain Delaware eyed the professor uncertainly.

"Which is — where, exactly? The orders don't say."

"All will be explained in due course," said Nimrod. "For now you should make all speed to Cagliari, on the island of Sardinia. When we have refueled there, I'll tell you the name of our final destination."

"Yes, sir. Well then. I'll convey you to some suitable quarters."

"Thank you, Captain. You've been most understanding."

"Is there anything else I could do for you and your party?"

"Yes, there is, Captain." Nimrod looked at the others and shook his head. "I don't know about them, but I'd love a cup of English breakfast tea." And because he was still speaking "American," he added: "With cream."

CHAPTER 10

A NEW POSITION

Guidonia is a smallish dump of a town east of the city of Rome.

It's a depressing, ugly place, with a lot of unemployment and crime, and everywhere and on everything there is graffiti, which was an ancient Greek invention, but much copied by the Romans.

As Vito's ice-cream van entered Guidonia, Groanin saw graffiti on the public buildings, on the hospital, on cars, on the bridges and overpasses, on the billboards, even on the coats of the local stray dogs. And he thought it was not unlikely that if he stayed still there for long enough he, too, would find himself adorned with a slogan or obscenity.

Some people like graffiti. Groanin wasn't one of them. He thought that the so-called "artists" who spray painted their unsightly slogans and tags on walls — and more especially dogs — should be hurled into the River Tiber inside sacks filled with wildcats, which was a punishment beloved of the Romans, who, in Groanin's opinion, knew a thing or two about real punishments — unlike the kind of soft, smack-on-the-wrist sort of punishments that are handed out today. If you are going to have an empire that lasts for the better part of a millennium, then, in Groanin's opinion, you need to ensure that folk behave themselves.

"Not much of a place is it?" he said. "I said, it's not much of a place. And I thought Manchester was depressing."

"I heard you the first time," said Vito.

Vito had been to Guidonia before and knew his way around. They found Decebal and some of his gang grouped around an abandoned lime-green sofa at the opposite end of town.

Decebal, a handsome, dark-haired boy of fourteen, was easily distinguished by the electric-blue tracksuit he was wearing — the same electric-blue tracksuit he had been wearing on the Italian TV program about the boy and his mostly Romanian gang — and by the white SUV that was parked a short way away with a personalized license plate that read 8 DECIBLES. The plate was well named because all of the SUV's doors were open, and loud, repetitive music of the kind that reminds most people of a distant antiaircraft bombardment was bruising the humid, early evening air.

Vito drew up alongside the SUV. "Keep an eye on the Englishman," he told Toni. "I will go and speak to the kid."

Decebal watched Vito suspiciously as he walked toward him and then spat onto the ground.

"Nobody ordered ice cream," he said.

"I brought you something better," said Vito. "An Englishman."

"What do I want with an Englishman?" said Decebal.

"He's rich," said Vito. "And the person he works for is even richer."

"Doing what, exactly?"

"He's a butler."

"So?"

"I was thinking that maybe you could hold him for ransom," said Vito.

"Why not hold him for ransom yourself?" Decebal asked.

"Because kidnapping people isn't my business. You, on the other hand, are good at it."

Decebal nodded but negotiations continued for several minutes before a deal was finally struck and Vito came back to the ice-cream van and Groanin.

"Get your stuff," Vito told Groanin. "These guys are going to look after the next stage of your journey."

Groanin did as he was told but he wasn't happy about it. In fact, he regarded young Decebal and his gang with deep suspicion. The butler might have had a superstrong right arm, but these young men were all carrying guns, and quite openly, too, as if they cared nothing for the law and the police. He'd tried very hard not to face up to the reality of his situation — that he was being kidnapped — but now he could hardly ignore it.

As Vito and Toni drove away in their ice-cream van with his bag of money, Groanin suddenly felt very scared and very alone.

"Just my luck," he muttered to himself through gritted teeth. "Just my flipping luck. I leave Nimrod's employment to avoid putting myself in danger and I end up getting myself kidnapped. And kidnapped by a bunch of horrible kids, to boot."

Decebal flicked away a cigarette, walked around Groanin like he was a baffling piece of sculpture, and shook his head. As he circled the Englishman, he made remarks in Romanian that seemed to greatly amuse his jeering gang of thugs.

"What's that you're saying?" demanded Groanin.

"You're bald," said Decebal. "And you're fat."

"And what of it?" said Groanin. "You cheeky young pup."

"I thought people like you only existed in books and movies," said Decebal, whose English was good. "English butlers."

"It's true that employment opportunities in domestic service are rather limited these days," said Groanin. "However, there are still a few discerning gentlemen for whom a gentleman's gentleman is considered the last word in gracious living."

All of this made perfect sense to the young gangster for whom the idea of gracious living had become something of a holy grail. As well as owning an SUV, Decebal owned a large apartment in the only nice part of Guidonia, and it was full of elegant, antique furniture and many stolen works of Renaissance art. He also liked fine food, expensive clothes, and reading books. But the thing he most craved was to have a servant and a proper servant at that, with pin-striped trousers and a clean white shirt and a black tie. Someone to press his shirts and his suits without a crease, and run his bath at the correct temperature, and make him a perfect cup of tea — the way that butlers did in movies.

That would really be the icing on his cake and everyone

would know that he was the boss. All the really important people, like the multibillionaire hedge-fund dealer Rashleigh Khan, seemed to have a butler; and of those people only the most important of all employed an *English* butler.

"It might be fun to have an English butler," said Decebal. Groanin was horrified.

"And what would you want with an English butler, sunshine? Butlers are for people who appreciate the finer things in life. People who are prepared to pay to have someone iron their shirts without a crease, and run their baths at the correct temperature, and make a perfect cup of tea." He shook his head. "A butler's not for the likes of you, sonny."

Decebal was shaking his head. "No, no, no. That's exactly what I want."

Groanin's horror kept on increasing. "What do *you* want with a perfectly pressed shirt? Look at you, wearing a T-shirt and a tracksuit. I doubt you could tell the difference between a good cup of tea and a glass of ginger beer. And as for a bath, well, you don't look like someone for whom a bath is that important. In short, you're an ill-bred pleb. I, on the other hand, I am a gentleman's gentleman. That means I only work for gentlemen, not scruffy-looking Herberts like you."

It was perhaps fortunate that Decebal — who had a gun under the waistband of his tracksuit bottoms — had no idea of what a "pleb" or a "scruffy-looking Herbert" was; but he guessed the thrust of Groanin's comments and might easily have proved the truth of Groanin's intemperate words — that Decebal was no gentleman — by behaving in a most ungentlemanly manner: waving a gun in the butler's face, punching him on the nose, or even shooting him. But Decebal was intelligent and realized all of this himself, which was how he came to nod calmly and to agree. Besides, he liked Groanin's spirit. No one ever spoke to him the way Groanin had spoken to him. Not even his father.

"Maybe you could help turn me into a gentleman," he said. "Like this other English fellow, Professor Higgins in a film called *My Fair Lady*."

"You're joking," said Groanin. "You can't make a silk purse out of a sow's ear. I could no more turn you into a gentleman than I could pop out of a lamp and grant you three wishes."

Beginning to lose patience, Decebal pulled his gun on the butler.

"On the other hand, I could just shoot you," he said.

Groanin smiled politely. "Since you put it like that, sir," said Groanin. "Well, perhaps I could offer a few top tips, as it were: on how you might make a little more of yourself, sir. Some finesse, so to speak. Yes, sir, now I come to think of it, I might brush on a veneer of good manners and breeding onto that rough surface you call a character. Why not?"

"Good. We start now."

"Excellent idea, sir. And if I might make an early suggestion, sir? The gun, sir. Please put it away. A gentleman never ever points a gun at his butler. Not even in America where they point guns at almost anything."

Decebal lowered his weapon and Groanin breathed a sigh of relief.

"Thank you, sir."

CHAPTER 11

SHOPPING IN FEZ

Following a speedy but uneventful Mediterranean voyage, the U.S. Navy hydrofoil docked at the harbor in Nador, where a stretch Mercedes met Nimrod, the twins, Professor Sturloson, and Axel at the foot of the gangplank and drove them straight to Fez.

"We're not staying in Nador, then," observed the professor.

"There's no time for sightseeing," said Nimrod. "We need to get to Fez as quickly as possible."

The fourth-largest city in Morocco, Fez was once the largest city in the world. Founded in A.D. 789, the city is situated just below the most prominently northwest point in Africa — a sort of continental thumb that pokes up at the soft underbelly of Spanish Europe. It was full of narrow, winding streets, minarets, and strange smells, not all of them good. Men in long, striped cloth hoodies stood around on street corners, shouting at one another and gesticulating wildly, while the women seemed all but invisible.

Everywhere — spilling out of bars and shops, blasting out of open car windows — there was the infectious sound of Arabic music.

Nimrod told the driver, a sleepy-looking Moroccan named Mohammad, to drive them to the old medina of Fez and, arriving at a dome-shaped gate in a high white wall, they all got out of the car.

"From here we'll have to walk," said Nimrod. "You'll soon see why."

"It seems familiar," said Philippa. "And yet I know this is my first time in Morocco."

"That's the curious thing about Fez," said Nimrod. "It always feels like an old friend."

"No, it's stronger than that," observed Philippa.

"You're right," said John. "It feels like I know the way."

"Perhaps you were here in an another life," suggested Nimrod.

And, of course, perhaps they had been, but that, as they say, is another story.

He led the way through the gate.

The twins considered themselves well traveled but the medina was like nothing they had encountered before. It was, thought Philippa, like stepping back into one of the seven journeys of Sinbad or, perhaps, the tales of Aladdin and Ali Baba. But Nimrod seemed to know the place like the back of his hand. He led them through a succession of streets — many of them too narrow for a car — and covered, shadowy alleys that were full of shopkeepers, tourists, chickens, and donkeys. Wonderful smells of spices and herbs assailed their nostrils, while their ears were filled with sounds of music and commerce that had changed little in centuries.

After ten or fifteen minutes, they arrived in a dusty, plain little square in the darkest and most ancient part of the medina, where Nimrod approached a small and very old-looking wooden door. And there he addressed his companions. "This is it," he said. "This is the place."

"You mean this old wooden door?" asked the professor.

"It doesn't much look like a rug emporium," observed John. "It looks more like a prison."

"Certainly somewhere very secret," said Axel. "And not like any other carpet shop I've ever been to. In Jerusalem, they virtually drag you into the shop to make you buy one."

"Yes," said Nimrod. "I know some of those shops. But they're rather more recent in origin than this place. This shop has been here for two thousand years. Mr. Barkhiya is the direct descendant of the vizier of King Solomon."

"You mean the chap in the Bible?" asked the professor.

Nimrod nodded.

"What's a vizier?" asked John. "No, wait, I think I know. It's a high-ranking minister or advisor to an Arab king, isn't it?"

"Yes, it is," said Nimrod. "When Solomon died, Mr. Barkhiya's ancestors inherited the king's famous flying carpet. Originally, this was an enormous carpet, sixty miles long and sixty miles wide, and when it flew, it was shaded from the sun by a canopy of birds. Thousands of djinn and people could ride upon it at any one time. On one occasion, so the story goes, the wind became jealous of King Solomon and shook the carpet, and over forty thousand people fell to their deaths."

"More than just a touch of wind, then," quipped John.

"Over the years, the carpet has been cut up many times," continued Nimrod, ignoring his young nephew. "Today all flying carpets are smaller pieces of that much larger one once owned by Solomon. Of course, in more recent times, flying on a carpet was deemed most unfashionable by us djinn. And over the last few decades, business has been slow for Mr. Barkhiya. But all of that is different now that we can no longer risk going anywhere by whirlwind. Which means that it may be hard to negotiate a fair price. So it would be better if you said as little as possible while I'm bargaining with him. Because it's certain that Asaf will want something more than just money. Is that clear?"

The twins nodded. "Clear," they said in unison.

"Clear," added Axel and the professor for whom, in truth, nothing was clear at all. Each of them still half expected to wake up in his bed at home in Iceland thinking he'd just had a most peculiar dream.

The rug emporium was more like a church inside — a huge, echoing, dark Byzantine church with a circular marble floor and many brass lamps hanging from a very high ceiling. The vast floor was surrounded with a series of enormous pillars that were unusual in that they appeared to be made out of giant rolls of carpet: a blue silk carpet with a gold weft.

Nimrod clapped his hands loudly, and lifted a hand in salute as a man wearing a plain, white turban and silken white robes, who was seated cross-legged on a little square of blue carpet, floated across the floor toward them like a cloud in a little bit of sky.

"Peace be with you," said Nimrod.

"And with you," said the man. Dismounting the carpet, which stayed floating several inches above the ground, the man bowed gravely and said: "Let tall mountains and vast deserts tremble. Let great cities shudder and turn in fear of the mighty Nimrod. Welcome, esteemed sir. Since I last saw you, great djinn, I have often thought of you and wondered how long it would be before you would grace my humble establishment with your august presence once more. And I bless this day, since we now meet again."

Philippa shuddered to look at the carpet seller. Mr. Barkhiya had the nose and eyes of an eagle, a large gap between his very white front teeth, and a long, shiny, black beard that was divided into two sharp points, like a pitchfork. He was not very tall but he carried himself like a man of enormous height, and his voice was as deep and almost as dramatic as that of a great actor.

"Permit me to introduce my nephew, John, and my niece, Philippa," said Nimrod.

"I am and always will be your most humble servant," said Mr. Barkhiya and bowed again. "May both of you continue to live happily until the very distant hour of your death."

"You too," said Philippa.

"Ditto," said John.

"May I also present Professor Snorri Sturloson and Dr. Axel Heimskringla," said Nimrod.

"The honor is all mine," said Mr. Barkhiya.

"We've come about a carpet," said Nimrod.

Mr. Barkhiya smiled as if such a thing was obvious. He bowed again and then lifted his arms to the ceiling as if someone up there was listening. "And when Solomon sat upon the carpet, he was caught up by the wind and sailed through the air so quickly that he breakfasted at Damascus and dined in Medina," said Mr. Barkhiya. "And the wind followed Solomon's commands." The carpet seller grinned happily. "Of course you have come about carpets, my dear Nimrod. Why else would you be here? Just the one carpet, is it? I could perhaps let you have a discount for three. A very special price."

While he talked, Mr. Barkhiya stroked one of the great blue carpet pillars, which rippled and undulated under his touch like a hide of some great beast. He nodded at John and Philippa. "Come, children, touch it."

John and Philippa glanced at their uncle, who nodded his assent, and the twins stepped forward to rub their not particularly clean hands up and down the smooth surface of the carpet pillar.

"Is it not smooth?" Mr. Barkhiya asked John. "Is it not silky?" he asked Philippa. "Is it not marvelous?"

The twins nodded.

"Very," said Philippa.

"It's like something alive," observed John.

"There's a vibration in every fiber," added Philippa. "I can feel the djinn power present in every fiber of the carpet."

"Then truly you are both djinn," said Mr. Barkhiya. "For only djinn like yourselves can feel this special vibration. I have never felt this sensation myself. I am merely the great carpet's custodian. Not its master."

"I suppose it's handmade," said the professor. "On one of those old carpet looms."

"Oh, yes." Mr. Barkhiya grinned his gap-toothed grin. "Handwoven by a thousand djinn. With one thread that was as long as eternity. Each knot of the carpet contains an uttered word of djinn power. What the djinn themselves call a focus word. Is it not so, Nimrod?"

"Quite so," affirmed Nimrod.

"And this is where the power of flying comes from. From the djinn power over mathematics and physics and the great Golden Ratio and the secret meaning of 1.61803."

"And is it easy to control?" asked Axel who, being an accomplished hang glider, thought he knew a thing or two about flying.

Mr. Barkhiya smiled his gap-toothed smile again. "I regret to inform you, Dr. Heinzkrinkle —"

"Heimskringla," said Axel. "My name is Heimskringla."

Mr. Barkhiya bowed politely. "I regret to inform you, Dr. Heimskringla, that no human being can fly one of these carpets. Many have perished in the attempt. Which is to say, they are dead. Only a djinn like Nimrod and, in time, these greatly gifted children may control such a carpet as this.

The tiny fragment of rug you saw me appear on earlier is as much as I am able to safely control myself. And even that is only because I was granted three wishes by another grateful customer."

"You mean three wishes," said Axel, "like in children's stories?"

"Are they children's stories?" Mr. Barkhiya looked at Nimrod and frowned. "Surely not. To have three wishes is surely more than any child would know what to do with."

"Axel's right," explained Nimrod. "In places like Europe and America, it's only children who believe in the idea of three wishes."

"In Morocco," said Mr. Barkhiya, "everyone believes in three wishes. Everyone dreams of releasing a djinn trapped for a thousand years inside a lamp or bottle and being handsomely rewarded for this humble service."

Nimrod shivered. "Please," he said. "Don't mention that kind of thing. It gives me claustrophobia just thinking about it." He rubbed his hands. "Talking of which. You haven't yet mentioned your price, Asaf."

"I will make a very special price for you, O great one. But for how many carpets? You have not said."

"I think an extra large one for me," said Nimrod, "and two juniors, one each for my nephew and my niece."

"Three wishes," said Mr. Barkhiya.

"That is fair."

"From each of you."

Nimrod shook his head. "No. That is too much."

"Nevertheless, that is my price. Three for the large one. And three for each of the two smaller ones. One wish for me and one wish for each of my eight sons."

"But nine wishes, Asaf," said Nimrod. "We'll be here all day."

"It's been a tough year what with the downturn in the economy and prices — don't talk to me about prices. It's not just carpets that are going up, it's everything. Besides, these carpets are works of art and art has no price."

Nimrod shook his head. "I tell you what I'll do. We'll take the large one now. In exchange for three wishes. But we'll defer the collection of the two juniors. My niece and nephew can return on another occasion. And we can haggle about a proper price then."

Mr. Barkhiya looked uncomfortable. "The thing is, Nimrod," he said. "It's not just European airspace that's closed. North American and Central African airspace have also closed because of volcanic ash. And Southeast Asian airspace looks like it's going to close as well. Very soon my carpets will be the only things flying. Which makes them more valuable."

"But only djinn know how to fly them," objected Nimrod.

"True," admitted Mr. Barkhiya. "However, I now anticipate a much greater demand for my carpets than of old. I am informed that already there are others like you traveling from the four corners of the earth, to my humble shop here in Fez, in order to purchase one of these rare and inestimable carpets. You wouldn't want these children of the lamp to be less than the birds of the air, would you?"

CHILDREN OF THE LAMP

"Three wishes for the large size," said Nimrod. "And three wishes in total for the two juniors. And that's my last offer. After all, there's a limit to how many people you can get on a junior."

"Agreed. One wish now for me and one wish now for two of my eight sons."

"And you will reserve two junior-sized carpets and my young relatives will return here to collect and pay for them when we are less pressed for time as we are now."

"This is also agreed."

Nimrod spat in his hand and shook hands with Mr. Barkhiya.

"One more thing," said Nimrod. "I know you to be a religious man, Asaf. And a man of your word. So, you and the two sons who are to be granted a wish today must all state these wishes in advance and confine yourselves to wishing for them and only them, by all that's holy to you. Is that agreed, also?"

Asaf grinned. "Don't you trust me, O great one?"

Nimrod shook his head. "You're only human, my friend. It's been my experience that wishing for whatever your heart desires is more than any mundane can cope with. For we djinn are compelled to grant exactly what has been requested. And it is always wise to remember to be careful what you wish for just in case you get it."

"True," said Mr. Barkhiya. "For power of such greatness as yours, O mighty djinn, it is wise that you counsel caution. I am a simple man of the desert and I know how a wish can turn like the head of cobra and bite a man who wishes foolishly. One time I was about to wish that I was 'dead rich,' as you English sometimes say. And it was my good fortune that I had explained this wish in advance to one of your tribe, Nimrod. A Marid. And not to an Ifrit or to a Ghul. Otherwise, my wish might easily have rendered me dead before I was rich."

"You were indeed fortunate," said Nimrod.

"So then. Let us find my two eldest sons. And we shall explain our wishes to you."

Mr. Barkhiya took Nimrod and the others up to the rug emporium rooftop where his sons had spread out Nimrod's flying carpet in the morning sunshine. The emporium's rooftop was castellated like a fortress and the highest in all of the old city so that local people might not be alarmed at the sight of a carpet ascending into the sky. The carpet itself was about a thousand square feet and as blue as a sapphire. Under the hot Moroccan sun, the gold thread woven into the carpet seemed to glow like it was molten metal.

"If the carpet has not flown for a while," explained one of the sons, "then you should always leave the carpet in the sun for a few minutes to warm the fibers up. Djinn power relies on heat, yes? Especially the heat of the sun?"

"Er, yes," said Philippa. "That's quite correct."

He handed her a hat pin and bowed.

John knelt and ran a finger along the edge. "It sure doesn't look like it's been cut."

"If the carpet is cut with a knife," said the other son, "the knife must always first draw the blood of the djinn who owns it."

"I see," said John. "A bit like a samurai sword. I'll remember that."

Professor Sturloson and Axel sat close to the center of the carpet and patiently awaited takeoff.

Meanwhile, Mr. Barkhiya and his two eldest sons debated their three wishes among themselves.

"What's the hat pin for?" asked John.

"I don't know," Philippa said. "One of Mr. Barkhiya's sons just handed it to me."

"I'll take that," said Nimrod. "It's so that I can personalize the carpet, and make it so that only I can fly it. You certainly wouldn't want another djinn to steal your carpet. Only, this requires the spilling of blood on the carpet. So my djinn blood will become part of the carpet. And the words of power that were used in its weaving will be mine to command."

Hesitating, he pulled a face. "Oh, Lord, I've always hated needles."

"Me, too," said John.

"Oh, here," said Philippa. "Give it to me." She took the pin back from her uncle. "Don't be such a wuss."

She grabbed her uncle's thumb and pricked it for him before he could protest.

"Ouch," said Nimrod. "That hurt."

Philippa squeezed his thumb hard and let a ruby of blood drop on the shining blue silk of the carpet.

Watching more closely, John noticed that the fibers seemed to emit a small cloud of smoke before the blood was completely absorbed, without so much as a stain.

"Er, thank you," said Nimrod, and sucked his thumb. "Very kind of you, Philippa, I think."

Mr. Barkhiya returned with his two eldest sons. "This is my eldest son, Hanif," he said. "And this is my son Salman."

"Have you decided what you're going to wish for?" asked Nimrod.

"Yes, O great one," said Mr. Barkhiya. He looked at Hanif and nodded urgently.

"Oh, right. It's me first, huh?"

"You're the eldest." Hanif's father looked at Nimrod and shrugged. "Educated in America," he said by way of explanation for Hanif's accent. "Like all my sons."

"Um."

"Hanif," said Nimrod. "Just spit it out."

"This is gonna sound kind of strange," said Hanif. "But I always wanted to play the horn. I mean the trumpet. Like Miles Davis. I play already but I'm not nearly as good as he was. Yeah, that's what I wish. To play the horn as well as him."

"That's nice." Nimrod nodded and then looked at Salman. "And you?"

Salman grinned and looked at his brother. "The sax," he said. "I wanna play sax like John Coltrane. All I ever wanted to do, man, was play the sax like John Coltrane. All my life that's been my wish. You might say it was a love supreme. Yeah."

Nimrod smiled and looked at Mr. Barkhiya. "And I suppose you want to play the double bass like Marcus Miller."

"Drums," said Mr. Barkhiya. "Like Philly Joe Jones or Billy Cobham."

"I certainly can't fault your taste," said Nimrod. "Any of you. However, before I grant your wishes and give each of you a little bit of talent, which is important, it's worth mentioning that most of their ability to play was the result of practice. Practice makes perfect."

As soon as Nimrod had granted these three wishes, he stepped onto the huge blue square of silk carpet, alongside the twins, Professor Sturloson, and Axel; sat down cross-legged; and then muttered his focus word.

A second or two later the carpet started silently to rise into the air like a very well-behaved helicopter.

"*Ótrúlegt*," said Axel. "Unbelievable." He rolled to the edge of the carpet and looked down at the retreating medina. "I feel like Sinbad. I never thought that I would fly on a real magic carpet."

"Don't say that word," said Philippa. "*Magic.* It irritates my uncle."

"Oh, right," said Axel. "Sorry. But this is very exciting. And it certainly feels like magic to a boy from Reykjavik. I used to think that a carpet was something for covering floors with. Or vacuuming. Not flying on."

"I agree." The professor grinned. He smoothed the carpet with the flat palm of his hand and thought it smoother than the velvet curtains at the White House in Washington where, once, he'd been invited to a dinner given in honor of the Icelandic ambassador by the U.S. president. "I'm afraid it's bound to feel very magical to us."

"*Frábær*," said Axel. "Fantastic." He rolled into a crouching position. "Is it safe?" he asked. "To stand? To walk around?"

"Isn't that a question you should have asked before you got on?" Philippa smiled at the big Icelander. With his blue eyes, light blond hair, peppermint-white teeth, and chiseled cheekbones, she considered him the most marvelous-looking man she had ever seen.

"I suppose it is," Axel said ruefully.

"Yes, it's safe," said Nimrod, and set a course east-north-east. "Only don't go too near the edge, Axel. As we pick up speed and altitude the most comfortable place to sit will be in the center of the carpet."

Axel grinned at Philippa. "I just wish I had my camera," he said.

And because Philippa liked Axel and wanted him to like her, she whispered her focus word and, of course, Axel's camera — a fine old Hasselblad — appeared in his big, strong hands.

"Did you do this?" he said, grinning from ear to ear. "For me?"

"Yes," she confessed, and blushed as he kissed her on the cheek.

CHAPTER 12

PIG MALE AEON

Groanin surveyed the mountainous pile of dirty dishes in the kitchen sink and uttered a profound sigh.

"Disaster," he muttered. "What a disaster." For once Groanin did not overstate the matter.

But he wasn't talking about the news on television, although he might easily have been: Another volcano — Bjarnarey, on the Vestmannaeyjar Islands, near Iceland — had become active.

He was talking about events that had occurred in Decebal's apartment in Guidonia the previous evening when Groanin had cooked an elaborate five-course dinner for ten, hosted by Decebal and his girlfriend, Bogna. Things had gone relatively well until the cheese course when Groanin had served a local blue Gorgonzola, which, the uncouth and ignorant Romanians insisted, was blue because it had spoiled; they proceeded to accuse him of trying to make a fool out of them and that he had intended to trick them into believing that the strong-smelling, blue-veined cheese was edible.

116

When Groanin had loudly protested that Gorgonzola was supposed to be blue veined and strong smelling, the skeptical Romanians had pelted him with the Gorgonzola as well as all the other cheeses he had purchased from the Guidonia Cheese Shop — d'Aosta, Grana Padano, Parmesan, and pecorino. They also pelted him with bread rolls, grapes, after-dinner mints, two antique silver salt and pepper cellars, and a television remote control. The butler had a large bruise on his head after being struck by a flying cell phone. And a couple of days working for Decebal already seemed like an age, an aeon.

"'You don't know what you've got till it's gone,' right enough," said Groanin. "And to think I used to complain about being in old Nimrod's service." He wiped a tear from his rheumy eye. "What kind of psycho throws a cell phone at his butler's head?"

No less disastrous than the dinner party had been Groanin's genuine attempts to educate the young gangster about good table manners and gracious living.

Preliminary instructions in the proper use of three sets of cutlery had been met with open hostility.

"What's the point of having three sets of cutlery on the table when you could just as easily make do with one?" demanded Decebal. "It doesn't make sense. Just more washing up."

"Nevertheless, sir, that is the proper way to do these things," insisted Groanin. "In restaurants — if you go to restaurants, that is, sir — it's customary to start by using the cutlery on the outside, and to work in, as it were."

"The whole world's about to blow up," said Decebal, "and you're worried about the right spoon to use."

"I'm not worried about it, sir," said Groanin. "The spoons, I mean. I'm merely telling you what is correct. What is right. What is expected in polite circles."

"I don't care about polite circles," insisted Decebal. "And I don't care about cutlery."

"Evidently, sir."

No more did Decebal care to have his bath drawn when he could have a shower instead; moreover, his shirts were all nylon and could not be pressed, and he hardly saw the point of Groanin polishing the silver — which is the principal occupation of butlers all over the world — when he was in the habit of stealing a new set of silver whenever the old set started to look tarnished.

But mostly, Groanin's attempts to teach Decebal how to behave had been thwarted by the boy's insatiable sweet tooth. To Groanin's obvious disgust and horror, Decebal was accustomed to eating chocolates from a large box before, during, and after any meal; he liked honey in his coffee and apricot jam in his sandwiches, and — after several attempts to drink the perfectly made tea that Groanin had prepared — he discovered he much preferred instant coffee with lots of sugar.

This was nothing, however, to compare with Decebal's reaction to being awoken by Groanin bringing him his breakfast on a silver tray. It was the adolescent's habit to sleep well past midday and into the early afternoon — a habit that Groanin considered to be nothing short of degenerate.

Nimrod liked to be awoken by Groanin at precisely seven A.M. with a breakfast tray and a newspaper. But Decebal didn't like being woken any more than he liked breakfast or wanted a newspaper, especially an Italian paper like *Il Giornale*.

Which was probably why he had pulled a gun from under his pillow and started shooting. Not actually at Groanin — Decebal wasn't crazy, just loutish — but almost everywhere else. And the bedroom now looked like a saloon in Dodge City — all broken mirrors and gunshot pictures.

Later on, in the afternoon, when Decebal finally got out of bed, he went over the criminal activities that were on the agenda with his number two, Costica. Or at least he tried to go over the day's business in hand.

"What's that infernal noise?" he asked Costica.

"It's the butler, boss, vacuuming the carpets and the curtains in the dining room," explained Costica. He got up and closed the living room door.

"The man is crazy. What does he want to go and vacuum the curtains for?"

"I don't know, boss."

Decebal may have been ignorant, but he wasn't stupid, and he knew that his idea of having a butler really wasn't working out.

"Get rid of him," said Decebal.

Costica drew his gun.

"Not like that, you idiot," said Decebal. "Sell him."

Costica frowned. "To whom? People around here haven't got the money for butlers. We should ransom him, like the Italians suggested. To this guy he works for. Nimrod."

"Maybe we could but the butler's cell phone isn't working." Decebal shrugged. "So we can hardly call this Nimrod and demand a ransom to set his butler free. Can we?" He shook his head. "Kidnapping is no business to be in when the entire cellular phone network stops working."

"So who are we going to sell him to?" asked Costica.

Decebal thought for a moment. "There's a ship called the *Shebelle* in the port at Civitavecchia," explained Decebal. "It's owned by some pirates from Somalia. We'll sell the butler to them. What those guys don't know about kidnapping isn't worth knowing. Plus, they're much more ruthless than we are."

"When shall we do this?"

The sound of Groanin vacuuming got nearer to the living room door.

"No time like the present," said Decebal. "Before he drives me mad with his cleaning and his cutlery."

CHAPTER 13

SIDI MUBARAK BOMBAY

The beginning of their lengthy journey on board the flying carpet took the fivesome over the island of Sicily, where they had an excellent view of Mount Etna, which, at almost eleven thousand feet, is the largest active volcano in Europe.

It was dark and they could not see the ash and gas plume that reached almost four miles into the air before trailing across Greece and Turkey some eight hundred miles away. What they could see, however, was a spectacular firework display of red-hot lava as it was shot one hundred and sixty feet out of the crater into the night sky, and several glowing streams of eighteen-hundred-degree Fahrenheit molten rock that flowed down the mountain slopes like a river of fire.

John and Philippa had crawled to the edge of the flying carpet to get the best possible view of Etna's eruption.

"Wow," said John.

"It's a sobering sight, right enough," said the professor.

"This is what lies in store for the whole of our planet unless we can put a stop to it," said Nimrod.

"That is, if you're right about this ancient Chinese curse," said Axel.

"I sincerely hope I'm not," said Nimrod. "However, I rather think I am."

"What was it again?" said Axel. "The curse. Something like '*yi wàng nián de huǒ zāi*,' wasn't it?"

"Your accent is very good." Nimrod put down the book he had been reading and smiled at the Icelander. "Sounds like you speak a bit of Chinese, Axel."

"A bit," said Axel modestly. "I used to have a Chinese girlfriend."

"That might come in handy. The language, not the girlfriend."

"She used to say I was terrible at speaking Chinese." Axel smiled ruefully.

"Well, you speak Icelandic really well," observed John. "And that sounds just as difficult."

Axel's smile widened and he rubbed the hair on John's head with affection.

"If you say so, little brother," he said.

"I must say, the lava from Etna doesn't look very golden," observed Philippa.

"All metal looks much the same at eighteen hundred degrees Fahrenheit," said Nimrod. "I would suggest we fly down to take a closer look, if it wasn't for what happened to your mother."

"What happened to their mother?" asked the professor.

"She got hit by a pyroclastic flow, in Hawaii," said Nimrod. "Much like you, Professor. Only she was less fortunate than yourself."

"I'm sorry," said the professor gravely. "I had no idea."

"Oh, she's not dead," said John. "At least, her spirit isn't. Her body was burnt to a crisp. But she was fortunate in that she managed to borrow another one. Well, not so much borrow, as take the body that had belonged to our housekeeper, Mrs. Trump. She had fallen downstairs and was in a coma." He paused, suddenly aware of what this must sound like. "Well, it's a long story."

"Sounds like it," said Axel.

"How fast can this thing go?" asked the professor, changing the subject.

"The carpet?" said Nimrod. "Well, it's been a few years since I flew one, so I'm a little out of practice, to be honest. Back in the day, I could get five hundred miles per hour out of my father's carpet. But now I'm lucky to get two or three hundred. All of which reminds me." He put down his book again. "John? Philippa?"

"Yes, Uncle?"

"It's high time you two learned how to fly a carpet."

"I thought the drop of blood you spilled on it meant no one can fly this carpet except you," objected John.

"Except that I give you my permission, of course," said Nimrod. "Not to mention the fact that I'm actually sitting on it. No, no, the blood spot is just to ensure that when I'm not there no one else can fly it."

"Er, right," said John. "What do I do? Is it anything like flying a whirlwind?"

"Yes, and no," said Nimrod.

"That's very helpful," said Philippa.

"A carpet is altogether heavier. Like driving a car that doesn't have power steering. Or an old bicycle without springs and proper inflatable tires. And, of course, flying carpets are not so good in storms as I sincerely hope we won't discover. It's altogether a harder ride than a whirlwind. And why wouldn't it be?" Nimrod banged the carpet hard with the flat of his hand. "This is solid whereas a whirlwind was just a cushion of air." He sighed. "A flying carpet is so much more primitive than a whirlwind. Like going back to a propeller aircraft after one has grown used to flying on the Concorde." He thought for a moment. "The action is more like a skimming stone on the surface of a lake. You must think of the carpet bouncing across the surface of one air pocket after another. Which accounts for the slight up-and-down sensation. Can you feel it?"

"I can," admitted the professor. "And it's making me ever so slightly seasick."

"You'll get used to it." Nimrod grinned at John. "Come on, then, John," he said. "Let's see you try it. When you're ready, just say *ready* and then I'll give you control, all right?"

John pulled a face. "I remember the first time I flew a whirlwind," he said. "In Kathmandu. I managed to flip over a car. And tore off someone's satellite dish. And then Dybbuk threw up on the heads of some tourists."

"Please don't talk about throwing up," said the professor. "Believe me, that's not so easy when you're wearing a mask."

"I remember." Philippa laughed. "All the hippies thought they had seen someone who'd actually mastered the art of yogic flying."

John grinned back at his sister. "We've had some fun times, haven't we?"

"Yes," agreed Philippa.

"Come on, come on," Nimrod said a little impatiently. "I haven't got all day."

"Oh. Right." John paused for a moment, and then said, "Ready."

"You have control," said Nimrod.

Except that he didn't. None by a long chalk.

Immediately, John felt the weight and dimensions of the carpet. It was as if someone had handed him a heavy barbell in a gym. For a moment he held it steady before the sheer bulk of it quite overwhelmed him and the carpet collapsed in on itself with everyone — Nimrod, Philippa, the professor, and Axel — wrapped up inside it like the contents of a tablecloth that had fallen through a hole in the middle of a table.

Everyone screamed as the carpet plunged toward the earth like a faulty elevator car, or perhaps a really terrifying theme park ride. Everyone except Nimrod.

"It's all right," he said. "Happens to everyone on their first attempt. Here. Let me straighten you out."

John felt Nimrod take control of the flying carpet again and a few seconds later they were level and still aloft.

"Ready for another go?" Nimrod asked John.

"I don't know about John, but I know I'm not," said the professor. "I don't think my nerves could stand another drop like that last one."

"Yes, it was rather sudden, wasn't it?" admitted Nimrod. "Like going over Niagara in a barrel." He chuckled. "And I should know, having done that."

"You're a man of many parts, Nimrod," said the professor. "But speaking for myself, I prefer to exist in just the one part, if you follow my meaning."

"Yes," said Nimrod. "Well, perhaps you're right, Snorri, old friend. Children? We shall have to postpone our flying lesson for another time. Out of courtesy for our fellow passengers."

The professor breathed a loud sigh of relief. "Thank you, Nimrod."

A few minutes later, a bird landed on the edge of the carpet. Axel said that it was a wild duck. A mallard.

"Yes, that's another problem with flying carpets," said Nimrod. "Other creatures sometimes hitch a ride."

"Still, it's rather a nice wild duck," said Philippa.

She crawled toward the bird with some cookie crumbs she had found in her pocket. "I've always thought of ducks as being friendly birds," she said. "Because of their smiley-looking beaks."

The bird quacked happily as Philippa tossed it the crumbs and then ate them, after which it allowed Philippa to stroke its head.

"Can I keep it, Uncle?" she asked after a while. "As a pet."

"It'll fly off before long," said John. "You'll see."

"But if it doesn't fly off. Can I keep it then, Uncle Nimrod?"

"On one condition," said Nimrod. "That you don't call it Donald."

"All right." Philippa thought for a second. "I shall call it Moby."

"Moby." Nimrod groaned. "Almost as bad, if not worse."

John laughed. "Oh, I get it. Moby Duck, yeah. Cool." He shrugged. "And if it doesn't work out as a pet, we can always eat it."

"What a crummy thing to say," protested Philippa. She hugged the bird to her and kissed its green head. "Of course he's going to work out."

John shook his head. "It's a long way to Mongolia, sis," he said. "And I'll bet you five bucks that Moby Duck will have taken off long before that."

"We're not headed to Mongolia," announced Nimrod. "At least, not right away. No, first we have to stop in Afghanistan." He tapped the book he had been reading. "According to this book, anyway."

"There would have to be a very good reason for going to Afghanistan," said the professor. "Especially since I could give any number of good reasons for not going to Afghanistan."

"Yeah," said John. "It's dangerous."

"Nevertheless," said Nimrod. "Afghanistan is where we're going."

"Why?"

"I don't remember you having any books when we got onto

this carpet," said Axel. "And now it seems that you have several. Too many to have fitted in that Louis Choppsouis bag you have with you. Where did all these old books come from?"

Nimrod showed Axel an old silver djinn lamp.

"Inside here," he said, "is a large library that belonged to an old friend of mine. Of ours. Mr. Rakshasas. He's no longer alive, I'm afraid, and I now have custody of the lamp and the library. Which is one of the best libraries on secret hermetic things anywhere in the world. Although strictly speaking, it isn't. In the world, I mean. It's sort of both in it and out of it at the same time, if you understand what I mean."

"Not really," sighed the professor.

"I sort of popped in and browsed around a bit back on the hydrofoil between Sardinia and Nador. When you were all asleep."

"A library? In a lamp?" Axel shook his head. "It's not possible, is it?"

"He says this while he's sitting on a flying carpet," murmured the professor.

"I can assure you it is possible, Axel," said Philippa. "A library with a reading room and shelves, and tens of thousands of books."

"Not to mention the creepiest librarian you've ever seen." John laughed. "Liskeard Karswell du Crowleigh. Although strictly speaking, he's the bottle imp. By the way, Uncle, how is Liskeard?"

"He's all right, thank you, John."

"Could I see the library inside the lamp, sometime, perhaps?" asked the professor.

"I'm afraid not, Snorri," said Nimrod. "A human being would suffocate and die inside a djinn lamp."

"I feel the same way about almost any library," said John.

Axel took the book from Nimrod's hands and inspected the title that was tooled in gold on the old leather spine. He paused for a moment to read the title, which was in Hindi, and then said: "'The Secret _Secret_ History of the Mongols by Sidi Mubarak Bombay, with the most useful help of my very good friend, Henry Morton Stanley.'"

"You read Hindi, too," said Nimrod. "Now I'm really impressed."

"Before I was a volcanologist," said Axel, "I was a mountaineer. In the Himalayas. I picked it up when I was there."

Philippa stared at Axel with unashamed adoration. There seemed to be no end to the man's talents.

"Well, you're almost right," said Nimrod, who spoke fluent Hindi. "But it's The _Secret_ Secret History of the Mongols."

"What's the difference?" asked Axel.

"Oh, quite a bit. My way of pronouncing the title makes it much more secret than your way. And certainly much more secret than The Secret History of the Mongols. That book is merely esoteric and only a bit secret. This one is hermetic. Which is to say, very secret indeed. And rare. And, I confess, so very rare that it was quite unknown to me until I got Karswell — the bottle imp librarian — to bring me all of the books on the subject of Genghis Khan and his secret mausoleum. In fact, I think there were only ever three copies printed."

"I haven't heard of Sidi Mubarak Bombay," said Philippa, "but, Stanley was a Victorian English explorer, wasn't he?"

"Yes," said Nimrod. "He's the chap who found Livingstone, in Africa. He wasn't really lost but Stanley didn't know that."

Axel turned the foxed pages of the book thoughtfully. " 'Dedicated to my great friend John Hanning Speke.' "

"Another Victorian explorer in Africa," said Nimrod. "But long before Speke was in Africa, he was exploring Tibet and the Himalayas with Sidi Mubarak Bombay, a slave brought to India by Arab slavers, but freed by Speke, with whom he went on many expeditions. Among them, the search for the tomb of Genghis Khan. After Speke died, in 1864, Bombay went to India to look for the tomb there. He didn't find it, I'm afraid. But rather usefully for us, he wrote this little book. With many important clues on what to look for. And one clue in particular."

"Which is why we're going to Afghanistan, right?" said John.

Nimrod nodded.

"And what's the one clue in particular we're looking for?" asked Philippa.

"A camel," said Nimrod. "A very special camel."

CHAPTER 14

TRAN2UILITY BAY

The pirates who owned the *Shebelle*, a cargo ship in the port at Civitavecchia, near Rome, were not the kind of Jolly Roger pirates most people would have recognized. None of them owned a parrot, or carried a cutlass, or wore a three-cornered hat, or drank rum; most of them didn't drink at all. Their flag was not a white skull and crossbones on a black background but a white star on a sky-blue background, which were the colors of Somalia, a country located in the so-called Horn of Africa, and that does indeed resemble the horn of a great white rhino gouging at the underside of the Arabian Peninsula and the countries of Yemen and Oman.

These modern pirates did, however, have a first mate called Mr. Khat, who wore a golden earring, and a captain with an eye patch called Rashid Ali Sharkey, and they were interested in treasure, although not the kind of treasure you put in a chest and bury on a remote desert island. For the Somali pirates, treasure wasn't gold doubloons or pieces of eight but a substantial ransom paid by electronic transfer into a no-questions-asked bank account in Switzerland, and they got it by demanding money from the families and governments of their kidnap victims — that is, when they weren't hijacking oil tankers and smuggling wild animals for private zoos, or stealing high-value cars, or just thumbing their noses at the British Royal Navy.

Captain Sharkey was less than convinced about the merits of holding Groanin for ransom and, squeezed around the tiny desk in his cabin, he told Decebal that he might have preferred an American.

"Do you have any Americans?" he asked the young gangster.

"No, just this Englishman."

"Pity."

"Next time I'll bring you a nice, fat American."

"Do that," said Captain Sharkey. "Only not a fat one, please. Americans might have plenty of money but they're expensive to keep, mainly because they're always eating, and you have to be very careful they don't also eat into your profits."

"So who are the best people to kidnap?" asked Decebal.

"Best of all to kidnap are your billionaires," said Captain Sharkey. "Like Rashleigh Khan. Because they have the most money. A man such as he could lose a million dollars out of his back pocket and he wouldn't notice. But the best race to kidnap are your Germans. They always pay immediately. Your French always pay, too, but it's best to count the money carefully before you let the victim go. Your Australians are too well traveled and wise to get themselves kidnapped at all. Your Canadians are too dull ever to get themselves kidnapped. Your Irish, they make better kidnappers than victims. As do your Italians. And of course, your Turks. Once I kidnapped a Swede and he was so miserable and cried so much I ended up letting him go because he was depressing me. This is the so-called Stockholm syndrome that you sometimes read about."

"And the British?" asked Decebal.

Captain Sharkey shook his head.

"Your British are not at all good to kidnap," he said. "They have principles, or at least that's what they tell themselves when they refuse to pay a ransom. The reality is that they just don't like spending money. Your Scots won't ever pay at all, because they have no money in the first place. They're even more mean than the English and that's saying something."

He thought for a moment. "And never ever kidnap a Russian," he said. "They take it very personally and will make it the business of a lifetime to track you down and have some horrible revenge on you."

"I'll try to remember that," said Decebal.

"You say this man Groanin is a butler, yes?"

Decebal nodded. "According to him he works for a very wealthy man called Nimrod. And has done for many years." He paused. "So. Do we have a deal?"

"I don't know," said the captain. "I must seek advice on the matter."

He shifted his eye patch and allowed a small golden scarab to crawl out of his empty eye socket.

Decebal tried hard to conceal his horror but it was no good; his jaw dropped like a drawbridge.

"Aiee," he gasped. "What is that?"

Captain Sharkey lifted the back of his hand up to the beetle and allowed it to sit on his prominent knuckles.

"Say hello to my little friend," said Captain Sharkey.

"You keep a beetle in your eye socket?"

"It's the safest place for him," said the captain. "That way I always know where he is. If I kept him in my pocket, I might easily sit on him."

Decebal smiled politely and decided these Somali pirates were much tougher than he had ever supposed.

"But why keep it at all?"

"This is no ordinary beetle," explained Captain Sharkey. "This beetle is the guardian of my future. He makes all my difficult decisions. Such as this one."

Captain Sharkey pointed at the table on which two words were written, each at opposite ends.

"This is the Somali word for *yes*," he said. "And this is the Somali word for *no*. When I do not know what to do, I ask the beetle and then put him on the table. If the beetle walks to yes, then that is the answer to the question; and when the answer is no, the beetle, he will walk there. Always he has led me in the correct way. Always his advice has been the right advice. I show you."

The captain kissed the beetle's back and then placed it in the center of the table.

"Ringo." The captain shrugged. "That is the beetle's name. Tell me, Ringo. This Nimrod. Is he as wealthy as the English butler says he is?"

The beetle hesitated for a moment, its antennae feeling the air thoughtfully. Then it walked, slowly but surely, toward one of the words written on the table.

Decebal, who neither spoke nor read Somali, shook his head.

"Which is it?" he asked. "Yes or no?"

"Ringo says yes, that this Nimrod is indeed wealthy."

The captain picked the beetle up and kissed it again. "Very wealthy?"

Once again the beetle walked smartly toward the Somali word for *yes*.

The exercise was repeated twice more and in this way the captain concluded, quite correctly, that Groanin was loved by Nimrod, that he would certainly be missed, and that Nimrod might pay a substantial ransom to have his butler safely returned.

The captain picked up the beetle and kissed it for a fifth time.

"But is this English butler dangerous?"

Once again, the beetle walked toward the Somali word for *yes*.

"The Englishman *is* dangerous," said the captain. "Interesting."

"Nonsense," said Decebal. "He's harmless. You only have to look at him."

"Are you calling Ringo a liar?"

"Er, no. But seriously, Captain, when you see the Englishman, you'll understand for yourself. He's fat and he wears a bowler hat, like some comedian in an old movie."

Captain Sharkey picked up the beetle and replaced it carefully in his empty eye socket. "I will look at this Englishman myself," he said, and called for his first mate, Mr. Khat.

"Where did you put the Englishman?" he asked.

"In one of the stolen sports cars," said Mr. Khat.

The three criminals went out of the cabin and looked down from a gangway into the cargo hold where six stolen Lamborghinis were parked.

Inside the yellow one, a Lamborghini Gallardo, Groanin's left arm was handcuffed to the steering wheel. There was little room in the supercar and, trying to keep up his spirits, the butler was listening to a football match on the car radio. Manchester City, his beloved football team, was doing rather badly in a game against Inter Milan F.C. The game was not going well for City and by the time the fourth goal went into the back of the Manchester net, Groanin was in a filthy, violent mood and, like any normal disgruntled English football fan, was ready to take out his disappointment on anyone or anything, including a two-hundred-thousand-dollar car.

For some people, football matters more than almost anything.

"Oh, that does it," growled Groanin. "It's quite bad enough to be dragged around this flipping country by one hoodlum after another. But it's more than a man can take to have to listen to his team playing like a bunch of schoolgirls."

First, he pulled the steering wheel off with his abnormally powerful arm; then he punched out the windshield and climbed out of the car onto the hood. And seeing the logo on the front of the car's elongated hood, Groanin realized that the car, like the team Manchester was playing, was Italian.

"I've had just about enough of Italians," he shouted. "And all things Italian."

Groanin proceeded to hammer a series of large dents into the hood with his big, clunking fist.

At this point, one of the Somali crewmen ran up to Groanin with a crowbar and was promptly thrown out of the cargo hold.

"You see? You see?" Captain Sharkey shook his head. "The man is dangerous."

"I had no idea," said Decebal, astounded that the butler appeared to be so strong and rather horrified that he had been ordering around such a man as this. "He is like Samson."

"Then we had better find Delilah," said Captain Sharkey. "And put him to sleep very quickly, or else I will have no cars to sell in Egypt."

The captain said something to the first mate, who saluted and ran off to fetch something.

Meanwhile, Groanin lifted one of the front wheels of the Lamborghini and then turned the vehicle onto its side.

"Silly, stupid car, anyway," roared Groanin. "Driven by silly, stupid people."

Mr. Khat arrived back on the gangway with a tranquilizer gun and handed it to the ship's captain.

"We keep this as a precaution," explained Captain Sharkey. "Because we are transporting lions and leopards from Africa to private zoos. No self-respecting Russian billionaire can show his face these days if he doesn't have his own big cat."

He loaded the rifle with a dart, took aim at Groanin's backside, and fired.

"Yaroo!"

Groanin plucked the tranquilizer dart from his substantial behind, flung it at another retreating crewman, and grinned fiercely as it speared the Somali's earlobe.

"Double top," he said with some satisfaction for, in his day, Groanin had been a skilled darts player.

But the damage to Groanin was done. A strong sedative was already coursing through the butler's bloodstream. Then he yawned and sat down on the floor of the cargo bay and went to sleep.

"Ringo never lies," said Captain Sharkey. "Clearly the man is dangerous. But equally, clearly he is also close to someone who is very wealthy. And who will pay for his safe return."

"So does that mean we have a deal?" repeated Decebal.

"Yes." Captain Sharkey handed Decebal an envelope full of money, which was the amount Decebal had agreed to for giving Groanin to the Somali pirates. "We have a deal."

"Good."

"There will be more," said the captain, "if he fetches a good price."

"How much were you thinking of demanding?" asked Decebal.

"One million dollars is a nice, round figure," said Captain Sharkey. "I like this number." He shrugged. "It's what we always ask. We don't always get that much but it's a very good place to start."

Decebal nodded. "One million dollars always makes people sit up and pay attention," he said.

"Until then, we could use a new cabin boy. The last one fell overboard and was drowned. Or eaten by sharks. Possibly both. This Mr. Groanin can make himself useful on the voyage back to Somalia. Perhaps by then the cell phones will be working again and we can start to turn the screw a little. When we get to Port Said, I'll send a letter to the British consul, explaining the situation. In that way, we shall get publicity and perhaps even more money."

CHAPTER 15

THE SADDEST STORY EVER HEARD (WITH APOLOGIES TO FORD MADOX FORD)

A camel?" said Philippa. "Why a camel?"

"Yeah," said John. He recalled a vividly unpleasant memory of his first animal transubstantiation, which had required his djinn-spirit self spending some time inside a camel's body, in Egypt. The stink of being that camel still lingered in his mind's nostrils, to say nothing of the taste in his mouth afterward. "And what's a camel going to tell us that doesn't sound like one enormous belch?"

"To understand that," said Nimrod, "it's necessary that I tell a sad story about the death of Genghis Khan. Not that there was anything sad in particular about him being dead, as he was a thoroughly nasty piece of work and seemed to take enormous pleasure in killing as many people as possible.

Sometimes whole cities were put to the sword when they resisted being conquered by him. Until the Nazis came along, there wasn't anyone who managed to kill more people than Genghis Khan. No, there was something else that made it sad. At least, I'm certain that you, Philippa, will think so. This is certainly the saddest story that *I* ever heard."

On the silky-soft carpet it was pitch dark with only a warm breeze in their faces to remind them all that they were actually flying through the air. Nimrod's velvet-lined voice sounded soothing and almost hypnotic so that even the professor struggled to stay awake and listen to what he was saying. He kept pressing a sharp fingernail into his own flesh to help keep alert enough to understand why they were going to Afghanistan at all. Like any other professor, Snorri Sturloson was someone to whom understanding was important.

Axel was no less attentive to Nimrod's voice especially since he had once been bitten by a camel spider that was the size of a hamburger, and that had left him on an antibiotic drip in a hospital. It didn't matter that camel spiders have nothing really to do with camels — they're called camel spiders because they live in the desert; just the word *camel* always left Axel expecting the word *spider* to scrabble after it at up to ten miles an hour, which is fast for any small creature. And in the dark, he flinched as the fingers of Philippa's hand walked their way into his own.

"I don't like sad stories," admitted Philippa.

"Me, neither," said John.

"Then ye that have tears prepare to shed them," said Nimrod.

"The great Lord of the Earth and the Sky and, of course, the Mongols, Temujin, also known as Genghis Khan, died in August 1227. His death was shrouded in much secrecy, as the Mongols were besieging some city or other at the time and they hardly wanted news of his death to give heart to their enemies. Indeed, Genghis himself had given strict orders to this effect.

"'Don't let the enemy know about my death,' he commanded his men. 'Don't mourn me in any way in case the enemy finds out about it. Just keep the siege going; and when eventually they surrender, annihilate them all.'

"It's certain these orders would have been obeyed by his sons and generals. Genghis Khan had always demanded unquestioning obedience. But as well as this particular campaign, there was of course the legacy of his sons and the security of the whole Mongol empire to think of. Imagine it: an empire one-fifth of the world's land area — almost thirty million square miles from the Pacific to the Caspian Sea. Genghis knew how hard it was to keep an empire this size in control and that news of his death would be greeted with joy and very likely revolt, too, as people all over Europe and Asia tried to throw off the cruel Mongol yoke.

"It's this strategic need for secrecy that may have contributed to the great and enduring mystery surrounding his burial. And it must have worked because for years after his death people still assumed he was alive, or that he was a god and could not die. All in all, as an exercise in public relations and media manipulation, the Mongols' handling of the death of Genghis Khan was extremely successful.

"Of course, it was customary for a great lord to be buried in some style, with many of his treasures and possessions. And, in the case of Genghis Khan, this included large quantities of gold plate, many jewels, his favorite saddle, his sword, several of his wives, and, of course, the Hotaniya crystals of the Xi Xia emperor, Xuanzong. Naturally, this created a problem for the Mongols. How and where to bury Genghis Khan with honor but without drawing attention to his burial place? For, as well as wishing to preserve the idea that Genghis Khan was still alive, his sons also wished to prevent the grave from being despoiled by robbers.

"A huge underground mausoleum was excavated by slaves who were then slaughtered to a man; the soldiers who had killed these slaves were themselves executed in their turn. A large part of the mausoleum was taken up with their corpses.

"Finally, when the grave was ready, the funeral cortege set off and, leaving nothing to chance, everyone it met on the way was also murdered. It's said that twenty thousand people died in order that the whereabouts of the grave of Genghis Khan could be kept a secret.

"Of course, the sons and brothers of Genghis Khan wished to be able to find his grave again, in order that they might come and do his memory homage. And this presented them with a difficulty. For if the grave was unmarked, how would they remember where it was? There were no accurate maps, no latitude and longitude, no satellite navigation aids to help them. What made things worse was that Mongolia, as you'll see for yourselves, is a land of immense plains called steppes, with very little in the way of geographical features like mountains and valleys to help them out.

"When a solution finally presented itself, it appeared to have been under their noses all along. Smell holds a significant place in Mongol culture. In fact, human body scent was assumed to be an important part of a person's soul. And, considering they never took baths, human souls must have been very smelly indeed. As a result, while other people were in the habit of kissing or shaking hands, Mongols were in the habit of sniffing each other like dogs. Anyway, they decided that the best aide-mémoire for finding the grave of Genghis Khan again was smell — but not his smell, although that would have been ripe enough. No, it was the smell of something else they decided to use.

"Being nomadic tribesmen, they knew a lot about animals — horses, goats, and camels in particular. They knew that camels have an excellent sense of smell, not to mention equally excellent memories. Camels are able to find water in the desert because they are able to detect the smell of something called geosmin, which is produced by bacteria in freshly turned earth. But they are even more adept at remembering and smelling their own offspring."

"I don't like the way this story is shaping up," said Philippa.

"Then brace yourself, Philippa," said Nimrod. "The Mongols took a female camel and its newborn baby to which it was giving milk and buried the baby camel alongside the body of Genghis Khan. *Alive.* They knew that the mother camel would always remember the spot. And that in the years to come they would only have to release and follow the mother camel for it to lead them to where the calf — that's what we call a baby camel — was buried."

"No!"

Philippa let out a wail, which, in the darkness, sounded much as a baby camel would have sounded as it was buried alive, and which made everyone jump, including Nimrod.

"That is awful," she exclaimed. "How could anyone do such a terrible thing? How could people be so cruel?"

John let out a loud guffaw.

"Typical girl," he said. "She says nothing when she hears about how twenty-thousand people were slaughtered in order to keep their mouths shut about the secret place where Genghis Khan is buried. And then she goes all gooey when some baby animal is killed."

"That *is* the saddest story I ever heard," insisted Philippa, ignoring her twin brother, which she was in the habit of doing.

"Perhaps it is," admitted the professor. "But all of this happened almost eight hundred years ago. But even you, Nimrod, cannot seriously be suggesting that this mother camel is still alive. I know, I've seen some remarkable things today that persuade me that there is more in the world than I ever dreamed was possible. But an eight-hundred-year-old camel? No, surely not."

"I haven't finished my story," said Nimrod. "You see, the Mongols thought they'd been very clever. Every spring the descendants of Genghis Khan, intent on honoring his memory, would release the mother camel and, without fail,

145

it would always return to the exact spot where the calf was buried. The camel, of course, was treated very well. It was named Dunbelchin —"

"Good name for a camel," said John.

"After one of the Khan's wives. It was fed with the best oats and grass and it was adorned with a jeweled bridle and a beautiful saddle, which of course made it a most valuable camel in the eyes of men. Too valuable, for one day it was stolen."

"Serves 'em right," said Philippa.

"The Mongols were beside themselves with anger and frustration," continued Nimrod. "For without the mother camel, how could they ever hope to find his secret burial place again? They searched high and low for the camel. And suspicion fell upon a notorious camel thief called Hotak, who came from a town called Parwan, north of Kabul in Afghanistan, and that today is known as Charikar. But Hotak eluded capture and fled with his camels to Kandahar.

"Meanwhile, a special clan of Mongols called the Darkhats was created in order to find the tomb, and to prevent anyone else from finding the tomb. The clan continues to this day, although it remains uncertain if the Darkhats ever found the tomb themselves."

"I'm getting confused now," said the professor. "What is any of this to do with Sidi Mubarak Bombay and John Hanning Speke?"

"Good question," said Nimrod. "They may not have succeeded in finding the grave of Genghis Khan but, according to Bombay's book, they certainly managed to see a beautifully tooled camel saddle and bridle, probably Mongolian, that belonged to a camel trader in Kandahar by the name of Ali Bilharzia. They themselves were convinced that the saddle and the bridle were more than five hundred years old and had once adorned Dunbelchin, the mother camel that was possessed of the knowledge of how to find the tomb of Genghis Khan."

"I'm beginning to see where you're going with this," said Philippa.

"I'm glad you are," said Axel. "I'm still in the dark." He blinked hard against the all-enveloping black night sky, as if he hoped he might see something that would help illuminate his understanding of their mission, but he remained wrapped in literal and metaphorical darkness.

"Me, too," admitted the professor. "Bombay and Speke made this discovery almost one hundred and fifty years ago. I don't have to tell you that things have changed a lot in Afghanistan since they were there. Four wars will do that."

"Four?" John sounded surprised.

"Two Anglo–Afghan wars in the nineteenth century," said the professor, "after which there was peace for a hundred years. Then the Russian invasion of 1979, which preceded a war that lasted ten years, and lately, the Americans have been fighting there, as part of Operation Enduring Freedom."

"And yet some things in Afghanistan never change," said Nimrod. "That's one of the things people never understand about Afghanistan. Trying to make that country change is always a mistake. It's just as much of a mistake now as it was a mistake at the beginning of the First Anglo-Afghan War in 1839."

"I take it you've been to Afghanistan before," said Axel.

"Oh, yes. When I was a student, it was a very popular place to visit."

"Let me get this straight," said the professor. "You're proposing that we go to Afghanistan to look for a camel that's been dead for almost eight hundred years. Is that correct?"

"All will be revealed," promised Nimrod. "In good time."

CHAPTER 16

WISH UPON A STAR

When the *Shebelle* left the Italian port of Civitavecchia early the morning after Decebal's coming aboard, it was shadowed by an Italian Navy submarine, the *Rodolfo Graziani*. For some time now, NATO had been keeping the ship under surveillance in the hope that it could track the pirates back to their secret lair in Somalia to destroy them for good.

To this end the submarine followed the ship as far as the Suez Canal where a U.S. military space KH satellite kept the *Shebelle* under surveillance until it reached the Red Sea.

A KH satellite is really just a gigantic orbiting digital camera with an imaging resolution of one inch, which means that it can see something one inch, or larger on the ground. In this way, the CIA had already managed to photograph Captain Sharkey and his entire crew of cutthroats while they were sunbathing on the deck of the ship. But back at the CIA headquarters in Langley, Virginia, they were surprised to discover a new man walking up and down the deck of the ship and concluded that he must have joined the crew in Civitavecchia.

Whenever he appeared on deck — which was always at the same time in the morning and in the afternoon — he was accompanied by his own armed bodyguard.

All the same, he was hardly like any of the other pirates in that he was rather fat and pink. He wore a white shirt and a black tie, a waistcoat, and pin-striped trousers; he also wore a bowler hat. In short, he looked like an Egyptian bank manager.

This new man closely matched the description of someone long sought by police forces and security services all over the world. A high-level meeting of CIA intelligence analysts and agents was convened at which it was concluded that this new, unidentified man might just be the Egyptian "Mr. Big" behind all piracy in the Gulf of Aden, the almost legendary Sheikh Dubeluemmdhi. This caused great excitement in Washington and plans were put in place to kidnap the man as soon as the *Shebelle* reached the Strait of Hormuz that led into the Arabian Sea.

Here, an unmanned aerial vehicle from the USS *Wisconsin* took over the task of watching the pirate ship from afar. The important thing was to keep the pirates under surveillance without them knowing they were being surveilled.

This was easy since the noise of the ship's old engines was more than loud enough to drown out the drone of the UAV's single engine. And the UAV stayed at the kind of height that made it all but invisible to the human eye.

Besides, most of the pirates were too busy watching television or Mr. Groanin to pay much attention to what was happening in the sky eighteen thousand feet above their heads.

Having given his word as a gentleman to Captain Sharkey that he would behave himself and not try to escape, Groanin was permitted the freedom of the deck; it seemed better than being locked up in the hold; all the same he was kept under the gimlet eye of a pirate armed with an AK-47.

When he wasn't taking exercise on deck, Groanin was kept busy in the galley. And unlike Decebal and his Romanian gang, the Somali pirates seemed to appreciate Groanin's home cooking, which, it has to be said, was without equal in that part of the world.

Of course, this was hardly enough to make Groanin feel good about his situation. And he spent most of his time on deck reproaching himself for his own failure to appreciate just how well off he had been working as Nimrod's butler.

" 'You never really know what you've got until it's gone,' right enough," said Groanin. "And to think I used to complain about being in old Nimrod's service." He wiped a tear from his rheumy eye. "First-class travel, the finest food and wines known to humanity, linen sheets, my own flat, a Rolls-Royce to drive, everything a man could ever wish for, and more."

He shook his head and glanced up at the sky, wondering exactly where Nimrod and the twins were at that precise moment. Surely, they would have left Italy by now. Nimrod wasn't the kind of person to let a little thing like the closure of European airspace, or a rail strike, stop him from traveling where he wanted to go.

"They're all back in London probably," he said. "What I wouldn't give to be back in London."

As he searched the sky, he saw what he assumed to be a star but was, in fact, the reflection off the American UAV's fuselage in the high-altitude sunshine.

"Wish upon a star," he muttered. "Why not?"

He thought for a moment and thinking that, perhaps, if only he wished hard enough and often enough, Nimrod, John, or perhaps Philippa might — if he believed they could — just feel or even hear his wish and make it come true.

"I wish I was back in London," he said. "I wish I was back in London. I wish I was back in London."

CHAPTER 17

SPY IN THE SKY

Daylight arrived with the flying carpet somewhere in the sky over Egypt. At that particular place and moment in time, the ancient city of Kandahar lay almost two thousand miles to the east.

As the crow flies this would have been an eight-hour flight on the carpet. But for safety reasons, Nimrod decided to avoid overflying several countries including Israel, Syria, Iraq, and Iran, none of which care for unidentified traffic over their airspace.

"This is another great disadvantage of the flying carpet as opposed to a whirlwind," explained Nimrod as they traveled farther south over the Arabian Peninsula to avoid these belligerent countries. "Being a solid object and about the same size as a decent-sized plane, the carpet shows up on radar. It's not much fun having to take evasive action when some fool of a general decides that you're unfriendly and sends up a military jet to shoot you down."

"That's something I'm glad I didn't know until now," said the professor.

"I'd have been glad not to know about it at all," said Axel.

"Can they fly these jets with so much ash around?" asked John. "I wouldn't have thought so."

"I rather suspect that military jets will fly when a lot of commercial ones stay grounded," observed Nimrod. "But, honestly. There's really not much to worry about. Even if we can't always outrun an F-15 or a MiG-17, their pilots are usually too nonplussed by the sight of people sitting on a flying carpet to shoot us down. More often than not, they report us as UFOs and that's the end of it."

"Well, that's a relief," said Philippa.

"No, it's the surface-to-air missiles that we have to worry about," added Nimrod. "They sort of arrive from nowhere and with no warning. So, from here on in we'd best start keeping a lookout. Even the Saudis are inclined to be a bit trigger-happy these days."

"Keeping a lookout?" John frowned. "How does that work?"

"The same as on a whaling ship," said Nimrod. "You and Philippa have keen eyes. Each of you, sit at one edge of the carpet and sing out if you see the spout of something coming our way. Better still, if either of you sees so much as a firecracker coming our way, you'd better use a little indjinnuity to deflect it."

John winced at his uncle's terrible joke.

"Like what?" asked Philippa. "What would you suggest to deflect a surface-to-air missile?"

"I don't know. A flock of wild ducks, perhaps. A sheet of hot corrugated iron. A piano. Use your imagination."

The twins did as they were bid and crawled to opposite sides of the carpet, where each of them looked very carefully over the side.

It was a long way down.

Philippa hugged Moby to her chest, feeling quite certain that the last thing she would use to deflect a surface-to-air missile would be a flock of wild ducks. Besides, making one living thing was hard enough, let alone a whole bunch of them.

John had his doubts about the whole idea. Being reasonably well informed about things military — in his time he'd watched a lot of action movies — he believed that surface-to-air missiles were attracted to the heat of a jet engine and since the flying carpet had no engine he wondered how it could home in on them at all. Then again, if it was aimed well enough, any rocket might just get lucky. And John concluded that Nimrod was probably right to be cautious about such things.

At one point, they actually saw the tiny pirate ship carrying their old friend Groanin as it steamed south on the Red Sea. And simultaneously, for just a few minutes, each twin thought fondly of him and wondered what he was doing, which was, of course, the immediate effect of all Groanin's hard wishing directly beneath them.

I expect he's back in London by now, thought John. *Or perhaps Manchester. Assuming he managed to get out of Italy before they closed the airspace. Gosh, I miss that guy. He may have groaned and moaned a lot but he was a loyal friend. This whole adventure's not really the same without Groanin.*

155

Philippa was thinking much the same. But because her djinn power was a little stronger than her brother's, she almost felt his presence and had to remind herself that he was not with them on their latest and perhaps last adventure.

Which is curious, she thought as she looked around just to check that Groanin was not actually seated beside Nimrod. *I've grown so used to Groanin being around it's hard to persuade myself he isn't. I expect that's what I was feeling just now. Yes, that must be the explanation. But why should I suppose that this might be our last adventure? That's harder to explain. Could it be what Nimrod said back on Vesuvius? Something about volcanoes being linked with the destiny of our djinn tribe, the Marid? Or perhaps it was just the portentous way he said it, as if he had always expected something like this would happen. Yes, that's probably it. At least, I hope so. I wouldn't like this to be our last adventure.*

Alone with their thoughts, the twins kept watch in this way for a couple of hours until they were over the Arabian Sea when they entered a bank of thick cloud and lost sight of what was below.

John returned to the center of the flying carpet. "No point looking out for anything," he said, "in all this cloud."

"Is it ordinary cloud, do you think?" asked Philippa. "Or cloud that's made of ash?"

"There's not much volcanic activity in this particular part of the world," said the professor. "The nearest volcano is probably Taftan, in southeastern Iran, which must be almost a thousand miles northeast of our position." He sniffed the air loudly and, behind the mask, he licked his lips. "Besides, the cloud doesn't taste or smell volcanic."

"Nevertheless," said Philippa, "I can sort of hear a kind of rumbling from within the cloud."

John listened carefully. "She's right," he said. "There is something. And it seems to be getting nearer."

Everyone except Nimrod stood up and looked anxiously into the cloud.

"That's not a volcano," said Axel after a minute. "That sounds more like a motor."

"A single-engine plane," said John.

"I hope they don't fly into us," said the professor.

"They won't," said Nimrod. "I'll make sure of that."

"But what if they see us?" said the professor.

"I wouldn't worry about it," Nimrod said cheerfully. "If you were a pilot, would you report sighting a flying carpet with five passengers?"

"Er, no," said the professor. "Probably not if I wanted to hold on to my pilot's license."

"Exactly," said Nimrod. "Besides, there's a limit to what I can do to disguise us while I'm flying this thing. A carpet requires a lot more concentration than a whirlwind."

John pointed behind the carpet. "It's coming from behind. There. Look."

A strange, insectlike plane emerged from the cloud immediately behind them. It had long, gray wings, rather spindly wheel struts, and a large rear-mounted propeller. Underneath the wings was an array of bombs and missiles, but under the nose was the lens of a large video camera.

"It's a surveillance UAV," yelled John.

"A what?" Nimrod frowned. "Speak English, boy."

"An unmanned aerial vehicle," explained John. "A remotely piloted drone that flies without a human crew."

"Yes, I understood as much when you said it was unmanned," said Nimrod.

"The propeller explains how it was able to take off at all," said the professor. "That kind of engine can't be damaged in the same way as a jet engine can, by sucking ash in with the air and causing it to overheat."

"The pilots are probably sitting in front of computer screens watching us from somewhere on the ground," added John.

Nimrod was horrified. "You mean we're being photographed? With a camera?"

"For sure."

"Then get rid of it," said Nimrod.

"Get rid of it?"

"I dislike being photographed at the best of times," said Nimrod. "But I especially dislike being photographed without my permission. There's too much of this sort of thing going on these days. Every time you open a celebrity magazine in the barber's chair, you find a picture of some poor actress with her hair in a mess coming out of a coffee shop with her mouth stuffed with muffin. It's rank, bad manners to photograph people in that way."

"I don't think they're doing it for a magazine," said John. "And it's quite possible they're not spying on us, but on someone else, and we just happened to get in the way."

"Well, perhaps that was true," said Nimrod. "But it's true no longer. If I'm not mistaken, that camera is now filming us. Besides, look at all those bombs and missiles the thing is carrying. Any minute now, whoever is watching us through that lens is going to conclude we're dangerous and start shooting."

"At five people sitting on a carpet?" Axel shook his head. "No, surely not. Why would anyone think we're dangerous? None of us is armed. Therefore none of us constitutes a threat. Even the U.S. Army wouldn't shoot at five people sitting on a carpet."

"Don't you believe it," said John.

"Might I remind you that this is a flying carpet?" said Nimrod. "Without a flight number. That makes us an unidentified flying carpet."

Axel shrugged. "So?"

"Did you ever hear of an unidentified walking object? Or an unidentified swimming object? No. Of course not. And that's because there's a lot less human understanding of anything when it's flying than when it's on the ground. Especially when it's an object that's not supposed to be flying at all. Like a saucer. Or a carpet. Even a commercial passenger jet that's in the wrong place. Especially when it's the military that is doing the understanding. Or not understanding, to be rather more accurate. 'Shoot first, ask questions later' is the motto of all army generals the world over.

"Then," continued Nimrod, "there's also the fact that the only flying carpets most people have seen are magic carpets in movies with Middle Eastern subjects like Sinbad and Aladdin. There's a lot less understanding of all things

Middle Eastern than there used to be. Philippa? Get rid of it."

Philippa hesitated. She wasn't the kind of djinn who destroyed things lightly. In her short life, she'd met several djinn who were of a destructive disposition and acquaintance with them had taught her more than a little self-restraint when the exercise of her own power was concerned.

"Need I remind you that we are on a mission to save the planet?" demanded Nimrod. "It's imperative that nothing interrupts our journey to Afghanistan. So get rid of it please, John, before it gets rid of us."

John had to admit his uncle had a point. Several points. But how to get rid of the drone? Blowing it up was not an option, not with all the missiles it was carrying.

Then, following another moment of thought, a simple but effective device presented itself to his juvenile mind and, with the aid of his special word, he focused all of his djinn power into the creation of a can of spray paint.

"ABECEDARIAN!"

No sooner was the can of paint in his hand than John had gone to the rear of the carpet, reached out, and sprayed over the fish-eye lens of the camera.

"Can't fly if it can't see where it's going," he said.

"Perfect."

Nimrod laughed and nodding his approval he increased altitude by several hundred feet, just in case the blinded drone fired off a missile in frustration.

"Well done. That'll teach them for spying on people."

Of course Nimrod was quite unaware that by spying on the Somali pirates, the drone could have assisted in the rescue of Mr. Groanin. In which case, he would probably have thought very differently about it.

Meanwhile, hundreds of miles away, in the technology-packed surveillance room on the USS *Wisconsin*, the two UAV operators stared at their screens and then each other with a mixture of anxiety and incomprehension.

"Did you see that? Did you see that?"

"I saw it, sailor. But I don't want to say what we saw. It doesn't make sense. And I'm not even tired."

"A bunch of people on a flying carpet is what it looked like," said the first operator. "One of them was wearing a black mask, like a Harlequin. He must have been the evil boss."

"But two of them were kids. And one of them was holding a duck. A mallard, I think."

"And the other kid had a can of spray paint in his hand. The little punk painted over my lens."

"That's sure what it looked like. You're right, sailor. The question is what do we do about it? If we report it like that, they'll bust us. They'll think we're a pair of crazy loons and then they'll bust us."

"They'll think we're crazy and they'll throw us out of the navy."

"So what are we going to do?"

"I dunno. We're blind now since that kid sprayed over the lens. There's not much we can do. Not even land the bird."

"Push the joystick down, fly the drone straight into the sea, and report the thing missing. Let the people who designed the UAV figure out what happened." The second operator shrugged. "It's the only thing we can do apart from hit the self-destruct button."

"Agreed."

"Who knows? Maybe we'll get lucky and the drone will hit the pirate ship."

Ten minutes later, the UAV crashed into the Arabian Sea a long way from the *Shebelle*, and NATO's plans for the destruction of the Somali pirates and the kidnapping of the almost legendary Sheikh Dubeluemmdhi — otherwise known as Mr. Groanin — were themselves destroyed.

The pirates sailed on, still quite oblivious of the airborne peril they had so narrowly avoided.

CHAPTER 18

A LITTLE LIGHT READING

Bored of sitting on the carpet, Philippa flicked through some of the books Nimrod had brought out from the Rakshasas Library. While these told her a great deal about the *secret* secret history of the Mongols and Dunbelchin the camel, they told her nothing about what she was really interested in, which was what Nimrod had said on Vesuvius — about the destiny of the Marid. And, after a while, she asked her uncle if he would mind her going inside the lamp and looking for a book of her own to read. She did not, however, mention her interest in discovering something more about his own words.

"No, of course I don't mind," said Nimrod. "I never mind when a child wants to go into a library. It's refreshing to hear it. Most children these days seem to think books are objects that furnish a room, not things to be read."

Philippa nodded patiently as her uncle continued speaking at her.

"You've been in there before as I recall, so you know about Liskeard, the bottle imp. And, more important, he'll remember you. Bottle imps can be dangerous to those who they don't know."

"Yes, I remember him."

There are the creatures of Beelzebub. There are mocking imps, and there are petty fiends. There are flibbertigibbets, which were once wont to hang about a place of execution, and there are imps that were once children. There are little demons and evil spirits, and there are bottle imps that some djinn employ to guard the lamps and bottles in which they occasionally live. Bottle imps are sometimes regarded as venomous but, strictly speaking — and there is no better way to speak to a bottle imp — this was not true of Liskeard Karswell du Crowleigh. It wasn't that he was venomous so much that his mouth was just dangerous, because of his unpleasant taste for rotting animal flesh, which meant that his teeth and gums were covered in lethal bacteria.

"I could hardly forget him," she said. "He's kind of unfortunate, to say the least."

"After Mr. Rakshasas died, I offered Liskeard three wishes as a reward for his long and faithful service," said Nimrod. "But he declined them on the grounds that having any kind of wish would have implied a strong longing for a specific thing he did not already have, and since his life was the library and nothing but the library, he could not conceive of an alternative to that."

"It's a point of view," said Philippa.

"Of course, I am, as you know, quite unable to change Liskeard's hideous appearance," continued Nimrod. "Many years ago, he made the mistake of trying to steal the synopados, the soul mirror, of a wicked djinn. The mirror was armed with a very powerful binding that turned him into the hideous-looking imp you've seen before. Since a binding made by another djinn is irreversible and since I have no idea whose mirror it was that he tried to steal, I fear he will be like that forever. Which is perhaps why he thinks it better that he remains as the bottle imp, where his frankly abhorrent appearance is an affront to no one."

"Not just his appearance," said Philippa. "His breath, too. Especially his breath."

"Yes," said Nimrod. "That's quite right. I have hesitated to bring it up. But you might get away with this, being young. You might just mention his breath. That it smells terribly. That it could turn milk to yogurt. Or butter into cheese. Yes, why not? Offer him a toothbrush, perhaps. Some floss. Some toothpicks. Some mouthwash."

"You want me to tell him to clean his teeth?"

"If you would, Philippa. But only if you think the moment right. It's never easy telling someone that their breath smells like a cheesy sock. Especially when their teeth are as sharp as Liskeard's."

"No kidding."

"It would make it so much more pleasant to go in there," said Nimrod. "And to have a conversation with him, if his breath could be tolerated."

"I'll see what I can do. But I'm not promising anything. It's one thing telling John he's got bad breath. Which he does because he's too lazy to brush his teeth. It's something else telling a really terrifying monster that he's got bad breath. Even if he is a librarian."

Philippa left Moby with Axel, retrieved Mr. Rakshasas's djinn lamp from her uncle's Louis Choppsouis bag, and, having become a thick cloud of transubstantiated smoke, entered the lamp. The interior of every djinn lamp is much bigger on the inside than on the outside. And this one was no exception. The Rakshasas Library was enormous. But it was also a library with no discernible organization, and for anyone who had never visited the place it would have been hard to believe that it was cared for by a devoted librarian who had curated the Rakshasas Library for fifty years.

It was several minutes before Liskeard appeared in the great Reading Room. He bowed gravely to Philippa and hissed a polite greeting to a person he recognized was his new lord and master's beloved niece.

"Good day to you, young missss," he hissed, for, despite his neat gray suit and vaguely human ways, Liskeard Karswell du Crowleigh most resembled a monitor lizard. "I'm sorry I did not come more quickly but I was in the lower library stacks."

"How are you, Liskeard?" asked Philippa, covering her own nose and mouth with the palm of her hand for his breath was much worse than she remembered. It was almost chemical. The little, red, forked tongue that flickered out of his mouth from time to time ought, she thought, to have been a little red flag, warning of the danger of getting near enough to Liskeard to get a whiff of his horrible, hair-raising halitosis.

"Very well, missss."

He smiled a hideous, malodorous smile.

"Were you looking for a particular book, young missss? Do please bear in mind that this is a wishing library. In this particular library, you only have to wish for a book and it will bring itself to you. Which is why we don't bother organizing the books in any alphabetical or subject or author order. I just return them to their proper place when your uncle has finished using them." He glanced at a pile of books that lay on the table. "Eventually."

"My uncle was here earlier on," said Philippa.

"That is correct, missss."

She pointed at the books on the huge library table. "Are those the books he was looking at?"

"Yes. Although it isn't my place to solicit or to receive explanations, why do you ask?"

Philippa shrugged. "Those are the ones I want to read."

"Very well, missss." He bowed again. "Then, since you have everything you need, I will leave you to read in peace."

"Um, Liskeard. Before you go. I was wondering if there was anything I can do for you. Out of respect for the memory of Mr. Rakshasas."

"I'm not quite sure I understand you, missss."

Philippa bit her lip. It's never easy telling someone with bad breath that they have bad breath.

"Have you ever heard of the ring of confidence, Liskeard?"

"Is that a book, missss?"

"Er, no, it's — well, sometimes you learn the most from books you aren't supposed to read, and er . . . words you aren't supposed to hear."

"So I'm led to believe, missss."

"And scientific research shows that there is a direct connection between germs in your mouth and er . . . unpleasant breath."

"And this is in reference to . . . what, exactly?"

Philippa smiled. "Nothing. I'll just get on with these books."

"Very well, missss."

Liskeard shuffled away, leaving Philippa alone in the huge, cavernous library with half of her wishing she'd thought to ask John along; it was true that he was often infuriating when she was trying to concentrate on something, nevertheless he was also comforting to have around in a place as spooky as the Rakshasas Library.

She sat down and noticed first that Nimrod had left his gold fountain pen on the table. Philippa knew it was his because it bore his initials and contained a special shade of maroon ink that sometimes her uncle joked was blood. Of course, it was always possible that the ink might have been real blood and that he wasn't joking at all. Anything was possible where Nimrod was concerned.

She glanced down the titles on the spines of the five books on the table that Nimrod had already perused and saw that they were all about twins. Anything on the subject of twins was always certain to stimulate her interest and she picked up the first book, *Dualistic Cosmology and the Power of the Twin*, by Professor Benito Malpensa, and, opening it, found that her uncle had already underlined the one passage that was of interest to him:

Almost every ancient society contains important myths about the power of twins. Castor and Pollux, collectively known as the Dioscouri, are perhaps the most famous. In this Greek myth, Pollux was immortal but Castor was not and when Castor died, Pollux asked Zeus to allow him to share his immortality with his brother in order that they could stay together. Zeus agreed and they were transformed into the Gemini constellation of stars.

There are many similar stories in Celtic, Hebrew, and Indian mythology.

But even now, there are still many human societies too numerous to list, in which twin children are treated as something special, as "children of the sky" and are held to possess magical powers over nature, especially over rain and the wind. It was often believed that they could summon any wind by motions of their hands, or by their breath, and that they could make fair or foul weather and could cause rain to fall by painting their faces black and then washing them, which may represent the rain dripping from the dark clouds. Some North American Indian tribes believed that they could cause rain by pulling down on the ends of spruce branches. Moreover, it was supposed that the wishes of certain twin children were always fulfilled; hence, they were often feared, because they might harm people who they hated. It is the author's opinion that this is mere superstition, though the extent of these powers is uncertain.

Another book, *Amphion and Zethus: The Twin in Semiotics* by Gilberto Echo, was also underlined:

Twins can, it is believed, call the salmon and trout to do their bidding. Some young human twins even have the power to turn themselves into salmon; hence, in some stories they must avoid water lest they should be turned into fish. For the same reason, some twins are forbidden to catch salmon, and they may not eat or even handle the fresh fish. No less intriguing are the stories in which young human twins develop the ability to become grizzly bears. Indeed, they are sometimes called young grizzly bears. According to these stories, twins remain throughout life endowed with supernatural powers.

The third book Philippa looked at was another about the nature of twins: *Children Are from Earth, Twins Are from Jupiter* by Prasad Vilma. And once again, the following passage was heavily underlined in maroon ink:

Now when there is a drought and the prospect of famine threatens your world, and all nature, scorched and burnt up by a sun that has been shining endlessly from a cloudless sky, is panting for rain, it is certain that twins can bring down this longed-for rain on the parched earth. If a village or town has no twins, the women must cover themselves with leaves and go and pour water on the graves of twins. For this reason the grave of a twin ought always to be moist, which is why twins should be buried near a lake. If all their efforts to procure rain prove abortive, they will remember that such and such a twin was buried in a dry place on the side of a hill. "No wonder," says the wizard in such a case, "that the sky is fiery. Take up the body of a twin and dig him another grave on the shore of the lake." His orders are at once obeyed, for this is supposed to be the only means of bringing down the rain.

Philippa yawned and then stretched. It was easy for her to understand why *she* was fascinated with twins. She was herself a twin. But, leaning back in her chair for a moment, she wondered why Nimrod was so interested in them, beyond the fact that he was uncle to twins. And while all of this was of mild interest, it didn't seem really important, at least not in the context of their urgent mission to save the world from some hidden hand that might or might not have used some mysterious ancient crystals from the tomb of Genghis Khan to bring all of the world's volcanoes simultaneously to life. Where was all of this going?

But then she picked up another book and things took on a darker hue, as if a cloud of volcanic ash had covered the blue sky in her own mind's eye. The book was rather more ominously titled, *Romulus and Remus Revisited: A History of Child Sacrifice*, by Professor Martin Moustache. And the underlined passage in this book left Philippa feeling very disturbed:

Child sacrifice to supernatural forces and figures has been prac-ticed throughout history. Perhaps the most famous story of child sacrifice is that of Abraham and Isaac in the book of Genesis, although, of course, God intervenes, and Isaac is spared. Almost all civilizations, without exception, have carried out child sacrifice, most notoriously the ancient Carthaginians. One burial pit in a Carthaginian archaeological site in modern Tunisia contains the bodies of as many as twenty thousand children. The practice of child sacrifice was equally common in ancient Rome: for example, Romulus and Remus, who were the twin infant sons of the god Mars. These two survived being tossed into the River Tiber and, having been raised by wolves, founded the ancient city of Rome.

But twins have always been especially susceptible to the practice of child sacrifice. Twins were put to death by some African societies such as the Nama Hottentots of southwest Africa and the Bushmen of the Kalahari because they were considered unlucky. Twins were routinely thrown to the sharks or into volcanoes to placate their gods by the ancient Hawaiians. The Kikuyu tribe of Africa practiced the ritual killing of twins and this may also have had something to do with the two dozen volcanoes that are to be found in Kenya.

There is much evidence of child sacrifice in the pre–Columbian societies of South America. The Aztecs made frequent sacrifices of children, and more especially twins, to Xiuhtecuhtli, who was the god of volcanoes, and these unfortunate children may even have been flung into the lava-filled craters to prevent eruptions. This practice was also common among the Incas for whom special children such as twins or physically perfect children were the best children they could give Apu, who was their god of mountains and volcanoes, and Catequil, the god of thunder and lightning.

Philippa wrinkled her nose with distaste and closed the book loudly.

"Horrible, horrible, horrible," she exclaimed. "Why must people always behave so horribly?"

And why had her uncle underlined this passage?

It was the fifth book, however, that left her most disturbed of all. This was the oldest book, entitled *Twice Upon a Time: The Importance of Twins and How They Will Save the World from Itself. A Prophecy by Taranushi.*

Of course, Philippa was well aware that Taranushi was the name of the first great djinn, which was why his memory was so important to the Marid. Before the time of the six tribes — of whom the Marid was the most powerful tribe for good — it was Taranushi who had been charged with controlling the rest of the djinn, only he was opposed by a wicked djinn named Azazal and was defeated.

Hardly knowing what to expect, Philippa opened the book and started to read another passage underlined in maroon ink by her studious uncle.

Among the djinn, twins are rare. Very rare, for even among the djinn they have special powers and deep bonds that all djinn — good or evil — would do well to fear, especially when these twins are still children, for their bonds will be closer than adult twins', who often grow apart. Their extra power lies in the fact that they are two halves of the same whole, which being multiplied by two, is twice as powerful as one. They are often partners on quests and that is their power. All djinn twins have a secret destiny, although it is very likely this destiny may never be fulfilled. Twins are especially powerful and important when they are male and female and the result of a djinn mother and a human father for mortal qualities are important to know a true sense of destiny. For just as the creation of the world was attended by the sacrifice of many human twins, so the saving of the world will require the sacrifice of one set of djinn twins. For it is written that when a sea of cloud arises from the bowels of the earth and turns the lungs of men to stone, the wheat in the fields to ash, and the rivers to liquid rock, then only djinn who are twin brother and sister and true children of the lamp can become true partners on a quest to save the world from inflammable darkness and destruction.

Philippa put the book aside and shook her head in disbelief. She could hardly ignore the fact that these passages had all been underlined with Nimrod's own fountain pen. Nor the fact that these words and ideas — many of them horrible to her — were now in her own dear uncle's head.

Was it possible that he was actually contemplating — she could hardly bring herself to think such a thing — throwing herself and John into a volcano in order to placate it in some way?

What was she going to tell John? Should she tell John anything? If they really were in danger, didn't he deserve to know?

Suddenly, the words she herself had uttered to Liskeard in relation to his horrible bad breath seemed to thrust themselves back into her memory.

"Sometimes you learn the most from books you aren't supposed to read, and words you aren't supposed to hear."

How very true that was, she thought. How true.

CHAPTER 19

THE SPIDER FROM MARS

Arriving in the ancient port city of Djibouti, on the Horn of Africa, the Somali pirate ship was met by two officials from the People's Rally for Progress, which is the largest political party in Djibouti. Other political parties are allowed in Djibouti but only the People's Rally for Progress (the RPP) is ever allowed to form a government.

The two officials were, as a result, members of the government as well as being senior officers in the Djibouti Secret Police. Following the arrest of several hundred people in the city, a ring of American spies had been uncovered by the secret police. The ring was actually just one man and everyone who was unfortunate enough to share the same apartment building with him; they were unfortunate because they were all tortured to reveal information possessed by only one man, and it was several days before the secret police found out who the man was. But this was how the two officials from the RPP knew that the Somali pirate ship was being watched closely by NATO, and why they told Captain Sharkey that it would be better if he left Djibouti, and why, not long after the *Shebelle* docked, it set sail again immediately, for the port of Aden, in Yemen, on the other side of the Red Sea.

Once there, Captain Sharkey and his first mate, Mr. Khat, debated what to do with Groanin.

"Now that NATO is onto us we should get rid of him," said Mr. Khat. "As quickly as possible. Before they have soldiers abseiling down from a helicopter onto the deck of our ship to rescue him and kick our behinds into prison."

"What would you suggest?" asked Captain Sharkey.

"Throw him to the sharks," he said. "It's what we usually do."

"I'm bored with throwing people to the sharks," said Captain Sharkey. "Once you've seen one person being fed to the sharks, you've seen them all. Besides, there's no profit in it."

"Then perhaps we could sell him to عصابة المجنون. Şābh al-Mjnwn. Here in Yemen."

"Şābh al-Mjnwn?"

"It means 'the Crazy Gang.' "

"I know what it means, Mr. Khat. But who are they?"

"Yemeni terrorists. Experts in kidnapping American and European VIPs. And extremely ruthless. Much more ruthless than us." Mr. Khat shook his head. "I mean, they're crazy. Everyone in Yemen says so."

Captain Sharkey nodded. "How crazy are they?"

"Really crazy."

"How crazy, out of ten?"

"Well, how crazy would you say we are, out of ten?" asked Mr. Khat.

Captain Sharkey thought for a moment. "Six or seven," he said at last.

"Then they are probably a nine. Take my word for it. These guys, they're really crazy."

Captain Sharkey nodded. "Okay, I'm gonna ask my little friend Ringo what we should do next."

Captain Sharkey lifted his eye patch, removed the beetle from his empty eye socket, and kissed its leathery back.

"Yes, we give the Englishman to the Crazy Gang, or no, we give him to the sharks."

Then he placed the beetle on the table and awaited its decision.

Ringo stayed motionless for a minute or more while it contemplated which way to walk. Finally, it made its decision and walked toward the Somali word for *yes*.

Which is how it came to be that later on that same afternoon, a group of very fierce-looking men with dark glasses, bright red beards, and white robes collected Groanin from the *Shebelle* and, with a great deal of shouting and gesticulating, they pushed the butler toward a new-looking green Toyota sedan that even now was being polished proudly by one of the other Crazy Gang members, almost as if he had just taken delivery of the car.

The leader pointed at the open trunk and indicated that Groanin should get inside.

"I'm not a suitcase, you know," protested Groanin. "I'm British."

"Don't ask questions, Englishman," said the man with the largest red beard. "Get into the trunk of the car."

"Where are we going?" asked the Englishman. "I said, where are we going?"

"Didn't I tell you not to ask questions? Get into the trunk of the car."

"A *please* would be nice," said Groanin. "Costs nothing to have good manners, you know. Even for someone like you who has no manners at all."

Captain Sharkey and Mr. Khat watched these proceedings nervously as the negotiations for the sale of Groanin to Şābh al-Mjnwn had been attended by a great deal of bad temper on the part of the Crazy Gang members. Captain Sharkey had rarely ever met people who were so cross and he was relieved to see the backs of them.

"Shall we tell them about the Englishman's enormous strength?" Mr. Khat asked his captain.

Captain Sharkey shook his head. "I don't think we'll mention it now that they've paid for him," he said. "Just in case they become even angrier than they are already."

"That hardly seems possible," said Mr. Khat.

"Do you think it's the fact that they have red hair?" wondered Captain Sharkey. "That makes them so angry? Or does being very angry make your beard turn red?"

"I don't know, Captain. But that looks like a new car. And I'd hate to be around to see how angry they get when the Englishman decides that he's had enough of being shut in that trunk."

Captain Sharkey grinned. "Don't worry. We'll be at sea by then. And perhaps we should stay away from Yemen for a while."

Groanin climbed into the trunk of the green Toyota and sat down. He was hardly happy about this new development, but the men from Ṣābh al-Mjnwn were heavily armed and, once again, he thought it best not to argue. Besides, there was a mattress in the trunk, a blanket, some jars of his favorite baby food, and several bottles of water. As the terrorists closed the trunk and then drove off with their new captive, Groanin settled down and, before long, managed to fall fast asleep.

He might have found this more difficult if he had known that as well as himself, the trunk of the Toyota contained one other living thing: the largest camel spider in Yemen. And while the butler was asleep, the camel spider, which looked like some sort of alien from the planet Mars, crawled onto his large, warm stomach.

Camel spiders are not true spiders and have nothing at all to do with camels. They are giant Solifugae, which are members of the class Arachnida, and while not particularly venomous, they do use their own digestive fluids to liquefy their victims' flesh into a soup, making it easy to suck this into their stomachs. They are also very, very fast on their *ten* legs. The reason they are called camel spiders is because some people think they gnaw on the stomachs of sleeping camels, which the beasts don't feel, due to the numbing effect of their anesthetic venom.

If Groanin had been aware of the presence of the camel spider . . . but, look, perhaps it's just fortunate that he remained soundly asleep.

For now.

CHAPTER 20

SUSPICIOUS MINDS

Philippa uttered her focus word and was quickly enveloped by white smoke. Leaving behind her transubstantiated self, she drifted up through the ceiling of the library and then the top of the old lamp and, once outside, she began to gather her atoms urgently. This was always a slightly nerve-racking moment for any djinn, especially one who was young and inexperienced. For Philippa, it always felt as if the string on a valuable necklace had broken and she was anxiously collecting lots of precious pearls that were still bouncing and rolling around the floor, worried that she would lose one and wondering what would happen if ever she did. A missing leg? An ear out of place? No teeth perhaps?

Finally, she heard herself take a loud, euphoric breath and then opened her eyes with a strong sense of relief that she seemed to be all in one piece.

"Is that painful?" inquired Axel, handing Moby the duck back to her.

She hugged the duck to herself. "No," she said.

"It looks as though it might be," observed Professor Sturloson.

"Transubstantiation?" Philippa shook her head. "No, not really. All the same it always feels kind of weird to be mundane again. I mean, human. To have a human body is, well, limiting. Being spirit, or smoke, is more natural to us. A more profound state. You sort of gain a better understanding of who and what you are when you're out of body. You know?"

"Not really," admitted the professor.

"No, I guess you couldn't. Sorry."

"And inside the lamp, or bottle," continued the professor. "What does it feel like? Rather close, I imagine. Like being shut into the trunk of a car, perhaps."

Philippa shook her head. For a moment, she was too distracted by what she had learned in the library to answer him; but after a moment or two longer she said, "No, not at all. You see, the inside of a djinn bottle or lamp exists outside time, and normal three-dimensional space does not apply. So it's impossible to imagine that you're inside anything at all. Unless, that is, you choose to have the interior of the lamp look like the inside of a house. Or in the case of this particular lamp, a huge library."

"I see," said the professor who, quietly, didn't see at all.

"Could you go inside another person?" said Axel.

"Yes," said Philippa. "But only with their permission."

This wasn't true, of course, but she hardly wanted to alarm the handsome Icelander, not when she was as fond of him as she was.

"So, if you were inside me," said Axel, "you could read my thoughts."

"Yes, I suppose I could."

Nimrod smiled at Philippa.

"Did you find the books you were looking for?" he asked her.

"Silly question," said Philippa.

"Yes, of course."

She showed him the book she had brought with her, only for the sake of appearances and again to elude her uncle's curiosity.

"*The Rime of the Ancient Mariner*," she said, surprised to find that this was the book that had come to hand as she was leaving the library.

"I'm pleased to see you're reading Coleridge," said her uncle.

"Why was it a silly question?" asked Professor Sturloson. "When your uncle asked if you had found the books you were looking for. Is the library as well stocked as that?"

And partly to deflect her uncle from further conversation on the subject of what she had been reading, Philippa explained that it was a wishing library.

"You just wish for the books you want to read," she said, "and then they sort of leave their places on the shelves and make their way up to the reading desk."

"How?"

"They sort of float through the air, like this carpet," said Philippa.

"Do you have to know the titles?" asked Axel.

"If you know the title or the author, that's an advantage, obviously. Otherwise, you just work by subject. A very specific subject, sometimes. For example, if you want a book on ice hockey in Hawaii, or whaling in the Congo, then that's what you would wish for."

"And if there are no books on those subjects?"

"There's always a book," said Philippa. "Whatever you can think of, there's always a book on it."

"I can't see the point of all these books," said John. "Just gathering dust, most of them. I mean, some of them never get read at all. What's the point of writing a book that no one is ever going to read?"

"I've written a few books like that myself, John," confessed the professor. "But sometimes you just feel you have to write them. Regardless of whether or not anyone will read them."

"That sounds like a waste of time," said John. "All that work. All that writing. All those words. Strikes me there are better things to do with your time than write a book that no one is ever going to read. That's like building a football stadium for a team that doesn't exist. Or making a record that no one is ever going to listen to. What's the point of them? That's what I want to know."

"I've written seven books like that," admitted the professor. "At least, that's what it feels like sometimes."

"Seven?" John looked aghast. "If I lived to be a hundred, I don't think I could ever write seven books. How old are you, anyway?"

The professor laughed. Behind his black mask and

without a smile the laugh sounded like something artificial to John. Something weird, anyway.

Philippa looked over the edge of the carpet and saw that they were no longer over the sea.

"Where are we?" She was hoping to change the subject again.

"Somewhere over Pakistan," said Nimrod.

"That's another country that doesn't much care for unidentified flying objects, isn't it?" said Axel.

"Yes, it is," said Nimrod. "But we have no choice but to fly over it, Afghanistan being landlocked like it is."

"What's *landlocked*?" asked John.

"It doesn't have a coast." Nimrod grinned at John. "So if anyone ever offers you a job as the head of the Afghan Navy . . ."

"I'll know they're pulling my leg," said John.

Philippa smiled at her uncle but there was no humor in her smile; it felt like the professor's laugh without a smile. She was only smiling because she needed time to think about what he was planning, if anything.

"So we should be keeping a lookout," said John. "All of us."

"Yes, indeed," said Nimrod.

Philippa saw an opportunity to speak with her brother out of Nimrod's earshot. She said to Axel, "All right. John and I will take the port side, and the professor can go on the starboard side with you."

"Any volcanoes in Pakistan, Professor?" said John. "Just so that we can tell the difference between the ash cloud of a volcano and a rocket launch."

"They're mostly small mud volcanoes," said the professor. "The only one of any note is Neza e Sultan, in the northwest of the country, on the Afghan border."

"We should be flying over it any minute now," said Nimrod.

"But it's been extinct for centuries," added the professor.

"You mean that pointy bit of rock that looks like two praying hands?" said John.

The professor crawled toward the port side of the carpet, where John and Philippa were now on watch.

"It doesn't look like it's extinct now," said John. "Look. There's a trail of smoke coming out of the top."

"My God, you're right," said the professor. "This is bad. This is very bad. If an extinct volcano has started smoking, this is very bad indeed."

Nimrod steered the flying carpet toward the curious little volcano for a closer look. And while he and the professor and Axel began to discuss this latest discovery, Philippa took John aside and told him what she'd discovered in the Rakshasas Library.

When she'd finished, she waited impatiently for John to say something.

"Well, what do you think?"

"And so you think that because of all those underlinings Nimrod has made in those books you were looking at, then maybe he's planning to sacrifice us to the gods of the volcano, or something like that?"

She shrugged. "I don't know what to think, John. Not yet. But they say two heads are better than one, so I wanted to know what you thought. So?"

"I dunno."

She glanced nervously at her uncle, who was still locked in conversation with the two Icelanders. "All right, one and a half heads," she said.

John shot her a sarcastic smile. "Funny," he said.

"Sorry."

John shrugged. "I don't mind volunteering for stuff that's dangerous. As long as it's for a good cause, mind you, as long as it's for a good cause. But there's no way that someone is going to fling me into a volcano to appease this Caterpillar guy or Shoetickelme."

"Catequil and Xiutecuhtli," said Philippa, correcting him patiently.

"Yeah. That's what I said, isn't it?"

"Look, I just mentioned those two pre-Columbian gods as an example. I really don't think they're anything to do with all this."

"That's good, because I don't ever think I could pronounce those names without a tongue transplant." John gave his uncle a sideways look. "He doesn't look like he's planning to sacrifice us."

"Oh? And what would that look like?"

"I dunno. Different. He might look a bit guilty or something. Like he might avoid your eye. I know I would avoid someone's eye if I was planning to sacrifice them. Especially if they were kids. You'd be kind of shifty, wouldn't you? Like it was already on your conscience."

"That's true," admitted Philippa. "But he did mention

Taranushi's prophecy and he did leave out some crucial parts relating to us. And there's another thing, too."

"What's that?"

"In all of our adventures, I've had the feeling that we weren't being told everything about ourselves. We've had little bits here and there, but never quite the whole story."

"What are you saying?"

"That just maybe we've been laid out for this all along. Set up. And that everyone's been in on it except us."

John thought about what his sister had said and nodded. "You're right, sis. All the other djinn kids seem to be different from us. Maybe that's because we have a mundane dad and a djinn mom. On the other hand, maybe there's another reason behind it, after all."

"Maybe that's the real reason Mom wanted nothing to do with the world of djinn," said Philippa. "Because she knew or suspected what destiny might — and I do stress the word *might* — have in store for us both."

"Nimrod didn't know that Vesuvius was about to become active again," said John. "Did he?"

"I think that's true," admitted Philippa. "But you can't ignore the underlinings in those books. In his ink. With his pen. I don't think it was Liskeard who did that. And who else does that leave? Nobody."

John shook his head. "After all we've been through," he said. "Hey. I just had a thought."

"At last."

"You don't suppose that Groanin's departure has anything to do with this, do you?"

"How do you mean, John?"

"Well, if he found out something about Nimrod planning to make sacrifices out of us, well, he wouldn't just stick around waiting for it to happen, would he?"

"You're right," said Philippa. "He wouldn't." She racked her brain for a moment. "It was a bit strange the way he quit like that. Even for Groanin. One minute he was on board and the next he'd jumped ship."

"That's what I'm talking about."

"I never thought of that. But it could be connected, yes."

"So what are we going to do? Nimrod's much too powerful to try and go inside his body to find out what's in his mind."

"We'll just have to keep a very close eye on him," said Philippa. "And take comfort in the knowledge that if the prophecy is true, then because we're twins, we're more than twice as powerful as one."

"That's right," agreed John. "We do have a bond that makes us stronger. Always did. Always will."

Philippa nodded. "I think the time has come when we have to start using that extra power."

"What are you two gossiping about?" said Nimrod.

"Nothing much," said Philippa.

"Really? The pair of you looked as thick as thieves a moment ago."

Philippa got up and went to sit beside Nimrod.

"We're just getting a bit bored, that's all," said Philippa, stroking Moby's green head absently. "It seems like we've been sitting on this carpet forever."

"We'll be landing soon," said Nimrod. "In the desert, near Kandahar. We wouldn't want to draw any more attention to ourselves than can be helped. It's the second-largest city in Afghanistan."

"Oh," said John.

"You don't sound particularly impressed, my boy," said Nimrod.

John shrugged. He was feeling distinctly cool toward his uncle. The prospect of being sacrificed has a very sobering effect on any child.

"But this is a historic place," insisted Nimrod.

"So?" said John defensively. "Everywhere's historic, if you think about it. I'll bet if you started digging up Des Moines, in Iowa, you'd find all sorts of historic stuff."

"Perhaps." Nimrod nodded, politely acknowledging John's point. "Only Kandahar is a bit more historic than most places. After all, it was founded by none other than Alexander the Great. Which is more than you can say for Des Moines, attractive as that particular city must be."

"What else has it got apart from history?" demanded John.

"Kandahar is famous for a number of things," said Nimrod. "It's a major trading center for sheep and camels. This is why we're here, of course. And for fine fruits, like pomegranates."

He paused for a moment, measuring the effect his next few words might have on his young nephew and niece.

"What else?" he said. "Ah, yes, it's also the home of my wife. Your aunt Alexandra."

CHAPTER 21

AT THE KANDAHAR CAMEL MARKET

Nimrod ignored all questions from the twins about an aunt of whom they knew absolutely nothing until the flying carpet was on the hot and arid ground, on which a deserted road led off to the north, where they could just make out the vague outline of the city of Kandahar.

The two Icelanders helped him to roll up the carpet into a long blue pillar.

"The carpet is too heavy to carry on our shoulders," said Axel. "Then again, we can hardly leave it here, by the roadside."

"No," said Nimrod. "We'll bury it." He glanced at the twins. "Perhaps you two could do the honors? With some shovels? I'm feeling rather tired after all that flying."

"Sure." John spoke his focus word and then handed everyone a nice new shovel.

"I was thinking of something a little more instant," said Nimrod. "Like a long trench. But these shovels will do almost as well. And now that I think of it, you're right, John. If you used djinn power to make a trench, then you'd have to make some earth or sand to put in it."

Everyone started to dig. In the hot sun it was hard work, but with five of them digging they quickly excavated a trench deep enough to hide the carpet, and then they filled it in again.

"How shall we mark the spot?" asked John.

"Oh, I shall remember where it is," said Nimrod.

"I imagine that's what the sons of Genghis Khan said," observed Philippa. "When they buried him." She smiled. "Anyone got a baby camel handy?"

"Touché, Philippa," said Nimrod.

He thought for a moment and then planted a small stone on the ground near the burial site.

"We're bound to spot that," said John.

Ignoring his nephew's sarcasm, Nimrod said that it was a special stone, but didn't explain in what way special.

"What about our clothes?" said Axel. "We shall stick out a mile dressed like this."

"Good point," said Nimrod. "Philippa? Perhaps you could oblige us all with some local costume. And I rather think the professor here had better wear a *chadri*. On account of his mask. Which might be alarming to the locals."

"What's a *chadri*?" asked John.

"It's like a burka," said Nimrod.

John was none the wiser.

"It's an all-enveloping outer garment for women," explained Philippa. "Not all women, just those who want to prevent themselves from being seen by men."

"Sounds like a good idea," John said pointedly. "Anything that covers your face, Phil."

Philippa flicked him a sarcastic smile. "It's not for kids," she said. "Just grown-up women."

"Pity."

A few minutes later, the little party of three djinn and two humans, dressed in local Afghan clothes, was heading into the ancient city. Along the way they passed almost a hundred wild camels grazing in a rough-looking field, which served to remind them all of why they were there in Afghanistan. But at that particular moment the twins were hardly interested in camels.

"You never said you were married," Philippa told Nimrod.

"You never asked," said Nimrod.

"I always thought you were, um . . ." John hesitated. "Single. After all, you never talk about — what's her name?"

"Alexandra," said Nimrod.

"Is she a djinn, like us?"

"Oh, yes. She's a djinn, all right. But she's not like us. For one thing she's an Eremite."

"That's the djinn cult whose believers seek to imitate the lives of angels and saints and go without possessions," said Philippa. "Yes, I remember."

"Many years ago, she and your mother became Eremites together, in New York City. Your mother was lucky enough to be rescued by your father. But Alexandra was not so fortunate. She persisted in the cult and came here after the Russian invasion of Afghanistan in 1979. On the basis that the Afghans needed her help more than any other mundanes. And has remained here ever since."

"But I don't understand," said Philippa. "How can you and she be married if she's an Eremite? Eremites believe in giving up not just possessions but relationships, too. Including marriage."

"We were married before she became an Eremite," said Nimrod. "It was partly me and my taste for the good things in life that drove her to it, I think. That and some other things."

"Are we going to meet her?" asked John.

"I sincerely hope not," said Nimrod. "She's half mad, you see. And that's another reason she's not like us. A lot of the Eremites are a bit eccentric, of course. But Alexandra is more than just eccentric. Possibly she's dangerous."

"Why?" asked John.

"Because she believes she has the gift of prophecy," said Nimrod.

"And does she?" asked Philippa. "Have the gift of prophecy?"

"That's a little hard to say," admitted Nimrod. "Alexandra has what you Americans call issues."

"What kind of issues?" asked John.

"Anger-management issues," said Nimrod. "She can manage to get cross about almost anything. Anything at all. And in the middle of all that, it's a little hard to remember her predictions at all. But whether she can or she can't, knowledge of the future is the most dangerous thing in the universe."

"I can't see why," argued John. "I reckon that it would be quite useful now, to know what's going to happen."

"I agree," said Axel. "That way we might know if we're on a wild-goose chase or not."

Nimrod shook his head.

"Take my word for it, every manner of things can go wrong if you attempt to act on a prophecy. Fortunately, the way my wife speaks makes it hard to understand her. However, people, including djinn, come here from all over the world to have her tell the future."

They reached the outskirts of Kandahar and found the city rather more modern than they had supposed. There were also a great many British and American soldiers on the streets, many of them heavily armed, and at almost every street corner, there was a large pile of sandbags and a military checkpoint where cars and trucks were stopped and searched. But mostly, the traffic was children on bicycles, heavily veiled women on donkeys and Pashtun tribesmen on mopeds and motorcycles, and local merchants leading camels laden with goods.

John glanced at Professor Sturloson in his bright blue *chadri* and then at a group of identically dressed but anonymous women and realized he could not tell the difference. Anyone could have been wearing this garment, anyone at all; even the aunt Alexandra he had never met and it now seemed wasn't going to meet.

"How are you doing, Professor?" he asked.

"I feel a bit of a fool," confessed the professor. "It's like wearing a tent. I'll be glad when we've found this camel trader and we can get out of here."

"As I recall," said Nimrod, "the camel market is north of Charsoo Square." He pointed to the right. "Which is this way."

He led the way through streets packed with rickshaws and scooters to a market where everything was for sale: fruit and vegetables, beautiful cloths and carpets, computer equipment, meat and bread, guns and ammunition. In a shop selling television sets, they stopped for a few moments to watch Afghanistan's Tolo TV. It was hard for the twins and the two Icelanders to understand exactly what was being said, but the drift of the news report was clear: Mount Damavand, the region's largest volcano at more than eighteen thousand feet, had blown its top, forcing many Iranians to flee their homes.

"This is bad," said the professor.

His deep and manly voice attracted a few strange looks from the locals but mostly he was ignored.

"This is very bad. Mount Damavand has been dormant for hundreds, perhaps thousands of years." He looked up at the sky, which was still the same color as his *chadri*. "No sign of any effects on the world's weather. But if this kind of thing keeps up, it's bound to create a volcanic winter. The eruption of Indonesia's Mount Tambora made 1816 the year without a summer. Crops failed, livestock died, and the world endured the worst famine of the nineteenth century."

"Then there's certainly no time to waste here watching television," said Nimrod, and snapped his fingers at the professor and his companions. "Let us quickly find this camel market. And, if we can, the descendants of Ali Bilharzia."

They smelled it before they saw it. And heard it, too. Hundreds of loudly belching, enormously smelly camels in a square the size of a football field. Flies, dust, and argument filled the air as gesticulating traders and their apparently indifferent customers haggled to buy and sell the strange-looking animals that patiently awaited their fate. This was not always to be a humpbacked beast of burden; here and there were hawkers carrying mountainous trays of camel livers — a local delicacy — to be eaten raw, or, even more deliciously, coated with peanut sauce.

Just to look at these trays and catch the strong smell of the meat in her delicate, young nostrils made Philippa feel like throwing up; once or twice she had to bury her face in the silky depths of her Afghan clothes to escape the pungent stink of liver. And it was fortunate that Nimrod was in a hurry as he might otherwise have eaten some of this camel liver of which once he had been extremely fond; or worse, obliged his nephew and niece to eat some, too.

As it was, he took several cups full of *doh*, which is the national drink of Afghanistan and made of yogurt, lemon juice, club soda, mint, and salt.

John took one look into a glass proffered by Nimrod and, disliking any drink on principle that looked like snot, he decided against tasting it.

"Besides," he said, "it sounds more like a swear word than a drink. Like the sound you'd make if someone had just stepped on your toe." He glanced down at his feet. "Which, in these sandals, would be kind of painful."

Nimrod grimaced. "And I thought Groanin was picky about what he'd eat and drink."

John smiled. "I expect the first thing he did when he got back to Manchester was make a cup of tea."

Nimrod frowned for he felt incomplete without his butler. "Yes, I shall miss his tea. No one, not even me or Mr. Rakshasas, could ever make tea like Groanin. In that respect, at least, the man was a genius."

"Followed by a large plate of sausages with fried eggs and buttered toast," said John. "And maybe some trifle for — what did he call dessert again?"

"Afters," said Philippa. "And stop it, John. You're making me feel hungry."

"Me, too," said Axel. "I'm not keen on raw liver."

"Don't know what you're missing." Speaking the local dialect of Pashto, which is the main language in Afghanistan, Nimrod began to inquire of the local camel traders if the Bilharzia family were still in the business of selling used dromedaries.

Finally, he was directed along to a group of handsome-looking men seated on the ground and leaning on their camel saddles. Of these men, one was taller and more distinguished than all the rest; he had a white beard, blue eyes, and a nose like a catalina macaw's beak. In his hand was a long length of cane with which he tapped the ground in front of him; from time to time, he would use this cane on the thickest part of a camel's neck to make it kneel down or stand up to be inspected by a prospective buyer.

Nimrod bowed politely and inquired if he was speaking to Mr. Bilharzia and, having established he was, Nimrod explained the purpose of his mission: "Many years ago, about one hundred and fifty years ago to be more precise, I believe that your ancestor Ali Bilharzia owned a saddle and a bridle of great antiquity and value, which were themselves more than five hundred years old and that had adorned Dunbelchin, the famous camel that once belonged to the sons of Genghis Khan."

Mr. Bilharzia frowned. "Who told you such a wicked lie?"

"This is what was written in a book by a man called Sidi Mubarak Bombay," said Nimrod.

"I have heard of this book," admitted Mr. Bilharzia. "But I have not read it myself. This is the book that was written with the collaboration of Henry Morton Stanley, was it not? The famous British explorer."

Nimrod nodded.

"This Stanley," said Mr. Bilharzia. "I have heard that he was a great liar. That many things of which he himself wrote were not true. That he never said 'Doctor Livingstone, I presume' and other things like that. So perhaps this man, Bombay, inspired by his friend Stanley, felt that he, too, could be similarly cavalier with the truth. Of course, this is true of all writers of books, to some extent. They are all wicked people who would never let the facts obstruct the telling of a good story. After all, there is only one book that is completely true and that is the holy Quran."

Nimrod bowed again. "Forgive me," he said. "It was my mistake, Mr. Bilharzia."

"My family has been in the business of selling camels for many centuries," said Mr. Bilharzia. "And I tell you that there never was any such camel as the one you mention. What was the name again?"

"Dunbelchin," said Nimrod.

Mr. Bilharzia shook his head. "No such camel called Dunbelchin ever existed. Or was ever stolen. Nor was there any such saddle or bridle that belonged to Genghis Khan, as you describe. No, sir, you have been cruelly misinformed."

Nimrod bowed again. "Please forgive the intrusion, sir," he said. "It was my mistake."

"You should be very careful making such allegations," said Mr. Bilharzia. "Perhaps you have not heard of the Darkhats. A dangerous clan of fanatics who claim descent from nine of the wicked Khan's generals and closest followers. For more than seven hundred years they have guarded his memory and I do not think it possible that they could allow any man not of their clan to remain in possession of the great and priceless treasures you describe. I think that they would cut many throats for such a bridle and saddle." He smiled. "That is, always supposing that they even existed." He stretched for a moment. "Myself, I have always believed that they were nothing more than the stuff of legends."

"Quite," said Nimrod.

"As for Dunbelchin, I believe she was not a white dromedary camel, but a Bactrian camel, with two humps rather than one. And as you can see, I only sell dromedaries. My family has only ever sold dromedaries. Bactrians are quite outside my family's expertise."

Nimrod bowed and made his apologies again and withdrew. John, Axel, and the professor followed at a respectful distance.

Philippa shooed away someone who wanted to buy Moby, and hurried after them.

"So what did he say?" said the professor. What with his mask, and the little cloth grille in his *chadri*, the professor almost had to shout to make himself heard.

"He said he'd never heard of Dunbelchin," said Nimrod. "And then said she wasn't a dromedary but a Bactrian."

"So he was lying," said John.

"I think so. In fact, I'm more or less sure of it. He denied that the saddle and bridle of Genghis Khan existed, too. Having also described them as great treasures. A most evasive man was our Mr. Bilharzia."

"So what happens now?" asked Axel. "We can't make him tell the truth."

"Oh, yes we can," said Nimrod. "I can. And I will. There's no time to be subtle with this man. But I'm not going to do it here. Not in the middle of the camel market. That would be unwise. Especially now that I've confirmed the existence of these Darkhats."

"So how are you going to make him talk?" said the professor. "Are you going to torture him?"

Nimrod looked horrified. "Certainly not. There are other ways of getting the truth out of people. I shall simply make him cough it up of his own free will. Well, almost free."

"You mean you're going to use a quaesitor binding, don't you?" John grinned. "Cool."

Nimrod shot his nephew an uncomfortable look. "I take no pleasure in this, John. And neither should you. I dislike using this kind of extreme djinn binding, but he gives me really no choice in the matter."

"So let me do it," said John. "I've never used a quaesitor on someone."

Nimrod stayed silent, thinking about it, and wondering if he could trust his nephew to get this right.

"Come on," pleaded John. "Please. You know I could use the practice. You were going to show us how to fly a carpet and you never did. And as our uncle you're supposed to be teaching us how to do djinn stuff, remember?"

"Very well," said Nimrod.

John punched the air. "Yes," he said. "That's fantastic. This is going to be fun."

"Sometimes, John," said Philippa, "I worry about you."

CHAPTER 22

VERBAL DIARRHEA

Later that evening, Mr. Bilharzia was followed home through a series of military checkpoints by Nimrod and the others who, speaking fluent English and equipped with the kind of impeccable documentation that only Nimrod's djinn power could provide, were quite above suspicion in the eyes of the mostly British soldiers guarding the city.

The camel dealer's house, a three-story neocolonial villa, was located in the southwest of Kandahar, which is the richest part of the city. Only half finished, it was still quite habitable with an enormous kitchen and a television room with all the latest equipment. At the rear of the house was an empty camel-shaped swimming pool, some stables, and a garage full of expensive cars. On one side of the house was a large poppy field, and on the other side, a large expanse of grass where several of Mr. Bilharzia's more expensive beasts were grazing. The front of the house was protected by several barbed-wire fences and a pack of almost-wild guard dogs.

"So how are we going to get past all of this security?" asked the professor.

"QWERTYUIOP," said Nimrod, and the fences disappeared. And as soon as the fence disappeared all of the guard dogs simply ran away. "That's how."

"Oh, right," said the professor. "Well, that's one way. Yes."

Nimrod led the way up the front door and rang the doorbell. It was clear that no one was expecting visitors because instead of the door opening, all of the lights inside the house were immediately extinguished, as if Mr. Bilharzia was frightened of whoever might be standing outside his house.

"I don't think they're feeling hospitable tonight," observed Philippa.

A shot rang out and they all ducked as something zipped over their heads.

"Or any other night."

"Yes, that was foolish, wasn't it?" said Nimrod. "I should have remembered that Kandahar isn't at all like Kensington, where the inhabitants don't mind when people ring their doorbells. Well, most people, anyway. In Kensington, we're never very keen on unemployed miners selling dishcloths and tea towels. Or shifty types selling bargain-priced garden furniture. Or young ruffians singing half a verse of just one carol at Christmas. And I'd certainly prefer it if religious people of any persuasion never ever rang my doorbell."

Another shot rang out and this one seemed to come closer than before, as if the hidden gunman's aim was improving.

"Perhaps," said the professor, "you might tell us this another time."

"Please, do something," said Axel. "Before we get shot."

"Yes, of course," said Nimrod.

He murmured his focus word again and a square of bulletproof glass (effective against all 7.62-millimeter armor-piercing ammunition) appeared around them like an invisible cage.

"There," he said. "That should keep us safe while I open this door." He turned the handle. "Which appears to be locked. No matter." He sighed and shook his head. "You know, I'm using rather a lot of power these days, much more than I feel comfortable with; but I can see no alternative if we're going to be in time to save the world from itself."

"Let me, Uncle," said Philippa, and muttering her latest focus word, PARASKAVEDEKATRIAPHOBIA (Philippa was always changing her focus word), which, as any fool knows, means having an abnormal fear of Friday the thirteenth, the door came off the hinges and fell like a drawbridge onto the marble floor with a loud bang.

"Thank you, Philippa," said Nimrod.

Advancing into the main hallway of the house, Axel found a big Maglite on a shelf by the door — because there are frequent power cuts in the city of Kandahar — and switching it on, aimed a thick beam of light ahead of them.

They were met by the sight of Mr. Bilharzia and his large family cowering in a corner and begging for mercy.

"Please," shouted the camel dealer. "Don't hurt us."

"My dear fellow, I have no intention of hurting you or

your family," said Nimrod. "But do kindly tell whoever it is who was shooting at us to desist forthwith, before someone really does gets hurt."

"It's my twelve-year-old son, Sirhan," said Mr. Bilharzia. "He is upstairs with a rifle."

Mr. Bilharzia shouted up the stairs and finally a boy came onto the landing. He was wearing a long, white *galabiya* and carrying an automatic rifle. His father barked an order at him and Sirhan laid the rifle on the floor.

"And do put the lights back on," said Nimrod.

Mr. Bilharzia flicked a switch that returned all the electric lights.

"Thank you," said Nimrod.

"You're the man who was looking for the saddle of Genghis Khan," said Mr. Bilharzia. "Why are you here?"

"I'm afraid I really do need some urgent answers to questions of an ungulate nature," said Nimrod.

"Ungulate? You mean camel."

"I most assuredly do." Nimrod smiled at his niece and then the professor. "Ladies? Why don't you take Mrs. Bilharzia and her children upstairs and keep them company while John and I and Axel ask Mr. Bilharzia some questions."

"I have nothing to say," said Mr. Bilharzia. "About anything. And certainly nothing about any camels, or saddles, or bridles that were once owned by Genghis Khan. I don't know anything."

Nimrod was staring at a mural — a copy of an Indian Mughal painting depicting the funeral procession of Genghis Khan and the murder of all those who had observed it.

"Oh, I think you do," insisted Nimrod.

He turned to examine a very old portrait of a white camel; it was encased with silver and resembled nothing so much as a religious icon.

"Is this a picture of Dunbelchin?"

"Really, I know nothing."

"Well," said Nimrod, "we'll soon see, won't we?"

"What do you mean? You said that you weren't going to hurt us."

"True," said Nimrod. "And I give you my word that it won't hurt a bit."

When Philippa and the professor had taken Mr. Bilharzia's family upstairs, Nimrod led him to the dinner table where the four of them sat down.

"What won't?"

"My young nephew's quaesitor," said Nimrod. "It's a djinn binding that's designed to find out the thing you find most unpleasant and then make it appear in your mouth until you start to tell the truth. My nephew here really detests vegetables. Which I don't think are so bad."

"Don't you believe it," said John.

"But I've seen all sorts of horrible things coming out of people's mouths. Cockroaches, rats, snakes, spiders. So what's it to be? Regurgitation or reality? Verbals or vomit. The truth or the taste of something you find vile."

"I don't know what you're talking about."

"One last time: everything you know about Dunbelchin and the saddle or else you'll have to eat your words."

Mr. Bilharzia was not convinced. He shook his head and

squeezed his lips tight, as if defying Nimrod and John to do their worst.

"I regret this," confessed Nimrod. "Really I do."

Mr. Bilharzia swore in Pashto.

"John?" Nimrod glanced at his nephew. "Whenever you're ready. "

John nodded and placed a finger quickly on the camel dealer's mouth just to help with the binding, and then he spoke his word of power.

"ABECEDARIAN."

Nimrod nodded. "Right. First of all. Do you speak English?"

"Yes, I speak English," said Mr. Bilharzia, speaking English. "Why?"

"It's just to help my nephew," said Nimrod. "He doesn't speak Pashto. Which means his binding doesn't, either. It's very much to your benefit that his quaesitor can tell the difference between a truth and a lie."

Mr. Bilharzia swore again, only this time in English.

"Oh, dear, it would appear that something horrible is already emerging from your mouth," observed Nimrod. "Let your next words be truthful, clean ones, or endure the taste of something truly abhorrent. Now then: Tell us everything you know about Dunbelchin."

Mr. Bilharzia was about to swear again but found something coming up his windpipe that was squarely in the way of the bad word. He gagged a little and finding the object now in his mouth, let it plop onto the palm of his outstretched hand.

The object was round and greenish brown and about the size of a small bread roll. John had no idea what it was. But Mr. Bilharzia recognized it instinctively.

"Camel dung," he said with horror.

"That seems appropriate," said Nimrod. "Given your potty mouth."

John snorted with horror. "That is so disgusting," he said. "I couldn't ever have thought of that on my own."

"I'm glad to hear it, John," said his uncle. "That's the great thing about the quaesitor. It does all of the nasty work for you."

"Aieee!" Mr. Bilharzia choked again, spat, and with his tongue, pushed another piece of camel dung out of his mouth. "Horrible! Horrible! Horrible!"

"Odd, don't you think, John?" said Nimrod. "That a camel dealer would find the animal's dung so disgusting? You'd think he was used to it by now."

"Used to seeing it and sniffing it, maybe," agreed John. "But not eating it. Yeeugh. Can't imagine how gross that must taste."

"I can't agree, given that a camel is vegetarian," said Nimrod. "The dung would be so much less palatable if camels were meat eaters."

"Yeeugh," said John, horrified at the effect his quaesitor was having on Mr. Bilharzia.

Nimrod was no less horrified than his nephew.

"I really don't like this sort of thing at all," said Nimrod, shaking his head. He sighed loudly. "But, given all of the circumstances, I suppose it can't be helped."

"The end justifies the means?" offered John.

"Perhaps," said Nimrod. "Yes. In this particular case it does, I'm afraid."

John's eyes narrowed. He knew that usually the idea of the end justifying the means was something his libertarian uncle had no time for; he was always saying as much. So Nimrod's admission that here the end did justify the means made John wonder just how far his uncle was prepared to go in order to achieve the end, which was, he imagined, to save the world from the threat of catastrophe caused by this sudden rash of volcanic eruptions. Recollecting what his sister had told him about the books their uncle had been reading in the Rakshasas Library and the passages he had underlined, John wondered if, in Nimrod's mind, the end might even justify the sacrifice of his nephew and niece.

More dung appeared from the camel dealer's mouth.

"Make it stop!" he wailed.

"There's a very easy way to make it stop, of course," explained Nimrod. "And that's simply to tell us everything we want to know about Dunbelchin."

"I cannot."

Mr. Bilharzia coughed and retched a fourth and a fifth piece of quite malodorous camel dung onto the floor.

"It's said that the taste of a quaesitor remains with you for many months afterward," said Nimrod. "And the longer it lasts, the more the memory lingers in your mouth. I once knew a man who used more than a hundred gallons of mouthwash to get rid of the taste of a really nasty quaesitor."

"Very well," yelled the camel dealer. "I will tell you everything, mighty lord djinn."

"Promise?" said John. "On your word of honor?"

"Yes! Yes! I promise. On my word of honor. As I hope to see heaven, yes."

"Excellent," said Nimrod. "I'm so glad. Doing this sort of thing to people always leaves a nasty taste in my mouth, too." He shrugged. "But not, I imagine, as nasty as the taste in yours."

"Please come this way," said Mr. Bilharzia.

He led them into the basement of the house, where he unlocked an ancient-looking door.

"The house is new," he explained. "But down here is very old. These cellars belonged to the original house and stables, which were destroyed by an American bomb in 2003. The cellars date back to the mid-sixteenth century, and possibly before that. I keep all the Bilharzia family records and accounts down here, not to mention the family treasures."

He ushered Nimrod, John, and Axel into the cellars, past a series of shelves that were full of leather-bound ledgers, to a room that looked like an inner sanctum if only because it was dominated by a rather threadbare-looking stuffed white camel that was wearing a fine old leather saddle and a jeweled bridle. Mr. Bilharzia switched on a light to properly illuminate his treasures.

"There it is," he said. "The saddle, the bridle, and most important, Dunbelchin herself. All of them bought by my ancestor from the thief who stole them: Kamran Hotak Mahomet of Charikar."

"And this is the original animal?" said Nimrod. "The camel that was stolen from Genghis Khan?"

210

"The very same. My ancestor, Ali Bilharzia, had Dunbelchin stuffed when she died in 1240. The taxidermist was the most skilled in all of central Asia. But she has been stuffed twice: once by the great Louis Dufresne in 1799, and again by the great Carl Akeley, in 1920. I keep these things secret, O mighty djinn. The Darkhats would kill to have these things in their possession. This is why security is so tight here. And why I have always denied even knowing about Dunbelchin. If they so much as even suspected that these things were here, our lives wouldn't be worth living."

"But don't they know about Sidi Mubarak Bombay's book?" asked Nimrod. *"The Secret Secret History of the Mongols."*

"They are not great readers, sir." Mr. Bilharzia shook his head. "Books are a foreign country for the Darkhats. They do things differently in their world. Besides, there were very few copies ever printed. Four to be exact."

"Hardly a bestseller, then," observed John.

"I have one here. There was one in the British Library but that was lost many years ago. The third copy was bought by the billionaire Rashleigh Khan, who is deluded enough to believe that he is the descendant of Lord Genghis Khan. And the fourth copy was bought from a bookshop in Calcutta by a Mr. Rakshasas in 1867."

"I have that one," said Nimrod. "In my own library."

"Then thank goodness they don't have it," said Mr. Bilharzia. "The Darkhats." He spat on the floor, hoping to get rid of the awful taste that remained in his mouth.

John fished in his pocket and produced a packet of mints and gave one to the hapless camel trader.

"Thank you, young sir, thank you." Mr. Bilharzia put the mint into his mouth and sucked it with considerable relief, like it was the choicest ambrosia. "But what more can I tell you, sir?"

"Is the story true, do you think?" asked Nimrod. "As described in Sidi Mubarak Bombay's book?"

"Oh, yes sir. Very substantially true, I am thinking. It was very remiss of my ancestor to tell Sidi Mubarak Bombay these things. But he was a most persuasive fellow."

"I'm still not sure how any of this helps us to find the tomb," said Axel.

"The tomb of Genghis Khan?" Mr. Bilharzia shook his head. "It is lost forever. Only the Darkhats know where it is."

Nimrod was wandering among the leather-bound ledgers in the adjoining cellar.

"What are these? Scrapbooks?"

"No, great djinn. They are my sales-and-purchase ledgers, invoices, profit-and-loss accounts, audit reports, camel-breeding records."

"Going back how far?"

"All the way back, sir. To Ali Bilharzia and beyond."

"Do you mean to tell me that you have records going back almost eight hundred years?"

"Yes, sir."

"So you could actually trace the descendants of Dunbelchin?"

"Oh, yes sir."

He opened one of the older ledgers and turned the vellum pages.

"This is the purchase ledger for the year 1227. And here is a record of Dunbelchin's purchase from Kamran Hotak Mahomet. This record is cross-referenced with . . ."

He opened another ledger.

"Here. Yes. You see? Bull camels and mare camels, their calves and their calves, when they were born, when they died. Everything. Dunbelchin had another calf after the one that was buried alive in the tomb of Genghis Khan. A male calf called Bigbelchin."

He turned some more pages of the breeding-record book.

"Bigbelchin had three calves himself. Two died. But Loudbelchin survived and sired three calves: Stinkibelchin, Burpbelchin, and Silentbelchin."

"Would it be possible to trace Dunbelchin's line to the present day?" asked Nimrod.

"Oh, yes sir. But it would take several hours."

"Please do it," said Nimrod. "Yes, please do it now."

CHAPTER 23

IT'S A, IT'S A, IT'S A, IT'S A SIN

The fierce men of Şābh al-Mjnwn drove northeast from Yemen across the great desert of Ar-Rub' al Khali into the United Arab Emirates and Oman, where they boarded a ferry that carried them across the Strait of Hormuz, into Iran.

From time to time, one of the three gang members listened through the backseat armrest of the Toyota to check that Groanin was all right and hearing the sound of loud snoring they concluded, rightly, that he was still alive and coping well with the discomfort of traveling in the trunk of the car.

Driving all through the day, the Crazy Gang reached the Afghan border, about four hundred miles from the coast of Iran, just before dusk.

For much of the journey the leader of Şābh al-Mjnwn, Sheikh Raat el Enrool, busied himself on his laptop trying to write the speech that he intended to make on Groanin's ransom video.

This was difficult, however, not because the poor condition of the road made it hard to type on the laptop's Arabic keyboard, but because the noise of Groanin's snoring grew louder and louder until it filled the interior of the car like the growl of an extremely large tiger. But it was the whistle that topped and tailed the sound of the butler's snoring that annoyed the sheikh most of all because, according to the sheikh's strict way of thinking, whistling was a kind of music and therefore immoral and forbidden.

"How are we going to stop this English dog from whistling?" he asked the driver.

"We could wake him up, perhaps," suggested the driver, whose name was Assylam. "Only he might escape. Or we might have to endure his unbelieving conversation that would surely be worse."

"Nothing could be worse than this infuriating sound," said the sheikh angrily. "The snoring is bad enough. It sounds like the rumble of thunder. Or an earthquake. But the Englishman's whistle is infinitely worse. It is making a nervous wreck out of me. I keep thinking that it is an artillery shell flying through the air toward us."

"In which case perhaps it is not music at all and therefore not forbidden," said a third member of the Crazy Gang, who was in the backseat of the car. His name was Ben Yussef.

"That might be true," said the sheikh, "if the whistle was always the same. But from time to time the pitch of his whistle doesn't descend like an artillery shell at all and actually holds a perfect C. If a note of music could ever be described as perfect. But you know what I mean."

"Yes, sir."

"It's a dilemma," said Assylam.

At this point, Groanin stopped whistling in and out of his snore for almost an hour.

"That's a relief," said the sheikh, and returned to his typing.

But when Groanin's whistle started again, it seemed that his whistling had acquired a much more musical character. Assylam tried to think of the tune he had heard that the Englishman's whistling snore was trying to pipe into his mind, and finally it came to him. With horror, he realized that the whistle sounded exactly like two notes from the whistling in the Monty Python tune "Always Look on the Bright Side of Life." He debated whether or not to inform the sheikh of this; finally, when the temptation to actually finish the rest of the tune grew almost too great for him, he decided that the right thing to do was to tell the sheikh even though he knew that this would make him very angry indeed.

As soon as Assylam had imparted this information, the sheikh realized he was quite right about the tune, and was properly horrified.

"Now we'll have to wake him up," said the sheikh. "We can't drive all the way to Kabul with this maddening tune in our heads."

"Agreed."

"The question is how to wake him up without opening the trunk and risking his escape."

"Tell you what, sir," said Assylam, "I'll aim the car at a few of these potholes and maybe their impact will wake him up."

"Good idea," agreed the sheikh. "And honk the horn while you're at it, for good measure."

"Wait," said Ben Yussef. "Isn't honking the horn making a kind of music, too?"

"Good point," said the sheikh. "Is it?"

Everyone thought for a moment.

"I think the horn would only sound musical if it was done in a rhythmical way," said Assylam. "Like the evil noise that is made at a football match when people clap together and then shout *Eng-land* or *Eee-gypt*. If I avoid any hint of rhythm when honking the horn, then no one is offended."

The sheikh nodded. "Agreed."

Assylam honked the horn loudly, and hit several potholes in succession, which made the car shudder like an aircraft enduring air pockets of turbulence. But none of this was enough to rouse the sleeping butler and, if anything, the noise emanating from Groanin's nose and throat actually seemed to get worse.

"It's not working," said the sheikh.

"No," agreed Assylam, "and if the car hits another pothole, I'll break the axle." He winced as, accidentally, the car hit another enormous pothole that almost loosened the fillings in his teeth. "This is a new car. And I don't want it damaged."

"How is it possible that any man can sleep so soundly?" said an exasperated Ben Yussef.

"Only a fool could sleep so much when he has been kidnapped to be held for ransom," said the sheikh. "It's wrong to have no fear, I think. And immoral to sleep so much."

"Most certainly," agreed Ben Yussef.

"You'd better stop in Kandahar," said the sheikh. "We'll get out and beat him there. It may not stop him from snoring again, but it will certainly make us feel better. And it will teach him to have better manners."

"Good idea," said Ben Yussef.

When they reached the southwest of Kandahar, Assylam slowed the Toyota and drew up next to a brightly lit, modern-looking house with a camel-shaped swimming pool.

"Wow, look at that pool," he said. "I have always wanted a camel-shaped swimming pool."

"It is immoral to swim if one does it for pleasure. And especially immoral if one does it without clothes."

"You think so?"

"I know so. Don't even look at it."

The sheikh and the others got out of the car and stood next to the trunk, ready to throw it open and give the Englishman a beating. Now that the car had stopped, Groanin's snoring sounded very much like a large polar bear and it was hard for the three Crazy Gang members to believe that there was only a human being inside the trunk.

But of course there wasn't only a human being in the trunk of the Toyota.

"I will punch him in the face," said the sheikh. "You, Assylam, will punch him in the stomach, and Ben Yussef will strike his thighs. We will teach him to sleep when he should be praying for his life."

The other two nodded. Then the sheikh nodded at Assylam who unlocked the trunk and then pressed the catch to release the lid.

Groanin opened his eyes. "Are we there yet?" he asked, and sat up. "I said, are we there yet, Mustapha?"

The three Crazy Gang members regarded Groanin with even more horror and distaste than might have been expected for, attached to the Englishman's chest and ample stomach like an enormous pink breastplate was the largest camel spider any of them had ever seen. All three screamed at once and ran in opposite directions as if Groanin had been carrying a deadly plague.

"What the heck's wrong with them, I wonder?" mused the butler. He yawned loudly and sleepily. Oblivious to the hideous creature that was clinging to his front, he stretched his arms and got out of the trunk. "Not that I'm sad to see the back of them, mind. I said, not that I'm sad to see the back of them. Treating a person like that. Making me ride in the trunk like I was so much baggage. I've a good mind to report them to the police. In fact, I think I will. Let's see now. I wonder if I have paper and pencil to make a note of this car number."

Groanin glanced down to find his trouser pocket and, in the red rear lights of the car, dimly saw something shift on his torso as the camel spider, sensing that the butler was no longer immobile, tightened its ten-legged grip on his portly person.

"What the dickens is that?"

At first, Groanin thought that the members of the Crazy Gang must have attached a bomb to him — not least because the bony pink legs of the camel spider resembled several sticks of gelignite, and the creature's thin and spindly antennae made him think of electrical wires. Naturally, he was very scared at the idea of exploding.

"And to think I used to complain about being in old Nimrod's service. What kind of lunatic, psycho, nutcase, weirdo-fanatic attaches an Englishman to a bomb?"

He took several nervous breaths and tried to contain his panic.

"No, wait a minute, lad. Wait a minute. If they've run away and the thing still hasn't gone off, then probably it's not going to go off. Aye, that's right. So, think, lad. Think. Think of Her Majesty the Queen, lad. What would she do in a similar situation? Yes, of course. She'd keep her cool. That's what she'd do. She'd stay calm. The way she always does in situations of adversity. Like when she has to shake hands with some spotty little Herbert with dirty hands. Or when she is obliged to eat the filthy food at a dinner in some nasty little pimple of a foreign country. Or when she has to knight some creep of a pop star. Or when she does her Christmas radio and television broadcast to the nation. That's it, lad. Keep calm, like Her Majesty does. What would she do? Yes. Yes, that's it. I can detach the wires and defuse the thing before the nutters who did this to me come back. Only I need a bit more light here."

Seeing that the headlights of the car remained on,

Groanin walked around to the front and then surveyed the problem before him. Then he gave one of the spider's legs an exploratory tug.

"What the dickens?"

At which point, the spider felt obliged to warn the creature pulling its leg not to mess with it, and clacked together its chelicerae — the substantial and venomous mouthparts or mandibles for which the camel spider is renowned.

Still dazed with sleep, it was another second or two before Groanin realized the true nature of the peril in front of him.

"Flipping heck," gasped Groanin. "It's a . . . it's a . . . it's a . . ."

Not a bomb at all. But something alive and rather horribly animated. Something creepy and very crawly. Something very large and quite repulsively disgusting.

And strange to say, something much more horrible and terrifying than an explosive vest.

CHAPTER 24

THE SCREAM

Mr. Bilharzia moved the big leather ledger toward Nimrod, John, and Axel.

"All of these books are bound with the finest camel skin." He smoothed the cover of the ledger with his hand and nodded at John. "Feel."

John rubbed his hand along the smooth surface and nodded his appreciation back as Mr. Bilharzia opened the ledger.

"So, here we are." He pointed to an entry on the old vellum page. "You see? Dated winter 1859. We have the last of the direct descendants of Dunbelchin: Morebelchin, Sourbelchin, Rudebelchin, and Vilebelchin, owned by the Bilharzia family. After that, the line, if you can call it that, disappears from our family's breeding records. Which means these camels must have been sold."

"And would you have kept a record of the purchaser?" asked Nimrod.

Mr. Bilharzia looked surprised even to have been asked such a question. "Of course. This is a respectable business. With everything aboveboard. But we shall have to look in the purchase ledger for the winter of 1859 to find the buyer's name."

They waited while Mr. Bilharzia fetched another ledger from the shelves and when he had blown the dust from the cover, he opened it and started to turn the pages.

"Yes. Here we are. Winter 1859. Morebelchin, Sourbelchin, Rudebelchin, and Vilebelchin were sold to . . . well now, this *is* most unusual."

"What is?" asked Nimrod.

"These four camels were sold not to an Afghan, or an Indian, or even the British Army." Mr. Bilharzia pulled a face. "These were four of two dozen camels sold to an Australian gentleman. A Mr. George Landells of the Victorian Exploration Expedition, Melbourne, Australia. The camels were delivered by my ancestor to Karachi, in what was then India, for loading onto the cargo ship, SS *Chinsurah*."

"What would an Australian want with two dozen camels?" said Axel.

"You'd think they had enough weird animals of their own," said John. "What with kangaroos and the duck-billed platypus."

"What do you mean, weird?" Mr. Bilharzia looked and sounded as if he had been insulted. "There is nothing weird about camels. Nothing at all."

He closed the ledger, with a loud bang that made John jump.

"The camel is the most beautiful animal ever made," insisted Mr. Bilharzia. "Not just beautiful but remarkable, do you hear? Tell me, American. Can you drink forty gallons of water at once? Does your skin reflect sunlight and insulate you from heat? Can your nostrils trap and recycle the water in your body when you breathe out? Can you carry a rider for one hundred and twenty miles in a single day? Can you see where you are going in a sandstorm? Don't talk to me about weird, sonny. There are one hundred and sixty different words for camel in the Arabic language. But only one word for a fool of an American who thinks that camels are weird and that word is —"

"Mr. Bilharzia, my nephew meant no offense," Nimrod said smoothly. "And in truth he has more acquaintance with camels than ever you might suppose. The boy has ridden camels. Raced camels. You might even say he knows camels inside out. He spoke as many young Americans speak, which is sometimes as he thinks. You don't really think camels are weird, do you, John?"

"Not in a bad way," said John. "Only in a good way. And if I said *weird*, I really meant that they're remarkable. I just thought that with the remarkable animals that Australians already have, that it was strange they should want any more. I mean, you don't think of camels when you think of the Sydney Opera House, do you?"

"As a matter of fact," said Nimrod, "you don't think of opera, either. But that's another story. The fact is, John, that deserts occupy almost a fifth of the Australian continent. About half a million square miles. And there are ten of them. Australia is the driest inhabited continent on earth. Even drier than Antarctica. And that makes it perfect country for camels."

John shrugged. "I guess it does." He smiled at Mr. Bilharzia. "Sorry, Mr. Bilharzia. No offense intended."

"Apology accepted," said Mr. Bilharzia.

"Here," said John. "Have another mint."

"Thank you."

"As a matter of fact," said Nimrod, "there are more than a million wild camels living in Australia. And many of them will be descended from the twenty-four bought by this Mr. George Landells of Melbourne, Australia."

"A million?" Mr. Bilharzia was astonished. "Wild, you say?"

Nimrod nodded.

"Perhaps I should set up my business in Australia," said Mr. Bilharzia.

"Indeed, they are considered to be agricultural pests," said Nimrod. "A bit like rabbits. And in some parts of the country they have even tried to eradicate them."

"Eradicate?" Mr. Bilharzia looked aghast. "You mean — ?"

"Yes," said Nimrod. "They shoot them."

Mr. Bilharzia opened his mouth and his eyes with horror and pressed his hands hard against the sides of his skull as if he thought it might explode.

For a moment John was convinced that Mr. Bilharzia, who was clearly very fond of camels, had screamed. And it was a moment or two before he realized that the scream had come and was still coming from outside.

It was a man's scream and to Nimrod's keen ears there was something about it that sounded almost familiar.

"Curious," he said.

Upstairs in Mr. Bilharzia's house, Philippa heard the scream, too, and went to look out of the window.

"Don't worry about it," said Mrs. Bilharzia. "We get all sorts in this neighborhood. It might be terrorists. It might be soldiers on R & R. Or an animal in pain. A dog. We get a lot of strays in this part of Kandahar and people are sometimes very cruel to them."

The scream continued like something infinite in the air.

"You know what? It's probably someone making a protest about the electricity cuts. 'Round here the power is always going off and people are really fed up with it."

"The lights seem to be working," said Philippa.

"We have a generator," explained Mrs. Bilharzia proudly.

Philippa moved the curtain aside and stared down into the street. It was almost dark outside, although the ash from the eruption of Mount Taftan, in Iran, had left the sky bloodred. An empty car was parked with its headlights on beside the glowing blue camel-shaped swimming pool at the back of Mr. Bilharzia's house. In the headlights she could see a bald, middle-aged, rather stout-looking man just standing in front of the car and, it seemed to her, screaming for no good reason. His hands were pressed to each side of his face and his eyes were wide open with fear and loathing.

The professor joined her at the window. But it was hard

for him to see anything through his mask and the eye grille in his *chadri*.

"What is it?" he said.

"It doesn't look like someone protesting against anything," said Philippa. "And it certainly doesn't sound like someone protesting."

Was he the driver, perhaps, and had just received some rather bad news? Or the victim of some crime — an attempted robbery, or even a hit-and-run? Or had he escaped from a lunatic asylum and was shrieking because he was suffering from some sort of mental disorder? Or perhaps was he shrieking at the top of his voice just for the fun of it? She couldn't imagine why anyone, let alone a grown man, would scream like that, and for so long, too. It seemed quite unmanly to her. And yet there was something about the man and indeed his screaming that was strangely familiar.

Something about the pin-striped trousers, and the vest, and the white shirt and the black tie and the pink bald head she seemed to recognize.

"It can't be," she said.

She removed her glasses, cleaned them on the back of Professor Sturloson's electric-blue *chadri*, and, putting them back on her nose, opened the window and leaned out to get a better look.

"It is," she said, and hurried toward the door.

Outside, she sprinted around to the back of the house, narrowly avoided falling into the camel-shaped swimming pool, and almost collided with the still-shrieking Groanin and the horrible thing that was attached to his torso. Indeed, so close did she come to colliding with her old friend and the Solifuga clinging to his belly that it hissed loudly at her with its stridulatory organ and then snipped its rattling and hideous mouthparts defensively in the air.

Philippa, who hated creepy crawlies of any size, let alone one as big as a dinner plate, screamed loudly. Hers was a loud, high-pitched, piercing scream, whereas Mr. Groanin's scream was now running out of energy and air; Philippa's loud and piercing scream was also over relatively soon, although to be fair to Groanin, it might have been a very different story if the camel spider had been attached to her.

Wringing her hands nervously, she took several steps back from the butler and, momentarily containing her horror and disgust, tried to stay looking at him long enough to figure out what to do.

"What is it?" she said.

Groanin, who was almost out of air because he had been screaming for so long now, just shook his head.

"Is it poisonous?"

Groanin shook his head and then whispered, "I don't know, miss. I don't even know what *it* is."

"It's a camel spider," said Axel, who was next on the scene. "A smaller one than that put me in hospital for six weeks."

"Thank you," whimpered Groanin, "for sharing that with me, whoever you are."

Next on the scene was John who stared openmouthed at the horrid thing stuck to his old friend and said, "That is an awesome-looking horror, Mr. Groanin." He shook his head. "*Alien* One, Two, Three, and Four. Hey, let's hope it hasn't laid an egg inside you, or you'll be eating breakfast on your own for a while."

"Please," whimpered Groanin. "Someone. Help me."

Nimrod appeared and next to him was the person wearing the *chadri*, whom everyone in Mr. Bilharzia's house assumed was Nimrod's wife, but was in fact Professor Sturloson.

"Oh, I say, Groanin," said Nimrod. "That is a magnificent specimen. You know, I think that's the largest female Solifuga or Pseudoscorpionida I think I've ever seen. Just look at the size of the creature's prosoma, to say nothing of those enormous biting parts — the chelicerae."

He leaned toward his butler to take a closer look. And so did Professor Sturloson.

"This one appears to have chewed through your vest and your shirt," said Nimrod. "But lucky for you, it hasn't yet tried to chew through your not insubstantial stomach."

Groanin whimpered again and shut his eyes.

"I was hoping to see one of these," said the professor. "I've heard so many stories about these little creatures."

"Little?" John guffawed. "It's huge."

"How clever of you to find it, Groanin," said Nimrod. "Normally, they're very shy and shun the light. That's what the name *Solifuga* means. It's Latin for 'the thing that flees from the sun.'"

"I didn't find it," whispered Groanin. "It found me. If I'd found it before it found me, I'd have dropped a rock on it. Or stamped on it. Or hit it with a hammer."

"Nonsense," said Nimrod.

"Is it?"

"Marvelous bugger, isn't he? When I was a boy we used to call them jerrymuglums. Don't ask me why, I don't know. But I used to have a South African friend as a boy who called them haarskeerders. And he was terrified of them. Used to claim they could cut your hair in your sleep and line their nests with it."

"Get it off," whispered Groanin.

"All in good time," said Nimrod. "All in good time. They're not venomous as such. But the bite is supposed to be extraordinarily painful and can easily get infected."

"I can testify to that," agreed Axel.

"Unfortunately, they don't much like being handled at the best of times," said Nimrod. "Even by someone like me." He took hold of the creature's abdomen and tugged gently. "Who knows what it's doing."

"If you don't get that thing off me soon," squeaked Groanin. "I'm going to die of heart failure. Do you hear? Either that, or I shall simply suffocate from lack of oxygen."

Nimrod bent closer and blew gently on the camel spider's back.

"Be careful," squealed Philippa.

"Why don't you just zap it with djinn power?" asked John. "Blast it into the next world."

"Because, my young zap-headed friend, I might also zap Groanin in the stomach, which would be a great pity. No, this has to be handled with care and precision."

He blew on the spider again.

"Try not to breathe for a moment," said Nimrod. "I think

230

it's attracted to the sound of your lungs. Not having any lungs of its own."

"Really?" said the professor. "How does it breathe?"

"With great difficulty, I hope," said Philippa, who was feeling thoroughly revolted by the spider.

"Through some slits on its trachea," said Nimrod. "Here we go. Nice and easy does it."

"I think it's shifting now, Groanin," observed John. "Get ready to be very happy."

Now there are lots of urban myths about camel spiders, but the one story about them that is actually true is that they can run incredibly fast; so that one moment Nimrod was lifting the spider clear of Groanin's bare belly, the next he was laying it down on the ground, and the moment after that it was running at ten or fifteen miles an hour but in no particular direction, and thus scattering a screaming Groanin, a yelling Axel, a howling John, and a shrieking Philippa, north, south, east, and west. Much to the amusement of Nimrod and the professor.

Gradually, everyone came back and Groanin got to explain what had happened to him after the others had left him at the hotel in Sorrento.

"I shall never ever leave your service again, sir," the butler told Nimrod finally. "It has been the worst experience of my life. Nothing that happens to us now could ever be worse than what I've been through these last few days."

Hearing this, Philippa exchanged a look with John. "Let's hope you're right," she said.

"Of course he's right," insisted Nimrod.

"What now?" asked the professor.

"Back to the carpet, I think," said Nimrod. "And then on with our journey."

He leaned into the Toyota interior for a moment and, touching the steering wheel and the gearshift, he uttered his focus word quietly, just so as to leave a small something for the three kidnappers, if and when they returned.

"Where are we going?" asked Groanin, fetching his luggage from the trunk of the car.

"Australia," said Nimrod.

"Follow that camel, eh?" said the professor.

"Exactly."

Groanin nodded and, putting on his jacket, he buttoned it up to cover the hole in his shirt.

"Just as long as no one asks me to follow that spider."

Philippa hugged him happily. "I don't think any of us can run that fast," she said.

CHAPTER 25

SHE WHO ENTANGLES MEN

They followed the road out of Kandahar and into the pitch-black and silent desert.

"That small stone you left near the spot where we buried the carpet should come in handy anytime now," John told Nimrod.

"If you mean," said Nimrod, "as I think you do, John, that we won't find it or the carpet in the dark, then you couldn't be more wrong. It's a beacon stone. It gets hotter, the nearer I get to it. And the hotter it gets, the more it starts to glow."

"Oh. I see. Well, why didn't you say so before?"

They walked on until seeing something very bright on the road ahead, Philippa said, "Is that it?"

Nimrod frowned. "No, that is much too bright for a beacon stone," he said. "That's something altogether larger. Besides, it's off the ground. Not on it."

"Looks military to me," said John. "Most probably a Solar Stik Remote Area Lighting System that's used by the EOD guys. That's explosive ordnance disposal to you."

"I presume you mean the bomb squad," said Groanin.

"Yes, sir."

"Then why didn't you say so?" muttered the butler.

Farther down the road, a British soldier waving a flashlight walked slowly toward them.

" 'Ere, you: Mustapha. You can't go up this pigging road." The soldier spoke first in English, and then in a sort of mangled Pashto that sounded quite unintelligible to Afghan ears. "It's closed."

"What seems to be the trouble, Officer?" said Nimrod politely.

"You speak English, then?" said the British soldier.

"I am English," said Nimrod.

"Where from?"

"London," said Nimrod. "Kensington, to be exact."

"You're a long way from pigging Kensington, mate," said the soldier.

"And these are my friends from New York, Iceland." Nimrod pointed at Groanin. "And Manchester."

"Manchester? Which team do you support?"

"City," said Groanin. "You?"

"Me, too," said the soldier. He grinned and clapped Groanin on the back.

For several minutes, the two Mancunians discussed the state of English football before Nimrod politely cleared his throat and asked again why the road was closed.

" 'Cos there's something big buried in the ground up ahead," explained the soldier. "Most likely a pigging bomb.

We're waiting for one of our lads from the squad to come and have a look at it."

"How big?"

"Pretty big. At least twenty or thirty feet long."

"I think there's been a misunderstanding," said Nimrod. "For which I am sincerely sorry. You see, we buried something by this road earlier on today. A carpet. For safekeeping. It was heavy and we didn't want to carry it all the way into Kandahar. No more did we feel inclined to leave it by the side of the road, in case it was stolen. So, as I say, we buried it. And now we're back to dig it up again. I should have realized how sensitive people are to that sort of thing in this country."

"You'd better speak to my officer," said the soldier. "Captain Sargent."

"Lucky he's not a sergeant," said Groanin.

"That's nothing," said the soldier. "We have a lieutenant colonel whose name is Major. And a brigadier whose name is Sirr, with two *rs*. You've no idea the pigging confusion that's caused when those three are in the room. Which is pretty typical of the whole mission, really. None of us really knows what we're doin' here."

The soldier led the way to his officer, Captain Sargent. The captain was a big, fat man with a very small mustache and a blue beret.

"This man is British, sir," explained the soldier. "From Kensington."

"You don't look very English," observed the captain.

"We're dressed to blend in," said Nimrod.

"He says it's not a bomb that's buried by the side of the road, sir. He says it's a carpet."

"A carpet?" The captain looked aghast. "What kind of Englishman goes around burying a carpet? Haven't you heard? You're supposed to put a carpet on top of the ground. Not underneath it."

"We buried it for safekeeping," said Nimrod.

"A carpet?"

"That's right," said Nimrod patiently. "It was too heavy to carry it into town."

"But not too heavy to carry somewhere else, eh? I don't see you here with a cart or a truck or anything. What are you planning to do, fly it away?"

Nimrod smiled patiently.

"My friends here will dig it up and show you."

"I suppose you'd like that, wouldn't you?" said the captain. "Dig it up and set it off with all of us standing around while you were doing it. You must think we're daft."

"I can assure you, Captain Sargent, that nothing could be further from the truth. But if you are at all concerned, then I suggest you and your men withdraw to a safe distance while we're digging up the carpet. That way the only people who could possibly get hurt if my carpet exploded are us."

"Couldn't do any harm, sir," said the soldier. "I mean, we're planning to blow it up, anyway, when the squad gets here."

Captain Sargent thought for a moment. "Very well," he said. "But no tricks, eh? We'll be watching you people carefully."

When the British soldiers had withdrawn to a safe distance, Nimrod, Groanin, the professor, Axel, and the twins started to dig. And a few minutes later they lifted the rolled-up carpet onto the road and waved at the soldiers.

"Look," said Nimrod. "It's perfectly safe."

The soldiers approached cautiously.

"Just an ordinary carpet," said Nimrod. "Blue, of course. Which some people think is unlucky." He nodded at the captain's beret. "But I wouldn't have thought that was a belief you shared."

"Are you sure you don't have anything rolled up in it?" said the captain.

"What, you mean like Queen Cleopatra?" said Philippa.

Nimrod smiled.

But the captain, who had never read Shakespeare, and didn't know who Cleopatra was, frowned. "Well, maybe, yes."

"Let's unroll the carpet," Nimrod told his companions, "and show the captain here that we don't have one of the world's most desirable and gorgeous women hidden inside it."

"Someone talking about me?"

Everyone looked around to see an astonishingly beautiful woman — perhaps the most beautiful woman any of them had ever seen. She was wearing a golden silk sari, and a variety of Indian bridal jewelery including a tiara, a necklace, and a nose ring that was hooked up to the tiara. She was very tall, and very black, with a spoiled, pouting mouth and an expression that was so haughty and proud, she looked like she'd been born in the most expensive palace in a city that was full of palaces. In her hand, she held a small clutch bag and a diamond-encrusted cell phone.

"I think I'm in love," whispered Axel.

Nimrod groaned. "Hello, Alexandra," he said.

"Trying to sneak out of Kandahar without saying hello, were you? No, don't deny it. Remember who it is you're talking to."

"Not at all."

"And you thought you could be here without me knowing about it." She tapped the middle of her forehead. "In here. With my third eye."

"No, of course not."

"That was stupid of you," she said. "I'm always ahead of you. You should know that by now. I know what you're going to say before you can even think it yourself."

"If you say so, dear," said Nimrod. "Philippa. John. This is your aunt Alexandra. Whom I was telling you about on the flight into Kandahar."

Alexandra stepped toward the twins and gave them a critical, unfriendly look, as if she had been inspecting a couple of tethered goats for a forthcoming barbecue.

"So these are Imelda's twins, are they?"

Philippa thought that Alexandra sounded English, like her uncle.

"You mean Layla," he said patiently. "My sister is called Layla, not Imelda, as you well know."

"I must say, they don't look like twins," said Alexandra. "Nor do they look particularly special. Hardly the stuff of prophecy, are they? I expected something much more impressive. Children who really look like the stuff of myth and legend. These two kids look more like a couple of local beggars. And look at their clothes. They're not much better than rags. What a pair of urchins."

"What do you mean?" asked Philippa.

"Oh, my God," said Alexandra. "You're Americans."

"Something wrong with that?" said John.

"No, sweetie. Not if you like *gum* on the sole of life's *sneakers*." She laughed. "Bad enough that your sister should have married a mundane. But you mean to say he's an American, too?"

"Yes, he is," said Nimrod. "And a very agreeable fellow, to boot."

Alexandra shrieked with laughter. "I'll bet he is."

Hoping to change the subject — or so it seemed to John and Philippa — Nimrod continued with the introductions to Professor Sturloson and then Axel, but these were ignored by Alexandra. She had big, clear-as-a-bell brown eyes only for the twins.

"You poor, poor dears," she said, touching John's face and then Philippa's. "Americans." She shook her head. "Doesn't it drive you mad? Living among such barbarians. The clothes are just rubbish. Even in New York. There's no decent tailoring to be had anywhere. And the food. How can you eat there? Hot dogs. Hamburgers. Milk shakes." She swallowed biliously and pressed her bag to her stomach with a heavily be-ringed hand. "Light my lamp, but it makes me feel sick just to utter these words. Really sick. I think I'm going to throw up."

Nimrod sighed. "Don't be so dramatic."

"Oh, it's not so bad," said John. "If you like hot dogs, and hamburgers, and milk shakes. Which I do."

"Me, too," said Philippa irritably.

"Oh, I can see that, dear," said Alexandra. "Let's face it. You could afford to lose a few pounds." Once again, she touched Philippa's cheek. "And your complexion is — well, it's not exactly flawless, is it? I've seen trays of gloves with better skin than you, honey. A little less grease in your diet might not go amiss, you know. And as for those glasses. Where did you get them? A bottle bank? A submarine?"

"Don't you know?" Philippa's tone was challenging.

"Believe me, little girl," said Alexandra. "I've forgotten more things than you've ever even remembered. And don't for minute doubt that I can foretell the future."

"Oh, yeah?"

"I know that the private is going to sneeze in five seconds, that the stupid captain with the ridiculous mustache is going to scratch his ear and wave away a mosquito. . . ."

The private sneezed and the captain scratched his ear and waved away a mosquito.

"Gesundheit," said John.

"See what I mean?" Alexandra jabbed Philippa on the shoulder. "Don't mess with me, shorty. Or I'll give you the full forecast on the rest of your young, soon-to-be-ending djinn life."

Philippa tutted loudly. "Really," she said, exasperated.

"Get off her case," John told Alexandra.

"And as for you, meathead. You have a fool's face. The world must be in a pretty poor state of repair if you're half of its best hope, sonny. Try closing your mouth once in a while. The way your jaw hangs down. It makes you look like the village idiot."

"I have trouble breathing through my nose, sometimes, that's all," protested John.

"If you are going to save the world, you should first try to look like you can save a couple of cents for your bus fare."

"I can see you've lost none of your talent for diplomacy, Alexandra," said Nimrod.

Alexandra snorted. "You talk to me about talent, looking like that. If you wanted to dress like an Afghan, why did you choose to look like a filthy peasant? Not that you ever had any taste in clothes, Nimrod. Tell me: Are you still wearing those stupid red suits?"

"She certainly doesn't sound like an Eremite," Philippa told her uncle.

"The Eremites." Alexandra laughed. "I gave up on them years ago. What a bunch of losers. These days I just stick to telling the future. Which is not looking good. At least not for you and your dumb brother."

"He's not dumb," insisted Philippa.

"No?" Alexandra looked at John with barely disguised contempt. "Hey. Brainbox. What's the capital of Afghanistan?"

John thought for a moment and then pulled a face. "I dunno."

Alexandra shrugged. "See what I mean? It's Kabul. How

can you be in a country and not know what the capital is? Oh, wait. I know the answer to that one, too. You're an idiot."

"I hate to interrupt this touching family reunion," said Captain Sargent, "but if we could get back to the main business in hand."

"Unless I'm very much mistaken, this *is* the main business in hand," snapped Alexandra. "These two children of the lamp. Eh, Nimrod? Your being here is to do with the Taranushi prophecy, isn't it? After all, this is the time that was surely foretold in that book you were always going on about. When 'a sea of cloud arises from the bowels of the earth and turns the lungs of men to stone, the wheat in the fields to ash, and the rivers to liquid rock.' There's no getting away from any of that, is there?"

She looked at Philippa and flashed a thin, insincere smile.

"Certainly not for you, niece of mine," she said. "The sooner you and your doofus brother here sacrifice yourselves to save the world, the better for the rest of us. My cell phone has been useless since this whole thing began. I don't know why I'm even carrying it. Habit, I guess."

"If you could just unroll the carpet, sir, and let us check that there's nothing concealed inside," insisted the captain.

"If you interrupt me again, Officer Dibble," said Alexandra, "you'll regret you ever left whichever neglected mouse hole of a town you sprang from. And I don't care if you are English." Alexandra gritted her teeth and stamped her stiletto heel angrily. "I won't be interrupted by a mundane. Not ever. Do you hear?"

"No need for unpleasantness, Alexandra dear." Nimrod stood on the edge of the carpet and kicked the rest of it hard — so hard that it unrolled completely. "The captain is merely doing his job."

"We're back to using these old things, are we?" said Alexandra. "Still, in the absence of commercial air travel, it's better than nothing, I suppose. But it'll never beat a whirlwind."

"You see?" Nimrod said to the captain. "There's nothing hidden inside. No weapons. No bombs. No Cleopatra."

"I wonder why you even bother trying to humor *him*," said Alexandra. "After all, he's just a mundane."

"Look, I'm still not satisfied that you people are on the level," said the captain. "If I could see some proper ID from you all."

As he finished speaking, Alexandra's jewel-encrusted cell phone flew through the air and struck him on the head.

"I told you not to interrupt me when I'm speaking," shrieked Alexandra. "Didn't I? Well, didn't I?"

Groanin rolled his eyes. He had seen this kind of bad behavior from Nimrod's wife before. "Now then, missus," he said. "No need for any unpleasantness, is there?"

"I've no reason for not throwing something at you, either, you old baldy," she said. "And count yourself lucky I don't foretell your future as well."

"That's it," said Captain Sargent. "I've had enough of you. Private Parz? Arrest them all."

"Yes, sir. Right you are, sir."

In truth, only the first two words of what the soldier said sounded at all human. The next four words amounted to little more than braying, which was not surprising as in the blink of an eye, the private, the captain, and several other British soldiers in the vicinity were transformed into a small herd of donkeys by Alexandra who was, after all, a powerful djinn, and a cross and angry one at that. All of this was accompanied by a bang, a strong smell of sulfur, and a loud exclamation of surprise from the professor.

"*Gœfa mín, Þeir eru sauðir,*" said the professor. This means "My goodness, the soldiers are all donkeys," in Icelandic.

"*Ótrúlegt,*" exclaimed Axel. "*Það er rifið það.*"

"That's torn it, right enough," said Groanin, who knew a little Icelandic himself. "I say, that's torn it." He looked at John and Philippa and threw up his arms in horror. "The woman's mad. Mad. Always was. Always will be."

The donkey that had been Captain Sargent began to bray in agreement with the butler.

"No wonder she and Nimrod don't live together," added Groanin. "This is why she lives in Afghanistan. Everyone here is mad or angry about something. So she fits right in. Isn't that right, Alexandra?"

Alexandra lowered her head in shame. "Yes," she said quietly. "Yes, it is."

"Alexandra, Alexandra, Alexandra." Nimrod sounded almost weary. "Why must you always get so angry?"

"People like you make me angry." She pointed at Groanin. "And him. Not to mention that stupid soldier." But already she was becoming calmer, as if the exercise of her power had purged something of her irritation and anger, which was always increased by seeing Nimrod again. "Anyway, it's not my fault I have the gift of prophecy. I didn't ask to be like this. It just happened."

Nimrod looked at the twins. "She's not a bad person, really she isn't. It's the gift of prophecy that makes her this way. Impossible to be with. Isn't that right, Alexandra?"

"It's a curse," agreed Alexandra, who seemed to be coming back to her senses. "Right enough. Every night I lie awake and hear the future. And the next day when I tell people what's going to happen, they just don't believe me." She shook her head. "It's a terrible predicament I've lived with for a long time now. This sense of understanding everything and yet being powerless to make anyone act upon that."

She sighed and shook her head. "Look, I'm sorry for being so rude to you both. I didn't mean anything I said. I often speak rashly, without thinking. I was just so pleased to see Nimrod again and yet mad at the same time that he was going away without speaking to me, that I got really angry and said all kinds of nonsense that simply isn't true." She stroked John's hair with affection. "Nonsense about you and Philippa and the dreadful fate that awaits you in the clouds after you have discovered that the price of chocolate is far above rubies. Nonsense about the death of a man in a black mask. About the ship that's inside a ship and a gray tiger. What can that mean? Oh, yes, and some nonsense about poor Axel winning the jackpot in the University of Iceland Lottery. And the shock he experiences when the worm turns. I don't know."

"*Því miður*, I haven't won the lottery," said Axel.

"You see?" said Alexandra. "I told you it was all nonsense, didn't I?" She laughed a hysterical sort of laugh and shrugged.

"Never mind that now," said Nimrod. "What about these soldiers? You can't leave them like this. As donkeys. It's hardly fair, is it?"

"No, I suppose not. But look, before I turn them back into men, you'd better sit down on that carpet and get out of here. Just in case that captain causes any more trouble for you. Believe me, I know what I'm talking about. He's going to cause a lot of problems for a lot of people before he's done in Afghanistan."

Nimrod took Alexandra's hand and, in the moonlight, Philippa saw that it was beautifully tattooed with *mehndi* — intricate henna markings that are considered good luck.

"Why not come with us?" he said.

"No," she said firmly. "We both know that wouldn't be a good idea. It's best I stay here where I can't cause too much trouble." She shrugged. "I mean, who would notice?" She tried a smile. "But thanks. Thanks for asking. And next time, don't leave it so long before you stop by, okay?"

Nimrod nodded and then kissed her hand.

A minute later they were airborne.

"She wasn't always like that," Nimrod said quietly. "Certainly not when I married her. But she had a brother. Who was killed. And the grief of that was so acute that it seemed to bring on her ability to foresee the future. While at the same time it made her so very angry about things. Until that happened she was the most wonderful woman in the world."

"She's very beautiful," said Axel. "I don't think I've ever seen a more beautiful woman."

Philippa smiled bravely and tried to contain her disappointment.

"I agree," said the professor who by now had thrown off his *chadri* and was looking like a man again — albeit a man in a black mask.

"I feel sorry for her," said Philippa.

"Me, too," said John.

Nimrod said nothing. But after a moment or two, Philippa noticed him wipe a tear from his eye. And she stopped feeling sorry for her aunt and started feeling sorry for her uncle.

CHAPTER 26

A SIMPLE PLAN

Past life regression," said Nimrod. "It's a technique that human hypnotists use to recover memories of past lives or incarnations. Of course, they got it from the Upanishads — the philosophical texts of the Hindu religion of ancient India."

He glanced over the edge of the flying carpet at a more modern India, which lay several thousand feet beneath them. It was dawn and Nimrod had been flying all night and because he was feeling tired, Groanin had just fetched him a reviving cup of his excellent tea, which Nimrod had declared was the best cup of tea in the world.

"Only the Indians called it karma from previous lives," said Nimrod. "Now, the Chinese believe that people are prevented from remembering their past lives by the goddess Meng Po, also known as the Lady of Forgetfulness. Anyway, all of them got the idea of PLR, or 'reverse birthing' as it is sometimes called, from us. From the djinn.

"Many years ago, a very holy djinn guru called Patanjali wished to purify himself of all worldly experience. And so he fasted and meditated very hard but it wasn't enough, and he decided that the only way he could really become pure was if everything that had happened to him since being born simply hadn't happened at all."

"Daft so-and-so," muttered Groanin, pouring his master another cup of tea.

"So he set out to go back beyond himself and to travel into the past, through his previous incarnations and, along the way, discovered that what he was really doing was traveling through the memories of all his ancestors."

"You mean in a Jungian sense," said the professor.

"Something like that, yes," agreed Nimrod. "You see, the brain, even the human brain, is very large indeed. It contains approximately one hundred billion neurons and perhaps ten times as many support cells, called glia. Hence, it has enormous overcapacity. Or so it was once thought. In fact, there's a part of all brains — djinn, human, actually all mammals have it — that the djinn call the Well. But instead of water, this is a well that contains thoughts and memories that belonged to our ancestors. And from time to time, our conscious and unconscious mind dips into it for ideas. This Well affects how and what we dream about. The Well makes us who and what we are."

"Utter rubbish," said Groanin, and buttered some toast that he handed to John.

"So the plan is very simple, really," said Nimrod, ignoring his butler. "As soon as we get to Australia we're going to retrace the steps of the explorers Burke and Wills across the continent, to try to find a wild camel descended from Dunbelchin. And —"

"Horrible beasts," muttered Groanin, and returned to the skillet where a large quantity of sausages were frying noisily. He poked the sausages around the skillet and wondered what a sausage made from camel meat might taste like.

"I get it," said John. "Because then we can go inside this camel's memories — its 'Well,' if you like — and find the memories that originally belonged to Dunbelchin."

"Exactly, John," said Nimrod.

Philippa nodded. "And that way we can find out where Genghis Khan is buried," she said. "And when we find out where that is, we can find out what happened to those Hotaniya crystals that were once owned by the Chinese emperor Xuanzong."

"Precisely."

"And when we find *that* out," continued John, "we'll know who's behind what's going on with the earth's volcanoes."

"On the button," said Nimrod. "Simple, really."

"Simple?" Groanin laughed a hollow-sounding laugh. "Very," he said. "I've seen advanced quadratic equations that looked more simple than what you just described. I've peeked inside computers that were children's toys next to that plan, sir. As a matter of common interest, how many wild camels are there in Australia?"

"About a million," said Nimrod.

"A million?" Groanin snorted back another guffaw. "And you think you're going to happen on the one that's descended from this Dunbelchin that was once owned by the sons of Genghis Khan? It'll be like looking for a needle in a haystack."

Nimrod grinned. "It's good to have you back, Groanin," he said fondly.

"Eh?" Groanin frowned. "How's that?" He forked some sausages onto a dinner plate and handed them around.

"I've certainly missed your input," said Nimrod. "Your positive outlook on life in general. Not to mention your tea. And your sausages. These are delicious."

"So's this toast," said John. "And those sausages smell fantastic."

"But you're missing the point," added Nimrod. "It's not *one* camel that's descended from Dunbelchin. Very likely it's tens of thousands of camels. Perhaps more. That's how genetic descent works. For example: You've heard of DNA."

"Of course. I'm not an idiot."

"Well then," continued Nimrod. "Recently, a group of scientists were able to isolate a Y chromosome particular to Genghis Khan. How many men in the world do you think share this same Y chromosome?"

"I dunno," said Groanin. "Half a dozen?"

"Sixteen million. Sixteen million men can claim to be directly descended from Genghis Khan. So you see, it won't be like looking for a needle in a haystack at all. In fact, it's my guess that we won't have to get into the bodies of more than a couple of camels before we find what we're looking for."

Groanin grunted. "I see. Well, either way it's very hot in Australia. Very hot. And very uncomfortable. And I've had more than enough of hot, uncomfortable places." He shook his head. "What were Burke and Hare doing in Australia, anyway?"

"Burke and Hare were grave robbers in early nineteenth-century Edinburgh," explained Philippa. "Burke and *Wills* were thirty years later, in the 1860s. They were two Victorian explorers who set out to walk two thousand miles across the Australian continent. From one coast to another."

"Why?" asked Groanin. "I say, why would anyone want to walk all that way? And in Australia, of all places."

"To find out what was in the middle," said Nimrod. "At the time Australia was largely unknown country."

"Still is," said Axel. "Most of it, anyway. Everyone lives on the coast and hardly anyone in the middle."

"Is that a fact?" said Groanin. "And what happened to them?"

"They died," said Nimrod. "Of thirst and hunger in the desert."

"Yes, that *is* encouraging," grumbled Groanin.

Axel clapped Groanin on the back. "Don't worry, Mr. Groanin," he said. "That's the advantage of a flying carpet. We don't have to walk anywhere."

"Axel is right," said Nimrod. "When we get to Darwin on the north coast of Australia, we shall simply fly directly south toward Melbourne, across the Northern Territory, along the same sort of route as Burke and Wills. And when we see some wild camels, as we surely will, we shall swoop down on them and pick out a few so that we might investigate their minds."

"Now I've heard everything," said Groanin. "Mind reading a camel."

"If you have a better plan, my dear fellow, I'd certainly like to hear it," said Nimrod.

"Well," said Groanin. "It seems to me that we're going about this all wrong. We need to be thinking more like detectives and asking ourselves some basic questions. Always supposing that it's not just a coincidence that all these volcanoes become active at once —"

"Impossible," said Professor Sturloson. "It's never happened before. Not even in prerecorded history."

"Well then," continued Groanin, "we need to ask ourselves who stands to profit from such a thing? And how?"

"You tell me," said Nimrod.

"Another djinn, perhaps," suggested John.

"It disadvantages us as much as it does mankind in general," said Nimrod.

"If not a djinn, then a human being?" said Philippa.

"What kind of human being could do this?" mused Axel.

"Aye, well, I'll admit it's not easy to see who could gain from such a thing," said Groanin. "I'm not a detective, see? But I would think that whoever it was would have to be mad for a start. I mean, you'd have to be mad to look for profit or advantage in this kind of thing. Then I think you'd have to be either rich or powerful, possibly both because to do this requires money and influence."

"Go on," said Nimrod.

Groanin nodded. "All right, sir. There's this. You say that the burial place of Genghis Khan has been lost for almost eight hundred years?"

"That's right."

"Then it stands to reason that whoever found this tomb might have spent many years looking for it. Perhaps all his life. It might be that this bloke's already pretty well known to the world as an enthusiastic collector of all things Genghis so to speak, and that he's wealthy enough to indulge this hobby. Perhaps, he's bought some bits and pieces at an auction: pictures, sculptures, Mongol objets d'art, junk like that. This bloke might even be someone who admires the character of Genghis Khan and all the nasty things that he did. Could even be that he's as daft as Genghis was. I say, this bloke might be as daft as Genghis was. A right megalomaniac who wants to be the most powerful man in the world, and all that imperial malarkey. A nasty evil so-and-so — pardon my French — who has about as little respect for human life as Genghis."

Nimrod frowned. "Groanin, that's brilliant," he said.

"Is it?"

"Yes. It is. Have you been eating fish?"

Groanin smiled a quiet smile. "Thank you, sir."

"Fish always improves Groanin's thinking," explained Nimrod.

"So," said John. "Let's see. We could be looking for a crazy guy who's very rich and powerful, who collects all kinds of weird stuff about Genghis Khan, who doesn't care about anyone except himself, and stands to make money or gain power or both from behaving like a James Bond villain."

"I think you have summed that up very well," said Nimrod. "But until we think of a precise motive, I still think we need to find the camel that will help us locate the grave of the tyrant conqueror who stole the crystals of the Chinese emperor to spike the volcanoes of the world to change the weather for power or money or —" He shook his head. "Or whatever. Something. I don't know what. I'm afraid I start to run out of ideas when I come to an explanation of how you could achieve power and money from doing this."

"Yes," said Philippa. "How could anyone profit by a volcanic winter and the failure of the world's crops and possibly the worst famine in history?" She shook her head. "It doesn't make sense."

Groanin thought for a moment. Being kidnapped — by at least four sets of kidnappers that he could remember — had given him a keener understanding of extortion and ransom, not to mention human nature and the perfidy and callous criminality that some people were capable of. There were, he knew, plenty of decent men and women in the world; but sometimes, it was easy to believe that there were almost as many evil ones. Especially after you'd been treated the way Groanin had been treated.

"No, miss," he said grimly. "It makes a lot of sense if whoever it is plans to hold the world to ransom in some way. Same as a Bond villain. Just like John said. And if so, then very likely he's in it for the same grubby reason as the folk that kidnapped me. *Money.* Money's still the reason most folk do things, good and bad. And probably always will be."

255

CHAPTER 27

THE RING OF FIRE

They flew low over India's Andaman Islands in the Bay of Bengal where Barren Island, one of India's only active volcanoes, was spewing ash and smoke into the atmosphere. But so was Narcondam, which the professor said had been dormant for centuries.

"The word *Narcondam* comes from the Sanskrit *naraka-kundam,*" added the professor. "Which means 'pit of hell.' And you could certainly be forgiven for thinking that's true. But this is as nothing compared with what lies ahead of us. We're about to fly over Indonesia?"

Nimrod nodded.

"Indonesia is part of the Pacific Ring of Fire," added the professor. "Seventy-five percent of the world's active and dormant volcanoes are ranged along the horseshoe-shaped ring. From New Zealand, all the way up to Siberia and Alaska, and then all the way down to Chile. That's about four hundred and fifty volcanoes, about a third of which are in Indonesia, including Kerinci and Dempo, which are massive by anyone's standard."

While the professor held forth to Groanin, Nimrod, and John about Indonesia's volcanoes, Philippa took a moment to chat with Axel:

"How did you get into the volcano business?" she asked him.

"It's hard to get away from them if you live in Iceland," he said. "They're everywhere. A bit like Indonesia. Only colder. Our history has always been closely related to volcanoes. When I was a boy, my family had a weekend hut near a lake and a village called Kirkjubaejarklaustur, which happens to be near the famous Lakagígar system of volcanoes that killed more than a quarter of Iceland's population in 1783. A cloud of poisonous gas drifted as far as south as Prague and Britain, where as many as twenty-three thousand people died from the poisoning. But the resulting Mist Hardships — which is what we called the terrible effect it had on the world's weather, not just our own — resulted in a famine that killed one-sixth of the population of Egypt. Can you imagine that, Philippa? The Mist Hardships may even have caused famine in Japan."

He shrugged.

"With a history like that it's hard to ignore volcanoes. But my family has extra reason to fear them. When I was thirteen years old, my father, a film cameraman, disappeared on a trip up a small and long-dormant volcano called Guðnasteinn that is near the much larger and much more active Eyjafjallajökull glacier. When the search team found his camera, it was still running. But of my father, there was no sign. They played the film back and found nothing. In part, I became a volcanologist in order to try to find an explanation of what happened to him."

"And did you?"

"For a long time, no. His disappearance remained a mystery. I even suspected that perhaps he had staged his own death to get away from me and my mother. But then one day, out of the blue, quite literally, there came an explanation. I said that Guðnasteinn was a long-dormant volcano. It was. For years. Until quite recently, when it erupted."

Axel sighed and shook his head.

"What is it?" asked Philippa.

"It's not a very pleasant thing to say this, little sister. But one day, there was a frightening explosion. Ash blackened the sky and numerous volcanic bombs were thrown up hundreds of feet into the air. Pieces of near-molten rock. One of these fell onto a car on Route I, the main road in Iceland. The driver stopped and when he got out to take a look, he found the remains of the body of a man that had been partly preserved in volcanic ash. Just like at Pompeii. That man was my father, Philippa. He was only identified by his dental records."

"That's a terrible story," said Philippa. "What I mean to say is that it's a really interesting story, but that it's really awful." She shook her head. "No, that's not what I mean, either."

"I know what you mean," said Axel. "It's all right. But that's just the half of it. You see, I was the driver of the car,

Philippa. After all the years of searching and study, suddenly, the volcano decided to give up its secret of what had happened to my father. Just like that. It was as if the volcano had been playing a game with me. I spend years looking for some clue as to what might have happened to him and then, the volcano tells me. The volcano's idea of a joke." He smiled bitterly. "Volcanoes are like that, Philippa. They are capricious. And I think they like surprising us. Just when you think they are asleep, they awake with a bang."

He clapped his hands loudly for effect. And it worked. Philippa jumped.

"Like Vesuvius itself. For eight hundred years the people of Pompeii thought it was just another mountain and then, one day, boom. It goes off and thousands of people are killed."

"Yes, they do seem unpredictable."

"Of course, after the ash from Eyjafjallajökull affected all those planes in and out of Europe, my country made contingency plans for the eruption of Katla. Katla always erupts soon after Eyjafjallajökull. But no one expected anything like this."

"No," agreed Philippa. "This seems much more extraordinary."

"And you, little sister," said Axel. "Do you mind me calling you little sister? It's just that I never had a little sister. And I always wanted one."

Philippa shook her head. "I don't mind," she said.

"How did you feel when you discovered that you are a djinn, little sister?"

Philippa shrugged. "At first," she said, "it all seemed like a bit of an adventure. And while there were plenty of scary things that happened to me and John, it was also a lot of fun. But lately, I've started to feel like it's all a bit too much, you know? That it's a lot of responsibility to have so much incredible power. You've no idea of how that can weigh on you, Axel. You give someone three wishes and then they wish for something horrible and then you have to make that happen. Or turning a person into an animal." She shuddered. "That's really horrible. Sometimes I think if I had a wish myself, I would wish that I wasn't a djinn at all. That I was just an ordinary kid, you know?" She smiled. "I know it sounds weird. Like the poor little rich kid. But my mom, she gave up being a djinn for that exact same reason. And I'm beginning to see why. Because being a djinn is a little like being surrounded by that ring of fire that the professor was talking about. I'm surrounded and there's no way out."

Axel squeezed her hand. "I understand," he said. "Understanding who and what we are is difficult for us all. Especially when we're young. But for someone like you and John it must be really difficult."

"I don't know if he feels the same way," admitted Philippa.

"I imagine he does. You're twins after all."

She nodded. "But there's something else that's preying on my mind. I'm haunted by the idea of something that woman said, back in Kandahar."

"Alexandra, yes." Axel smiled. "I'm afraid I can't remember anything she said. I confess I was rather dazzled by her remarkable beauty."

"I could see that." Philippa nodded. "That's okay. You're only human, right?"

"Just as one day other men are going to be dazzled by you, little sister."

"Do you really think so?"

"I know so. So, what did she say that haunts you?"

Philippa shrugged. "It's strange but all I can remember now is the horrible, unpleasant things she said. It's weird but everything else is a blank. And yet . . ."

"What?"

"I don't know. I feel there's something she said that was important to me and John. But I can't for the life of me say what it was. Weird, isn't it?"

"Have you spoken to him about it?"

"Yes," said Philippa. "He says he stopped listening to her after she called him an idiot."

"Understandable. And Groanin?"

"He says he was too traumatized by that camel spider to remember anything of what she said."

"Can't say that I blame him," said Axel. "They are uniquely horrible."

"Professor Sturloson says that he finds it easier to understand what people are saying in English when he watches their lips, on account of the fact that he's a little deaf."

"That's true," said Axel.

"And because he was wearing that burka thing, with a little cloth grille covering his eyes, he found it hard to keep track of what my aunt was saying. So he doesn't remember what was said, either."

"And your uncle?"

"He says that if I don't mind, he'd rather not talk about it. I think he's upset by seeing his wife again."

"Well, of course. That's to be expected, under the circumstances."

Philippa sighed. "So as you can see. I'm really none the wiser."

"Well, I always say that if you can't remember something, it wasn't worth remembering in the first place," said Axel.

"I hope you're right," said Philippa.

Their first sight of Indonesia was of several columns of ash on the horizon. John said it looked as if a small nuclear war had been fought in the area, and Nimrod was soon obliged to find higher altitude in order to escape the worst of the smoke.

"Now I know what a kipper feels like," said Groanin.

"What's a kipper?" Philippa asked.

"A smoked fish," said Groanin.

"I fear that unless we solve this mystery soon," said Professor Sturloson, "and put an end to all this volcanic activity, we shall be too late."

Nimrod agreed and tried to make more height and speed for the north Australian coast.

A short while later, the professor pointed at the sea beneath them.

"According to my calculations, that is the approximate site of the island of Krakatoa. A volcanic island that exploded in 1883, killing tens of thousands of people. It's said that it was the loudest explosion in history — about thirteen thousand times as powerful as the bomb that destroyed Hiroshima — and was heard three thousand miles away, in Western Australia."

"I'll bet that bang broke a few windows," said John.

"Oh, it did."

"If you don't mind me saying so, sir," said Groanin, "I'm beginning to wonder if any of us is really equal to the enormous task we seem to have set for ourselves. I know that you're a powerful djinn, sir, and that gives us a bit of an advantage, but aren't you worried that this time, we've bitten off more than we can chew?"

"Of course I am," said Nimrod somberly. "Of course. And I have the distinct feeling that by the time this is over, none of us will ever be the same again."

CHAPTER 28

FOOD, GLORIOUS FOOD

I'm cold," said Groanin. "Perishing cold."

"Me, too," agreed the professor.

"It's the altitude and our air speed," said Nimrod. "I think what we all need is a coat. Perhaps, a good, old-fashioned duffle coat. It's cold at night in the desert, too, so now's as good a time as any to have one, I suppose."

"Aye, that's the ticket," agreed Groanin. "A duffle coat. Just like Field Marshal Montgomery used to wear in the western desert during the war."

"I've seen those," said John. "They're really cool."

"I hope not," said Groanin. "It's a warm coat I need, not a cool one."

"Philippa?" said Nimrod. "John? If you could oblige. I'd do it myself but for the fact that I'm flying this carpet."

"Sure," said John, and uttering his focus word, he made a camel-colored duffle coat for Groanin.

"Perfect," said the butler. "For once that's exactly what I need."

"It suits you, Groanin," said Nimrod. "Makes you look like a general. All you need is a beret and a pair of binoculars and you'll be the perfect picture of an army man."

"Well, I was, as you know, an army man, sir," said Groanin proudly. "In the paratroops."

"I don't like that color," said the professor. "Could you make mine red, please?"

"Red?" Groanin was appalled. "What do you want a red one for? These coats are supposed to look military. You wouldn't last five minutes wearing a red duffle coat in the western desert. An enemy sniper would pick you out in no time."

The professor shrugged. "I like red," he said. "Besides, we're not in the military or, for that matter, in the western desert. And I don't think there are any enemy snipers where we're going."

"But red." Groanin shook his head. "Navy blue, perhaps. But not red, Professor, old chap. I say, not red. A red duffle coat isn't quite right, if you see what I mean. It isn't done. Not for a man. Besides, going near camels, it might be wise to have a camel-colored coat. So as not to alarm the beasts."

"What nonsense," said Philippa. "If he wants red, he can have red. What difference does it make if it's red, or any color, so long as it is warm? I shall have a pink one myself. So there."

Uttering her focus word, she made two duffle coats, one in red and then one in pink, while John created three camel-colored coats — one for himself, one for Axel, and one for Nimrod. And soon they were all of them wrapped up warmly against the cold.

They flew all day and made good progress to Darwin,

which is the northernmost city in Australia, and soon were flying low across the desert, keeping a close lookout for camels.

"According to the map, that's the Great Sandy Desert over there, I think," said Nimrod, pointing to the west to where the sun was already going down.

"And what else are you likely to find in a desert but sand, I wonder?" said Groanin. "Calling it a sandy desert is hardly helpful. That's like calling a sea the great watery sea, isn't it?"

"They do have rather a lot of deserts here," said Nimrod. "I expect they were running out of ideas by the time they named that one."

Their route south took them across the Northern Territory. Even when it wasn't desert the land looked as dry as a bone.

"I haven't seen any camels yet," said John. "Not one. I thought you said there were millions of them."

"No, I said there were a million of them," said Nimrod. "That's not quite the same thing in a country as large as this. Besides, it's getting dark and soon it will be hard to see anything, let alone a camel, so I rather think we ought to land and set up camp."

"Couldn't we try to find a decent hotel, sir?" inquired Groanin. "Or even a Holiday Inn?"

"Can't be done," said Nimrod, steering the flying carpet nearer to the ground. "It gets dark very quickly in the outback, which is what Australians call their countryside. Besides, this is a vast country. We might fly two or three hours before we even see a town, let alone a decent hotel. No, we'll land, and set up camp."

"Very good, sir."

They landed by a small billabong, which is Oz for a water hole. This was surrounded by a few gum trees and a seemingly endless supply of sky and stars. The night was full of the noise of exotic-sounding birds, some of which proved to be fruit bats.

While Nimrod used his djinn power to conjure several large tents from the cooling night air, creating an elegant and comfortable encampment that would not have disgraced any modern cross-continental expedition, Groanin and Axel collected wood for a fire, in the conventional way, and the twins walked around the growing camp to see if there was anyone about. They saw no one, but they were not unobserved. Several hundred living things were watching them, and two of them were human.

In a matter of minutes, Groanin had made a fire and was boiling water because, being English, he and Nimrod were unable to function without a cup of freshly brewed tea. Tea was soon followed by dinner and, in honor of Axel and the professor, Nimrod used his powers to make a special Icelandic feast that included caviar, smoked lamb, rye bread, shrimp, and, as a special treat, some special Icelandic dishes including *kæstur hákarl*, *svið*, and *selshreifar*.

Groanin and the twins regarded the *svið* — which is a dish of singed and boiled sheep heads — with something close to horror.

But Axel and the professor were delighted.

"I don't believe it," said Axel. "We're here, in the middle of the Australian outback, and we're eating *svið*."

"You might be," said Philippa. "But I'm not."

"And *kæstur hákarl*," said the professor. "It's been ages since I ate *kæstur hákarl*."

"I'm not surprised," said Groanin. "You'd have to forget a great deal before you could eat that stuff again."

"I don't think I've ever smelled anything as disgusting," said John, his nose wrinkling with distaste. "What is that stuff, anyway?"

"It's a great delicacy in Iceland," insisted the professor, tucking into the feast with relish. "My father used to make it. But I think yours is better, Nimrod."

Even through his mask, they could tell that he was really enjoying the feast.

"Yes," said Groanin, "but what is it?"

"Iceland's answer to fugu," explained Nimrod.

"You mean that poisonous fish the Japanese eat?" said John. "At least, the ones who can afford it."

"Yes," said the professor. "*Kæstur hákarl* is simply putre-fied Greenland shark. Prepared and cooked to remove the high concentration of poisons from the shark flesh. Trimethylamine oxide and uric acid."

"But that's —" John look horrified.

"Yes, John," said Nimrod. "That's exactly what it is."

John shook his head. "I feel sick just smelling that stuff."

Axel grinned. "You don't know what you're missing, lit-tle brother," he said, eating some putrefied shark with, it must be said, some considerable relish that was perhaps increased by the look of repulsion that was displayed on the faces of Groanin and the two Americans.

268

"I'll stick to caviar, if you don't mind," said Groanin.

"I don't know how you can eat that stuff, either," said John. He tore off a piece of bread and stuffed it into his mouth unhappily.

"It's not so bad," said Groanin. "When you get used to it." He shook his head and grinned. "I've eaten some wonderful food being around you, Nimrod, sir. And been to some great restaurants. But I've also had to eat some terrible things. A curry so hot I thought my head would explode. Beer made from human saliva. Rats at that foul restaurant in China. And I'm just glad I'm not going to have to eat anything as disgusting as that dead shark. Not on this trip."

The strong smell of the *kæstur hákarl* did have one useful function in Groanin's opinion: It kept away the many insects that otherwise would have plagued him, but it served only to fascinate Jimmy and Charlie, a couple of aborigines who were hiding nearby in the bush.

"What do you think, mate?" whispered Jimmy.

"Well," said Charlie. "We know they came from the sky. So I reckon that narrows it down a bit. And so does the way they made all sorts of stuff appear from thin air. Like the tents and the lights and the rest of their gear. Which narrows it down even further. I mean, I don't think they're from Oz. At least, not the Oz I know. Then there's the bloke in that black mask and the red coat. You ask me, no bloke goes around wearing a black mask unless he's not a bloke at all, but something else."

"Too true, mate."

"But I reckon the real clincher is the grub they're eating. Because I certainly don't reckon that no white feller could ever eat grub like that. Not when it smells so bad."

"Too true, mate," said Jimmy. "Smells like a dead window cleaner floating in Sydney Harbor."

Charlie grinned. "That's exactly what it smells like, mate. Exactly. Couldn't have put it better meself."

"But they don't look like bunyips, neither." (A bunyip is an Australian evil spirit that lives beside water.)

"That's true. Not that I've ever seen a bunyip, mind." Charlie thought for a moment. "You know what? I reckon they must be sky gods."

"Could be right. But do you think they're friendly?"

"The way I look at it is this, Jimmy. If they are sky gods, they probably know we're here already. Very likely they know we're on walkabout and they're just waiting for us to come and introduce ourselves." Charlie thought for a moment. "But here's a clincher. Instead of speaking to them in English, try speaking in Laragiya. You're about the only person I know who still speaks Laragiya, Jimmy. And if they really are sky gods, they'll be able to answer you."

"Good thinking, mate."

"Hang on. What if they can't speak Laragiya?"

"Then maybe they'll kill us."

"I don't like the sound of that."

"Me, neither."

"Maybe we should call the cops, back in Alice Springs."

"With what? In case you've forgotten my cell phone isn't working. Anyway, do you think the cops'd believe us?"

"Nah. Probably not. Here, maybe we should take these sky gods a gift?"

"Good idea."

"Like what, mate?"

"Some better food, of course. Fresh food. That stuff they're eating is just rotten."

A few minutes later, the two near-naked aborigines, painted with white dots, and carrying spears and a gift of fresh food, walked into camp.

At first Philippa and Groanin, and John to some extent, were afraid of them, but Nimrod assured them that there was nothing to fear as aborigines were peace loving and friendly and much more sinned against than sinning. He stood up politely and welcomed them into the camp.

"They don't look friendly, dressed like that," said Groanin. "Or rather not dressed like that. They're wearing war paint, aren't they?"

"That's not war paint," said Nimrod. "It's just decoration."

Jimmy hailed Nimrod and addressed him in Laragiya.

Nimrod spoke back to him in Pama-Nyungan, which is a bit like Laragiya, and it was a while before he was able to identify the precise dialect that Jimmy was speaking; but as soon as he did, and had spoken a few words, Jimmy appeared satisfied and started speaking English.

"I reckon you blokes are all right," said Jimmy. "I just wanted to see if you were the real McCoy or not. And I reckon you are what you seem to be. Which is pretty impressive."

"We're not gods, if that's what you were thinking," said Nimrod.

"Go on," said Jimmy. "I believe you, boss." But of course he didn't. "Well, what brings you out here to the middle of nowhere, mate?"

"We're looking for some wild camels," said John.

"Camels?" said Charlie. "There's none around here. Not for a long while. We ate the last of them a few months ago."

"'S'right," agreed Jimmy. "You need to go farther west, mate. I heard of a big herd making a nuisance of itself over at the town of Docker River. That's five hundred miles west of Alice Springs."

"Is that a big town?" asked Philippa.

"Nah. Blink and you'd miss it. Not that you would miss it, if you'd ever been there. A few houses on a Monopoly board. That's the kind of town we're talking about."

"Could you show us where it is, perhaps?" asked Nimrod.

Jimmy pointed at the flying carpet. "You mean fly there, on that floating rug of yours?"

Nimrod nodded. "I can't think of a quicker way to get there," he said. "Can you?"

"Maybe not."

"Perhaps you might like something to eat?" said Nimrod. "While you were thinking about it?" He pointed at the *kæstur hákarl.*

Jimmy's nose wrinkled with disgust. "No offense, mate, but whatever is in your pot smells like a dead dingo that's been eating a dead koala bear. I wouldn't eat whatever that is if you paid me."

"Yeah," agreed Charlie. "With stomachs like yours, you folks can't be human. That's what we reckon, anyway. Which is why we brought you some real, good, fresh tucker." He opened a broad leaf to reveal a handful of large witchetty grubs. Each of them about the size of a man's little finger, these were still alive and as such considered to be a special delicacy among all aboriginal peoples. "There you go. One each."

Handing them around, Jimmy said, "Dug 'em especially for you. Just a few minutes ago."

Groanin and Philippa stared at the wriggling grubs with horror. So did Axel. Only John, who had once eaten locusts, was not perturbed at the idea of eating "bush tucker"; after eating locusts, witchetty grubs don't look so bad.

"Well, that's very hospitable," said Nimrod and, without a moment's hesitation, he popped one into his mouth, chewed it several times, and then swallowed. "Delicious," he said.

John was next and with only a little hesitation, he ate one, too.

"Come on, you lot," murmured Nimrod. "They'll be offended if we don't all eat one. And it looks like we're going to need them to find this herd of camels they were talking about."

"In the spirit of scientific inquiry," said the professor, and collecting the smallest grub from off the leaf, he pushed it through one of the holes in his mask and into his mouth. He chewed for a moment and then said, "A bit like a prawn, I suppose. Not bad."

"Have another?" suggested Charlie.

"Er, no thanks."

Quelling his own instinctive disgust, Axel quickly followed the professor's example and then it was only Philippa and Groanin who had yet to eat one of the grubs.

"Come on, sis," said John. "If I can do it, then you can do it, surely."

Philippa nodded, for this made perfect sense to her and always had. They were twins after all and if her brother could eat a live witchetty grub without throwing up, then so could she. She picked one up and trying to ignore the movement of the grub in her fingers, she closed her eyes, steeled herself, and then put the grub in her mouth.

That left Groanin, lips sealed, eyes closed, and shaking his head, resolutely opposed to putting anything in his mouth that was still moving.

"Look here, Groanin," said Nimrod. "You wouldn't want to hurt their feelings, would you?"

"What about my feelings? Me, with my digestion? If these lads knew anything about *my* feelings, they'd be a lot more circumspect about asking *me* to eat something objectionable that, to my eyes, belongs under a stone. Besides, sir. That white worm wouldn't be in my stomach for very long, if at all, before it was coming back up again and then where would we be? Just think. How much more hurt would their feelings be if I threw up on their toes?"

"You make a fair point, Groanin," agreed Nimrod. "I suppose I'd better help you out with this one. For the sake of diplomatic relations, you understand. We certainly wouldn't want you being ill, now would we?"

Groanin smiled at his master's kindness. He thought that Nimrod meant that he would eat the last witchetty grub himself, to save Groanin from having to do it. At least he did until he felt some unseen power taking hold of his hand

and place it on the leaf, and then making him collect the witchetty grub and bring it toward his mouth, which seemed to be opening of its own volition.

"No," said Groanin. "You can't make me eat it, Nimrod."

Except that Nimrod *could* make him eat the witchetty grub, and did; and before another minute had elapsed, Groanin found himself placing the large, writhing larva squarely onto his tongue and then closing his mouth, where it remained for several seconds, shifting around like an insect in a tiny cream-colored sleeping bag — which is what it was, after all — and then biting into it so that his mouth was filled with what felt and tasted like the yolk of a runny, boiled egg, and then swallowing the entire contents of his mouth with one loud and quite involuntary gulp that was also half whimper.

To his own surprise, Groanin did not even so much as gag, and gradually, as he felt himself released from Nimrod's powerful control, he felt able to relax and even to detach his mind from the thought of what he had just swallowed. It was perhaps the first time the fastidious English butler had eaten anything quite so spectacularly unusual with quite such little effect.

"There," said Nimrod. "Now our two guests are satisfied. And you, my dear fellow, you're not going to throw up."

The two aborigines grinned happily, pleased that their thoughtful gift had been received so well by such illustrious visitors from the songlines in the sky.

"I don't know why I stay with you, Nimrod," said Groanin. "Really, I don't." He shrugged. "Then again, as I discovered recently, the alternative might be so much worse."

CHAPTER 29

DEEP THOUGHT

Early the next morning, Nimrod, Groanin, the twins, Axel, the professor, and their two aboriginal guides, Jimmy and Charlie, flew directly west, on the large blue carpet. Against the red ocher of the dry ground, the sky appeared to be a bright shade of azure and the flying carpet an even brighter blue. But nothing could compete for brightness with the smiles of the two aborigines.

"When we get back to Sydney, this is going straight onto my next painting, mate," Jimmy told Charlie.

"Too right. Flyabout sure beats walkabout, doesn't it?"

Several hours later, and as many hundred miles west of Alice Springs, Jimmy checked the horizon and the position of the sun, and told Nimrod to fly a bit lower and farther south as they were now nearing the little town of Docker River.

"Let's hope we miss the storm," he said.

"What storm?" said John.

Jimmy pointed at the northwestern horizon. "Look," he said. "Over there."

To everyone else but Charlie, the horizon looked much the same as before but Jimmy was adamant. "Lot of dark cloud coming our way," he said.

And gradually, as they looked, the rest of them did see something, as if someone had drawn a very faint line with a pencil between the sky and the land.

"It must be all those volcanoes along the Pacific Ring of Fire," said the professor. "There's probably so much ash in the atmosphere that it's filtering out the sun and cooling the air. When that happens there's likely to be an almighty thunderstorm around here."

Nimrod shook his head. "Flying carpets don't perform at all well in thunderstorms," he said. "We'd better hope we can be away from here before those clouds arrive."

"Amen to that," said Charlie. "Could be bad with the camels, too, if it rains."

"How's that?" asked Philippa.

"Camels are a real nuisance around these parts," explained Charlie. "Most people think that they don't need water. Of course they *do*. They just make it last longer than other animals. Water's pretty scarce out here and they go berserk if there isn't any. And even more berserk when there is, smashing down fences and cattle stations and generally causing damage, so the local folk just hate them. A thirsty camel is one of the most dangerous animals in Australia."

Jimmy sniffed the air and said, "We're getting closer now. I can smell 'em. The camels."

"I can't smell anything," said Groanin.

"You will," promised Jimmy. "You will."

Half an hour later, he pointed at a large group of braying dromedaries that was grouped around a very small billabong. The camels looked altogether scrawnier and meaner than their domesticated cousins in Afghanistan. In their haste to get near the dwindling supply of local water, they had knocked over the few acacia and bloodwood trees that were shading the water hole.

"There are thousands of them," said John. "Not nearly enough for that little bit of water. They've more or less drunk it dry."

"That's why some of the bulls are fighting," said Charlie. "Look."

A pair of bull camels seemed to be wrestling. One camel's neck was wrapped around the other's and they were each of them biting ears, lips, noses, and faces — anything they could get hold of with their large yellow teeth.

John pointed at another pair of male camels who, foaming at the mouth, were locked in a desperate struggle on the ground, with blood pouring from their wounds.

"Kind of vicious, aren't they?" said John.

"You bet." Charlie grinned. "Reckon I'd rather get bit by a croc than a camel."

Philippa put her hands over ears. "And noisy, too."

Nimrod steered the carpet a safe distance away from the herd of camels and then landed. But almost immediately some of the camels started to run toward them.

"They're trying to drive you off from what's left of the water," explained Jimmy. "We better get out of here fast, or risk being trampled down like them trees."

Nimrod had little choice but to take off and he spent the next few minutes landing and then taking off again as the camels persisted in trying to run them off.

Hovering over the heads of the loudly braying camels, he wondered how to proceed.

"Maybe you should just land a bit farther away," suggested Groanin.

"Easier said than done, Groanin," said Nimrod. "By my reckoning, there are almost ten thousand camels over an area of two or three square miles."

Spooked by the carpet flying overhead, some of the camels ran one way and then the other, kicking up a large amount of dust that included quite a lot of dried camel dung.

"They don't half stink," said Groanin, holding his nose. "You were right, Jimmy."

"I reckon a herd of camels is about the smelliest thing this side of that stuff you blokes were eating last night," said Charlie.

"The *kæstur hákarl*?" said the professor. "It's an acquired taste, right enough. What do you say, Nimrod? You seem to like it all right."

Nimrod wasn't listening.

"If I land down there and leave the flying carpet," he said, "so that I can go inside the mind of one of those beasts, there will be no one to fly us out of trouble if the rest stampede."

"There's only one possible solution to that," said John. "I think me or Phil will have to go."

"Why not both?" said Philippa. "With two of us mind

reading the camels it should take half the time it would take with just one person doing it. We can leave our bodies here on the carpet and then float down. That way there's no need even to land."

"Good idea," said Nimrod. "All right. It's a plan. You two will go down there and do it. And I'll keep hovering over the herd like this. To keep an eye on things. But here's the thing: To search for the Well of ancestor memory in a camel's mind, you will have to delve deep into the beast's subconscious."

"And where will we find that?" asked John.

"Well, most of anyone's mind is subconscious," said Nimrod. "As much as ninety-five percent. With only five to ten percent being devoted to what you might call taking care of business."

"Yes, but where is it?" persisted John. "I mean, where inside the camel's head?"

"Well, that's a little hard to explain," said Nimrod. "It's not like the subconscious mind has an exact location, like front or back, or next to an ear. It's sort of beneath your conscious mind's awareness, if you like. You'd best search for the subconscious by looking for deep thoughts and emotions the animal has about its mother and father, and perhaps also its grandparents. These thoughts and emotions are probably in the same place you would keep them in your own mind. For example, if you were to start thinking about Christmas with your family, five or ten years ago, that would probably lead you nicely to the top of your own Well of ancestor memory. And then, you just dive in."

"Think of Mom and Dad," said John. "Right. I can see how that might work."

"But beware," added Nimrod. "You'll be very much on your own, I'm afraid. Because you'll be just spirit when you leave your own bodies, you'll be invisible to us on this carpet and I won't have any idea which camels you choose to be inside. Got that?"

The twins nodded.

"And remember that while you are in the camel's unconscious mind, you won't actually have control of the camel's conscious mind. So the camel will still be free to do anything it wants: run away, have a fight, you name it. And of course while you're inside the camel's unconscious mind, you'll have no sense of what's happening in the outside world. No sight, no sense of smell, no hearing. In other words, it's possible that when you leave the camel's body it's probable that you will be in a different spot from the place where you went in. So, this is not without risk. If you get lost, I don't have to tell you what can befall a djinn who can't get back to his or her body. If that happens, try to stay put and we'll come and find you, all right?"

The twins nodded and lay down to go into a light trance.

"Good luck," John told Philippa.

"You too," she said.

"Whisper in my ear as you leave your bodies," said Nimrod. "Just so that I'll know you've gone."

Several minutes passed, without result.

"Whenever you're ready," said Nimrod.

"I'm finding it difficult to get into a trance," said John.

"Me, too."

"I'll take us a bit higher," said Nimrod, and lifted the carpet farther up in the air where the noise and stink of the camels were less obtrusive. "There. How's that?"

Philippa sat up and shook her head. "Nope. It's still not working. It's like there's something preying on my mind. But I don't know what."

Of course, what she'd forgotten was Alexandra's prediction; but then no one ever remembered Alexandra's predictions, and if they did, then they never took them seriously. But it wasn't just her aunt's ominous, terrible prediction she had forgotten, but also what she had learned in the Rakshasas Library.

It was the same for John.

"And Phil's affecting me," he said, mistaking his own mental turmoil for hers, which is common enough between twins.

"If I had my *yirdaki* with me," said Jimmy, "I might help you two blokes."

"What's a *yirdaki*?" asked John.

"White fellers call it a didgeridoo," explained Jimmy. "It's a length of hollow, cylindrical wood, about ten feet long. You blow in it and you get a great drone sound. Perfect for getting into a trance."

No sooner had he explained it than John had made one with djinn power — a polished wooden tube, about the size of a largish organ pipe. He'd even thought to add a few aboriginal-style decorations.

Jimmy blew into it experimentally and a deep, almost electronic sound emanated from the opposite end.

"That's a beaut," said Jimmy. "Nice one, John."

"I saw one on TV," said John. "And made one just the same as that."

Jimmy got up onto his knees to get a better grip on the *yirdaki*, put his mouth to the beeswax mouthpiece, and when he was satisfied he had a really airtight seal, he started to blow. Breathing through his nose while at the same time expelling air from his mouth, he produced a continuous, steady, and vibrating tone that was an aural kaleidoscope of low-frequency sound.

The noise seemed modern and primitive at the same time, and uniquely Australian.

For John, the *yirdaki* seemed to illustrate what was going on inside his own head, like hearing the passage of one enduring thought as it made its way 'round and 'round his own mind.

For Philippa, it was like going to a place deep in her thoughts she had never before been; at the same time, it was like joining up with Jimmy's breath. She took a deep breath of her own and closed her eyes.

And it wasn't long before Jimmy's playing began to produce the desired effect: Groanin fell soundly asleep.

CHAPTER 30

IN SEARCH OF THE LOST TIME OF A CAMEL

Philippa had liftoff almost immediately once she gave herself up to the soothing sound of Jimmy blowing on the *yirdaki*. She floated out of her body and across the carpet to where Nimrod sat cross-legged and keeping them all airborne, and whispered in his ear. Then she slipped silently over the silky edge of the carpet and allowed her spirit to sink down toward the herd of camels which, thankfully, she was unable to smell now, not having a nose.

Meanwhile, John floated over his own body and seemed almost to rest on the sound coming from the *yirdaki*. He could not hear it that well, but he could feel it and the ancient vibrations that were contained in Jimmy's breath. As soon as he had his bearings he swooped, wraithlike, beside Nimrod, whispered in his uncle's ear, and then sank toward the ground.

Neither twin was without fear. A large herd of camels is an intimidating sight, especially when it is cranky with thirst, and the twins were wise to be wary. And while there was no chance of John or Philippa incurring any physical injury, they were both mindful of what their uncle had said about getting lost among the several thousand animals. But more than that, they were acutely conscious of the real danger that the world was in and the fearful consequences to the planet's climate that might result from their failure to find what they were looking for.

Sixth-sensing something unusual in their loud and malodorous midst, the herd of camels belched and brayed and shifted around nervously, moving one way and then the other as if they expected to be attacked by a herd of wild dingoes. Others bit, shoved, kicked, or simply spat at their neighbors as they tried to hold the ground nearer the billabong. It was like a New York subway station at rush hour.

Just above the hump of a tall female dromedary, Philippa paused for a moment before taking possession of the beast and braced herself for the shock of being in a camel's shape instead of a humanoid one. That was the thing about animal possession: The first few seconds were always a tremendous affront to anyone who was used to having hands and legs, not to mention being clean and free of parasites.

John hesitated about which camel to pick before selecting to possess one that at least bore a resemblance to the picture of Dunbelchin he had seen in Mr. Bilharzia's home back in Kandahar: a camel a bit whiter-looking than some of the others and therefore perhaps more likely to be one of Dunbelchin's descendants with hidden knowledge of the whereabouts of the burial place of Genghis Khan.

These two camels growled irritably and trotted a few dozen yards in opposite directions as they felt themselves taken over by John and Philippa.

For a moment, John took control of the camel's conscious mind and found himself suddenly obsessed with thoughts of water, plum bush, quandong, curly-pod wattle, native apricot, and bean tree, which, as any fool knows, are the principal elements in the Australian feral camel's diet. He winced with pain and bellowed loudly as he felt another camel bite his hindquarters and, looking quickly around, he found himself face-to-face with a much larger bull camel that was already frothing angrily at the mouth and spitting at him in a most unpleasant way.

To avoid a fight, John gave yet more ground and tried to find himself a spot that might allow the camel carrying his spirit to remain quiet and unmolested while he raked through the deepest drawers in the animal's subconscious. Seeing a large gum tree, he galloped over and parked himself in the small amount of shade that was available and, hoping to settle the animal even further, he began to eat the leaves — not of the gum tree, which are toxic to ruminants like a camel — but of a wattle bush. Much to John's surprise he found himself enjoying the flowers of the wattle most of all; he'd never before eaten a flower, but this one was delicious and it was all he could do to tear himself away and leave

the camel in control of its own conscious mind and its appetite while he went walkabout inside the beast's memory.

It was, thought Philippa, a lot less complicated being a
camel than being a djinn with all that responsibility of power
and wishes and saving the world. Two toes per foot was so
much simpler than having five. Everything was. A lot of a
camel's life was just foraging for food and roaming around
looking for the next water hole. And there was, of course, no
shame but only comfort in having the hump, knowing it was
there with enough stores of fat to trap the heat-minimizing
insulation that made life in such hot climates at all possible.
She gave herself up to it, just as she had done before, for
Philippa had a few vivid memories of being a camel herself.
Not long after discovering that she and John were djinn,
they had visited Cairo with Nimrod and Mr. Rakshasas, and,
at a little perfume shop near Giza, they had been introduced
to a Mr. Huamai who, as well as being a great perfumer, was
also the proprietor of a business renting camels to tourists
who wished to see the pyramids from the relative comfort of
a saddle instead of on foot. Mr. Huamai's wonderful perfume had been a useful antidote to the strong smell that
adhered to the twins following their first experience of
being an animal and a strong-smelling animal at that. But
she particularly remembered how her initial disgust of being
a camel had been quickly replaced by a feeling of enjoyment,
and, for a while, a camel had seemed like the most natural
thing to be in the world, even with a large, sweaty tourist
complaining on her back.

Philippa had really taken to the idea of being a camel, and Nimrod said he was pleased because camels were of great historical importance to the Marid, which was the tribe of djinn to which she belonged. And she wondered if there was more to that apparently innocent experience than, at the time, she had supposed. Was there some extra purpose behind the Marid affinity with camels that even Nimrod had not realized? Was that visit to Mr. Huamai an important preparation for what was happening now? Perhaps. But only time would tell. And there was little enough of that now. She was wasting precious minutes, surely. Except to say that this little moment of reverie had brought her closer to her own deep subconscious, which seemed to overlap the camel's, and swiftly, she set about plunging herself into the Well of ancestor memory that seemed more like the camel's than her own.

Meanwhile, John felt very strange. Indeed, it was the strangest feeling John had ever had. The memories he was experiencing — of his life as a calf, of his camel mother, of her untimely death at the hands of an Australian farmer (she'd been shot as part of a camel cull) — these felt like his own memories; of course, John knew they weren't his memories, not really, but they were no less painful for all of that.

Whatever kind of mammal you are, losing your mother is the worst thing that can ever happen to you.

These strong emotions now gave way to something more broadly ungulate in character, which is to say that he now encountered feelings and things and ideas that were about camels in general rather than one camel in particular. Among camels as a species there were habits, customs, even myths, and artifacts, which meant that there was a lot more to being a camel: more than just life as an even-toed ungulate, bearing a distinctive fatty deposit known as a hump on your back. John could now see that to be a camel was to be a thing of beauty, as the Arab word for camel, جمل (pronounced ğml, which means "beauty"), surely recognized.

Perceiving that he now stood within the animal's subconscious and at the very edge of the Well of ancestor memory, John gave himself up to it and found that he was now remembering things long forgotten: of building roads in the Australian outback; of serving with the British Army in Egypt, and before that on India's North-West Frontier; of being part of a Persian baggage train; of fighting as part of a Roman army force in the eastern Roman Empire; of the Egyptian Ptolemies; and even the time of Philip of Macedon.

He had gone too far back. Surely, he thought, the Romans were from a time long before the Mongols. It was the Mongol Empire he was looking for, not the Roman Empire and certainly not the Ptolemies. And thinking that Persia was at least geographically closer to Mongolia, he returned to those memories and, carrying them into the future like a camel laden with a merchant's silks and spices, he tried to find his way through a cornucopia of history to those of his ungulate ancestors that had lived in the early thirteenth century.

Suddenly, John encountered a vivid memory whose details he recognized: ancient Kandahar. There was no mistaking the plain on which it stood, the ancient citadel, that distant mountain range, and there was a man, who strikingly resembled Mr. Bilharzia, buying him from a thief, except that he wasn't a him anymore, but a her — a female camel. Then John felt the saddle he/she was wearing and the beautiful bridle with which he/she was adorned. Yes. There could be no mistaking that bridle. Surely, he/she, whatever he was, had found Dunbelchin at last.

But the pain of this discovery was intense, for was there not a great grief here? The grief of the loss of a child. This was an easy memory to track down and find. It was like a piece of jagged bone sticking out of a broken leg. . . .

How could anyone do such an evil thing to something so young and defenseless and innocent? The little gray-white baby camel with spindle-thin, unsteady legs that was taken away from me when it was just an hour old; when it had just stood up; before it had even been suckled. Those soft brown eyes. The most beautiful baby I had ever seen.

To bury it alive was beyond all monstrosity. I can still hear the calf's plaintive, high-pitched cries. These were almost human, which ought to have made it harder for the cruel tribesmen to take the calf from me. But the Mongols, who were not known for their soft hearts, took it, anyway, and tied its legs and placed it into the mausoleum with all of the khan's treasures, and then sealed it up while I, the calf's mother, tethered to a post, was forced to look on in appalled horror. How long did they leave me there bellowing in distress after the grave was sealed? It seemed like several days. And long enough to know that when they took me away, the calf was still alive and crying for its mother. Long enough for me to remember that spot for all eternity. Yes, I could have found that grave from the other side of the world, with my eyes closed. Just by smell. It was etched indelibly on my memory as if by very strong acid.

How could anyone ever have forgotten this terrible site where so many others — not just my own calf — had died, thousands of them, just to keep the secret of the great Lord Temujin's grave?

I pictured the remote spot carefully in my mind's eye: Burkhan Khaldun, also called Khan Khentii, a small and insignificant but carefully chosen mountain about 124 miles from the modern capital city of Mongolia, Ulan Bator, a spot so close to Genghis Khan's birthplace at Deluun Boldog; a trackless waste close to the confluence of three tributaries of the River Kherlen and west of the River Onon; north of the Blue Lake and the ancient Mongol capital of Anurag; near a shoulder of reddish rock, a high plateau that was a forbidding place of mist and permafrost.

Only when he was quite certain that he knew exactly where the burial place of Genghis Khan was to be found did John withdraw from the eight-hundred-year-old memories of Dunbelchin, and make his way up through the Well of ancestor memory and back into the conscious mind of the Australian feral camel.

But once there, possessed of the wild camel's own sight, sound, and smell, John was in for an unpleasant surprise.

CHAPTER 31

DON'T LOOK NOW

It was dark and it was raining very heavily. Water bounced off John's furry head and ran down his hill-shaped body; his two-toed feet were already several inches deep in an ever-widening puddle. A flash of white light as bright as a rolling artillery bombardment illuminated the black sky and a twisting fork of electricity split a gum tree in two; this was quickly followed by a clap of thunder as loud as Krakatoa — or so it seemed to John — and the next thing he knew the whole herd of camels, himself included, was fleeing the burning tree in terror. John ran, too, because when he tried to stop, other camels ran into him and since there were almost ten thousand of them, he knew that not to run was to risk being trampled to death. After a few hundred yards, the stampede ended but this was immediately followed by another loud thunderclap that set them all running again. This happened at least a dozen times in an hour before finally the storm passed overhead where, to John's acute discomfort, there was now no sign of Nimrod and the flying carpet. Unlike the rest of the camels that were now gulping up as much water as they could — gallons of it — John was the only camel staring up at the already brightening sky. He brayed loudly in the hope that he would attract some attention, but there were only a few straggler clouds heading southeast in pursuit of the rest of the storm.

"This is not good," he told himself. "This is not good at all."

He considered his choices. Either he could remain inside the camel for a while longer, which seemed like the sensible option. Or he could leave the camel's body, float above the herd a bit to see if he could spot the others, but that meant he would have to risk getting lost. The right thing to do, he knew, was to remain in the camel's body and wait for Nimrod to come back and find him. Probably, they had been forced to seek shelter from the storm.

And yet he also had to consider the possibility that they might have been hit by lightning, like the gum tree. Which wouldn't have been good. And John began to patrol the area just in case Nimrod and the others were lying stunned on the ground, or more accurately, in a pool of water, for the ground was now entirely waterlogged. None of his surroundings seemed at all familiar. The billabong was gone. Now everything was one huge water hole.

Half an hour passed in this way, before finally, John spied a small object approaching on the horizon and, realizing with a loud belch of relief that it was them, he flew out of the camel and headed quickly their way.

A minute or two later, John was back in his own body,

which was very cold and wet, but otherwise he was quite unharmed. Sitting up, he spat several times over the side of the damp carpet, to try to rid himself of the horrible taste of the wattle flowers. Groanin handed him a packet of mints, and a small bottle of eau de cologne. But of Philippa, there was still no sign. Her body lay motionless, exactly where she had left it, beside his own, awaiting the return of her own life's spirit. Moby, the duck she had befriended, was waiting for her, too. He was the only one on the carpet who looked not to have minded the heavy rain. Not a bit.

"When the storm broke," explained Nimrod, "the camels ran every which way. We had no idea of which ones to follow. So we flew a bit higher, above the rain clouds, and waited for it to pass."

"What do we do now?" John looked anxiously at his sister.

"Keep looking for her," said Nimrod. "There's nothing else we can do for now. I expect she'll turn up, before long. But look here, how did you get on? Were you successful? Did you find what we're looking for? The location of the secret tomb of Genghis Khan?"

"Yes," said John. "I found it."

"Excellent. Well done, my boy. Where is it?"

John told him the geographical details as best he was able. "But I'll certainly recognize the place when we see it."

"As soon as Phil shows up," said Nimrod, "we'll head to Mongolia. To see what clues we find inside the tomb. You'll like Mongolia. I always did."

But after another hour, Philippa still hadn't returned and Nimrod was worried.

"If she was down there," he said, pointing at the herd of camels, "surely she would have seen us by now." He winced as he thought of something.

"What?" asked Groanin.

"Nothing," said Nimrod.

"What?" repeated Groanin, only more loudly this time. "Spit it out, man."

Nimrod glanced at his niece's silent body.

"Well, it's just that if she left the body of any camel she'd previously taken possession of when the air was full of lightning, the electricity in the air might have stunned her spirit. Left her disorientated and floating around with no sense of where and what she is. In those circumstances, she might never find her way back to her body."

"What can we do?" asked John.

"I'd go looking for her myself," said Nimrod, "but I daren't land this thing anywhere near those camels. Not with them being so nervous. Also it's important that I stay aloft, where she can see us, just in case she does show up."

"Then I'll go myself," said John, pulling on his duffle coat.

"Can you go?" asked Nimrod. "Look at you. You're freezing, John."

John felt within himself and shook his head. "Yes, you're right," he said. "My body's much too cold for my djinn power to work."

"I'm feeling rather cold and wet, as well," admitted Nimrod. "It's all I can do to keep this thing in the air." He shook his head. "Besides. Even if your powers had returned, I couldn't let you go. Not now that you know the location of the tomb, John. I can't risk you both getting lost. What's at stake here is far too important for you to go and look for her. Do you understand?"

John nodded grimly. "Yes, sir," he said.

There was a long silence.

"This is important, right?" said Charlie. "For the future of the world and our weather and all that?"

"I can't overstate just how important this is," Nimrod said gravely. "If we don't put a swift end to all these volcanic eruptions, the world is facing catastrophe." He paused. "And I suspect my nephew and niece are the only ones who can put a stop to all of this."

John shrugged and, thinking his uncle was talking about his most recent adventure inside the body of a camel, he shrugged and said, "It was nothing."

Charlie thought for a moment.

"Then I'll do it," he said brightly. "I'll go and look for your niece."

"You?" said Nimrod. "How?"

"You djinns aren't the only ones who can get out of your heads," said Charlie. "We have been doing it, too, since way back when. Believe me, I know what I'm doing. I've tracked more spirits than I care to remember." He pointed at the ground that lay beneath the flying carpet. "Down there is a whole labyrinth of invisible songlines and pathways. But I reckon I can find her all right."

"He's right," said Jimmy. "If anyone can track your niece in the spirit world, mate, it's Charlie here."

"You can track spirits?" Nimrod sounded surprised. "How?"

"Charlie can track anything," said Jimmy. "In this world or the next."

"Then, please," said Nimrod. "I'd be very grateful if you would go and look for my niece, Charlie."

"Me, too," admitted Groanin. "I say, me, too."

"Is there anything I can do to help?" asked Nimrod.

Charlie shook his head.

"Reckon all I need is a bit of a tune on Jimmy's *yirdaki*, to put me in the proper mood, like," he said. "That and a mask to stick on my mug, to disguise my true identity from the spirits. Just in case they get a bit annoyed with something I do and come looking for me afterward."

"We always wear a mask when we visit the spirit world," explained Jimmy. "They can get a bit narked when you turn up unannounced, like." He picked up the *yirdaki* and gave it a couple of experimental blows, like a man tuning up for a concert.

"What kind of mask?" asked Nimrod.

"I dunno," said Charlie. "Black is best. But it doesn't have to be too fancy like the ones we sell the tourists. Those masks are just for making money. So the more elaborate they are, the better. Nah, plain black is good enough, I reckon."

A smallish figure wearing a red duffle coat walked toward him. It was Professor Sturloson.

"Will this do?" he said, and handed Charlie his own black face mask.

Charlie's jaw dropped several inches and his eyes widened as he stared hard at the professor for a long moment. And he wasn't the only one staring. Anyone would have found it hard not to stare at the face framed by the hood of the red duffle coat. For the face was not one horribly burnt and blackened by a superhot pyroclastic flow; it was that of a child with rosy cheeks and a cute little dimple in its chin, a child not much younger than John or Philippa.

"Blimey," said Groanin, and looked away.

"*Blóðugur helvíti*," said Axel.

Remembering his manners at last, Charlie looked sheepishly at the mask he now held in his hands. "Er, yes," he said. "That'll do nicely, mate. No worries. Cheers."

"It's all right," said the professor. "I don't mind any of you looking. Not now, my friends. But perhaps I do owe you all an explanation. Especially you, Axel. Yes, especially you, my old friend."

"None of my business what you look like," said Axel. "Seems to me that if a man wants to wear a mask, it's his own affair."

"Don't you want to know why?" asked the professor.

Axel shrugged. "Not if you don't want to tell me."

"I told you all I'd resisted having a face transplant," said the professor. "When, in fact, the truth is I did have one. However, there was a mix-up at the Edvard Munch Memorial Hospital in Oslo, and the surgeon had taken off my face — or what remained of it — before he found out that the donor face came from an eleven-year-old girl. By then, it was too late to stop the operation and he was obliged to go ahead and give me this face you see now. Since then, I've been stuck with it. It must seem ridiculous to you, I know; but the fact is I wear the mask because, well, I was worried that no one would take me seriously with the face of an eleven-year-old girl; and in a field like volcanology, it's always important that people take you very seriously. After all, who's going to evacuate a whole city that's threatened with a lava flow on the say-so of someone with a face like this?"

John nodded. "I get it," he said. "When you're wearing a black mask, people can't help but take you and your scientific field very seriously indeed." He shrugged. "I mean, if Batman looked like some kid in elementary school, well, it just wouldn't work, would it?"

"Makes perfect sense to me," admitted Groanin. "I say, that makes perfect sense to me, Professor."

The professor nodded and smiled an angelic smile. "I still wish that eventually I might be able to grow a beard or something." He shrugged. "But, so far nothing."

"I can see you don't know many eleven-year-old girls, Professor," said John.

"Why not get another face?" said Axel. "If that one bothers you. I know the Edvard Munch hospital. It's a good hospital. But people die there all the time."

"Aye, that's hospitals for you," murmured Groanin.

"What I mean is," said Axel, "there must be new faces available all the time."

"I thought about it," said the professor. "But I sort of think that now that I have a face, a proper, unscarred, recognizably human face, that there are probably many more

299

deserving people than me who need one. This might be a little girl's face. The wrong face. But it's still a face. So I decided just to leave things as they are."

For a moment, everyone was silent.

Then Charlie said, "Talking of young girls, I'd better get cracking if I'm going to find Philippa." He nodded to Jimmy and put on the professor's mask.

"Yes, you must," agreed Nimrod. "When a spirit is missing from a body, there's no time to lose." He looked at John. "You remember what happened to Faustina."

"Yes," said John. "She ended up being displayed in the catacombs at a place called Malpensa, in Italy. They were passing her off as their own mummified corpse: the Sleeping Beauty, they called her."

Jimmy began to play the *yirdaki*. Charlie stood up and, starting to clap and stamp in time with Jimmy, he danced.

"If I fall over, don't worry yourselves none," said Charlie. "That'll be me achieving separation of mind and body. When that happens, just leave me be for a while. Even if I sound like I'm in trouble."

It was a slow and very repetitive dance and, to an untutored eye like John's, it resembled someone directing traffic.

Possessed of a no-less-untutored eye than John's, Groanin thought the way Charlie moved his hands looked a bit like a conjurer he'd once seen at the Manchester's Theatre Royal. It was all a bit too camp for his taste.

It was a good hour before Charlie finally collapsed, writhing and jerking onto the carpet, and Jimmy said that his spirit was now free to leave his body and go walkabout for a while.

"That's why we came out here, anyway," he explained, laying aside the *yirdaki* and catching his normal breath again. "To keep in practice. You see, when it comes to the spirit world, if you don't use it, you lose it."

Suddenly, Charlie stopped moving.

"Is he all right?" John asked anxiously. "I mean, there's some weird stuff coming out of his mouth." John put his ear to the mouth of the mask the aborigine was wearing. "And I can't hear him breathing."

Jimmy gave his friend a cursory glance. "No worries," he said. "That's just a bit of froth. You see, John, you fellows make it look easy. But for us it's hard, sweaty work separating mind and body."

John nodded.

"Relax, sonny," said Jimmy. "If anyone can find your sister, Charlie can."

CHAPTER 32

THE SONGLINE
OF CHARLIE GARDIPY

Is this a better place than the last one? Or a worse one?

Philippa's spirit was between camels when the first bolt of lightning hit the billabong, and the impact left her feeling like a cartoon character hiding in a trash can that someone hits with a sledgehammer. For several minutes afterward, she had no idea where or even what she was, only that she was not a camel; for a while, she just lay on the sodden ground and tried to gather herself together. This was almost impossible to do, however, as water is an excellent conductor of electricity and every time the lightning hit the ground, a small part of the charge passed through the water and into her stricken spirit.

Is this death? Has my body ceased to function? If I'm climbing up, why does the correct direction seem to be down?

By the time the storm had cleared, the camels were all gone and Philippa thought she was a ghost, a confused spirit

302

abroad on the darkened face of the earth, lost for all eternity in a confusing maze of visible songlines and spirit pathways that were more visible than she was.

Who was I? Why am I here?

This electric-blue maze was not like any other maze she had ever seen for there were no walls, just tracks on the ground, footprints left in rock, landmarks, shapes in the land left by the spirits of people, animals, plants, as well as darker things of which she had no knowledge or understanding.

What did I look like? Was I horrible, like that face? If it was a face. I'm not sure what it is.

For this reason it was a frightening place, where strange faces leered at her and silent hands tried to take hold of her spirit and draw her after them.

I don't think I can deal with this. It's beyond me. It's too much to expect anyone to have to deal with this.

It was not a quiet place. All around, there was the confused sound of songs that were more than just music; they were visible, too, like long lines of vibrating sound waves you could see but which were animated with strong ideas and powerful emotions and life itself. She sensed that these songs were somehow connected with a world she had left behind, but she could not understand how.

They should have someone to explain things to you. When you arrive here, it's too much to expect that you will know what's happening.

And yet there was something she recognized. A sound that seemed to touch her somewhere deep in herself, if deep and self there were. A sound that was more than just a noise, for it was full of meaning, a sort of line that she could take hold of. If she dared.

Do I dare take hold of this? Suppose it means me harm? I should try to understand it before I take a hold of whatever it is.

She looked around in fear and dread. And having once turned, walked on. And turned no more her head. Because she knew a frightful fiend did close behind her tread. She took hold of the line of the sound that seemed to present itself to her shapeless understanding and realized that the sound was a word, full of meaning and significance to her, more than any other. Or was it her imagination? But where did imagination end and reality begin?

What does it mean, Philippa?

She held tight and let the line draw her along for a while and gradually she perceived that the word was part of a song. Not a great song, it was true, because the song only seemed to have the one word and that one word was *Philippa*. But a catchy song nonetheless because, although she was not yet caught, she was content to trust the word that was the song; for wasn't the alternative worse? Something foul really was behind her in the dark. Something fiendish.

Hold tight. Hold tight. Don't let go or you'll never again have this opportunity. You'll be lost forever. You do realize that, don't you? If you hold the line of the song for long enough, surely you will find out who and what you are and why the word means so much to you.

She held on tight. And let the line of the song guide her through the spirit maze, certain now that the word *Philippa* meant something near to her.

"Philippa."

Yes. That was my name. Of course. Someone is calling to me! Singing to me to come to them! I'm coming. Don't go. Don't leave me here, whoever you are! I'm coming to you. Wait a while. It's hard to reach you. Will I know you when I see you? Please don't stop singing to me. Surely, I will see you soon. And then will you take me away from this dark place? Say that you will! Oh, say that you will take me away.

The song was stronger in her hand now. Thicker. Not thin like before. And it was moving more quickly. Helping pull her along. Back to her friends, her family. Back to Life! That was it! The song was pulling her back from this half world to Life! And yet.

She could see him now. A figure who was holding the other end of the line. And surely it was no one she knew. A near-naked man wearing a loincloth and a sinister black mask. Dancing in a little circle, and singing her name.

"Philippa."

Should I fear him?

Seeing her, the man stopped dancing for a moment and beckoned. She hesitated.

"Can you see me?"

"Yes, I can see you."

"Who are you?"

"Come," he said. "Philippa. Come. There's nothing to fear. But you must take my hand, sweetheart. And you must come back with me."

Still she hesitated.

"I can take you back with me, Philippa. But you must trust me."

She heard herself speak in a voice she hardly recognized. "I don't know you," she said.

"It's me, Charlie," he said. "Remember? I'm one of the two aborigines you met in the desert the other day. Charlie and Jimmy? The blokes your uncle Nimrod asked to help him find this herd of camels. Do you remember? Don't worry about the mask I'm wearing. I wear it because of my fear. My fear that I'll be recognized when I'm here. Fear of what's here, Philippa. But never mind that now. Come with me. I'll show you where your body is if you come with me, Phil. But you have to trust me."

"My body?" Still Philippa hesitated.

"There's not much time, Philippa." Charlie glanced anxiously over her faintly visible shoulder as if there really was something horrible waiting there if she refused to go with him.

"If I could only see my body, now," she said. "Then I'd know I could trust you."

"I can't bring your body here, Philippa," said Charlie. "That's not possible for me. I can only show you where you left it. Will you come with me? Please. You have to. There's not much time left if I'm going to help you. There's a limit to how long I can stay down here."

Philippa shook her head. "I can't," she said. "I'm afraid."

Charlie sighed. "That's all right," he said.

"I'm sorry."

Charlie thought for a moment and concluded there was only one thing he could do.

"That's all right." Charlie nodded. "Look, your uncle

said this was very important. That you and your brother were going to save the world. Well, I reckon if you guys can't, no one can. But I reckon you're going to need a bit of help. So, let me see now. Yes, that does look like it's the only way to do this. Look, I can't fetch your body down here, Philippa. But I can fetch another one. If I bring you another body to get you home again, Phil, will you do it? Will you take that one? Just to get you home again. It'll be just a few feet to your own body. I promise. All right?"

Philippa nodded. "Yes," she said.

Charlie sighed. "How did you get yourself into this, Charlie mate? Streuth. All right, Phil. Don't be alarmed now. I'm going to be away for just a few seconds. And when I come back I don't want arguments. You just do as you're told and get inside this body. Fair enough?"

Philippa nodded.

"And above all, don't look around, Phil. On no account are you to look around. There are things down here that aren't nice, okay? And I don't want you losing your nerve while I'm gone."

"All right. But promise me you won't be long."

"I'll be back before you know it," said Charlie. "See if I'm not."

The next moment, Charlie disappeared and Philippa was alone among the songlines and the spirit pathways.

Except that she knew she was hardly that. She was quite certain that there was something standing close behind her. Something foul and fiendish and very, very frightening.

CHAPTER 33

THE DIRGE OF
JIMMY SHEPHERD

Jimmy had stopped playing the *yirdaki*. Now that Charlie was in a trance, there was no need. Besides, Jimmy's playing had left him out of breath and exhausted. And yet even though he had stopped playing, the sound of that ancient drone seemed to linger in the air like a powerful smell or a strong taste. Groanin was fascinated with the instrument and said that he was keen to learn how to play it. But mostly, he said this because it helped to distract him from his worry for Philippa of whom he was very fond.

Jimmy showed him how to hold the instrument and how to get a noise out of it.

"To play the *yirdaki* you have to master circular breathing, Mr. Groanin," explained Jimmy. "Sucking in and blowing out at the same time."

"You're good at both of those," observed John. "So you should be an expert already."

Groanin ignored him. "In and out at the same time? Sounds difficult," he said.

"Nah," said Jimmy. "Not at all. 'Sides, playing the *yirdaki* has important medical benefits."

"Like what?" inquired Groanin. "I say, like what, Jimmy lad?"

"My dad used to say that it stops a bloke from snoring," said Jimmy. "Playing the old didgeridoo strengthens the muscles in your upper airway. And they're the ones that collapse during sleep and that make you snore."

"Oh, please learn it, Groanin," said Nimrod. "And soon. Anything that stops you from snoring is to be welcomed with open arms and a cup of sugar. Sometimes, when you're asleep, it's like living in a sawmill."

"I don't snore," said Groanin.

John laughed. So did the two Icelanders.

"Nay, give over," insisted Groanin. "I don't snore. Never have."

"You could enter an Olympic snoring event," said John. "And win the gold medal."

"Your snoring is something almost primeval," said Nimrod. "When you hear it, you can almost believe that it predates human life on this planet; that some extinct antediluvian beast is still abroad in this world."

This good-humored conversation made the sudden snorting noise all the more startling to everyone. They all turned around to see what had caused it, as even now another, louder stertorous snort emanated from Charlie's unconscious body. But even more startling to them all was the alarming discovery that in his trance state, Charlie had managed to roll over to the very edge of the carpet and was in imminent danger of falling off. He almost seemed to be wrestling with himself.

Jimmy yelled. "Charlie! Look out, mate!"

Charlie's body moved again, almost as if someone invisible was rolling it, like a log. For a moment he seemed to pause, balanced halfway between heaven and earth, but the next second, Charlie's body disappeared over the edge of the carpet.

"Blimey!" exclaimed Groanin. "He's fallen off."

Nimrod did not hesitate. He turned the flying carpet around as quickly as he could and swooped toward the ground with the aim of catching Charlie before he landed. And if he had started from a position of greater height he might have succeeded, too; but from only sixty or seventy feet in the air, Nimrod simply didn't have time to intercept the man. And they were still ten or twenty feet from the muddy ground by the time that Charlie was already lying there.

The aborigine had landed mostly on his head and neck and it was immediately clear to everyone that he had landed badly. Very badly indeed. His whole body weight had crushed all of the vertebrae in his neck.

Not that it seemed to bother the camels very much, at least not right away. Now that they had drunk their fill of water, they were much calmer and viewed an aborigine's broken body followed by the arrival of a flying carpet with complete indifference. But, gradually, they moved slowly away, as camels often do in the presence of mortal injury, almost as if they instinctively feared the contagion of death.

As soon as they were landed on the ground, Nimrod and Jimmy, followed closely by Axel, John, and the professor, hurried toward their motionless Australian friend and turned him gently onto his back. Meanwhile, Groanin tore off his jacket and, arriving last of all, tucked it under Charlie's head in an attempt to make him more comfortable.

"Are you all right?" Jimmy asked desperately, and wiped a trickle of blood from his dearest friend's mouth.

Charlie opened his brown eyes and moved his lips silently for several seconds before any sound was heard, and when he spoke, with an effusion of yet more blood, the voice was not his, but Philippa's.

"Where am I?" she said. "What's happened? John? Uncle Nimrod? Groanin? Where's Charlie? He was here a second or two ago. Where's Charlie? Let me up. Let me go and look for him please. No, wait. What's the matter with me? John. Help me, John. I can't feel my legs, John."

John winced as the same feeling spread to his own body by the telepathy that existed between him and his twin sister. It was uncanny but he felt the strength in his legs ebbing away and so strong was this sensation that he was obliged to sit down.

"In fact," added Philippa, "I can't feel anything very much. Just my right hand, I think. I've got a terrible pain in my head and I don't feel very well at all."

Charlie's eyes rolled in their sockets, and Philippa, whose spirit was inside his body, now caught a glimpse of her own unconscious body lying on the carpet a few yards away and, lifting invisibly out of Charlie, she quickly floated over there and climbed back inside herself before it was too late.

Almost immediately, she felt much better. The pain she had felt in Charlie's body, especially in his head and neck, was gone now. Her limbs all moved normally. Everything was back to normal. But the strong taste of plum bush leaves in her mouth was alloyed with the more bitter taste of fear for Charlie's life. She felt sick to her stomach with worry.

"Charlie!" said Jimmy. "Speak to me, Charlie. Speak to me, mate. Are you all right?"

Charlie grinned feebly. "I'm feeling a bit crook, mate," he whispered. "But I reckon the little girl be all right now."

Philippa hurried to the stricken aborigine's side and, kneeling beside Charlie, took his hand in hers, understanding exactly what had happened now. How Charlie had used his own living body to aid her escape from the spirit maze and how doing this had cost him his own life.

"It was Yowee, the skeleton spirit, who was standing behind you," said Charlie. "With a big head and fiery eyes. His coming always means just one thing: death. It was just as well I turned up when I did, I think."

"Yes, it was," said Philippa.

Charlie winced with pain as Philippa squeezed his hand anxiously.

"Not so hard, darling," he wheezed. "In a minute or two, I reckon you can squeeze the hand all you like, but right now leave it out, there's a good girl."

Philippa grinned even as tears burst out of her eyes.

"Geez," whispered Charlie. "Is it raining again?"

Philippa looked at her uncle. "Can we help him?" she said.

Nimrod shook his head gravely.

"Reckon we needed all that rain." Charlie swallowed but with some considerable difficulty. "I just love this country after it rains. You wait. There'll be flowers all over this desert in a few hours. I just wish I could be there to see it."

"Why did you do it?" sobbed Philippa. "Why, Charlie? Why?"

"'Cos if your uncle Nimrod is right, *Queanbeyan*, the earth is going to need all three of you to fix this disaster. And if that's not worth taking a dive for, I don't know what is."

Jimmy laid his big hand on Charlie's forehead. "Say hello to Mum for me, will ya, mate?"

"No worries," whispered Charlie.

His lips continued to move for a moment without sound. And then he died.

The professor pressed his ear next to Charlie's barrel chest for a minute and then sat back on his haunches. His strange, young girl's face remained inanimate — indeed, it was quite like a mask, so little emotion was written on it — but, from the evidence of his shaking hands and his tremulous voice it was clear to everyone that he, too, was upset.

"I'm afraid he's gone," said the professor. "Poor Charlie is dead."

Philippa lay prostrate across the aborigine's body and wept bitterly.

Jimmy stood up and walked away. John and Nimrod waited for a few minutes and then followed.

"Best mate I ever had," said Jimmy.

"I don't know much about aboriginal funeral ceremonies," said Nimrod, placing a hand on Jimmy's shoulder. "But I'd like to help. I'm sure we'd all like to help. If you'll allow us."

"Yes, please," added John. "It's the least we can do for a bloke like Charlie."

Jimmy nodded. "Thanks, *pittong* Nimrod. Thanks, *poolya* John." He wiped a tear from his eye. "A *toorooga*. A hollow log," he said, half choked with grief. "A dead tree trunk that's been hollowed out by termites. That's where we folks usually leave our dead. At least, out here, it is."

Nimrod nodded. "I think I can find a hollow log," he said.

"But I'll decorate it meself," said Jimmy. "If you don't mind." He swallowed hard and then tousled John's hair. "The decoration on that didgeridoo you made was a bit crook, mate." He grinned at the boy djinn. "Some of it was upside down."

"Sorry," said John.

"No, mate. No need for that. 'Cos I reckon all of this was meant to be. And you can't go kicking against that. Or else why are we here?"

A little later on, when Charlie's body had been placed carefully inside a hollow tree trunk, Groanin — following a little bit of instruction from Jimmy — managed to play the *yirdaki* so that the aborigine could be free to dance and sing in order to ensure his friend's spirit might leave the area and return to his birthplace, where it might be reborn.

Philippa thought that for as long as she lived she would never ever forget the sound of the *goohnai-wurrai*, or dirge, that Jimmy sang as he danced a slow but graceful corroboree step around the hollow tree trunk that now contained his best mate, Charlie. And the dirge seemed to stay inside her head and heart long after they had climbed back aboard the carpet and taken flight for Mongolia. And whenever she thought of Jimmy's dirge and of Charlie she thought of a good man who had bravely sacrificed his own life for hers and for something he believed in. It was a very humbling thought.

They asked Jimmy to come with them, but he declined.

"Please come," said Philippa. "You can see the whole world from a flying carpet."

"I've got no use for seeing the world." Jimmy shrugged. "Not without me mate. Besides, why would I want to see the world when I haven't yet seen all of Australia?"

For a long time, Philippa just sat silently at the rear of the carpet, as they crossed the continent, heading northwest, back to Asia. It was, she thought, one of the most extraordinary places she had ever seen. With its unending red deserts and dry irrigation channels, Australia looked like the surface of the planet Mars. And now, since Charlie's death, it felt almost as alien to her.

As they left the land behind and reached the shore of the ocean, she reflected that it could hardly have been denied that perhaps Jimmy was right, that there was a great deal of

Australia to see. Not that there seemed to be anyone who was actually seeing it. She'd never seen anywhere that looked so unpopulated. There were just hundreds and thousands of miles of empty land, without roads and without towns and without people.

Of course, people were there, although mostly on the southeastern coast. People for whom Charlie had been almost happy to give up his own life. And that unselfish sacrifice touched her in a way that nothing had touched her before.

It left Philippa feeling inspired by his example.

CHAPTER 34

THE FALLOUT

Strongly affected by the misery his sister was feeling, John left Philippa alone for the first few hours of the flight up into east Asia.

But the sight of so many smoking volcanoes in Sumatra and the rest of Indonesia — the sky looked like the aftermath of a nuclear war — prompted him to go to the back of the carpet and sit beside his sister and put his arm around her shoulders.

"Looks pretty bad," he said.

"Hmmm," she said, stroking Moby's head. "Pretty bad, yeah."

"Professor Sturloson says that if we can stop it in time, all this volcanic activity could actually be a good thing. Because it makes the soil very fertile. Like on Vesuvius. Volcanic ash provides all sorts of useful soil nutrients. He says there are parts of the planet where nothing grows very much that might actually benefit from all this extra volcanic activity."

"Always provided that there's enough sun getting through to make things grow," said Philippa.

John glanced over his shoulder. "I think I preferred him wearing that mask," he said.

"Me, too. I can't get used to him looking like a girl I know from school."

"Does he?"

Philippa mentioned a name.

"For Pete's sake," said John. "You're absolutely right."

"Maybe we should speak to Nimrod," said Philippa. "And see if we can't organize him a new face."

"Nimrod says it's only polite to wait until we're asked," said John. "But as a matter of fact, I already did something to help him out. It's only something he said he once wished would happen, so I didn't think Nimrod would mind."

"What is it?"

"Can't you guess?"

Philippa thought for a moment and then nodded. "Yes. I approve. It's a good idea. I'd have done the same. Anything so as not to have to look at that face and be reminded of —"

"Daisy Bohemio."

Philippa nodded again.

John grinned. "What were you thinking?" he asked. "Before I sat down."

"As if you didn't know," she said.

"I guess I do," he said. "But I'd still prefer to hear you say it. I'm not as good as tuning into your thoughts as you are at tuning into mine."

"It's telepathy," said Philippa. "Why not just say it?"

"Because it scares me." He shrugged. "Besides I feel it, rather than know it, if you know what I mean."

"It's the same for me," said Philippa. "You think I'm better at it, bro, but I'm not. I'm just more in touch with my own feelings than you are. Because I'm a girl, I guess."

"I thought it was because you're more intelligent."

"We both know that's not true. You have a different kind of intelligence, that's all." She shrugged. "Well, since you ask, what I was thinking was this: I was thinking that if I'm dealt the same cards as Charlie, I hope I would have the guts to do what he did."

"I hope so, too," said John. "All the same I don't think you can tell what you'd do in that kind of situation until you have to do something, do you? I mean, everyone aspires to be brave but not everyone can be that self-sacrificing."

"So what are you saying, bro?"

John shrugged. "I'm just saying that I don't really know if I could actually be as brave as Charlie, that's all. And I don't think you can ever know that until the moment arrives."

"I think *I* know," said Philippa.

"Good for you," said John. "But *I* don't. Not yet. That's all I'm saying."

"Don't you think that some causes are worth dying for?" asked Philippa.

"Of course I do. But to be really brave I think you also have to be afraid first. And that's where I am now. You have to be afraid first, otherwise it's not really brave you're being; it's, I don't know, crazy, I guess. Reckless. Foolhardy." John smiled. "But look, Phil, this is just talking, right? This discussion we're having now, it's only theoretical, yeah? There's no real call to be talking about sacrificing your life in a cause, is there?"

Philippa shrugged. "No, I suppose there isn't. I just wanted to let you know what I think about these things."

John smiled. "As if I didn't know," he said.

Nimrod, too, was deeply impressed by Charlie's heroic self-sacrifice and had thought about little else since leaving the burial ceremony at Docker River. It was easy to see that the brave aborigine's death had had a profound effect on the children, too. He watched and heard the twins talking and wondered if perhaps now was the right time to mention to them the very sensitive matter of the Taranushi prophecy and the somewhat barbaric idea that in order to save the world a set of djinn twins would have to be sacrificed.

Not that he believed in the Taranushi prophecy — at least the part about sacrificing a pair of djinn twins; but it could hardly be denied that there were certain aspects of John and Philippa's existence that seemed to fulfill what Taranushi had said about two djinn who were twin brother and sister and true children of the lamp, and how only they could become true partners on a quest to save the world from inflammable darkness and destruction.

At first, Nimrod had concluded that it was best not to mention the prophecy to the twins at all, reasoning that no one would ever care to be told that the planet's future survival might depend on his or her death.

But after Alexandra's mention of these uncomfortable things in Kandahar, Nimrod had been expecting John and

Philippa to bring the matter up with him themselves. And when neither twin had spoken to Nimrod about the subject, it was another day or so before he realized that it was always thus with Alexandra: No one ever remembered the predictions she made for them.

That was her curse. Never to be believed.

Now he was of the opinion that he *should* tell them about the prophecy — after all, knowledge is potentially, at least, a kind of power, and to be forewarned is to be forearmed — but he'd been awaiting the right opportunity to do so. And overhearing their conversation about Charlie's sacrifice prompted Nimrod to think that the twins were now in the right frame of mind to talk about these things.

He would have preferred to discuss the subject with John and Philippa on his own, without Groanin and the professor and Axel hearing everything that was said. Groanin was certain to say something unhelpful. For a while, Nimrod contemplated landing somewhere and finding a quiet spot where he could talk to the twins on his own; but the sight of so many ash plumes in the air above Indonesia had persuaded him that there was no time for such diplomacies and that they must get to Mongolia as quickly as possible.

And finally, he just called the twins over and told them the unvarnished truth about what Taranushi, the first great djinn, had prophesied.

To Nimrod's surprise, Philippa actually looked relieved.

"So that's what I've been trying to remember," she said. "Ever since Kandahar. It's been nagging me for days."

"You forgot about it because people always forget the predictions that Alexandra makes," explained Nimrod.

Philippa nodded. "I guess that's why I also forgot about those books you underlined in the Rakshasas Library," she said.

"You saw those, did you?" Nimrod nodded. "Yes, well, it's all the same subject, so you would have forgotten that, too, yes. Undoubtedly. But I wonder why you didn't mention it to me then. Before Kandahar."

Philippa shrugged. "I wasn't sure if we could trust you," she said.

"We're still not sure," added John. "Why are you telling us now?"

"Look," said Nimrod. "It's not something that I believe myself. Obviously."

"Obviously," murmured John.

"But I just thought you ought to know."

The twins said nothing.

"I certainly hope you don't think that I'd ever contemplate something like that," added Nimrod. "I mean, that sort of thing — human sacrifice — it's nothing more than primitive superstition. The Incas practiced mountaintop child sacrifice for centuries, but no gods were ever placated, no crops grew as a result, nor any rain fell. It's nonsense, of course."

"But suppose it wasn't just a primitive superstition," said John. "Suppose it was true. What would you do then?"

"Why suppose it when it couldn't ever be true?" asked Nimrod.

"Suppose it was," insisted John. "Suppose there was no other way to save the world but to sacrifice me and Phil. What would you do then?"

Nimrod shook his head. "No one intelligent could ever believe that by killing someone, someone else could be saved. Least of all me."

"That's not answering," said John. "That's not answering at all."

"I'm sorry you think that, John," said Nimrod. "Very sorry indeed."

"We don't know what to think," said Philippa. "That's just the point."

"Perhaps if you'd been straight with us from the very beginning, things might be different," said John. "But you only told us half of the Taranushi prophecy. You left out the most crucial part. The part that affects us."

Groanin scowled at the twins. "I never thought I'd see the day when you two kids fell out with your uncle Nimrod," he said. "I say, I never thought I'd hear the day when you stopped trusting him. You ought to be ashamed of yourselves. After all he's done for you." He looked at Nimrod and shook his head. "If you ask me, that's the trouble with kids today. All they think about is themselves."

"With all due respect," said Philippa, "child sacrifice concerns us in a way that it doesn't concern any of you."

Groanin uttered a loud sigh.

"After all we've been through," he said. "The four of us. After all the adventures we've had and the dangers we've faced. Together, mind. Together. Through thick and thin.

One for all, and all for one. After all that, you still have the nerve to ask him what he would do if the world and the good of mankind depended on you two being sacrificed."

"If I might say something," said the professor.

"Please do," said Nimrod.

The professor looked at John and then at Philippa.

"Forget what your uncle might or might not do in these peculiar circumstances. If this prophecy was indeed true — although that seems highly unlikely to me — then what would *you* do? What would *you* do?"

John looked at Philippa, who shrugged back at him.

"Aye," said Groanin. "I thought not. You've no idea what you would do. You expect your uncle to have all the answers when you've none of the answers yourselves."

"No, she's right, Groanin," said Nimrod. "They're both right. I should have told them everything from the beginning."

"Why didn't you?" asked John.

"It's not the sort of thing that's easy to say," said Nimrod. "Besides, it's not like I know much more than you about all this. You might think I do, but I don't. It's my manner. It looks omniscient, but it isn't really."

The carpet turned slowly in the air and started to head back toward the coast of Sumatra. At the same time, they started to descend through the air.

"What are you doing?" asked Philippa.

"Landing," said Nimrod.

"Landing?"

"I think it's best that I let you both off," said Nimrod. "I'll cut off a piece of the carpet, show you how to control it, and then you can both fly back home to New York. Shouldn't take you more than a day or two at most."

"Perhaps I could cut this one for you, sir," offered Groanin. "Hmm?"

"My dad was a carpet fitter all his life," declared Groanin. "In Burnley. For sentimental reasons, I keep his carpet knife in my suitcase alongside a picture of the queen. Sometimes, I just get it out and hold it. It's amazing but I can always think of the smell of a new carpet when I hold that knife. Perhaps I could cut this carpet for you, sir."

"Yes, Groanin," said Nimrod. "Why not? Thank you, old fellow."

"What about you?" John asked his uncle. "Where will you go?"

"We'll keep on going to Mongolia," said Nimrod. "And just hope that we can find the grave of Genghis Khan from the description of the site you gave me, John."

"And if you don't find it?"

Nimrod kept the carpet headed for the ground and didn't answer.

They landed on a long, deserted beach that was covered with a thin layer of volcanic ash, as was the vegetation that lay behind it. But this was hardly the thing that impressed them the most. Almost immediately, Axel found a dead gray bird with a large, curving beak, and then another. Axel handed one of the dead birds to the professor.

"*Buceros bicornis*," said Axel. "The great hornbill."

The professor nodded. "Looks like it," he said. "Poor thing."

"I thought hornbills were black and white," said John. "With a yellow beak."

"They are," said Axel, and blew off a thin layer of gray dust to reveal the dead bird's true coloring.

"What happened?" asked Philippa.

"It's a bit hard to say, little sister, without performing an autopsy," said Axel. "Either it flew through an ash cloud and suffocated" — he looked around at the flora and fauna. Even the berries on the bushes were covered with ash — "or perhaps they ate some of these berries that are covered in ash." He rubbed his stubbly chin and sighed unhappily. "Such a waste of beautiful birds."

"Not just birds," said Groanin. "Look."

He pointed at the bushes under which there lay a large animal, half concealed in the gray undergrowth, breathing loudly but erratically, as if it was in some distress.

It was a tiger.

Groanin did not approach the stricken beast himself; he had good reason to feel nervous about these big cats because, several years before, he had been attacked by a tiger.

"My goodness," said Axel. "It's a *Panthera tigris sondaica*. A Javan tiger."

Except that it was more like a black-and-white photograph of a tiger, for it, too, was covered in a thin layer of ash. Its beautiful, yellow-striped coat was now the color of a dirty fireplace and its previously pink tongue, which lolled out of the big cat's mouth, was like an old strip of overcooked bacon. The tiger's eyes were glazed and milky and it was too tired or too sick to flick away the many flies that buzzed about its head.

"I thought they were extinct," said Axel as something rattled in the big cat's throat and the animal appeared to breathe its last.

"It is now," observed Groanin. "At least this one is."

Cautiously, the professor lifted the creature's mouth to inspect the discolored tongue and shook his head.

"It must have licked the ash off its fur," he said. "The way any cat does when it's trying to keep itself clean. And, in the process, poisoned itself."

"Is the ash poisonous, too?" asked Philippa.

"Oh, yes," said the professor. "Volcanic ash contains fluoride. This creates acid inside the animal's stomach, which corrodes its intestines and causes internal hemorrhage. It also *binds* with the calcium in the bloodstream that — well, that isn't good, either, as you can judge for yourselves."

Philippa looked at Nimrod. "Is there nothing that can be done for it?" she asked her uncle.

Nimrod placed a hand on the tiger's chest, near where he guessed its heart must be and shook his head grimly.

"The impossible I can sometimes do," said Nimrod, "but miracles are very definitely beyond my powers. This animal is dead, I'm afraid."

"What a tragedy," said Axel. He glanced around at the jungle bordering the beach. "I think we're probably looking at an environmental disaster of the kind that makes an oil spill look like a storm in a teacup. Quite probably there are hundreds, perhaps thousands of animals already lying dead in that jungle. It's like the fallout after a nuclear explosion."

"Perhaps because there are so many volcanoes here in Sumatra — thirty-five — the island is suffering more than anywhere else," said the professor. "So far."

"Except perhaps Iceland," Axel said gravely. "This makes me wonder how bad things are back home in Reykjavik. First, the banking crisis. And now this."

The professor rubbed his chin again. Against his leathery hand the stubble on his chin sounded like sandpaper. "I shudder to think what things are like there."

"How many volcanoes does Iceland have?" asked John.

"One hundred and thirty," said Axel. "Although until this phenomenon started, there were only eighteen that were at all active. After what we've seen lately, we might have to revise that figure up."

"In a few days from now," said the professor, "if things keep going like they are here, everywhere on earth might well look like this place."

"Now there's a comforting thought," said Groanin.

He went back to the carpet and fetched his carpet knife from his suitcase. Then he brought it back to Nimrod. For a moment, Nimrod, deeply affected by the sight of a dead tiger, regarded the Burnley carpet fitter's knife blankly. It was small and hooked and sharp, like the beak of the dead hornbill.

"Crain?"

"To cut the carpet, sir," explained the butler. "This 'un's German. But the Germans make the sharpest carpet knives on the market. And the best German knife is a Crain."

"Oh, yes. Of course. Well, look, perhaps you should do it, Groanin. Perhaps this is a talent you inherited from your father. Skills like that tend to run in families, you know."

"Aye, well, it's true, no one could cut a carpet like my old dad," said Groanin.

"Only you'd better give it to me, first," said Nimrod. "You'll need some of my blood on that blade before you can cut the carpet safely."

Groanin handed over the knife, and Nimrod cut himself and then gave it back, dripping with blood.

The butler returned to the carpet and prepared to slice a piece off.

"How much would you like me to cut, sir?" he inquired. "For the twins."

"How much would you suggest?"

"A four-foot strip from the edge ought to give them enough room for wherever it is they're going," said Groanin.

Nimrod, who was still caught up in the sad death of the tiger, nodded distractedly. "Oh, yes. Whatever you think is right, Groanin."

Groanin put the curved tip of the blade to the edge of the carpet and was just about to cut when John said, "Don't, Groanin. Don't cut it."

Groanin sat back and looked around. "Eh? What's that you say?"

"Don't cut the carpet," repeated John. "At least not on my account. Because I'm not going home. At least not yet. I'm coming with you. To Mongolia."

"What about you, Philippa?" asked Nimrod.

"Of course I'm not going home," said Philippa. "How could I go home after seeing all this? No, I'm coming with you."

"Besides," added John. "The description I gave of the location of the tomb of Genghis Khan is only very approximate. You'll need me to guide you to where it is, exactly."

"Thank you, John," he said. "Thank you both."

John grinned. "Anyway, if I go home now, I'll be missing out on the first sight of the professor's beard."

"What are you talking about?" asked Professor Sturloson.

"Haven't you noticed?" asked John. "You're growing a beard."

Axel laughed. "He's right, Professor," he said. "You do look like you need a shave."

The professor rubbed his face but instead of finding his young face smooth to the touch — as he expected — he found it rough and stubbly.

"A while ago I heard you wishing you had a beard," said John. "Or some words to that effect. I kind of took the liberty of granting you that wish."

Groanin found a hand mirror in his suitcase and handed it to the professor, who proceeded to examine the reflection of his transplanted face — especially the chin and upper lip — with no small fascination.

"You're right," he said. "I am growing a beard." He grinned at John. "Thank you, my boy."

"Beard suits you," observed Groanin. "Makes you look distinguished. More professorial, if you like. I've never hankered after growing a beard myself. A beard looks wrong on a butler. It makes him look unkempt. Even a tad careless."

"Thank you very much indeed." The professor pumped John's hand gratefully. "A beard is just what I wanted."

"Don't mention it," said John. "The mask was good. I mean, that really made a statement. But Groanin's right. In my opinion, a male professor should always have a beard. Or at the very least a big and bushy mustache." He shrugged. "How else are you going to convince people that you're wise and that you know what you're talking about if you don't have a few mad-looking whiskers?" He shrugged. "I mean, Einstein wouldn't ever have looked like a genius without his mustache and his mad hairstyle. Obviously, he'd still have been very intelligent. But he wouldn't have looked like a genius, would he?" He shrugged again. "Well, would he?"

"Now that's what I call a general theory," said Philippa.

CHAPTER 35

GRAVE HUNTERS

Mongolia is a landlocked country that lies between China and Russia. It is the nineteenth-largest country in the world — five times larger than Germany, twice as large as Turkey — and yet it is also the largest, most sparsely populated country in the world. Australia, five times larger in square miles has a population of twenty-two million people; Mongolia has just three million people living in a country the size of Iran, which, by comparison, has a population of seventy-five million people.

To the south of the country is the Gobi desert and to the north are high mountains, but most of the country is just grassland plains called steppes.

Philippa thought it the most beautiful country she had ever seen. She imagined the open prairies of America would have been like this before the wagon trains brought the people who built the cities. It was untouched, unspoiled, like the beginning of the world before cars and airplanes, with vast rainbows and endless plains of grass that looked more like the open sea. If Australia looked like Mars, then Mongolia, no less alien in her eyes, looked like something much more lush and fertile, which made it all the more surprising that no one was there. Once or twice, they saw a herd of sheep, or some wild horses; another time they thought they spotted a moose, but mostly the land looked deserted.

The sapphire sky was a different story, however. It was full of birds, many of them — eagles, cranes, and vultures — that were easily mistaken for small planes. These seemed to fly in comparative safety, for unlike in Sumatra, here the air was fresh and clean and absent of smoke clouds and ash plumes, which seemed ironic given that they were reaching the end of their quest.

The professor said there were only five volcanoes in the whole country — Bus-Obo, Dariganga, Khanuy Gol, Taryatu-Chulutu, and one in the Gobi desert he said he'd forgotten — and that the last time any of these had erupted was more than ten thousand years ago.

For John, Mongolia was quite at odds with his perception of Genghis Khan and a horde of warlike, nomadic Mongol cavalry riding swiftly across the steppes and putting all who opposed them to the sword. What could they have thought was worth conquering? The next empty grass plain? The grass plain after that? A tented village that, next week, might exist somewhere else? There were no cities, no towns, no villages, and no castles. It was hard to imagine how someone like Genghis Khan could ever have existed.

It was curious, but Dunbelchin's memories were now John's own and for all the fact that the country seemed an unlikely place for a great tyrant and conqueror to have gotten started, it also seemed very familiar to him and quite like home, so that he felt like he belonged there — almost as if he had walked every mile of the country over which they were now flying. Which, of course, Dunbelchin almost certainly had. That memory was also the smell of something indefinable in the air that perhaps only a camel's large and sensitive nostrils could have detected; at first, it eluded John what this might be, and it was only when offering precise navigation for Nimrod to steer by, and when they finally neared the site of the hidden tomb, that John was able to put a word to what this smell was. It was death: the death of the slaves who had dug the tomb, the death of the soldiers who had killed them, and the death of the baby camel that had been cruelly buried with them. And the memory and the smell left him feeling edgy and disturbed, almost as if these events had taken place in his own life and not Dunbelchin's almost eight hundred years earlier.

"That's Darkhan," said John, pointing to the first town they had seen for hundreds of miles. "From here, we keep flying north, with Ulan Bator, the Mongolian capital, on our left to the west."

A little later on he said, "All right. This is good. We're entering the Gorkhi-Terelj National Park."

"Doesn't look much like a park," observed Groanin, peering over the edge of the flying carpet. "It's not like there are any playgrounds, or park benches, or anything like that. In fact, there's nothing much of anything."

"It's not that kind of park, Groanin," John said irritably.

He pointed at a river. "There. That's the River Kherlen. Just keep following that river northeast and it'll take us straight to the mountain called Khan Khentii, also called Burkhan Khaldun."

"Right you are," said Nimrod.

A hundred miles farther north, John sniffed the air to the east and said, "Over there is Lake Khar. The Blue Lake. Which means we're still right on course."

"I can't see anything," said Axel. "And I certainly can't smell anything."

"That's because you're seeing things as a human being," said Nimrod. "John is seeing and smelling everything from the point of view of a camel. Isn't that right, John?"

John belched loudly by way of confirmation. Reliving Dunbelchin's memories was really starting to affect him now.

"Not much farther now," he said. "They used to let me off the bridle about here and I'd start running toward the site."

Groanin pulled a face as if to indicate he thought John was going mad.

"And about ten tribesmen," continued the boy djinn, "who were the sons of Genghis Khan, they would mount their horses and ride after me. This was always in summer, August, right? Because that's when Genghis died, on August 25, 1227, the Year of the Pig. So that's when we always visited the tomb. And then the ground was good, of course. So it took about three days to get there. It would have taken much longer if Genghis had died in winter."

"Naturally," said Groanin.

"Do shut up, Groanin," said Nimrod.

"Yes, sir."

A little farther north, above a trackless waste close to the confluence of three tributaries of the River Kherlen, John declared that they were getting close to the high plateau where the tomb was hidden. Night was coming and a mist had started to close in, but John was not deterred.

"Don't worry," he said, sniffing the cool, conifer-scented evening air. "I could always find this place with my eyes closed." He pointed ahead of them. "There. That shoulder of reddish rock. There's a plateau behind it. That's where you should land, Uncle."

Nimrod did as John directed and brought the big blue carpet to a smooth landing on a high grass-covered plateau at the summit of a rather ordinary-looking hill. The plateau, which was entirely unremarkable, covered almost a square mile and was boggy in parts and rocky in others. And just as the purple sky began turning black, John pronounced that they had finally arrived.

"Arrived at what?" said Groanin.

A cold wind stirred the longer grass and smaller stones and whistled its way around the deserted plateau, almost as if something malign and invisible was already alerting the general area to their presence. Gradually, the mist that surrounded them turned to fog.

"Arrived at what?" repeated Groanin. "There's nothing here. Nothing at all. I've never seen a more desolate place."

"Or a more creepy one," observed Philippa.

"The lost tomb of Genghis Khan wouldn't be lost if it was obvious where it was, Groanin," said Nimrod.

"No, I suppose not," said Groanin. "But Philippa's right. This place is creepier than a loud noise in a mortuary at midnight."

"I wouldn't mind it if it wasn't so dark," said Axel. He had his small, pencil-thin flashlight in his hand and was waving the almost solid beam around the plateau like a white stick. "I must say it doesn't look like anyone's been here in quite a while." He looked at John. "Are you sure this is the right place?"

"It's the right place," said John.

"Perhaps we should wait for morning before we go and look for the tomb," said Nimrod. "We ought to make camp and build a fire. And have something to eat. That will improve our spirits."

"No," said John firmly. "That wouldn't be a good idea."

"Why not?" asked Nimrod.

John didn't answer for a moment. He walked a short distance from the others and stared hard into the thickening fog, almost as if he suspected it of containing something more threatening than some damp night air. And when finally he answered, his voice sounded distracted — even a little mysterious.

"I think it would be best if we were to find the tomb now," he said quietly.

"You can't be serious," said Groanin. "It's pitch dark. We couldn't find an airship in this darkness."

"Aren't you forgetting something?" said Philippa. "John knows where it is. The tomb, I mean. Not the airship." She looked at her brother and smiled politely. "By the way, where is it?"

"We should find it now," said John. "*Because* it's dark. And because I don't think we can afford to delay until morning."

Nimrod came and stood beside his nephew, staring into the fog. After almost a full minute, Nimrod whispered John's name.

"John?"

"There's something in the fog," John said quietly.

Groanin shook his head fearfully and found Philippa taking his hand. "I don't like this place at all," he whispered.

"Me, neither," she confessed. "We'd better stick together, huh?"

"Yes, miss, that sounds like a good idea."

"What is it?" Nimrod asked John. "I can't see or feel anything."

John did not reply at first. "I'm not feeling this as a djinn, or even with my human half," he finally confessed. "I'm feeling this with the part of me that was Dunbelchin."

"The camel part." Nimrod nodded. "Yes, of course that makes sense. With an animal's sixth sense."

John nodded. "Whatever it is that's in that fog," he said, "it's something that's always been here, in this place."

"Can you tell what it is?"

John shook his head.

"An evil spirit?" said Nimrod. "A demon? An elemental, perhaps?"

"No. Just that it's there."

He kept on staring for a moment and then seemed to relax, shaking his head. "It's gone for the moment, whatever it was."

Nimrod muttered his focus word, which produced a large, blazing fire in the middle of the plateau.

"That feels better," admitted the professor. He rubbed his hands and held them up to the flames. "I don't mind admitting I find this place most uncomfortable, although, to look at, it's a bit like Iceland."

The wind strengthened and this time there was moisture in it.

"Rain," said Axel. "That's all we need. Now it really is like Iceland."

"It's just a shower, I think," observed Groanin.

The next second, there came an inhuman-sounding groan that seemed to persist for several seconds before dying away.

"What was that?" hissed the professor.

But just as soon as the groan faded away it came back again, only louder this time. Louder and more horribly desperate.

"What is that?" Groanin shuddered.

"It seems to be coming from that shoulder of rocks," said Nimrod. "At the edge of the plateau."

There was a flashlight in his hand as he started to walk toward the rocks.

"Where are you going?" Groanin said, standing closer to the fire. "Don't leave us, sir."

"I'm going to find out what's making that noise, of course," said Nimrod.

"It's a soul in torment, that's what it is," said Groanin. "Perhaps even more than one. Which is hardly surprising given the terrible history of this place. We should get out of here right now before I — before *we* die of fright."

Nimrod scrambled up the nearby shoulder of red rock and, shining the flashlight around him, he searched the area until he saw where the sound was coming from.

"Interesting," he said.

"What is?" said Philippa, following.

"There's a piece of rock here that's exactly like the pipe in an old church organ," he said. "And when the wind catches it just right it makes —"

The groaning sound came again.

"Oh, yes," said Philippa. "It makes that rather frightening sort of noise."

"Well, I always thought there would be a perfectly logical explanation for it," said Groanin.

He wiped his face as another pulse of rain swept across the plateau. Absently, he glanced at his hand in the firelight and then let out a cry of horror.

"What is it now?" asked the professor.

"There's blood in the wind." Groanin showed him the

reddened hand with which he had wiped his face and cried out again as he saw the professor's heavily stubbled face. "You too, Professor," he added. "On your face."

The professor swept his face dry with his hand and found it covered in what looked like blood. He swore in Icelandic and shook his head. "What's happening here?" he said. "There is indeed blood in the wind."

Nimrod wiped the moisture from his own face, and having inspected his hand under the flashlight and tasted what, he had to admit, looked very much like blood, he said, "Relax, it's not blood. It's just rain with a bit of red mud in it. Probably mud that came off this reddish-colored rock. Sandstone or, perhaps, hematite." He broke off a piece in his fingers and handed it to the professor. "Here, you're the geologist, Professor."

"A very soft type of hematite, yes," said the professor. "After all, hematite is derived for the Greek word *ιρα*, meaning 'blood.'"

"You know," said Nimrod. "I wouldn't be at all surprised if this is the very reason why the Mongols chose this place to locate the tomb of Genghis Khan. Because of all these natural phenomena that anyone superstitious might easily misinterpret as something supernatural. The so-called blood in the wind, this natural organ pipe that sounds very much like a soul in torment. You're absolutely right about that, Groanin. Yes, there's that and some natural phenomenon that exists in the fog around here, perhaps. Although I don't know what. Not yet, anyway."

"Why not just say the place is evil and leave it at that?" said Groanin. "Better still, let's just leave the place altogether. Natural phenomena or not, we shouldn't be doing what we're planning to do. And if the spirit of Genghis Khan is listening, then I'd just like to say it's nothing to do with me, Your Majesty. I'm just a humble servant whose opinion seems to count for very little in these matters."

"Do shut up, Groanin," said Nimrod.

"Yes, sir."

"Where's the entrance to the tomb, John?" said Nimrod.

"Search me," said John. "All I know is that it's somewhere under this plateau. Beneath our feet are the bodies of at least twenty thousand men, as well as the one man whose secret they were killed for. After the tomb was closed up, the whole area was covered with earth and trampled by horses for several weeks. Then grass was allowed to grow on top of it. I doubt that even the sons of Genghis Khan could have said where the original entrance lay."

"And yet," said Nimrod, "if the Hotaniya crystals were taken from the tomb, we could expect to see some recent sign of an entry here."

"Not in the dark we can't," murmured Groanin.

"That is what we must look for," insisted Nimrod.

"Like looking for a needle in a haystack," said Groanin. He thought for a moment and then added, "In a giant barn without a light."

"Excellent, Groanin," said Nimrod. "You've given me an idea."

"I have?"

"As always, your grumbling has managed to provoke a useful thought in my brain."

"It did?"

Nimrod muttered his focus word and, in the blink of an eye, an enormous wooden barn appeared over their heads. It covered the entire plateau and from its raftered ceiling there hung several dozen powerful halogen lights that illuminated everything on the ground.

"*O'trúlegur.*" Axel laughed with amazement. "This tomb will have to be something to be beat this," he said. "Nimrod? That's the most impressive thing I've seen since I climbed aboard your flying carpet in Fez."

"Thank you, Axel," he said. "But it has left me feeling rather tired." Nimrod sat down on the carpet. And then lay down wearily.

"Are you all right, Uncle?" Philippa asked him anxiously. Under the bright lights of the barn ceiling, he looked pale, and there were bags under his eyes she was sure had not been there before.

"I'm fine, I'm fine. Just a little tired, like I say. Using djinn power to make something as big as this barn is always going to be rather exhausting. Especially after a long flight."

He closed his eyes as everyone came and knelt beside him.

"Sir," said Groanin. "Perhaps a cup of tea would help to revive you."

"Yes," said Nimrod. "That sounds ideal. Perhaps in a little while. Only right now, I'd like to sleep."

"I don't think he's slept since Fez," said Groanin.

"Fez," whispered Nimrod. "That does seem like a long time ago now."

"Didn't he sleep in Australia?" asked John.

"No, not him," said Groanin. "Not after that beastly Icelandic stew he ate."

"It's always hard to sleep after you've eaten a good *kæstur hákarl*," said Axel. "That's one of the reasons people eat it." He shrugged. "I didn't sleep well myself."

"Besides, he's been too worried to sleep," added Groanin. "About all these flipping volcanoes going off."

"I'm afraid you will have to search for this entrance yourselves," Nimrod said quietly. "Can you do that?"

"Yes," said John.

"Tell the professor to use his pocket transit. He's a geologist, so he's bound to have one in his bags."

"I'm here," said the professor. "I have a Brunton with me. Tell me what I'm looking for."

"I think you'll find that the main part of the plateau is perfectly flat," said Nimrod. "At least that was my impression when I first looked at it. However, I wouldn't be at all surprised if there's a slight dip in it somewhere, and you'll need the Brunton to find it. When you do, that's the most likely place to look for an entrance to the tomb of Genghis Khan."

"All right," said the professor, and went to find the instrument in his bag.

Nimrod pushed himself up on one elbow. "When you find the entrance, be very careful. It's possible that the

Mongols or even the person who was here before us may have left some sort of trap to protect Genghis Khan or to cover his tracks, respectively."

"You mean like a booby trap," said John.

"I mean exactly a booby trap, "said Nimrod. "Good luck."

Then he closed his eyes, lowered his head onto his forearm, and went straight to sleep.

CHAPTER 36

GRAVE ROBBERS OF GENGHIS KHAN

Philippa and John stood up and exchanged a worried look over Uncle Nimrod's sleeping body. A horrible, unthinkable thought now passed between them that neither wished to utter in so many words. And it was finally John who, gathering all of his courage in his mouth, gave utterance to half of their joint-ventured thought.

"Are you sure he's asleep, Groanin?" said John.

Groanin knelt down beside his master and nodded. "Aye, lad, he's sleeping like a baby."

"I've never seen him like this before," said Philippa. "Five adventures we've been on and not once has he ever so much as yawned."

"Has it been so many?" asked Groanin. "Five. It seems like more than that. And yet not that many. I often thought we would all go on much longer than this. But lately —

lately, I've had a strange feeling that things were ending, somehow."

"What do you mean?" asked John.

"You're growing up, of course," said Groanin. "You're really not children anymore. You, John, are becoming a young man. And you, Philippa, you are becoming a beautiful young woman."

The twins stared awkwardly at each other for a moment, looking for some sign that what Groanin had said was true; but they could see nothing, no sign that they were any different from before.

Surely, he was exaggerating. Perhaps, he was actually saying something else.

Philippa glanced down at her uncle.

"You don't think —" Philippa hesitated. Nothing Groanin had said had put her mind at rest. If anything, she was more worried now than she had been before. "Oh, Groanin, you don't think Uncle Nimrod's dying, do you?"

"Dying?" Groanin frowned. "Whatever makes you say that, girl?"

Philippa shrugged. "I don't know. But he's not getting any younger, you know."

"It's just that suddenly he looks older," observed John. "Haven't you noticed? His hair seems much grayer than when we were in Naples. Doesn't it?"

"So does yours, lad," said Groanin. "So does everyone who's got hair, unlike me. It's volcanic ash that's made it gray, like everything else. Ash from that beach in Sumatra." And so saying, he leaned down and blew some of the gray from Nimrod's hair.

Philippa breathed a sigh of relief.

"I'll look after him, don't you worry," said Groanin and, taking off his duffle coat, he laid it carefully over Nimrod's shoulders. "You two go and help the professor find the entrance to the tomb so that we can get out here before something awful happens to us all." He shook his head. "I must say, I do fear it."

The professor had a little instrument in the palm of his hand that looked like a complicated type of compass. He held the instrument at waist height and, looking down into a small mirror, he lined up target, needle, and guideline, and then read the azimuth.

"A Brunton compass," he told the twins, who'd never seen such a thing before. "Properly known as the Brunton pocket transit. No self-respecting geologist is ever without one of these little compasses. Fault lines, contacts, foliation, sedimentary strata, craters, there's no surface geological feature this can't find."

Axel had one, too, and was taking readings from the opposite side of the barn.

"Well, that is extraordinary," said the professor.

"What is?" asked John.

"How your uncle recognized that this plateau is completely level. It's like the surface of a billiard table. Hard to believe this place was ever trampled down by horses. Now, if you'd said they had flattened it with a heavy garden roller, I might have found that easier to believe."

"They did," said John. "I was there. Or at least, Dunbelchin was there. And I remember what she remembers."

"Nimrod's always had a good idea for proportion," said Philippa. "He can draw a perfect circle, you know. With an equal diameter whichever part of the circumference you measure it from."

"Interesting."

Eventually, the two Icelanders came together to compare their compass readings, and after a minute or two's conversation in Icelandic, they walked toward the center of the plateau. John and Philippa followed.

"At the approximate center of the plateau," explained Axel, "is an area about ten feet in diameter that dips by as much as three feet from the edge." He shook his head. "You hardly notice it with the naked eye. But with the Brunton, it's obvious."

John knelt down and examined the ground. "The grass here is different," he said. "Not nearly as coarse as the grass on the outer edge. It must have been covered in new turf."

Axel knelt down beside him and started to go around the dip on his hands and knees. Every so often, he stopped and pushed a finger into what looked like a hole in the ground.

"These look like holes made by tent pegs," he said. "As if this dip on the plateau was protected from the elements by some sort of canopy or tent."

"For an archaeological excavation, perhaps," added the professor.

"Remember what Nimrod said about booby traps."

Philippa's tone was suddenly urgent. "Please be careful, all of you."

Axel pulled an old, broken tent peg out of the ground by way of confirmation and waved it at the others.

John went and fetched the shovels they had brought with them from Afghanistan and started to dig. So did the others. It was hard digging because the earth was partly frozen but after twenty or thirty minutes, they had uncovered a section of a large and heavy green tarpaulin sheet made of a rubberized canvas.

"It's only a guess," said John. "But I don't think the Mongols knew about rubber, do you?"

"This has been used to cover up a hole." The professor patted the tarpaulin with the flat of his hand. "See? Underneath this part, there is earth, but underneath this part, there's nothing at all."

From his trouser pocket, Axel produced a knife and began to cut into the tarpaulin. This revealed a dark hole from which cool, damp, stale air drifted up onto the plateau. Swinging his legs over the edge of the hole he glanced up.

"Here, John, fetch me one of those flashlights will you? We'll take it inside the excavation."

John carried the light and shone it into the hole as Axel climbed inside. For a moment he held on to the edge and then, letting go, disappeared from view.

"There's a sort of platform in here," said the Icelander.

"Do be careful," urged Philippa.

"It's quite safe, I think. Although I don't believe it's of recent construction."

They heard the sound of his leather-soled, hobnailed climbing boots move heavily along the platform.

"The platform itself is attached to an intricate system of wooden ladders that go down a long way. And that looks a bit like Escher's impossible staircase. The hole I just climbed through appears to have been made in a sort of curving leather roof. Quite a thick leather roof, I think, with wooden rafters and leather bindings. A bit like one of those framed leather tents that Mongol nomadic tribesmen use."

He paused and then added, "Fantastically well made, really. I mean, extremely strong. And —"

"I believe it's called a yurt," said the professor.

Axel gasped audibly.

"What is it?" asked Philippa.

"If it's a yurt, it's the biggest yurt I've ever seen," said Axel. "It must be at least a hundred and fifty feet in diameter. And probably as far down to the floor."

"Hold on," said John. "We're coming down."

John and Philippa climbed in after him. John went first and then helped his sister climb in.

John sighed with exasperation when he saw that his sister had brought Moby.

"Do you have to bring that stupid duck everywhere?"

"He's not doing you any harm," said Philippa.

They found themselves on a solid wooden frame that extended into the darkness. There was a sort of handrail and, peering carefully over it, John saw that the platform was perhaps a hundred feet off the floor. And that the system of ladders was, indeed, as Axel had described, like

Escher's impossible staircase. Except that it did actually look possible to climb down.

Axel was standing at the far end of the platform and staring down at something. Something that had been tied on to the platform.

"There's something dead here," he said.

The professor passed John another flashlight and followed the twins into the excavation. All three walked carefully toward Axel.

"It's the remains of something that had a peculiarly long neck," he said, shining his flashlight onto a weird-looking skeleton. "Perhaps a horse. But something very old, I should say."

"Or something very young," John said grimly.

"It's a baby camel," said Philippa. "Dunbelchin's calf, most probably."

"Yes," said John. "That's exactly what it is." He shook his head. "No wonder Dunbelchin remembered this spot. Even with a few feet of soil on top, she could easily smell and hear it through this leather roof."

"These were very calculating men, those Mongols," said the professor. "Very calculating and very cruel."

Axel took hold of the ladder.

"This ladder might be over seven hundred years old, but it looks safe enough." He started to climb down. "Everything is amazingly well preserved. But cold. Yes, it's very cold down here. It's the cold permafrost on the ground that's probably kept things preserved for so long."

"That's a pity," said Philippa.

"Why?" asked the professor.

"Our djinn power doesn't work when we get cold," said Philippa.

"Let's hope we're not here long enough for that to happen," said John, and climbed down the ladder after Axel.

Philippa left Moby on the top platform and went after her brother.

It was the echo of John's voice and Moby's quacking that first told Philippa how big the mausoleum of Genghis Khan really was. And glancing down the ladder herself, she was astonished at the size of the burial chamber. It was huge. Despite this, it wasn't very long before she started to suffer from the claustrophobia that often afflicts djinn when they find themselves inside confined spaces. But in Philippa's case, her claustrophobia had more to do with the fact that she was inside a mass grave, an uncomfortable fact that the smell of death and decay in her nostrils only seemed to underscore.

After climbing down the complex series of ladder and platforms, the four explorers found themselves on the floor of the burial chamber.

It was John who made the first two discoveries. It was an ossuary, which is what you call the final resting place of several sets of human skeleton remains. Except that this was no ordinary resting place and no ordinary ossuary, for there were many more than several human skeleton remains in this mausoleum. And while there were too many of the neatly stacked skeletons — most of which were still wearing Mongol armor — for John to count, there were also so many that one particular round number — twenty thousand, to be precise — seemed to present itself immediately to his mind. Indeed, it was more like a pyramid than an ossuary and it now occurred to him that the system of ladders and platforms down which they had just climbed seemed to have been built not only as a means of access up and down the height of the mausoleum but also to keep the carefully built mountain of bones firmly in position.

"You remember all those soldiers the sons of Genghis killed to keep this place a secret?" he said.

"Yes," said the professor. "Twenty thousand, wasn't it?"

"I just found them," said John. "All of them."

The others came to take a look.

"Incredible," said the professor. "Like sardines in a tin. They must have been killed as they lay one on top of the other. Absolutely incredible."

"*Horrible* is the word I'd have chosen," said Philippa.

"I've never seen such a large pile of bones," remarked Axel. "It's like an Everest of human bones."

John was already walking around the base of the pyramid. "Here," he said. "I think I found our man."

They followed him around to the far side of the ossuary to find another skeleton, seated on a throne that was set into the wall of bones. He wore better armor than the dead soldiers who surrounded him in death; but he was no less dead for all that. He wasn't very much taller than the long sword that lay across his thighs.

"You really think it's him, little brother?" asked Axel.

Philippa shone her flashlight onto the floor where underneath the dead man's feet was painted a map of Asia and central Europe, from Peking to the Danube.

"These look like his conquests," she said. "So who else could it be?"

John bent down to retrieve a piece of shiny wastepaper off the ground. He glanced at it and then put it in his pocket.

A little farther away, they came across what had once been the great khan's treasury; they knew this because there were wall paintings of stewards and slaves filling chests with coins and jewels, silks, perfumes, and most eloquently, a golden casket with a picture of an exploding volcano on the front.

"The Hotaniya crystals," said the professor. "They must have been in that golden casket."

But of this and the other treasures in the tomb of Genghis Khan, there was no sign because all of the chests were gone or empty.

"It looks like everything of value that was here has been stolen by the grave robbers," said Philippa.

"That's what grave robbers do, little sister," said Axel.

"I wonder why they left that sword on his lap," said John.

The professor inspected the hilt more closely. "For the simple reason that if you were to pull it away, you would bring this entire mountain of bones down upon your head. It's very cleverly positioned. Look."

John bent forward to take a closer look at the sword. "Yes, you're right." He shrugged. "Ingenious."

"To protect a rusty old sword?" Philippa frowned. "I

think not. More ingenious would have been a way of protecting what was in the khan's treasury."

"You sound almost disappointed," said Axel.

"We're not out of here yet," said John.

"Well," said Philippa. "We've confirmed what we always suspected. That one of the things that was here but that is here no longer were those Hotaniya crystals. We've also confirmed that someone robbed this grave. And, most probably, that this must have been someone who lived in the age of rubberized tarpaulins."

"And chocolate." John held up the wrapper from a bar of chocolate. "It's the wrapper from a chocolate bar. I found it on the floor here in the treasury."

"I'm not sure that tells us very much more than we already know," said Philippa.

"Except that one of the grave robbers has a sweet tooth," said John. "It tells us that, at least."

"Someone with a taste for expensive chocolate," said Axel, examining the wrapper. "It tells us that, too."

"It's still not much to have found out," objected Philippa. "After all this effort."

"We're not finished looking yet," insisted Axel, glancing around the mausoleum for another clue. "Surely."

But after another thirty minutes they still hadn't found anything that might have provided an answer as to the identity of the grave robbers.

But there was a last discovery in the mausoleum, and it was the professor who made it after patrolling the walls of the mausoleum.

"Only the roof and the ladder system are man-made," he said. "The walls and the ground underneath the floor are natural."

"Natural?" Axel laughed. "How ironic."

"Does that mean what I think it means?" asked Philippa, shivering.

"Yes," said the professor. "All this time we thought we were in a man-made pit, and we're not. Fantastic. And, as you say, Axel, kind of ironic, yes."

"Will someone please tell me what this is?" demanded John.

"Certainly," said the professor. "We appear to be inside a volcano." He laughed. "Well, how marvelous. We're in a volcano. And given the size of that plateau, we're in what may be the largest volcano in all of Mongolia."

CHAPTER 37

THE OLGOI-KHORKHOI

That's a comforting thought," said Philippa.

"Oh, I wouldn't worry," said the professor. "This one is from ten thousand years ago. And like the animals that used to populate the earth at that time — the dodo, the giant lemurs, the moa, the elephant bird, Haast's eagle, the Mongolian death worm, and two species of Malagasy hippopotamus — this particular volcano is extinct. Like those other Mongolian volcanoes I was telling you about earlier. Bus-Obo and Khanuy Gol. I doubt this one has erupted for at least ten or twelve thousand years."

"Haast's eagle," said Axel. "That was a true raptor, wasn't it?"

"That's right," said the professor. "The largest eagle ever to have existed. At least twice the size of any eagle that exists today."

"I think I might have met one of those before," said John.

"Really?" said Axel.

"Remind me to tell you about it," said John.

"Only not now, eh?" said Philippa. "Come on. Let's get out of here. I'm freezing to death in this dreadful place."

They climbed back up the ladders to the top platform where they had found the skeleton of Dunbelchin's baby camel.

"I almost feel that one should offer the poor creature a decent burial," said John.

"That's just the camel in you," said Philippa. "And in case it slipped your mind, it *was* buried. Here. For almost eight hundred years."

"You know what I mean," said John.

"Not really," admitted Philippa. "But if it makes you feel better, then take it with you." She picked up Moby and put him under her arm.

John looked at the camel bones, of which there were a great many and decided to take only a thigh bone. He did not take the bone as a souvenir but as a keepsake of a memory that was now precious to him. Strictly speaking, this was Dunbelchin's memory but in John's mind it was difficult to know where his memory ended and the camel's began.

Axel climbed to the hole that led up to the surface. "Did you really see a Haast's eagle?" he asked.

"Actually, no," said John.

"I thought not," said Axel.

"It was a Rukhkh," said John. "But it might easily have been related to the bird you were describing."

"It must have been a pretty big rook," said Axel as he climbed out of the hole.

"Not that kind of rook," said John. "Actually, it was a prehistoric Quetzalcoatlus. A large pterodactyloid that could have picked up an elephant as easily as an owl takes a field mouse."

Axel started to ask where John had seen this bird, but his words were immediately swallowed up by a very loud scream of pain that was accompanied by a flash of blue light. This was followed by a profound silence.

"What was that?" said the professor.

"Axel?" called John. "You okay?"

There was no answer.

John was about to poke his head out of the hole to see what had happened when Philippa restrained him.

"Remember what Nimrod said," she whispered. "About booby traps."

Remaining in the hole, they called Axel's name again, and hearing no reply they called Groanin and then Nimrod, from whom no answer came.

The professor fumbled in his pocket and took out his Brunton compass. "The mirror," he explained. "I can hold it up to the edge of the hole and take a look outside without the risk of injury."

Sweeping the compass around the circumference of the excavation's lip, he stopped and then closed his eyes for a moment.

"What is it?" asked John. "What can you see?"

"Axel," he said quietly. "He's dead."

"What?" Philippa gulped loudly. "No, he can't be. How do you know he's dead? Here, let me have a look."

"He's dead," insisted the professor as Philippa took the

Brunton from his numb hand and held it up to take a look out of the hole herself.

What she saw left her feeling both horrified and then astounded.

Axel's incinerated body lay smoking and wholly unrecognizable on the ground a few feet from the excavation. And there was no doubt in her mind that the professor was right. Axel was quite dead. But the cause of his death still eluded them all. Steeling herself against the tears she wanted to shed, for she was more immediately concerned for Nimrod and Groanin than for her own grief, she continued to use the Brunton mirror to survey the scene on the surface of the plateau for some explanation of what had happened.

And then she saw the culprit. It was a thing easily seen under the lights of the barn ceiling. Bright red and about ten feet long, it appeared to be a very large and disgusting-looking worm with spiked projections at both ends.

"This Mongolian death worm you mentioned earlier," she said to the professor. "Sadly, I don't think it's as dead as the dodo."

She handed the professor the Brunton compass and when he had taken a look for himself, he handed the compass to John.

"I think you're right," said the professor. "It was supposed to live in the Gobi desert, but frankly, I always thought it was little more than a harmless legend."

"Not anymore," said John.

"Poor Axel," whispered Philippa.

CHILDREN OF THE LAMP

"Yes, indeed," said the professor. "Poor Axel. He was like a son to me. A very dear son. How am I going to tell his poor wife?"

"I don't want to sound insensitive, Professor," said John, "but that won't be a problem unless we can figure a way of getting out of this hole without being killed by that thing." He took another look at the mirror on the Brunton. "It seems to be guarding the entrance to this excavation. But let's make sure of that, eh?"

He took the baby camel's bone, hurled it out of the excavation and up into the air, and then watched the reflection of how the red worm reacted to this in the little mirror.

The reaction was instant. The worm reared up on its end, whereupon its intestine-like body rippled like a wave and directed a bright blue pulse of electricity at the bone, which, being very old, was affected only slightly. But the worm's behavior was clear enough; anything that came out of the hole was likely to be attacked by the worm.

"It seems to behave exactly like an *Electrophorus electricus*," said the professor. "An electric eel, which is of course not a true eel at all, but a fish. Instead of generating a current of electricity that conducts through water, this worm generates a current that travels through air, like a bolt of lightning. An electric eel can generate up to five hundred volts, which could be fatal to a human being. Given what happened to Axel, this looks much more powerful than that. Perhaps ten times as powerful."

"Fascinating," said John. "But what are we going to do

about it? Anyone who lifts his head through that gopher hole is liable to find himself with a permanent haircut."

"Can't you use your powers to get us out of here?" said the professor. "To kill it?"

"I'm afraid that when we get cold our powers desert us for a while," explained John.

The professor nodded. "I remember you telling me."

"Which," added Philippa, "could be some time given how cold it's getting. I'm freezing."

"Me, too," said John.

"Where's Nimrod?" said the professor. "Why doesn't he fix that horrible thing?"

"I wish I knew the answer to that," said John. "I really do. After what happened to Axel, I'm really worried about him, and Groanin, too."

"These eels," said Philippa. "You seem to know a lot about them. Is electric eel a delicacy in Iceland, too? Like rotting shark?"

"No. The electric eel lives mostly in the fresh waters of the Amazon and Orinoco Rivers. I was down there a few years ago to observe Ubinas, which is the most active strato-volcano in Peru. And I spent some time on the river with local Indians. *They* eat them. For *them*, they're a delicacy. But *I* didn't have any."

"You surprise me," said Philippa.

"Wait a minute," said John. "If the Indians killed an electric eel, they must have worked out a way of not getting hit with five hundred volts."

"Oh, they did," said the professor. "But it takes time. I believe that what they do is to make the eels keep discharging electric current until they tire. The organs generating the eel's electric power simply runs out at which point they can be safely handled — for a while, anyway. But as you can imagine, that's a difficult judgment to have to make."

"So maybe we have to tire this one out in the same way," said John. "Until it's no longer generating so much power."

Philippa who was already reading John's mind saw the beginnings of his plan.

"Yes, that's a good idea," she said. "We could use some of those bones from the dead camel and, if necessary, the ossuary, and keep throwing them out of the excavation until the death worm tires itself out."

"And then what?" asked the professor. "Even a smaller amount of electricity from that thing could leave you lying stunned on the floor."

"Good point," admitted John.

"Well, we certainly can't stay here," said Philippa.

"I think we'll have to until we can think of a way of protecting ourselves against the death worm's power," said the professor.

They sat down on the platform and tried to think of a way forward. The professor rubbed his growing beard, which helped him think; John tapped on his own head with a knuckle, which helped him think, sometimes; and Philippa pulled her feet toward her and stretched the muscles on the backs of her legs, which served to concentrate her mind wonderfully because almost immediately she nodded and said that maybe she had half the answer.

"Axel was wearing leather boots, right?" she said.

"Oh, yes," said the professor. "He bought them in England. Axel was very proud of his English boots."

"Maybe so." Philippa lifted her foot and showed off her own boot. "But rubber soles are better when it comes to insulating us from direct contact with the earth's magnetic field, right?"

"A bit, yes," said the professor. "But not enough to stop you from getting hurt, I'd have thought. No, you need something else. Some way of insulating your whole body."

Again they thought for a moment.

Suddenly, John punched the flat of his hand. "I've got it," he said. "The tarpaulin covering this hole is rubberized. If we can wrap the thing in the rubber tarpaulin, then, perhaps, we can safely handle it."

"Brilliant," said Philippa. "Of course. That's the only solution."

"I'll have to go," said John.

"Why you?" asked Philippa, hauling the tarpaulin down into the hole.

"Because I'm also wearing rubber-soled boots," said John. "In fact, if anything, my rubber soles are thicker than yours."

"There's a hole in it," said the professor. "There's a hole in the tarpaulin."

"Do you have a better idea?" asked John.

"No," admitted the professor. "But I'm not wearing rubber-soled boots. And I can't allow you to go. It wouldn't be right. You're — *children*."

"Maybe so, but there's another reason it makes sense for one of us to go," said Philippa. "Djinn like us are made of fire. Not earth, like mundanes. I mean, humans. So, it has to be assumed that we stand a much better chance than you of surviving a bolt of electricity from the Mongolian death worm."

"She's right," said John. "She's always right." He shrugged. "But it should be me who goes. I'm a much faster runner than you."

Philippa nodded. "I'll buy that."

The twins started to throw bones out of the hole, one after the other in quick succession, and each time a bone appeared the death worm sent a bolt of electricity in the same direction. This continued for almost an hour, with the professor keeping the creature under observation in the mirror of his Brunton.

"Is it tiring yet?" asked Philippa. "Because I am."

"No, not yet," said the professor. "Not obviously."

"Keep throwing," said John.

"When I bought this thing," said the professor, "I hardly suspected that this is what I'd use it for."

"If it saves our lives, it will have been worth every penny," said Philippa.

"You know, we should really use something else before one of us goes out there," said John. "It's hard to tell how much current it's using against old bones." He was looking at Moby while he said this and it was quite clear to Philippa what her brother was driving at.

"Oh, no," she said, stroking Moby's green head. "You've never liked him. I let him fly out of here and we end up with roast duck."

"You'd prefer I get roasted, is that it?"

"No, of course not."

"Well then." John hurled another bone into the air with frustration. "You ask me, it's about time that duck earned its passage."

"He's right, Philippa," said the professor. "We need something living with which to test the worm's power." He shrugged. "And look, it's quite possible that the worm won't be expecting something that flies out of the hole and keeps on flying."

Philippa said nothing.

"You know," continued the professor, "I used to go duck shooting when I was a boy. And I never ever managed to hit one. Not ever. Ducks are pretty quick in the air. Much quicker than you think. I seem to remember that ducks can fly at up to sixty miles per hour."

"And what will we learn if the worm misses him?" said Philippa. "Only that ducks can fly fast."

"We'll know that the worm is getting tired, perhaps," John said lamely. "But you're right. We'll find out a lot more if Moby does get hit." He threw another bone out of the excavation. "What can I say? I'm all out of good ideas. And unless you want me to go down that ladder and risk obliteration under that ossuary thing, we're all out of bones, too."

Philippa nodded. Without a doubt, John and the professor were both right but that didn't make it any easier to risk the life of her pet. She stood up and collected Moby off the platform. She kissed him on the head and spoke gently into his all but invisible ears. Then she lifted him to the hole above their heads and threw the bird into the air as if he were a homing pigeon she was sending on an important mission.

There was a loud flapping and quacking as Moby quickly ascended through the air.

"Go, Moby, go!" she shouted as the duck flew out of sight.

Then there was a blue flash and with a scream of fear, she grabbed the Brunton from the professor's hand and was just in time to see Moby drop with a thud onto the plateau as if shot by a hidden duck hunter. But he was not dead. For a moment he lay there, stunned, with one wing trailing to the side before he shook his head, collected himself, and got up onto his feet again, quacking a little and preening himself where some of the feathers were now missing from his body.

All of which seemed to draw another bolt of electricity the poor duck's way.

Moby quacked loudly and somersaulted as the impact of the electricity knocked him over again.

"Stay still, Moby!" yelled Philippa. "Don't move. It's the movement that makes the worm attack. Stay still or you'll be killed."

But John had already arrived at a very different conclusion.

CHAPTER 38

SCHADENFREUDE

Groanin had not moved a muscle since the arrival of the horrible, slimy, giant red worm onto the plateau. The lethality of this hideous creature was quickly confirmed to the butler when a poor bat, attracted by the lights of the barn, had fluttered in and was apparently hit by a powerful current of electricity generated by the creature's throbbing and slimy body. By the time it hit the ground, it looked like a burnt Frisbee.

As a consequence of the bat's incinerated fate, Groanin had recognized the importance of remaining completely still for fear of attracting the worm's attention and, in this respect, it was fortunate that he had been sitting down beside a sleeping Nimrod when the nasty, great, wormy thing — as he now thought of it — slithered out of the damp Mongolian fog. It was easier keeping still when you were sitting down: The one thing Groanin knew about all large and nasty-looking animals that killed things was that it was always best to keep still. But through clenched false teeth and in the hope of awakening the sleeping djinn, he had spoken to Nimrod as loudly as he dared; yet despite this, his employer remained more soundly asleep than would have seemed possible. In all the many years Groanin had worked for Nimrod — and, being his butler it was duty, at home in London, to waken his employer with a handsome breakfast and a freshly ironed newspaper — Groanin had never known Nimrod to sleep so solidly.

"No one would believe that a man employed by a powerful djinn could find himself involved in so many scrapes as me," he muttered quietly to himself. "One scrape after another. If I ever get out of this alive, I might just go to bed and stay there for a week."

An hour had passed in this way during which time Groanin had worried that the others would not come out of the hole and rescue him, and then worried that the others would come out of the hole and be killed themselves, as poor Axel was the minute he had climbed back onto the surface of the plateau.

"Poor lad," Groanin muttered. "Such a nice young fellow, too. Hey, Nimrod, you great, fat pudding, wake up and do something before your nephew and niece are killed as well."

But Nimrod remained asleep.

Even when someone — John? Philippa? — started throwing old bones out of the excavation and these had been noisily zapped by the beast, one after the other, like clay pigeons, the djinn had stayed asleep.

Then Moby, Philippa's duck, had flown out of the hole and, despite being electrocuted, too, had not been killed, at which point Groanin had recognized the cleverness of throwing the bones out of the hole, which previously he had regarded as nothing more than stupid folly. Now he perceived that the creature was tired and that, like a common alkaline battery, its electricity-generating organs were running out of power.

This realization was quickly followed by the sight of John leaping out of the excavation, holding a large sheet of rubberized canvas in front of him and running bravely toward the worm with the evident intention of rendering the worm harmless.

"Attaboy, John," he yelled, and got to his feet to help.

It was as well he did because the bolt of electricity the creature had intended for John came Groanin's way instead and knocked Groanin off his feet and left him lying stunned on the ground and gasping like a newly landed salmon. It was this impulsive action on Groanin's part that gave John sufficient time to throw the rubber tarpaulin over the Mongolian death worm, thereby insulating its electrically charged body long enough for him to deliver a well-aimed kick at each end of its body, and with the not-unreasonable assumption that one of these ends was the creature's head.

The creature lay still, at which point, cheering and shouting loudly, John jumped on its thicker section, up and down, as heavily as he was able, which was part triumph and part determination to make sure the creature was beaten.

"I've beaten it!" he yelled. "It's dead. The rotten, murderous, slimy thing is dead. Hooray! Hooray!"

Nimrod sat up and rubbed his eyes. "What's all the shouting about?" he yawned.

On top of being hit twice by a bolt of electricity, all of this shouting and cheering was too much for Moby. He flew off and was not seen again.

Groanin pointed. "It's a nasty, great, horrible, red, wormy thing that John has killed or immobilized," he said. "For the last couple of hours while Your Majesty has been asleep, it's been patrolling the plateau, killing poor Axel and keeping the rest of us in terror. And John killed it. At least I hope he did. I feel like cheering myself."

There was no time for Nimrod to say anything. But recognizing the huge danger John was now in, he had just enough time to create a strong gust of wind that blew John from off the worm's body and several feet through the air.

Emerging from the excavation, Philippa screamed, for she thought that John must have been hit by another bolt of electricity from the Mongolian death worm. Instead, John landed harmlessly on the ground and scrambled to his feet just in time to see Nimrod bring all of his remaining djinn power to bear on the worm and render it completely harmless.

"Thank goodness you're all right," said John. "We thought the worm had got you both. We were worried about you."

"Not as worried as I was when I saw you jumping on that *olgoi-khorkhoi*. That's Mongolian for 'large intestine worm.'"

Nimrod drew back the rubberized canvas sheet to take a closer look at the creature.

"That is what it looks like, all right," said John. "But I had it licked."

"Perhaps you did," said Nimrod, "but jumping up and down on a Mongolian death worm is never a good idea. Which is why I blew you off. This kind of polychaete is very rare, you know. Almost extinct."

"That was you?"

"Of course."

"I like that." John scowled. "Here am I trying to kill it and you're worried about it being extinct."

"You might have been extinct yourself," said Nimrod. "The Mongolian death worm's body is filled with a particularly powerful sulfuric acid. If it had burst while you were using it as a trampoline, you might have been severely burned, my boy. Perhaps even killed. That's why I blew you off and then neutralized the acid inside the worm."

"Oh, I see. I didn't know."

"No, well, why should you? These things aren't exactly common, thank goodness. I expect it was created by Genghis Khan himself before he died and set here by his sons to guard the tomb. That seems to be the only explanation for the worm being so very long lived as this one."

Philippa wiped the tears from her eyes and came and hugged her uncle, and Groanin, too. "I thought you were both dead," she said.

"No," said Nimrod. "Just asleep."

She looked at Axel. "What are we going to do with Axel?" she asked. "We can't leave him here." She swallowed with difficulty. "He was so — so very nice."

"No, of course, we're not going to leave him here." Nimrod went and placed a hand on the professor's shoulder. "We'll take him with us, poor fellow."

"Thank you, Nimrod," said the professor.

No sooner had Nimrod uttered these words than he had spoken a diminuendo, reducing Axel's burnt body to the size of a tiny doll so that they might easily carry him with them on the flying carpet. Then he placed the cadaver inside a cigar tube and handed this to the professor.

"In this way you can easily carry him back to Iceland, and have him buried there," explained Nimrod. "All you have to do is take his body out of this cigar tube when you get back home and it will be returned to its previous shape." He shrugged. "What's left of it. I'm so very sorry for your loss, Snorri."

The professor nodded and slipped the cigar tube into his coat pocket.

"Ten years he's been with me," said the professor. "I shall miss him very much."

"Groanin?" said Nimrod. "Would you be kind enough to drag the worm's body over to the excavation and drop it in the hole?"

"Very good, sir."

Nimrod looked at the twins. "Now then. To business. There's no time to lose if we're going to prevent a climatic disaster. What did you two discover in the tomb?"

"Very little, I'm afraid," said Philippa. "And only what we always suspected: that one of the things that was there but which is there no longer was those Hotaniya crystals. We've also confirmed that someone robbed the grave. And, quite recently, too."

"Good grief, is that all?" Nimrod sighed irritably. "Groanin, wait a moment. Before you tip that worm into the hole I'd better go down there and take a look for myself."

"Very good, sir."

"You won't find anything," said John. "Just a lot of bones. And a sword."

"What, nothing at all?" said Nimrod.

"There's a skeleton on a throne that looks as though it must be Genghis Khan," said Philippa. "And he's sitting under this mountain of bones."

"How did you know it was him?" asked Nimrod, approaching the excavation.

"For one thing, the sword that was lying across his thighs," said John. "And because his feet were on a map of the Mongol conquests."

"A fair assumption," said Nimrod. "Anything else?"

The twins shook their heads.

"Professor?"

"Nothing," said the professor.

"No matter how small," insisted Nimrod.

The twins shook their heads.

"You're sure?"

"Sure, we're sure," said Philippa.

"Well, there was some wastepaper they dropped," said John. "But it was nothing important."

"What sort of wastepaper?" asked Nimrod.

John shrugged. "A chocolate bar wrapper, that's all," he said. "Nothing that really helps identify who could have robbed the grave."

"Let me see." Nimrod snapped his fingers at John urgently.

John frowned. "I'm not sure if I even kept it," he confessed, searching his trouser pocket. "What with the worm 'n' all, it kind of slipped my mind that I had it." He shook his head and then tried the other pocket. "Hey, it's only a candy wrapper. What's the big deal?"

"The big deal, as you put it, is this, John," said Nimrod. "It is almost invariably the case that the important clues to crimes are apparently small and insignificant. That is the first principle of forensics. You must learn to overlook nothing, no matter how inconsequential, for all detectives worship at the altar of coincidence and small things."

John moved on to his coat pockets and finally he found what he was looking for. He handed the golden wrapper over to his uncle who spread it flat on his palm.

The chocolate brand was not one either of the twins — who liked chocolate — had ever heard of. Indeed, the only reason John had recognized that it was a chocolate bar wrapper was the fact that the word *chocolate* appeared under the logo RAKHA.

"This is no ordinary chocolate wrapper," said Nimrod. "This is the wrapper from a box of the most expensive chocolate in the world. A box of RaKha plain chocolate costs almost a thousand dollars a pound."

"For a box of chocolates?" Groanin was appalled. "You're joking. How could a box of chocolates ever cost a thousand dollars a pound? And who would be mug enough to buy it?"

"I believe the chocolate is obtained from cacao beans grown in the finest plantations in Ecuador, Trinidad, and Venezuela," said Nimrod. "And people do buy it. After all, everyone likes chocolate."

"At a thousand dollars a pound?" said Philippa. "It doesn't seem possible."

"That isn't RaKha's most expensive box," said Nimrod. "They have a line of chocolates called RaKha Eldorado that costs almost twice as much because Eldorado chocolate is made by applying real flakes of twenty-four-karat gold to each praline by hand."

"So you're eating gold, as well as chocolate," said John.

"Just like that unspeakably disgusting Roman emperor Heliogabalus," said the professor. "Who abandoned himself to the grossest pleasures, including, I believe, a drink made from gold."

"Precisely," said Nimrod.

"Give me a Hershey bar any day," said John. "But what does it tell us apart from the fact that the grave robbers had a taste for very expensive chocolate?"

"It tells us a great deal," said Nimrod. "According to Mr. Bilharzia, there were only four copies ever printed of *The Secret Secret History of the Mongols* by Sidi Mubarak Bombay, the book he wrote about the search for the tomb of Genghis Khan with the help of his friend, Henry Morton Stanley. And one of those copies is owned by a man called Rashleigh

Khan, who believes himself to be the descendant of Genghis Khan."

"Along with sixteen million other people," remarked Groanin.

"Exactly so," said Nimrod. "The man is deluded, certainly. However, he is very rich and very powerful and he is the owner of a large multinational corporation called RaKha that makes, among many other things, this very expensive chocolate."

"Wasn't his yacht anchored in the Bay of Naples?" said Philippa. "When we were on vacation in Sorrento?"

"The *Schadenfreude*," said John. "I remember. It's supposed to be the largest yacht in the world. Six hundred and fifty feet from bow to stern."

"Yes, that's right," agreed Nimrod. "And it's a yacht that's well named in the case of Mr. Rashleigh Khan. *Schadenfreude* is a German word, but a loanword in English. It means 'pleasure derived from the misfortune of others.'"

"Then I must have been feeling Schadenfreude when I was cheering as I was jumping up and down on that horrible worm," said John.

"Indeed, you were," said Nimrod. "And, in that particular situation, your sense of Schadenfreude was entirely justified. However, when we think of Mr. Rashleigh Khan, we must imagine a man cheering while jumping up and down on the bodies of the people he has stepped on in order to reach the top. Who delights in their ill luck. A man who once confessed during a television interview that nothing confounds him so much as a good friend's success."

"He sounds perfectly awful," said Philippa.

"So are you saying that he's the grave robber of Genghis Khan?" asked the professor.

"I'm saying that he, or perhaps those working for him, is now our number one suspect," said Nimrod.

"But what possible advantage could he gain from using the Hotaniya crystals of the Xi Xia emperor Xuanzong to affect the world's weather?" asked Philippa.

"Aye, that's the sixty-four-thousand-dollar question," said Groanin.

"Say that again, Groanin," said Nimrod.

Groanin frowned. "What?"

"One would hardly think you needed an invitation to say things twice," said Nimrod with some exasperation. "You say so many other things twice, unbidden. Say it again."

A little bewildered, Groanin said, "I said, that's the sixty-four-thousand-dollar question."

Nimrod nodded. "And when we were flying over India, on our way to Australia, you said something else of great wisdom, didn't you?"

"I did?"

"You said that whoever is doing this is very likely doing it for the same reason as all of the people who kidnapped you. *Money.*"

"Aye, money. I did say that. Money's still the reason most folk do things, good and bad."

"Precisely," said Nimrod. "Dollars. Thousands of dollars. Millions of dollars, probably. Perhaps more."

"How could Rashleigh Khan be making money from causing volcanoes to erupt?" asked John.

"That I don't know," said Nimrod. "But it's what we're going to find out."

He walked briskly to the carpet.

"Where are we going?" asked Groanin.

To his surprise Nimrod was singing a song in Italian:

"Ma nun me lassà,
Nun darme stu turmiento!
Torna a Surriento,
Famme campà!"

"Very nice, I'm sure," said Groanin. "But what does it mean? Where are we going?"

"It means that we're going back to Sorrento, Groanin," said Nimrod. "Back to the Bay of Naples."

CHAPTER 39

SITTING ON THE DOCK OF THE BAY

Sitting on the elegant terrace of the Excelsior Vittoria hotel high above the local docks in Sorrento, Nimrod watched Rashleigh Khan's enormous yacht, the *Schadenfreude*, which was still anchored in the Bay of Naples, through a pair of powerful binoculars while a waiter in a white jacket served afternoon tea to him, Groanin, the professor, and the twins.

Bigger than two football fields, the white motor yacht dwarfed every other boat in the bay. On the foredeck was a black helicopter and, from time to time, another smaller supply boat would leave the yacht's side and visit the Italian coast. Nimrod noted that the yacht was sailing under an American flag, which seemed to indicate that Rashleigh Khan was a citizen of the United States.

"Feels like déjà vu all over again, us being here," said Groanin. "If you believe in such things."

"I think you can believe in the feeling at least, Groanin," observed Nimrod. "It's the interpretation you choose to put on the feeling that is open to question."

"So much has happened since we were here," said Philippa, staring out to sea. "Makes you wish you could turn the clock back on all of this."

"Yes," agreed Nimrod. "It does."

Meanwhile, Philippa just wished that Axel could have been there with them to see the view. She hadn't told anyone that she loved him and now it didn't seem to be appropriate to mention it. So she just looked at the view and wished he could have seen it, too. And what a view it was. As a volcanologist, Axel would surely have appreciated it. The great pyramid of Vesuvius was connected to the summit of another inverted pyramid, only this one was made of smoke and ash. The sight dominated the whole landscape like the bearded, gray stone head of some giant Roman god — Jupiter or Mars — and she had an insight into what it must have been like for the poor citizens of Pompeii in A.D. 79.

Sorrento, on the other side of the bay from Vesuvius, was far enough away from the volcano for the ash cloud not to be a problem for the resort and its visitors. But the population of the city of Naples had been evacuated as a precaution and the local airport — like other airports all over the world — remained closed until further notice.

Nimrod was the only one on the terrace watching the yacht; everyone else was watching Vesuvius, many of them with telescopes in the hope of seeing something more spectacular than what was already taking place. It was hard to imagine just what this might have been: the mountain blowing its top, perhaps. Or molten lava pouring down the slopes of the volcano.

"Funny to think that just a short while ago, we were all sitting here enjoying our holiday," said Groanin. "Without a cloud in the sky to spoil things. Blissfully unaware of all that lay ahead of us. Funny thing, life. It seems to be what happens when you're making plans to do something else."

"As always, Groanin," murmured Nimrod, "you provoke my mind to cogitate in a way it did not cogitate before."

"Eh? What's that you say? I say, what's that you say?"

Nimrod did not answer his butler. He was too busy thinking.

So Groanin shrugged and looked at John.

"How big did you say that daft yacht is?" he asked John.

"Six hundred and fifty feet," said John.

"I'd be embarrassed to arrive anywhere in such a boat," said Groanin. "Even Queen Cleopatra in her barge, like a burnished throne that burned on the water, attracted less attention than that."

"Well said, Groanin," murmured Nimrod.

"Thank you, sir."

"Rashleigh Khan had it built just to spite another billionaire, Victor Pelorus, whose yacht until then had been the world's largest," explained John. "It cost four hundred million dollars and it's got its own missile defense system. It's even got a submarine and a tennis court." John lifted up his digital camera and took another picture. "It must be true," he added. "I read it in your newspaper, Groanin."

"Who on earth needs a submarine?" said Philippa.

"They're not much good on earth," observed John.

"Or a tennis court," said Groanin. "Who needs a tennis court? I said, who needs a tennis court? Beastly boring game."

"According to the newspaper it costs him a hundred thousand dollars just to fill up the fuel tanks," said John.

"How does anyone afford a garage bill like that?" said Groanin.

"You've heard of a hedge fund," said John. "Well, he's an expert in what the newspaper calls financial topiary. That's like an extreme hedge fund. Rashleigh Khan shapes whole economies into whatever shape you like. Tigers, pigs, you name it."

"I've never understood all that financial stuff," admitted the professor.

"Me, neither," said Groanin. "And if you ask me, most of them that are in it are just spivs and cowboys."

Nimrod was still watching the yacht through the binoculars. "It's an interesting yacht," he said. "All of the curtains in the staterooms are drawn. There's very little activity on deck."

"Well, I think it's a horrible yacht," said Philippa. "With a very horrible name. Imagine naming a yacht after a thing like that."

"What's most interesting about the yacht," said Nimrod, "is that it doesn't appear to move. I've been watching it quite closely and I swear this one hasn't moved by so much as a foot."

"It's at anchor," said Groanin. "It's not supposed to move."

"Not true," said Nimrod. "All ships at anchor move around a bit. The sea moves them. But this one hasn't moved an inch since I've been looking at it, which is" — Nimrod glanced at his watch — "almost an hour now. And that's even odder when you consider that the engines are running." Nimrod shook his head. "The engines on that yacht are running all the time."

"That is odd," agreed the professor. "The man's carbon footprint must be enormous."

"Bigger than we yet know, I'll warrant," said Nimrod.

John took another picture, which gave Nimrod another idea.

"John? Did you take any pictures of the *Schadenfreude* when we were last here?"

"Yes, sir," said John. "Would you like to see them?"

"Yes, please."

John found some pictures he had taken on the day before the earthquake. "There's one," he said, showing his uncle the screen on the back of his camera. "I took that one off this terrace as well." John looked up at the *Schadenfreude* and then back at the picture on his camera. "Hey, Uncle, I think you're right. It was in exactly the same position as it is now."

"I thought as much," said Nimrod.

"I don't know what that tells us," muttered Groanin. "Other than the fact that some folk are so rich and bone idle that they can't even be bothered to move their boats and have nothing better to do than lie around all day and watch the rest of us poor idiots try to scratch a living."

"It tells us that the *Schadenfreude* doesn't behave like any ordinary yacht," said Nimrod. "Even one that's six hundred and fifty feet." He put down the binoculars. "No, I think we shall have to go aboard and take a look for some answers."

"At last," said John. "We're going to see some action."

"But I suspect the answers have a lot to do with Vesuvius. It was you, Groanin, who reminded me that it was Vesuvius that was the first volcano to erupt, when last we were here, enjoying our holiday. This is where it all got started." He shook his head. "What would I do without you, Groanin?"

"Don't mention it, sir," said Groanin.

"That's right," agreed the professor. "That's absolutely right. The earthquake that struck this region was what started all of the world's volcanoes to erupt at once. Which doesn't ever happen. At least it never did before."

"Rashleigh Khan was here then and he's here now," said Nimrod. "And he's up to no good, I'll stake my life on it." He frowned. "Did you say that the yacht has its own submarine, John?"

"Yes, sir. A luxury submarine."

"Now, why does anyone need a luxury submarine?"

"To go underwater in comfort," Groanin offered helpfully. He enjoyed being Watson to Nimrod's Sherlock Holmes. "Without getting wet? To run silent and sleep deep?"

But this time Nimrod ignored his butler.

"How are we going to get on board?" asked John eagerly. "Fly over there on the carpet? Steal a boat, maybe? Borrow a submarine of our own from the U.S. Navy base in Naples?

Scuba gear: We could wear wet suits, swim over underwater, and go aboard under cover of darkness, perhaps." He grinned. "Man, this is going to be fun."

"There's no time for any of that feature-film nonsense," said Nimrod. "Stealing. Wet suits. Swimming. Ugh. Even the flying carpet might not be a good idea if it has a missile defense system."

"Then how are we going to go aboard?" asked John. "Wait for an invitation to dinner?"

"Have you forgotten what we are?" Nimrod smiled and placed his hand on top of his nephew's. "We shall go aboard the *Schadenfreude* invisibly, of course. We shall float across the violet bay like the sweet breath of Zephyrus. Like three ghosts, we shall see what we shall see but we shall not be seen. So." Nimrod clapped his hands loudly. "We have to go up to our suite right now and leave behind our bodies, immediately."

"Hmm. Maybe you're right," admitted John. "I had forgotten about invisibility."

"Good," said Groanin. "That lets me out."

"Yes, and myself," said the professor.

"Me, too," said Philippa.

"You, Philippa?" said Nimrod. "Whatever do you mean? Surely you're coming with us."

"If you don't mind, Uncle Nimrod," said Philippa. "It feels much too soon for me to leave my body behind again, especially after what happened the last time with Charlie, in Australia. It scares me. But for him I might be dead."

"Yes, of course, my dear," said Nimrod. "I'd forgotten. It

was insensitive of me even to suggest it. John and I will go, just the two of us. Eh, John?"

"Yes, sir."

"You three can stay here and await our return."

"And I shall float, like the west wind, toward the hotel bar," said Groanin, heading across the marble terrace. "I feel the sweet, cold breath of a cocktail coming on," he said.

John chuckled.

"You're absolutely right, Uncle Nimrod. Being invisible is the best fun anyone can have."

CHAPTER 40

INVISIBLE TOUCH

John lay down on his bed and, leaving almost all of his power inside his body — which is the great disadvantage for any djinn, young or old, who steps out of his or her body — and set about raising his own spirit up to the ornate ceiling of the hotel bedroom.

In some ways, it always felt like he was growing taller — much taller — and it was only when he looked down and saw a figure lying on the bed that he hardly recognized as himself that John was absolutely certain he was hardly more substantial than the air-conditioned air around him.

"Are you there?" said a voice tinklingly close by the chandelier. It was Nimrod, whose spirit he couldn't see but whom he could smell quite distinctly. His uncle's body was lying on the other bed in John's room and, like John, his eyes were closed and he was for all intents and purposes, deeply asleep.

"Yes, I'm here," said the disembodied John.

"Since we have to travel a mile or so across the Bay of Naples to reach Rashleigh Khan's boat, it might be a good idea to hold hands," said Nimrod. "Sea breezes can be quite treacherous when one is out of body. One can be easily blown away."

John, who disliked holding hands with anyone unless they happened to be a girl who was not his sister, declined Nimrod's offer. "Er, no thanks, if you don't mind, I'd rather not."

"As you wish," said Nimrod.

Suddenly, he became almost visible, at least in outline, for Nimrod had moved in front of the air-conditioning unit on the wall up near the ceiling. "If you do get lost, then move somewhere cold, like this air-conditioning unit, so I can see you a bit."

"I remember," said John.

"Only try not to do it where there are people around or some hapless mundane will think you to be a ghost. Which is fine if you want to scare someone, but not so fine if it isn't. People have been known to have heart attacks when they see a careless, disembodied djinn."

"Yes, Uncle."

"And if you feel yourself starting to panic a bit about being a free and disembodied spirit, or if you're beginning to suffer from astral sickness, then just step inside a mundane's body and have a breather. Most likely, they'll think they had a daydream or something, and leave it at that."

"I have done this before, you know," said John. "Several times."

"I know you have," Nimrod said patiently. "And, of course, it's natural that you should think you know it all. I was the same when I was your age, John. To think you know everything is the enormous advantage of all young men; to realize for a fact that you know almost nothing in the scheme of things is the greater curse of old ones." He sighed loudly. "It must be so. It was always so. All right, listen. We'll rendezvous on the bow of the boat. Inside the helicopter if there's no one in it. Got that?"

"Yes, sir."

The two djinn floated out of the window, across the red roof of the hotel, down over the terrace with its marble balustrade and Roman statues, over the dock with its smaller pleasure boats and passenger ferry to Capri, and out to sea.

It was a warm day but not as warm as it had been before the eruption of Vesuvius; the huge cloud of ash and smoke in the sky acted like a screen to prevent the sun from raising the temperature in the Bay of Naples to the normal seasonal levels. As well as the air temperature, which seemed to be part of him, John could taste the salt in the sea, and smell the sulfur in the breeze; these were almost part of him, too. To be a free spirit was, for a djinn, to be at one with the universe.

John found that he moved much more easily as a spirit than as a physical body. Faster, too. Faster than any speedboat could have traveled. He skimmed the surface of the water like an invisible missile and, thinking he had left Nimrod far behind, he reached the gleaming white bows of the *Schadenfreude* in less than ten minutes.

The foredeck landing for the helicopter was more than twenty-five feet above the waterline and gradually John let himself rise up the bow until he was on the deck and standing next to a little black helicopter that neatly occupied an encircled H. A few yards away, a helicopter landing officer was talking to the pilot. John stepped through the solid that was the monogrammed door of the helicopter and found Nimrod already there ahead of him.

"What took you?" said his uncle's voice as John looked around the aircraft's interior.

"How did you do that?" he asked. "I was going pretty fast."

"But I was going faster," said Nimrod.

"I thought you were tired," said John.

"I was. I am. Very. In fact, I believe I've almost come to the end of myself. To the end of all that makes me what I am. But this is more important, wouldn't you say? That's why I hurried here just now. Because this is much more vital — this quest of ours, to rescue the world from itself, ironic as that might sound — than the mere matter of my own vitality. You know, I've never felt safe in these things. Even on the deck of a ship."

"What do you mean?" asked John. "I don't understand." And he felt this lack of understanding more because he could not see Nimrod's face, only hear his voice.

"I mean a helicopter seems so inherently non-aerodynamic," said Nimrod. "Just the nickname *chopper* sounds like it could be you that gets the chop, if you see what I mean."

"I'm not talking about the chopper," said John. "Nimrod? Are you saying you are losing your powers?"

"What happened to Dybbuk can happen to us all," said Nimrod. "He exhausted his Neshamah: the source of all his djinn power. He used it all up in sheer vanity, with trying to be a cheap cabaret magician. Remember?"

"How could I forget? But you're not saying that this is happening to you? Are you?"

Nimrod sighed loudly. "I suppose I am rather. Really, it will be all I can do to get us back to Fez to see Mr. Barkhiya and collect those other carpets we ordered."

"Don't say that," said John. "There's nothing wrong with you. Is there?"

"No one can keep going forever," said Nimrod. "And it's not that I'm losing *all* my powers, John. It's just that, like dear old Mr. Rakshasas, it's not what it was. Nor am I. I get tired more easily after using it. I need to rest more than of old."

"Why are you telling me this?"

"In case something happens to me. Like poor Charlie. And Axel. I'm afraid they've been on my mind, rather. Which is something else that happens when you get older."

"Nothing is going to happen to you, Uncle," insisted John.

"Let's hope so. Look, what I'm saying is this: that I can't do this without you, John. Or Philippa. Whatever lies ahead of us, I'm going to need your joint strength to help me through it. For all our sakes, you must promise me not to give up on the world of mundane. They have need of us now more than ever, my boy."

"Of course, I'm not going to give up on them. My dad's a mundane. And yes, I promise."

"Good. Come on. Let's go and snoop around. I think

393

we'll head belowdecks and look for Mr. Rashleigh Khan himself, shall we? Follow me."

"How shall I do that? That is, follow you."

"Oh, yes. I was forgetting. Tell you what, I'll hum. That's it. Just follow my humming."

"And if someone hears you? I thought you were worried that some poor mundane might think us a ghost."

"That's their problem. Now that I'm here and see the size of his boat, I realize I'm too tired to care much about the feelings of the people who work for Mr. Rashleigh Khan."

"What will you hum?"

"That's an excellent question, John. Let me see, now. It ought to be something appropriate, I think. Ah, yes. How about 'Coming Through the Rye'?"

"I don't know it."

"Of course you do. You just think you don't."

They went down the polished wooden stairs into the dining room with John following the sound of Nimrod humming "Coming Through the Rye," which, of course, he did recognize. A couple of times in the yacht's narrow gangways and passageways, they passed close by members of the *Schadenfreude*'s smartly uniformed crew who, hearing the sound of Nimrod humming, looked around nervously to see from where it was coming.

After several minutes, Nimrod stopped abruptly in what looked like a finely furnished study and, for a brief second, John passed straight through his uncle's spirit. Momentarily, he experienced his uncle's great worry for the world as well as a little of the weariness he had been talking about, and he let out a gasp as he felt the weight of them on his uncle's shoulders.

The study was like a museum and decorated with many Mongol treasures in glass cases that had obviously been looted from the grave of Genghis Khan: a golden breast-plate, a shield, a golden helmet, several Mongol swords, and a collection of priceless Mughal paintings. A small man sat in a big leather chair behind a large custom-made desk on which was ranged a whole battalion of telephones. He looked European but he wore an Asian-looking chin beard. And he was wearing a pair of chocolate-brown silk pajamas on which was the monogram RK.

"I think that's our man," whispered Nimrod as the man got up from his chair and knelt down beside a safe from which he took an ancient-looking gold box. The box was inlaid with the design of an erupting volcano and looked Chinese.

"The Hotaniya crystals," whispered John. "It has to be them."

For a moment, the man stopped and looked around, as if he had heard something; but then he shook his head, closed the safe, and left the room.

"Come on," whispered Nimrod. "Let's follow him."

John and Nimrod followed Rashleigh Khan into the center of the ship, where there was a sort of control room with a large indoor pool. But the pool was not for swimming. Floating in the bright blue water was a small submarine. Khan climbed aboard, followed invisibly by John and Nimrod; a few minutes later one of the submarine's crew members closed the outside hatch and they began their enclosed and rapid descent.

It was a short voyage to the bottom of the sea — no more than five minutes — where the midget submarine docked again with some other vessel. And this time, when the outside hatch opened, the two djinn were met with an astonishing discovery.

Anchored on the seabed underneath the *Schadenfreude* was a submersible drilling platform equipped with a viewing bubble, a small crew, a gymnasium, and a radio-control room. The drilling platform was tethered to the hull of the ship by several long cables which, thought John, probably explained why it was that the *Schadenfreude* never moved from its anchor.

Rashleigh Khan greeted the men aboard the drilling rig with an affable silence and carried on walking through a set of double doors that opened automatically and then closed behind him, but not before, once again, John and Nimrod had followed; as soon as they felt themselves rising slowly to the leather-lined ceiling, the two djinn realized they were in an elevator car and that this time they were descending at some considerable speed into a borehole made by the drill rig.

Their descent lasted almost fifteen minutes, by the end of which John was feeling decidedly queasy and told himself that if he'd had a stomach, he might have thrown up; it was only when the elevator car stopped moving and they emerged into a small and very warm cave that John realized he was actually feeling claustrophobic.

Other than Rashleigh Khan himself, there was only one person in the dimly lit cave: a short, fair-haired woman with a pointy nose and glasses. She was dressed in a white coat and holding a clipboard and, according to the name badge she wore on her breast pocket, her name was Dr. Björk Sturloson.

This was not a common name and John wondered if she might be related to the professor.

On the floor of the cave was a metal hatch like the one in the submarine and, once Khan arrived, the woman in the white coat put on a pair of thick leather gauntlets and began to turn the wheel on the hatch to open it.

As soon as the hatch was laid open, a wave of intense heat filled the undersea cave. Undeterred by the temperature, Khan put on some goggles, knelt beside the hatch, and carefully opened the inlaid golden box he had brought from the surface. Inside was what looked like a handful of small, uncut yellow diamonds.

John thought they might easily have been part of a meteorite from outer space; they looked to have an extra luminosity and sparkle that no terrestrial, earthly diamond ever had.

He glanced down the hatch and saw, at the bottom of a deep drill hole, a point of intense light that resembled a little sun, and it was a second or two before John realized he was looking into the actual molten bowels of the earth.

"Let's have some fun with Mr. Khan," whispered Nimrod.

"Yes, let's," whispered John.

"Did you say something, Mr. Khan?" asked Dr. Sturloson.

"No."

"My mistake."

Khan removed one of the crystals from the golden box and held it up to the light for a moment; he was about to drop it down the drill hole when the hatch closed abruptly with a loud bang.

"I think not, Mr. Khan," said the woman in the white coat. But the voice was not a woman's. It belonged to Nimrod and as soon as he heard it, John realized that his uncle had taken possession of Dr. Sturloson's body. "This horrible endeavor is now at an end."

Rashleigh Khan stood up and frowned.

"What on earth's the matter with you, Björk?" he said. "And why in the name of Sam Hill are you speaking in that ridiculous English voice?"

John almost laughed because Mr. Khan's own voice — thin, lisping, effete, with a distinct flavor of the American Deep South — was almost cartoonish in its delivery, and reminded John most of Droopy Dog.

"Well? I'm waiting. Explain yourself."

"I'm afraid that would take much too long to explain now," said Dr. Sturloson/Nimrod. "Let's just say that I've had a complete change of heart about what we're doing here."

"Look, Doctor," said Khan, "if this is some elaborate scheme of yours to persuade me to pay you more money, it isn't going to work. Considering all you have to do is keep an eye on the magma level and the temperature in the shaft, I think I pay you quite handsomely already."

"Next to the billions you're making from this criminal enterprise?" said Dr. Sturloson/Nimrod. "It's chicken feed."

"So it *is* about money." Khan smiled. "I thought as much. Where I am involved, it's always about the money. Sometimes it seems as if I've spent my whole life walking three steps behind my wealth."

"Stop, I almost feel sorry for you," said Dr. Sturloson/ Nimrod. "If you carry on like this, I shall have to take out my violin and play 'Hearts and Flowers.'"

"How rude you are. Well then, let's negotiate. I'm not an unreasonable man. Just an obscenely wealthy one. Only let's drop the soppy, stern, limey voice, shall we? Perhaps I do owe you something more than our agreed fee. After all, it was your idea to drill down into the gap between the Eurasian tectonic plate and the African tectonic plate. So, how much? Shall we say another hundred million dollars?"

Nimrod hesitated for a few seconds, just long enough to read what was in Dr. Sturloson's mind.

"Yes, of course, I see now," said Dr. Sturloson/Nimrod. "You've been dropping the Hotaniya crystals into the magma that's produced by the subduction of one tectonic plate below another. *That* magma also flows into the planet's surrounding mantle and produces the startling effect on all of the earth's volcanoes. It is clever. Clever but completely reprehensible and horribly criminal. And you'll probably get life in prison for this."

Rashleigh Khan sneered. "What is this? An attack of nerves? A crisis of conscience? Guilt? Or have you just lost your mind?"

"Like I said, it would take much too long to explain."

Nimrod read a little more of Dr. Sturloson's mind. "And

that's how you're going to make money out of this? From owning the world's entire supply of chocolate?" Nimrod shook Dr. Sturloson's head and gasped. "I'm not often shocked, Mr. Khan. But this is shocking. I can't believe anyone could be so selfish. Or greedy. Or trivial. That you should be prepared to risk millions of people dying of starvation *for chocolate*."

"You know? Now that I come to think of it, that voice suits you better than the Icelandic quaver I'd gotten used to. I do declare I prefer it. There's something annoying about anyone that can't actually pronounce the word *actually*." Khan shook his head. "And what do I care if millions of people starve?" He laughed cruelly. "Let them eat cake. The earth has an unsustainable level of population, anyway."

"Think of the world's children. What about them?"

"Children?" Rashleigh Khan's face wrinkled with disgust. "Children? I hate children. Always did. What do I care about children? They're nasty, horrible, greedy, dwarfish little creeps. Always whining. Always asking for more. 'I want I want I want.' Revolting. None of them has ever done a day's work. Oh, no. They want stuff, but are any of them prepared to find a job in order to get it? Not a bit of it. They're like locusts, I tell you. Parasites. It beats me why people have children. All they do is eat and consume and watch television and sleep until midday and live off the work of adult people. No, I hate children more than anything in the world. Besides the money, the reason I'm doing this is to spite all those horrible kids the world over." He laughed a cruel little laugh.

Nimrod had heard enough. He made Dr. Sturloson tighten the wheel on the hatch and then throw the leather gloves into the back of the cave.

Rashleigh Khan laughed. "What is this? You really think that's going to stop me?"

"It's over, Mr. Khan," said Dr. Sturloson/Nimrod. "I just want you to know that before we take your helicopter and fly to the police station in Naples. I believe there's a helipad on the city carabinieri roof, so that should make things nice and convenient for you. I know you value your own comfort and convenience above almost anything. Except money. And chocolate, of course."

Rashleigh Khan turned away and pressed the button on the elevator door. "This conversation is over," he said quietly. "And so are you, Dr. Sturloson. I do believe I will have some of my men come back down here and lower you very slowly, an inch at a time, into that magma shaft."

"John," said Dr. Sturloson/Nimrod. "Take control of Mr. Khan, will you?"

"Yes, sir."

"What?" Rashleigh Khan looked above his head. "What is this? What is going on here?"

But it was too late. John dropped off the ceiling and slipped into the billionaire's body and nodded back at his uncle.

"Okay," he said. "I'm in, sir."

Quickly, he read Rashleigh Khan's thoughts, which were all about Genghis Khan, and making money and yet more money, and chocolate, of course. Khan seemed to like that more than anything. John had never before encountered anyone who seemed to like chocolate better than Rashleigh Khan. So much that he was quite prepared to —

"What?" he said out loud. "That's disgusting."

"I assume you're referring to Mr. Khan's scheme, John."

"I am. Let me get this straight in my own mind. Well, in Rashleigh Khan's mind. But you know what I mean, Uncle."

"Yes, John."

"Rashleigh Khan has three obsessions in life: making money, Genghis Khan from whom he believes he is descended, and chocolate. Which is why he already makes the most expensive chocolate in the world."

"That's right."

"Having already tried and failed to buy up all of the major cacao tree plantations in the world, he did the next best thing: He bought the world's entire supply of cacao beans, from which chocolate is made. But not content with this, he then set about with his plan to destroy all of the cacao trees in every plantation on earth, using the Hotaniya crystals to drastically affect the world's weather."

"That's about the size of things, yes," said Dr. Sturloson/ Nimrod. "It's simple market economics. Having control of the supply, he then tried to drastically affect the demand."

"And in this way, he planned to raise the price of chocolate from the current level of four thousand dollars a ton to four hundred thousand dollars a ton; so that a chocolate bar currently costing a dollar would in the future cost a hundred dollars. He was actually planning to have cameras installed in candy stores around the world so that he could photograph the faces of kids who couldn't afford to pay a hundred bucks for a chocolate bar."

"Horrible."

John shook Rashleigh Khan's head. "But would anyone actually pay that kind of money for a chocolate bar?"

"I'm afraid that there's no limit to what people will pay for things they like. Caviar is nothing more than lightly salted fish eggs. But it's the scarcity that makes it expensive. Years ago, American bars used to serve it as a free snack to make customers thirsty. These days, it's three hundred dollars for just an ounce and three quarters."

"This whole scheme is the most evil thing I've ever heard of."

"It's pretty bad, isn't it? But tell me, John. Dr. Sturloson — who, as you may have gathered, is the professor's estranged wife — she has no idea how any of this can be prevented. Is there anything you can see in Rashleigh Khan's mind that tells you exactly how this might be achieved? If any of this can be reversed?"

John thought for a moment, which is to say he looked through some of what was in Rashleigh Khan's memory.

"There was something in the box that contained the Hotaniya crystals," said John. "Something in the safe. A parchment. Only Khan hasn't a clue what it means or how it works."

"Well, let's hope it *does* work. For all our sakes. Right you are, my boy. We'll collect that parchment on the way to the police station in Naples."

"But what are we going to tell them?"

"As Dr. Sturloson and Rashleigh Khan, we shall simply make a full and frank confession of everything. Make a clean breast of it. The whole dirty, rotten scheme."

John hesitated as, for a moment, one of Rashleigh Khan's own selfish thoughts managed to intrude upon his own.

"Do you think they'll believe us?" he asked.

"Don't worry about that," said Dr. Sturloson/Nimrod. "I speak fluent Italian. And I can assure you, John, that there's nothing or nobody the police in Italy like more than a billionaire who walks in off the street and confesses to a major crime."

CHAPTER 41

AUBADE

John and Nimrod returned Dr. Sturloson and Rashleigh Khan to the *Schadenfreude*, where the billionaire immediately ordered his pilot to make ready the helicopter for a flight to Naples. Then they went back to the study to retrieve the parchment from the safe.

The combination was the date of Rashleigh Khan's birthday, which was easy enough for John to recall. But the actual script on the ancient yellow paper was quite incomprehensible to both him and Rashleigh Khan. But luckily, Nimrod was able to understand it.

"I thought it would look a bit more Chinese," said John. "But it doesn't look even remotely Asian. Frankly, it looks more like Elvish."

"Until Genghis Khan, the Mongols were illiterate," said Nimrod, examining the parchment in Dr. Sturloson's hand. "They had no writing. Now Genghis Khan recognized the importance of writing but he also recognized that the Mongols could never have adopted Chinese script. Because they hated the Chinese. So Genghis had the Mongols adopt a style of writing that was an offshoot of Hebrew. And it's still in use today in some parts of Mongolia. Which is how I can read it. And you're right. It is like Elvish."

On the short flight into Naples, Nimrod read the parchment over and over and had to rehearse what he was going to tell John about it several times before he felt able to mention to him what it contained.

"It was Genghis Khan himself who wrote this parchment," said Dr. Sturloson/Nimrod. "Being half djinn, I daresay he knew rather more about how to counter the probable effects of the Hotaniya crystals on a volcano than the Chinese emperor Xuanzong."

He was silent for a minute while he thought about what he had learned from the parchment.

"Well?" asked Rashleigh Khan/John. "Does he say that there's a way of reversing this catastrophe?"

"Yes."

"Good."

"But it won't be easy. It won't be at all easy."

"I thought not."

Nimrod shook Dr. Sturloson's head. "In essence, what's written here is the Taranushi prophecy." He read out half of what was written on the parchment. "'For when a sea of cloud arises from the bowels of the earth and turns the lungs of men to stone, the wheat in the fields to ash, and the rivers to liquid rock, then only djinn who are twin brother and sister and true children of the lamp can save the world from inflammable darkness and destruction. Just as the creation of the world was attended by the sacrifice of many human twins, so the saving of the world will require the sacrifice of one set of djinn twins.'"

"Oh," said Rashleigh Khan/John. "I was afraid you might say something like that."

"But at least Genghis Khan suggests just what that sacrifice might entail," added Dr. Sturloson/Nimrod. "Which is bad, although not as bad as perhaps you might think, John, all things considered. I mean, it's really bad, there's no doubt about that. But it could just be worse."

"So, let's hear it."

Dr. Sturloson/Nimrod told him what Genghis Khan had written.

Rashleigh Khan/John let out a loud sigh. "That's just great," he said. "Are you serious?"

"I'm afraid so, John."

"Well, that's just great."

John turned Rashleigh Khan's head in the direction of Vesuvius, which now threatened the eastern part of Naples. There were, he knew, at least a million people living in the city before the evacuation, whose houses would be destroyed if the volcano blew its top the way it had back in A.D. 79. He couldn't let that happen.

"It does sort of make sense, rather, I'm afraid," said Dr. Sturloson/Nimrod. "I wish I could say it didn't. But it does. If I'm honest, I suppose I've always suspected that it would require something like this."

"It doesn't seem fair," objected Rashleigh Khan/John.

"What you're suggesting is way more than seems reasonable, Nimrod. At least to me. If I do this. If Philippa does this. Well, it's the ultimate sacrifice is what you're talking here, isn't it? For us, anyway. And what's more, you've had your life. We haven't."

Dr. Sturloson/Nimrod didn't answer.

"Is everything all right, sir?" asked the pilot.

John wanted to tell him it wasn't; he wanted to tell him to turn the helicopter around and go back to the yacht. After all, who would know that he wasn't the real Rashleigh Khan? The life of a billionaire might be fun. But, of course, he didn't.

"Yes, everything is fine, thank you," said Rashleigh Khan/John. "All things considered."

"It's just, well, you don't sound very much like yourself, sir," said the pilot. "If you don't mind me saying so."

"I have a summer cold," said Rashleigh Khan/John, by way of explanation. "We both have. Don't we, Doctor?"

"Yes," said Dr. Sturloson/Nimrod. He was silent for a moment as he stared out at the Tyrrhenian Sea and thought of his niece and nephew and all they had been through together. He knew this meant the end of their adventures and he allowed himself to shed a small tear.

"Rashleigh?"

"Doctor?"

Nimrod collected himself and thought of something less sentimental to say, something practical. "I just wanted to say that we shall have to stay long enough at the police station to make signed confessions. So I think it may be a while before you and I can return to the hotel in Sorrento."

"The others will be starting to worry about us."

"That can't be helped. What's important is that we leave these two characters behind bars. It doesn't matter if they're themselves again, even protesting their innocence and asking to speak to lawyers, provided the police have it all on tape."

"Yes. I understand. I understand everything now."

They landed on the roof of the police station in Naples and asked to speak to some detectives, who were surprised both by the manner of their arrival, and by their apparent willingness to confess to such heinous crimes. The Commissar himself came into the interview room and took their statements and, after several hours, the two signed their confessions and were led down to the cells at which point, Nimrod and John exited these mundane bodies. Immediately after this happened, Rashleigh Khan and Dr. Sturloson began, as Nimrod had predicted, to shout for lawyers and to protest their innocence and to demand bail.

"I'm not sure how an Italian court will view a defense of possession," Nimrod said to John. "Then again, Mr. Khan might just argue that he should be regarded as a special case because he's so rich. The *Animal Farm* defense. All animals are equal but some animals are more equal than others. I believe that sometimes works."

"I hope they throw away the key," said John who, understandably, was feeling less than charitable as far as Rashleigh Khan was concerned. "I hope they sink his stupid yacht.

I hope they — I don't know what I hope as far as what happens to Mr. Khan is concerned, but I hope it's something really crummy."

They floated out of the police station and down to the city's ancient port.

"It's a long way back to Sorrento," said Nimrod. "Perhaps a little too far to float through air. I'd suggest the local Circumvesuviana train — the one we took before — only it's probably not running because of the eruption. So we'd better take the ferryboat to the island of Capri, and change there for the ferry to Sorrento. You'll like Capri. It's one of the most beautiful islands in the world."

John growled his doubt. In other circumstances, he might have enjoyed a trip to Capri; after all, it was where the Roman emperors had gone on vacation. But since learning from Nimrod what needed now to be done, he had quite lost his previous mirth and found that he cared nothing for the island's famous beauty. Now all he wanted to do was return to Sorrento and enjoy one last night with Groanin and Philippa before doing — according to Nimrod's interpretation of the parchment — what needed to be done, first thing the following morning.

It was dark by the time they got back to the Excelsior Vittoria hotel and reclaimed their bodies, after which they found Groanin, Philippa, and the professor on the balustraded terrace, again, almost as if they had not moved from the last time. The professor and Groanin were each facing a large cup of coffee. Philippa was nursing a soft drink and holding the binoculars.

"We've been watching the *Schadenfreude*," said Philippa. "Waiting for something to happen. But apart from the helicopter taking off, so far nothing has."

"That's what you think," said John, and confirmed what they all suspected — that it had indeed been Rashleigh Khan who had robbed the grave of Genghis Khan, and how the yacht was full of stolen treasures including the golden box containing the Hotaniya crystals.

"So how come the Mongolian death worm didn't attack him?" asked Groanin. "Back on the plateau."

"It did," said John. "When I was inside his body, I learned that several of his men were killed before a thick fog descended on the plateau and they managed to make their escape."

"Then who covered up the excavation?"

"I rather think that must have been the Darkhats?" said Nimrod. "The special clan of Mongol tribesmen who Mr. Bilharzia spoke of and who are dedicated to keeping the grave a secret."

"We also found out why Rashleigh Khan is doing this in the first place," said John. "And while I understood it during the time I was in his loathsome body and I was using his enormous financial brain, I really don't think I understand it now because it's all economics and stuff."

Nimrod explained exactly how Rashleigh Khan had hoped to use a drastic alteration in the world's weather in order to drive the price of the world's chocolate supplies through the roof.

"The rich *are* different," said Groanin. "Truly it is easier for a camel to go through the eye of a needle than for an obscenely rich so-and-so like Mr. Khan to behave like a decent human being." He shrugged. "I suppose that's how they got so rich in the first place."

"Don't talk to me about camels," said Philippa. "If I never see another camel again, it will be too soon. I can still taste that Ozzy camel's mouth. Which makes me think a piece of chocolate might be just the thing right now."

Groanin noticed her eyeing the chocolate lying on the saucer of his coffee cup and handed it over. "Here," he said. "Have it. This is dark chocolate. I never much liked dark chocolate. It's much too bitter for me."

"Thanks," said Philippa, and ate it.

"Chocolate," remarked the professor. "It doesn't seem possible that someone should behave with such criminal disregard for his fellow human beings over something as mundane as chocolate."

"I prefer milk chocolate myself," admitted Groanin. "I say, I prefer milk chocolate. I don't know what I'd do if it was more expensive."

"None of that is important now," insisted John. "What's important is that we've stopped Rashleigh Khan from pouring yet more Hotaniya crystals into the borehole between the two tectonic plates in the Mediterranean Sea. And now we have to try to reverse this catastrophe. To turn the clock back to how things were when we arrived here in Italy."

"If only such things as turning the clock back were possible," said Nimrod. "Unfortunately, they're not."

Of course, if he had been aware of their previous adventure, their sixth together — which he wasn't — then he would have realized that such things *are* possible, in which case, there would have been nothing of which he could have been aware because it would never have happened in the first place. Time is like that and it's only the present you can ever be really sure of.

"So what are we going to do?" asked Philippa.

Nimrod nodded to John who proceeded to explain to his sister what needed to be done. To John's surprise, she seemed quite prepared for what he told her. And, in the light of Charlie's self-sacrificing and inspiring example, more than equal to what lay ahead.

"I told you before," she said to him bravely. "If I'm dealt the same cards as Charlie, I hope I have the guts to do as much as he did."

"I can help a bit," said Nimrod. "But only you two can do this. I think that perhaps I've always known that you two were marked out for some sort of special mission."

John nodded. "Then we're agreed," he said. "Tomorrow morning, we'll go back up Vesuvius and sort things out, if we can."

"Yes," said Philippa. "Agreed." She shrugged. "I'm sort of glad, really. Honestly, I am. I mean, it'll be hard. But so be it."

"I've something to tell you, too, Professor," said Nimrod. "Something that's also rather hard to hear, perhaps. But all the same, I think you ought to know about it."

Then Nimrod told the professor of how he and John had

413

made the acquaintance of the professor's wife, and how she was now in a Neapolitan prison.

"Best place for her," said the professor. "But, I am still married to the woman, so I suppose I'll go to Naples and see what I can do for her. At least I will after we've been back up Vesuvius."

"What about you, Groanin?" asked Nimrod. "Are you coming tomorrow?"

"Of course," said the butler.

"You didn't come the last time we decided to go up Vesuvius," said Philippa. "You resigned."

"Aye, and shall I tell you what that taught me? That you don't know what you've got until it's gone. I learned that I didn't know how well off I really was with you and your brother and your uncle."

"It could be dangerous," said John.

Groanin laid a hand on John's hand and then took Philippa's in his own. "You honestly don't think I'd let you do this by yourselves, do you? Not after everything that we've been through. Hot lava couldn't stop me from coming this time. I say, hot lava couldn't stop me from coming this time. Nor all the fire and smoke and ash that's in the earth. And just remember this, you two: Fortune favors the brave."

CHAPTER 42

THE SACRIFICE

The twins slept little that night. They had far too much to think about. John watched television in his room for several hours. Philippa wrote a letter to their mother, which she signed from both of them.

They were up at seven A.M. and somehow John managed to eat a large breakfast in the hotel's spectacular dining room. Philippa had a cup of coffee. Groanin, who had already breakfasted, shimmied into the dining room carrying a picnic hamper.

"Just in case we have need of refreshment," he said. "That's the thing with climbing a mountain. It gives you an appetite without the means of satisfying it."

"I don't think I shall be wanting anything to eat, Groanin," said Philippa.

"Me, neither," said John. "Take it from me, the condemned man just ate a very hearty breakfast."

"I'm very glad to hear it," said Groanin.

The Circumvesuviana train was, as Nimrod had supposed, not running; so they hired a Land Rover locally and drove north, around the bay, to the Parco Nazionale del Vesuvio. As before, this was closed and closely guarded by several dozen policemen and, this time, it was the professor who talked their way through. Which ought to have been a little easier now that he was no longer wearing a mask, but wasn't; it was only when he pulled his black polo-neck sweater over his head and had Groanin cut him two eyeholes that the police finally recognized him.

They drove up the mountain to the end of the winding road, and then, leaving the Land Rover, set out to ascend the last thousand feet on foot.

The ground was warm underneath their boots. In other places, it was a lot more than warm. Steam poured out of fissures in the rocks in a way that reminded John of a New York hot dog stand on a cold day. A strong wind was carrying a plume of ash and smoke as tall as the Empire State Building away from them as they climbed. A couple of times Groanin stopped, almost out of breath, wiped his pink forehead, and looked up at the tumbling gray cloud and tried to contain his mounting fear for the sake of the twins.

"I feel like Pliny," he said with a brave smile. "That Roman writer fellow who popped up here to take a look when Pompeii was first threatened with destruction. I think he was writing a book about natural history at the time and he thought that coming here might be good research, as they say."

"What happened to him?" asked John.

"Er, I don't know," admitted Groanin. "But I do know he got married three times. And his book got published. So he must have done all right for himself. Anyone who writes a book seems to do all right for himself." He pulled a face. "Can't imagine it were a bestseller, though. There wasn't much that was natural that them Romans liked."

"It was Pliny the Younger who got married three times, Groanin," said Nimrod. "You were thinking of Pliny the Elder. And in spite of the fact that his book was published without a final chapter, it was a great success. Indeed, it is one of the few works of Roman literature that have survived to the present day."

"But why no last chapter?" asked Groanin. "Did he run out of inspiration, or ink, or what?"

Nimrod shrugged, pretending that he couldn't remember. "I've forgotten," he said. "It must have slipped my mind." Changing the subject, he added, "You know, it's lucky the cloud is blowing the other way, so that we can enjoy the view. Local people come and get married up here, you know. Because of this marvelous view."

The professor, however, wasn't much interested in the view; he'd seen it many times before. He was much more interested in Pliny the Elder.

"Pliny the Elder was killed," said the professor bluntly. "Right here, on Vesuvius." He also stopped on the narrow path for a breath, and stroked a beard that was now as bushy as Pliny's own.

"I suppose the poisonous gas from the volcano got him, did it?" said Groanin. "Or the lava, perhaps?"

"No, he had a heart attack walking up the slope," said the professor. "He was rather a fat man. And not very fit."

"Oh," said Groanin, who was quite fat himself. "I see."

"But even today," added the professor, "we volcanologists still use his name as a term for a very violent eruption of a volcano that is marked by columns of smoke and ash that extend high into the stratosphere. We talk of a Plinian eruption. Like this one."

Groanin smiled thinly. "How very fascinating," he said, although in truth, he was more horrified than fascinated. "Thank you for that. I say, thank you for that."

"Don't mention it," said the professor, whose own thoughts were mostly of his poor wife. Despite what he had said the previous day, he still loved her. Love is like this, sometimes.

Noting Groanin's obvious disquiet, Philippa said, "Don't worry, Groanin. It's not far to the top now. About half an hour."

"That is a relief," said Groanin as a jet of hot smoke and gas hissed out of a large hole in the ground next to him as if from the wheels of a waiting locomotive train. "I'm sure I'll feel a lot more relaxed when we reach the top." He opened the picnic hamper, took out a bottle of water, and poured the contents down his throat.

John reached the top first and, as before, the crater rim offered a sight worthy of Dante's *Inferno*, at least that was what Nimrod — who arrived close behind him — said. John didn't have much of an idea who Dante was, but he knew an inferno was a place of fiery heat or destruction where sinners were supposed to suffer eternal punishment, and that looked like a pretty good description of the volcano, which was even more daunting to the eye and mind than the last time he had been there. Whereas before, the crater had been mostly filled with hot dust and gravel, now it was full of dull molten rock that, at any moment, might be blasted high into the air. John knew that he could no more have rappelled safely into the crater than he could have skied down a lava flow.

The professor, arriving a few minutes after Nimrod, let out a breath and a loud gasp at the horrid spectacle that met his expert eyes.

"Incredible," he said. "I think we must be in the final volcanic phase before there is a violent eruption. Which makes me suppose that many other volcanoes in many other countries are about to blow, as well."

"In which case, we have arrived in the nick of time," said Nimrod. "Possibly these would already have erupted but for the fact that we were able to prevent Rashleigh Khan from adding yet more Hotaniya crystals to that borehole."

Philippa and Groanin, still carrying the picnic hamper, brought up the rear.

Groanin sat down heavily on a rock and then stood up abruptly as the heat from the rock scorched his trousers.

"Flipping heck," he yelled, rubbing his painful backside. "Fetch the sauce. I say, fetch the sauce. It's like sitting on a barbecue up here."

"Yes, do be careful, Groanin," said Nimrod.

In response, Groanin muttered something about locking a stable door after the horse had bolted.

"So what do we do now?" Philippa asked her uncle. "Hold hands and wait for you to shove us into the crater like those Inca kids? Hey, Apu? Here we come. Look out, Catequil, you've got a couple of visitors."

"Very amusing," said Nimrod.

"Who are they?" asked Groanin. "Apu and thing-ummybob?"

"Inca gods," said Philippa. "Apu was their god of mountains and volcanoes. And Catequil was the god of thunder and lightning. The Incas used to throw twins into an active crater, as a sacrifice."

"As you do," remarked John drily. "Now and then."

Groanin's jaw dropped and he looked at Nimrod and then at Philippa. There was a look of alarm on his face. "You're not thinking of doing that, are you? Nimrod?"

"No, of course not," said Nimrod. "What do you take me for?"

"I thought for a moment I must have gotten hold of the wrong end of the stick," admitted the butler. "Well, it wouldn't be the first time."

"So what *do* we do now that we're here?" John asked Nimrod.

"We already talked about this, John," said Philippa.

"Yes, we did," agreed John. "But what we haven't yet talked about is if this can work or not. Maybe it's a waste of time. Maybe what we're doing will be done in vain."

"Maybe," said Philippa.

"But that's what I want to know," insisted John. "I mean, I really don't mind making this sacrifice if it's going to work, but I can't see the point if it's done more in hope than expectation."

"I don't think anybody can tell that until you try," said Nimrod. "We're on uncertain ground here."

Groanin glanced at his boots. A strong smell of burning rubber was coming off his soles. "You can say that again, sir."

"At least we are as far as I'm concerned," continued Nimrod.

"That makes three of us," said John.

"Groanin? I shall require you to keep quiet from now on."

"Yes, sir."

"You too, Professor."

"Anything to help," said the professor.

"Being 'children of the lamp' is one thing," said Nimrod. "But 'children of the sky' is something else. It was often believed that the children of the sky could summon any wind by motions of their hands or by their breath, and that they could make fair or foul weather and could cause rain. But remember what makes you unique: You are both children of the sky and children of the lamp. So then. I suggest you stand on the rim of the crater and hold hands."

John pulled a face and took his sister's hand.

"This will, of course, help you to concentrate your djinn power," said Nimrod. "And you should let the sound of my voice help you to shape your will. At least, in the beginning."

Philippa looked at John and nodded.

"Ready?" she said.

"Let's do it," said John.

"I want you to concentrate every iota of your power and for as long as you can endure," said Nimrod. "I want you to start to drag and drop the biggest rain clouds over this volcano. As many as you can until the sky is dark with them. You may have to keep uttering your focus words in order to do this. But as you bring rain clouds here, I want you to imagine doing the very same over every volcano in the world. Here, in Italy. In Iceland. And all along the Pacific Ring of Fire. And then I want you to make it rain like it never rained before. Right into every one of these craters."

John and Philippa closed their eyes and began to think very, very hard of the many volcanoes the professor had told them about: the fifty most active, and the six or seven hundred volcanoes that had been active since the beginning of recorded time. They thought about the volcanoes of Hawaii. The volcanoes of Sumatra. The volcanoes on the Canary Islands. The volcanoes in Japan and Alaska. The volcanoes in Ecuador, Chile, and Peru.

They thought of thick rain clouds gathering immediately above the craters of these volcanoes. The biggest rain clouds anyone could have imagined. And all the time that they concentrated on drawing weather systems and small anticyclones directly onto these craters, they uttered their focus words and gathered their djinn power.

And as their concentration of mind and power increased, gradually they forgot about Nimrod, and Groanin, and the professor; they forgot about Axel, and Charlie, and Moby; they forgot about Rashleigh Khan; they forgot about Mr. Bilharzia and Genghis Khan; they forgot about their mother and father; they almost forgot about each other. The only thing they did not forget was why they had come there.

It was, perhaps, the greatest concentration of power John and Philippa had ever felt. Certainly, it was the most power that either of them had ever used.

Or would ever use again.

Gradually, each twin lost all sense of time and place. There was just their awesome power, and the four elements: earth, water, air, and fire. Indeed, the longer they persevered with their collective thought process, the more their will came to resemble an elemental force itself so that there were four elements that were required to submit to the fifth element that was their two minds.

And after a while, it began to rain.

John and Philippa hardly seemed to notice. They just stood on the edge of the crater, hands locked together like two mythological twins', staring at the sky, and making the rain fall.

And what rain it was.

For a while Groanin, Nimrod, and the professor gathered under the umbrellas they had brought with them from the supermarket in Sorrento, but as the day wore on they were forced to take shelter in the gift shop that occupied the beginning of the path around the crater rim.

"Do you think they'll be all right, standing on the edge of the crater like that?" Groanin asked Nimrod.

"I don't really know," admitted Nimrod. "But I daren't touch them now that they're doing this. It might be dangerous for them, and it would certainly be dangerous for me."

Seeing Groanin raise an eyebrow at that, he added, "Oh, yes. Together, they're much more powerful than me. That's rather the point, you see. There's no djinn alive who could make rain like this. That is, apart from them."

Groanin glanced out of the window of the gift shop. He had to admit there was something in what Nimrod had said. Coming from Manchester, on the western side of England, Groanin thought he knew a bit about rain. Manchester is surrounded by the Pennine Hills to the north and the east. When a southwesterly wind blows over England, it brings damp Atlantic air. The Atlantic air reaches Manchester, is forced up over the Pennines and, as it rises, it cools and turns into water droplets. This is what is known to climatologists and geographers as a rain shadow. Which is why Manchester has more than twenty-seven inches of rain a year, and rains, on average, for between fifteen and twenty days a month. Groanin knew rain like a Spanish orange grower knows sun. There was probably quite a bit of rain in Groanin's soul. But he had never seen rain like the rain that fell on Vesuvius. It was almost a solid sheet of water.

"Look," he said, pointing through the rain and down the slope at the Bay of Naples. "There's blue sky down there. It seems to be clear in Naples and Sorrento. It's only raining up here, directly into the crater."

"That's the whole idea," said the professor.

"What we need is a television set," said Nimrod. "Then we could check the international news bulletins and see if it's raining on any of the other volcanoes."

"There's one down at the old observatory," said the professor.

"Yes, of course," said Nimrod. "Well, let's go there."

"If you don't mind, sir," said Groanin, "I'll stay up here with them. Just in case they need me."

"This could take a while, Groanin," said Nimrod. "You'd probably be more comfortable down at the observatory."

"Thank you, no, sir. I think it's best that someone remains up here with them. They're only children, after all. Besides, I think they'll need to see a friendly face when this is all over, don't you? Not to mention some refreshment." He nodded down at the picnic hamper.

"If you say so, Groanin." Nimrod nodded. "We'll come and find you when the rain stops, shall we?"

Groanin watched Nimrod and the professor walk carefully along the already treacherous path down the mountain in the direction of the old observatory. Finding the driest spot in the gift shop, he opened the picnic hamper and poured himself a cup of tea from one of several thermos flasks he had filled in the kitchens of the Excelsior Vittoria hotel. Then, he took out his silver-framed photograph of the queen (recently repaired), placed it carefully on the gift shop's empty ice-cream chest, and, with a cup of tea in one hand, found his newspaper and started to read.

CHAPTER 43

A MUNDANE
WAY OF THINKING

John opened his eyes and looked up at a beautiful, cloud-less blue sky. High in the troposphere, a jet was moving as slowly as a silver snail, leaving behind a thin white contrail. The sun was shining and warmed his face pleasantly while the early morning air was filled with birdsong and a strong smell of flowers. His clothes were a little damp, but surely that was to be expected after so much rain. And remember-ing where he was, he sat up and looked around.

He was sitting on the edge of the path on the crater rim of Vesuvius. The skyscraper-high plume of ash and smoke that had existed there the day before was now gone. And in the crater below his feet, where once there had been molten rock and fire, and prior to that an enormous dust bowl, now there was just a large expanse of water.

Philippa was lying next to him, in a similar state of bedrag-gled wakefulness. Her red hair was matted onto her skull like it was a head scarf. Her face was already pink from the sun, which, he thought, was something he'd never seen before.

She sat up and picked her damp shirt from her shoulders. Then she took off her glasses, cleaned them on the end of her shirt, and put them back on her face.

"Are you all right?" he asked.

"Yes," she said. "I guess so. A bit tired. You?"

"Okay, I think." He nodded. "It must have worked. At least it has worked here on Vesuvius. Look." He pointed at the lake below them. "The rain has filled the crater."

"It looks kind of peaceful, doesn't it? Like one of those Swiss lakes, but smaller. Hard to believe it's the same crater, don't you think?"

"Hmm."

"I wonder if it worked anywhere else," said Philippa. "On any other volcanoes."

"I can't imagine it didn't, given the way I'm feeling now." John shrugged. "But time will tell, I'm thinking."

Philippa yawned — a big, stretching, loud yawn that echoed across the crater like a yodel.

"It feels like it's really early in the morning," she said, and glanced at her watch. "I guess it must have rained all day and all night."

"How do you feel?" he asked. "Really."

"Wet," she said. "My clothes are stuck on like postage stamps."

"Mine, too. No, I meant, you know. Inside."

"Inside?" She thought for a moment. "Different. Very different. Like I'm seeing things with different eyes. Or that

427

I've forgotten something. Except that I know what it is that I've forgotten." She shrugged. "If you see what I mean. You? How do you feel?"

"Really, not as bad as I thought I'd feel," said John. "Considering everything that's happened." He shrugged. "I ache a bit, all over. And I have this feeling of loss." He shook his head. "Maybe that's too strong a word for it. But I sort of feel like a car that just ran out of gas."

Philippa stood up, stretched, and looked around. "I wonder where the others are."

"Let's go and find them."

They walked down the crater path to the gift shop and found Groanin asleep on the concrete floor. Seeing the hotel picnic basket reminded John that he was hungry and he helped himself to some of the delicious things that Groanin had thoughtfully brought along: pastries, fruit, orange juice, sandwiches, cakes, coffee, and tea. There was even some chocolate, which, under the circumstances, seemed a little ironic.

John poured himself some coffee but found there was no sugar.

"I wish I had some sugar," said John. "I don't like coffee without sugar."

But he drank a cup, anyway.

Groanin woke up and sat up. "Forgive me," he said. "I must have fallen asleep." He rubbed his eyes and straightened his tie. "What must you think of me, sleeping while you went through that terrible ordeal." He glanced at the children. "Was it terrible?"

"It was hard work," said John. "I don't mind admitting it. Probably the hardest thing I've ever done. But I guess it wasn't so very terrible." He shrugged. "We're still here, aren't we?"

Philippa was hungry, too. She helped herself to a slice of cake, and then another.

"I wish this cake wasn't so delicious," she said happily. "But it is. I can't help myself." She pushed some John's way. "Here. Try some."

"Thanks. I will." John stuffed a whole slice into his mouth and nodded his agreement.

"How long have we been up here?" asked Philippa, embracing Groanin fondly.

"We came here three days ago," said Groanin. "And it's been raining ever since. All day and all night. It rained so much that I half expected to see Noah floating up here in an ark." He glanced up at the sky. "Looks as if it's worked, then."

"Looks like," said John. "Here, anyway."

"Where's Nimrod and the professor?" asked Philippa.

"They went down to the old observatory," said Groanin. "To watch the television news. See what was happening in volcanic countries around the world." He felt in his pocket. "I wonder. Now that the ash cloud is gone, it might just be that my cell phone is working again."

He switched it on. "There's a signal, all right," he said excitedly, and keyed in Nimrod's number. "I wonder if that means some things are getting back to normal."

"Yes, they are," said John. "They must be. I saw a jet in the sky a few minutes ago. So the airspace must have reopened already."

"I can hear a phone ringing," said Philippa, and step-ping out of the gift shop, she saw Nimrod and the professor coming slowly up the path. Both of them were grinning broadly and it was plain from their faces that they were the bearers of good news.

Philippa ran to greet her uncle and embraced him, too.

"Did it work?" she asked keenly. "Did it?"

"Did it?" yelled the professor. "And how!"

"Yes," said Nimrod. "It worked."

"Everywhere?" shouted John.

"Everywhere there was a volcano threatening to erupt, there is now an attractive mountain lake or reservoir, like this one," said Nimrod.

"Everywhere?" Even John sounded surprised, in spite of the fact he knew that he and Philippa were responsible.

"Everywhere," said the professor. "From Iceland to Hawaii. From Sumatra to Chile. In Africa and in Japan. It's incredible. The world's media are talking about a mountain miracle."

"Aye, well, they would," said Groanin. "It's been a while since we had one of those."

"Already the skies are clearing of smoke and ash and the world's weather seems to be returning to normal," added Nimrod. "And the threat of a global catastrophe has passed."

John punched the sky. "That's great news," he said. "The best."

"How do you feel?" asked Nimrod.

"A bit tired and wet," admitted Philippa. "And —" She shrugged. "A bit ordinary, I guess. I suppose I'll get used to that. Eventually." She thought for a moment and then added,

"A bit like when you lose an arm or a leg and yet you have the sensation that it's still there."

"A phantom limb," said Groanin. "Aye, well I remember that, all right."

"That's the way I feel, too," said John. "I don't know. Like something went out inside of me."

"Well, that may change, of course," Nimrod said brightly. "You're cold. A young djinn's power never works when he or she is cold, you know that."

"No," said Philippa. "This feels different from just being cold."

"And of course you're tired," said Nimrod. "Both of you. Exhausted. You need time to recharge your batteries, so to speak. Like that Mongolian death worm. You know, I'll bet that in just a few days you'll find that your powers are back to normal. You wait and see if I'm wrong."

"No," said Philippa. "I'm certain they won't. It's over. You know it. I know it. And John knows it. We always knew we would have to use absolutely every last candle of power that we had to make this work."

"Philippa's right," said John. "I made a wish a minute or two ago. For more sugar. And I didn't get any. As soon as I felt the word in my mouth I whispered my focus word but I knew it was no good. There's nothing there anymore. Like an electric light when there's no electricity. I'm flicking the switch but there's no power. Nothing. Nothing at all."

"And never will be again," added Philippa. "What's gone is gone."

"Just like Dybbuk," said John. "Burnt out. Remember?"

431

Groanin let out a big, unsteady sigh. "What, my pets, no djinn power left at all?"

"None." Philippa smiled through her tears. "I'm not crying because I'm sad. I'm crying because I'm happy."

"Happy?" Nimrod frowned. "How is that possible?"

"I'm happy because I can be normal now. I'm happy because I can be mundane like everyone else."

"I never thought I would say this, but I agree," said John. "And, what's more, I'm glad I gave it up — the djinn power — not because I couldn't handle it, or something lame like that, but because there was something truly worthwhile to sacrifice it for."

Nimrod nodded. "I'm proud of you," he said. "I'm especially proud because the world will never know how much it owes you."

"I wouldn't have it any other way," said Philippa.

John smiled. "No normal person would," he said. "Besides, who would believe us now?"

"You know what I'm looking forward to most?" asked Philippa.

"No," said Groanin. "Tell us."

"Going back home," said Philippa. "Going back to school. Hanging out with some friends. Having an ambition. Living a normal life."

"Doing things the hard way." John shrugged. "Not being special. Not being important. Just being ordinary."

"Staying at home. Not having adventures. Not being children of the lamp anymore. Just being — like other kids, I guess."

"Not smelling like a camel, or tasting what a camel had for its breakfast."

"Not worrying about having to give someone three wishes. What they're going to wish for. That's a heck of a responsibility." Philippa shook her head. "I won't miss that at all."

John nodded. "Not turning someone into an animal. Or a bird. I hated that."

"It's all very well having three wishes and stuff like that," said Philippa, "but I really think the only things worth having are the things you work for."

"Still," said John, "it was fun while it lasted."

"Yes, it was," agreed Philippa. "A lot of fun. But now it's over."

Nimrod sighed. "What have I done?"

"You didn't do anything," said Philippa. "We did. And what's more, we knew what we were doing. So don't blame yourself. There wasn't any other way."

"That's right," said John. "Look on the bright side, Uncle Nimrod. We won't be needing those two junior flying carpets now. So you won't have to go back to Fez and see Mr. Barkhiya."

"And now that the airspace is open again," said Philippa, "we can all fly home in the normal way. On a plane."

"Going home." Groanin rubbed his hands. "What could be better, eh, John? Philippa? I say, what could be better than going home to your mum and dad. You can't ask for more than that. It's always a blessing to go home."

The End

AUTHOR'S NOTE

Good-byeeee! Good-byeeee! Wipe the tear, baby dear, from your eyeeee!

I have often been asked where I got the idea to write Children of the Lamp. I'm afraid the answer is not a particularly enlightening one: It seemed like a good idea at the time. Many times have I been asked this same question and it always seems curmudgeonly to answer the question with the apparently anodyne reply that is "my brain"; nevertheless, that is the truth. Duh! How could it not be? Where else do ideas come from?

And yet, perhaps, there *is* more. For perhaps the question begs a better question: Where do ideas go? Obviously, when you're a writer the ideas go into a book. But the book is merely the manifestation of the idea; the thought processes that accompany the book are of enormous importance to the writer. Because every book one writes becomes a real experience and effects some change.

For example: While writing these books I have especially enjoyed getting in touch with my inner twelve-year-old — a scrofulous, bucktoothed, swarthy-looking Scottish boy I never again thought to meet — and I can honestly say to anyone who loves the story of Peter Pan (as I do) that writing for children is easily the best way I have found of getting some of his plentiful supply of fairy dust to rub off on you. Not growing up, not getting old, that is what writing Children of the Lamp has, for a while, meant to me.

As a result, I have had a great time over the last seven years writing these seven books that now make up the complete Children of the Lamp series. I had not intended that the seventh book should be the last. However, when I began to write the story it seemed to me that the characters — especially John and Philippa Gaunt — were asking me to end it for them. And, unlike Rashleigh Khan, I am a great believer in listening to children. Well-drawn, full-fleshed characters in books do this from time to time, and there is nothing that an author can do about it.

So, at their behest, it seemed best to finish the series now and certainly do so while I was still enjoying myself. I sincerely hope those readers who have read all seven titles will forgive me for not writing any more of them. But seven is quite a lot of books to have written in seven years. And I had no wish to repeat myself or become tedious as a storyteller.

I shall be sorry, however, to hang up my magic lamp and put away my flying carpet after what has been an adventure not just for John and Philippa, and I hope my readers, but for me, too. Because I have learned a great deal as a writer from writing for children. I think that the most important thing I have learned — and this is crucial for anyone who writes books for children — is to listen to your own imagination, and to trust what it tells you. It's not for me to judge the results of my endeavors, but I have the feeling that my imagination has served me well these last six or seven years; on the odd occasion when it has looked as if it was going to let me down, I was lucky to have enjoyed the advice of my son Charlie, whose unfettered, tangential way of thinking has been, sometimes, inspirational. He is quite a character.

I am often asked who in the books is my favorite character. Like a lot of writers, I must confess that all of the characters are merely facets of my own peculiar character and, as a corollary, there are none I regard with especial fondness, for that would be to say that I am fond of my faults and boastfully proud of those few virtues I do possess. Nimrod is every bit as pompous as I can be; John and Philippa represent my own personality split between action and bookishness. I especially loved writing the axiomatic djinn philosophy of dear Mr. Rakshasas, but the character who comes closest to the real me is probably Mr. Groanin. *I say, the character who comes closest to the real me is probably Mr. Groanin.*

Another question I am asked is why did I choose to call myself P. B. Kerr? Was I really, as one Scottish newspaper suggested, trying to pass myself off as a writer *like* J. K. Rowling in order that I might make more money? Well, no, actually. As Philip Kerr, I am the author of many crime novels and thrillers, some of which contain violence and quite a bit of bad language, and I wanted to make sure that children did not mistake these for books that were suitable for them. Incidentally, the *B* stands for Ballantyne, a name that I hated as a child and that even now I cringe at when I confess to it. I often wished I had another.

Which leads me neatly to the subject of wishes and the small but important philosophical message that lies at the heart of all seven books: This is that there is great importance in thinking before one speaks and of learning how to use language to indicate precisely what one means. Being careful what one wishes for is a lesson well learned on the rare occasions when you get exactly what you wish for. I still smile when I remember the looks of horror on the faces of some children who had told me what their three wishes might be and I proceeded to tell them in some detail how, if I were a wicked djinn, I might just give them what they wanted, which, of course, was a lot more than any of them expected.

There is also an important life point at the heart of the books and it is this: the enormous value of ambition and working for what you want, rather than having someone — a djinn like the ones on television talent shows, perhaps — come along to make your wish come true. *If it's worth having, it's worth working for.* I am the proof of the importance of having an ambition. As a child of about ten, it was my dearest wish to become a professional writer. And that was when I started first to write. Twenty-three years later, after many valuable failures, I achieved that ambition. Fortunately, it was I who made my wish come true and not Nimrod or John or Philippa.

Author Message: You can make your own fondest wish come true provided that you are prepared to work hard. Now all you have to do is to decide what that wish is.

P. B. Kerr
Wimbledon, London, 2011.

ACKNOWLEDGMENTS

After seven books, there are a great many people to thank.

The most important people to thank, of course, are my wife and three children. It's not easy being married to a writer or having one as a father. Perhaps, one day my own kids (like the children of poor Enid Blyton) will write a book about what an ogre I was. (And if you do, then remember this: I did my best for you.)

Now I have to thank three people who are excellent agents but, more importantly, even better friends. These are Robert Bookman at CAA, and Caradoc King and Linda Shaughnessy at AP Watt. These people are the nearest thing I have found to powerful but benign djinn who can help to make a writer's wishes come true.

I should also like to thank everyone at Scholastic USA, of course, many of whom I didn't get to know by name. I should especially like to thank Dick Robinson, Ellie Berger, and the wonderful Lisa Ann Sandell, who was my very patient and long-suffering editor, and the charming Charisse Meloto.

Thanks are also due to the talented Barbara Marcus, the brilliant Jean Feiwel, the loyal Richard Scrivener, the delightful Jo Hardacre, and my fellow in lunch, Amanda Punter. To each of them I say, "Best wishes to you all."

I should like to thank Walter Parkes, Laurie MacDonald, and Nina Jacobson at Dreamworks for all their help and kindness.

But most of all, I must thank you, my readers — readers of all ages — many of whom have written to me with good ideas and kind words. The best thing about writing for children is the letters and e-mails from readers who almost invariably never write unless they have something nice to say. Apologies for not answering all of you. I'm a hopeless correspondent, as many of you will know by now. So thanks, guys. Warmest regards to you all.